Cobiah was ... *when the ship* ... *beneath his feet.*

Caught by surprise, Cobiah fell toward the gunwale and skidded precariously toward the *Indomitable*'s edge. With one arm wrapped around the bundle, he grabbed desperately for the central mast. The ship was shuddering violently, boards protesting in high-pitched shrieks, and there was a horrible crunching sound from the rudder at her stern.

The ship pitched again, and Cobiah's hand slipped on the damp wood. Toppling down across the deck, Cobiah crashed painfully into the butt of one of the massive cannons. He desperately grabbed its iron cap, wrapping his legs around the gun and holding on for dear life. Other sailors, not so lucky, were cast into the sea. Cobiah could hear men screaming beyond the gunwale.

With a lurch and a groan of her arched keel, the *Indomitable* righted herself in the waves. Water splashed onto the deck in huge swells, toppling over the sides of the ship as the galleon settled into the ocean once more. Cobiah lifted his head and tried to ascertain what had happened. Had the ship hit the rocks? Was the bottom of the ship torn, taking on water that would drown them all?

Fingers of stone towered above the ship to either side, pointed tips clawing toward a gray, boiling sky. Yet they were still distant. The ship couldn't have struck one. Cobiah glanced over the lip of the deck and saw only deep blue ocean—no sign of reef or coral. That left only one answer.

If they hadn't hit anything, then something—something *big*—must have hit *them*.

Don't miss these other thrilling novel-length fantasy
adventures from the world of GUILD WARS®

Edge of Destiny
by J. Robert King

Ghosts of Ascalon
by Matt Forbeck and Jeff Grubb

GUILDWARS®

SEA OF
SORROWS

REE SOESBEE

Based on the Acclaimed Video Game Series
from ArenaNet

POCKET BOOKS

New York   London   Toronto   Sydney   New Delhi

Pocket Books
A Division of Simon & Schuster, Inc.
1230 Avenue of the Americas
New York, NY 10020

This book is a work of fiction. Names, characters, places, and incidents either are products of the author's imagination or are used fictitiously. Any resemblance to actual events or locales or persons, living or dead, is entirely coincidental.

First Pocket Books paperback edition July 2013

POCKET and colophon are registered trademarks of Simon & Schuster, Inc.

For information about special discounts for bulk purchases, please contact Simon & Schuster Special Sales at 1-866-506-1949 or business@simonandschuster.com.

The Simon & Schuster Speakers Bureau can bring authors to your live event. For more information or to book an event contact the Simon & Schuster Speakers Bureau at 1-866-248-3049 or visit our website at www.simonspeakers.com.

Manufactured in the United States of America

10 9 8 7 6 5 4 3 2 1

ISBN 978-1-4165-8962-4
ISBN 978-1-4391-5605-6 (ebook)

For my friend and sidekick Emily,
whose courage inspires me to inspire others

Time Line

10,000 BE: Last of the Giganticus Lupicus, the Great Giants, disappear from the Tyrian continent.

205 BE: Humans appear on the Tyrian continent.

100 BE: Humans drive the charr out of Ascalon.

1 BE: The Human Gods give magic to the races of Tyria.

0 AE: The Exodus of the Human Gods.

2 AE: Orr becomes an independent nation.

300 AE: Kryta established as a colony of Elona.

358 AE: Kryta becomes an independent nation.

898 AE: The Great Northern Wall is erected.

1070 AE: The Charr Invasion of Ascalon. The Searing.

1071 AE: The Sinking of Orr.

1072 AE: Ascalonian refugees flee to Kryta.

1075 AE: Kormir ascends into godhood.

1078 AE: Primordus, the Elder Fire Dragon, stirs but does not awaken. The asura appear on the surface. The Transformation of the Dwarves.

1080 AE: King Adelbern of Ascalon recalls the Ebon Vanguard; Ebonhawke is established.

1088 AE: Kryta unifies behind Queen Salma.

1090 AE: The charr legions take Ascalon City. The Foefire.

1105 AE: Durmand Priory is established in the Shiverpeaks.

1112 AE: The charr erect the Black Citadel over the ruins of the city of Rin in Ascalon.

1116 AE: Kalla Scorchrazor leads the rebellion against the Flame Legion's shaman caste.

1120 AE: Primordus awakens.

1165 AE: Jormag, the Elder Ice Dragon, awakens. The norn flee south into the Shiverpeaks.

1180 AE: The centaur prophet Ventari dies by the Pale Tree, leaving behind the Ventari Tablet.

1219 AE: Zhaitan, the Elder Undead Dragon, awakens. Orr rises from the sea. Lion's Arch floods.

1220 AE: Divinity's Reach is founded in the Krytan province of Shaemoor.

1230 AE: Corsairs and other pirates occupy the slowly drying ruins of Lion's Arch.

1302 AE: The sylvari first appear along the Tarnished Coast, sprouting from the Pale Tree.

1319 AE: Eir Stegalkin forms a band of heroes known as Destiny's Edge.

SEA OF
SORROWS

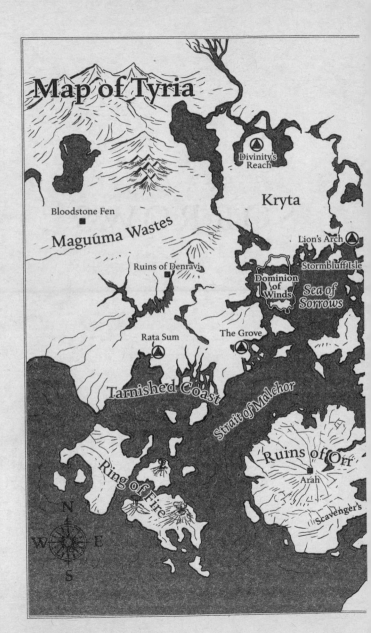

ACT ONE

1219 AE
(AFTER THE EXODUS OF THE GODS)

You don't know a storm 'til you ride the wind
Beneath cold and blackened skies, O
'Til you're sailing through a thunderhead
With the lightning in your eyes
Death, he laughs in the sails and the jags
And the bloody sun won't rise, O.

—"Weather the Storm"

1

A sharp breeze swept through Lion's Arch, the curious offspring of cold ocean currents and warm southern winds drifting inland. It wove through the streets of the city, whispering in doorways and slipping down alleys. The cold season had been a long one, and ice still glinted on puddles of melt between stones in the uneven streets. Yet even in Kryta, winter must eventually yield to spring.

The wind broke into a gust, and the ships at harbor shook and quavered in their moorings, pitching uneasily against the salt-soaked boards of the docks. Spray leapt up from a whitecap, foam trickling around sharp barnacles that freckled the mighty galleon's hull. Sailors clapped their hands to their hats, and merchants grabbed their goods, keeping them close. On one of the larger vessels, a youth jumped down the ship's gangplank, leaning into the wind and propelling himself forward with long, uneven strides.

"Thanks for the extra work, Vost!" the young man yelled over his shoulder with a wave. He loped forward on the edge of balance, hardly caring about the wind that shoved against him. Torn, too-short pant legs flapped about his calves, and his shoes clung to the salty boards despite their cracked leather soles and worn stitching.

Aboard the massive galleon, an older man waved down from the railing. With a leathery grin on his face, he called out, "Are you sure you don't want to sail with us this time, Coby? We've plenty of berth and could use a good spotter out at sea!"

"Sorry, Bosun Vost, but I can't go!" Cobiah waved back. "There's a pretty girl waiting in the city, and I can't let her down!"

"A girl? Ha! Good for you, lad." The older man laughed. "See you on the horizon, then."

"Aye, aye, Vost. Take care!" The youth leapt over a crate at the bottom of the ship's ramp, darting among slow-moving fishermen in the hustle and bustle of the crowd as he headed back toward shore. Whistling, he bounded over fishermen's buckets and dodged through nets hung to dry, squeezing through the sailors at work without so much as an apology.

He was a skinny youth, only just out of boyhood, legs ungainly and arms akimbo. Taller than most, Cobiah had not yet grown into his height, and he ran like an awkward colt still finding its balance. He was pale, with white-blond hair flopping about his forehead. Sharp blue eyes glinted in a lightly tanned face. The gawkiness of adolescence did not diminish a handsome face. It was perhaps a bit too long in the jaw, but it had a firmness and intelligence stamped on every feature.

Cobiah skidded around the end of the dock, ducking under a thick wooden board being laid as a gangplank. He leapt up onto one of the wooden pillars of the dock to make the long jump to a second towering above the sandy beach. Thirty feet over the rocky shore, he balanced for a moment to enjoy the view.

The Lion's Arch docks stretched out like fingers from the sandy shore, reaching out to touch the ocean. Beyond that, a great stone city rose from the coastline, its ancient buildings shining white and yellow in the gentle morning sun. A soft whisper of green tinged the rocky cliffs around it, and mountains rose toward the clouds inland, beyond the city's sculptured outline. Lion's Arch had stood since the days when humans first colonized the nation of Kryta, like a foundation stone of the kingdom, and of civilization itself.

Cobiah grinned and felt the wind shifting all about him. He smelled the bitter tang of the sea and the faint hint of sweetness from the spring's first growth in city gardens and in distant plains. With a smile, he threw himself forward toward the streets of the city. Recklessly leaping onto the high crates of a loading area, Cobiah climbed down a stiff wooden piling until he reached the hard-packed ground below. Once there, he strode down small, wandering streets where scattered beach sand gave way to cobblestones and city dirt. Cobiah hurried as if Grenth, the god of death, were on his heels, and he didn't stop running until he plowed face-first into the proverbial immovable object.

Standing in the doorway of the Iron Tankard, a burly man threw his hand across the opening and held his ground. A hat hung low over his heavy-lidded dark eyes, protecting them from the sun and giving the man a perpetual scowl. "Well, well." A lousy, lopsided sneer spread beneath the hat. "Cobiah. Late again." The tavern keeper shoved the youth backward. "Yer not welcome here no more."

"Jacob!" Cobiah protested with a winning smile. "You know it's not my fault. I was helping out at the docks, carrying crates to the *Indomitable*. She's to set sail at dawn, and—"

"Din't ya hear me?" the big man snarled, dark skin flushing with anger. "*Yer not welcome!*"

"One of the crates broke," the youth claimed quickly, ducking under the man's muscular arm with eager abandon. Cobiah was quicker than the tavern owner, his skill at dodging honed by a childhood on the streets. "I had to get it all back together and in the hold before the stores got damp, and that's why I'm late. It won't happen again."

The tavern keeper gripped the back of Cobiah's belt, hauling him out the door and onto the street. "Don't care." A grin spread across his features, showing long rows of sharp alligator teeth. "My tavern don't need somebody that sweeps the floor *after* the patrons show up." The gruff man's malicious snarl never faltered. "You're fired."

Cobiah paled. "Jacob . . . you can't do this to me. I need this job." He folded his hands together, begging, though hesitation replaced the friendliness in his eyes. "C'mon. I get it, you're strong-arming to scare me straight. Let me in, and I'll sweep up now, and tonight, too. Without pay." Wheedling, Cobiah reached for the broom inside the doorway, but Jacob grabbed his wrist so hard that he bruised Cobiah's flesh.

"*I don't care!* I'm tired of it, Cobiah. I'm done." The man's angry glare softened. "I know yer family's got it rough, boy, but I can't make no allowances. I got a bar to run." Cobiah started to argue again, but Jacob thrust him back, releasing the youth's wrist with a forceful shove. Jacob growled, "Now get goin' before I cuff ya!"

People on the street were staring, judging Cobiah with stern, unforgiving eyes. Someone brushing past muttered, "Lazy skale. Shiftless layabout!" Others shook their heads or whispered in mocking tones. A woman in a rich gown cast the pale-haired youth a glance that could have boiled eggs as she swept past. Cobiah didn't bother to argue. He'd been called worse.

It was as much as he could do to keep his face straight and his jaw square as he slunk away from the dockside bar. Jacob's laughter rang mockingly in Cobiah's ears, but it was nothing compared to what was ahead of him. He'd lost his job. The *Indomitable* was leaving port, so the extra money from loading the galleon would vanish, too. Few other ships were willing to trust a street kid to heft valuable cargo. There was little work in the crowded city of Lion's Arch, and with no real skills or training in a craft, Cobiah was completely adrift. Just six silver coins in his pocket, all his prospects in ruins, and now he had to return home and explain it all . . . to *her*.

The populace of Lion's Arch hustled about their lives, ignoring the tow-haired youth wandering dejectedly through its cobbled streets. The city hadn't lost any of its beauty; sunlight glistened on the waters of Lion's Bay from the sandy cliffs of Lion's Gate through the strait of Claw Island, illuminating soft white waves in the distant Sea of Sorrows. White sails hovered on the horizon like wave foam. He could hear bells ringing in the harbor, signaling the passing of ships in and out of dock. None of it meant anything to Cobiah.

Yet despite the lost, desperate feeling, Cobiah couldn't stop a smile from creeping to his lips at the sight of the most beautiful thing in the city. It wasn't a sculpture or one of the magnificent buildings. It wasn't sunlight, or sea waves, or even glittering gold. It was a little girl, squatting in the gutters outside Hooligan's Route, playing with an earthworm that wriggled in the muddy dirt. She looked up at Cobiah with eyes the color of a clear summer sky. "Coby!" the four-year-old squealed, her grubby face breaking into a wide smile of joy. Leaving the worm to its own devices, the little girl dove into Cobiah's arms, wrapping her hands around his neck as if to climb right up onto his shoulders.

Cobiah laughed and whirled her about. She giggled, careful not to drop her faded rag doll. Though its yarn hair had worn to threadbare patches and its dress was little more than a dyed bit of burlap, the little girl cradled it close as he held her to his chest. "Heya, Bivy-bear. Sleep well?"

His sister didn't answer at first. Instead, she pushed her dolly into Cobiah's hand. "Kiss for Polla?" Cobiah obediently gave the dolly a kiss on its forehead and handed it back to the girl. Only then did she reply softly, "No." The little girl pouted, lower lip jutting out like a slice of ripe plum. "I had night-horses."

"Nightmares, Biviane?" Cobiah bounced his sister lightly, watching her pale curls tremble across her chubby, dirt-stained cheeks. She clutched his neck tightly and laid her head on Cobiah's shoulder. In her hand, the dolly's stitched lips smiled prettily, and her button eyes matched Biviane's, for all that they stared out of a weary-looking yarn head.

"I dreamed there was a monster outside. Polla was scared. I tried to sing a little song to make her feel better, but . . . that made Mama yell." Biviane sighed heavily, kicking her feet in exasperation. "Mama took Polla away and put her in the dark place."

Cobiah's blood ran cold. "Polla went into the dark place?" he asked carefully. "Just Polla. Not you, Bivy. Right?"

Biviane lay her head on his shoulder, curls tumbling down onto Cobiah's chest. In a small voice, she whispered, "Not me. I was very, very quiet, and Mama let me sleep." A pause. "This time."

A breath he hadn't known he'd been holding eased out of Cobiah's lungs. "Good girl." His hair lay against hers along the curve of his shoulder, matching like two skeins of the same thread. It was probably a good thing that Biviane couldn't see his expression, for it took him several moments to get it under control. At last, with infinite care, he lowered his sister to the ground. "Here." He forced a happy smile onto his lips. With a wink, Cobiah drew a silver coin from his pocket. He held it up, giving it a flourish so that the metal sparkled in the sun. "Do you know where I got this?"

Biviane clutched her dolly close to her chest and opened her rosebud mouth with awe. She shook her head, eyes wide, staring at the money.

Cobiah let the coin dance over his fingers. "See those big masts out at the last dock? That's the *Indomitable*. She's got three masts and three decks, and a hundred guns on each side. The king of Kryta built that ship himself, and she's the finest one on the sea!"

Biviane stared out over his arm, glancing back and forth between white sails and yellow gold. "That's King Baede's ship?"

"His biggest one. And it's a sight to see. It could fit a hundred soldiers on it, and still have room for fifteen houses, a thousand cats . . ." He smiled to see her mouth purse into a little O of astonishment. "And Polla, too."

"Wow." Her eyes were big and trusting. "And you were on that ship?"

"I was. I was helping to load it last night, and while I was putting a crate in the hold, I looked out of a porthole at the sea. Do you know what I saw there?" Cobiah leaned in close and whispered in Biviane's ear. "A *mermaid*."

The little girl's blue eyes grew as wide as china plates. "A real one?"

"Yes, indeed. She'd come to see the king's galleon. She had green scales from her shoulders to the tip of her tail, and she wore a dress made out of kelp and pearls. Her eyes were pale, like stars on the water, and her hair looked *just like yours.*" Cobiah tugged gently on a curl as Biviane giggled. "She said I was so handsome that she wanted to take me to the bottom of the ocean and keep me for her very own. But I told her that I wouldn't leave my sister for the whole wide world." He shook his finger teasingly. "Then she told me she'd give me some of her treasure if I gave her something in return. And do you know what she wanted?"

"A kiss!" Biviane breathed.

"I did, and she gave me this piece of silver. Now that I've told you the story, little miss, I'll make you the same deal. If you give me a kiss, it'll be yours."

With a gasp, Biviane threw her hands around Coby's neck and kissed him on both cheeks, giggling. Hugging his sister tightly, Cobiah pressed the coin into her palm.

"Did you really see a mermaid, Cobiah? A really-real one?" Biviane squealed, and her face glowed with delight. Cobiah couldn't help hugging her again, breathing in the warm scent of his sister's hair.

"Go get some breakfast, Bivy. And buy a piece of candy for Polla. I have to talk to Mom." Cobiah set the girl down on her feet and waved to one of the sailors passing by. "Romy? Are you headed into town?"

"Aye, young Cobiah. What can I do you for?"

"Can you take my sister to the muffin cart and help her pick out a nice sweet one? She's not allowed to go into the city alone." Cobiah smiled at the old man.

"Why, of course I can." Romy smiled, his green eyes adrift amid a sea of wrinkles and white beard. "C'mon, little lass. Ooh, is that your dolly? What's her name?"

"Polla!" Biviane said, taking Romy's hand trustingly. She turned to look back over her shoulder. "I love you, Coby!" she squealed. "I'll see you soon!" With a leap, she followed the old man, clutching her rag doll close to her chest. Cobiah straightened, watching his sister dance along the sand at the edge of the row of houses. Romy headed for the vendors at the docks, just a little ways down past where the big ships were moored, chattering happily to the little girl all the while.

Cobiah watched as the two vanished into the press of people moving back and forth on the pier. Even after she was gone, he stood there, imagining that he could still see her bouncing golden curls here and there among the crowd. Finally, with a sigh, Cobiah turned toward the shanty and headed inside.

The rotted door swung gently on ruined hinges. Inside the dark, filthy hut, the smell of tar and whiskey hung on foul air. The window glass was cracked and clogged with spiderwebs, and its wooden floor was thick with grime. The hut was composed of one choked-looking room. A faded red-and-blue rug lay dejectedly on the mud-and-slat-board floor. It was wrinkled and limp, looking very much as if it had died trying to crawl to freedom. The room's central table tottered in uncertain balance, tilting precariously on three warped legs and a half leg resting on a rusted bucket. In the rear of the cottage stood a large bed behind a wide, withered-looking threefold screen of paper.

The only bright spot in the little shanty was a trail of thin pink ribbons on a rickety-looking ladder. They'd been woven in lumpy braids by uncertain fingers, and hung down in tatters like tiny banners. The ladder, its rungs half-rotten and dripping wooden flakes onto the floor, led to a thin ledge tucked under the roof of the hut, where a flat, musty-smelling mattress of reeds had been shoved into the nook, covered by a small, faded quilt.

A harsh throttling noise shook the shoddy boards of the cabin. Cobiah jumped within his skin, unable to control an instinctive wash of revulsion. He steeled himself and stepped inside. Across the rickety table lay a woman, her snores echoing so loudly that they shook a trio of empty glasses arrayed on the board. Her hair was pale gray with care and years but bleached and tinted to give it a sickly echo of its original yellowish cast. Wrinkles clustered like vultures around her eyes, and her teeth were gray like stones. She snored again, choking on her breath, and absently mopped at her crooked nose with one half-aware hand.

Cobiah crept into the room warily. He gulped, unwilling to wake her, and fingered the five silver pieces left in his pocket. Maybe he could give them to her and leave, go find another job in the city. Making leather, maybe, down at the tannery . . .

The woman snorted, choking, and turned her head to spit a thick mass onto the floor. She peeled one bloodshot eye open to regard Cobiah. Grunting, the woman lurched upward in her chair and fixed him with a nasty gaze. "Filthy, useless boy. Why are you standing there like a gape-jawed idiot?" she snarled, muffling a belch. "Give me my money!" Her eyes were sharp and cold, deeply bloodshot and staying open due more to anger than to interest. She pawed at him greedily, hand snatching out like a hunting bird trying to catch a mouse.

"Yes, Mother." Biting his lip, he quelled the waver in his voice. Cobiah held out the five silver coins.

With a snarl, she snatched them from him. She peered at the coins in her palm and then held one up, fingers pinching the metal skeptically. Cheeks purpling, she growled, "Only five? There should be at least eight. Are you hiding money again, Cobiah?" She said the last words so strongly that a chill ran up Cobiah's spine.

Clearing his throat, he managed to say, "I never had more than six. I gave one to Biviane, so she could get breakfast—"

"You *what*?" Cobiah's mother lunged forward, rising to her feet between chair and table. Clumsy with the leftover effects of drink and sluggish sleep, she raised her hand and struck him to the ground. "That girl doesn't need breakfast—she's fat enough! She's like a little gutter pig. Wish I could sell her like a pig . . ." The drunken woman stood over him and scowled. "Bah, you lazy boy. Just like your father. Every day I thank the Six Gods for the storm at sea that drowned him. Wish one would come and take you, too! Useless, hopeless . . . worthless!" With each exclamation, she struck him, kicking him broadly as he lay curled on the floor. "You hear me? You're worth nothing! I should have drowned you myself, when you were small . . ." He could smell the rotten alcohol on her breath, feel the mud from her shoes falling on him in chunks. For a moment he wanted to fight back, rage flaring up and causing his hands to clench so hard that he could feel the curves of his fingernails splitting his palms. But he couldn't fight. If he did, she'd just take it out on Biviane. Forcing himself to lie still, Cobiah accepted each stinging slap and fierce, degrading kick.

"Cobiah!" Suddenly, a frantic shout from outside drew their attention, causing her hand to pause in the air. "Cobiah! Come quickly! Biviane's hurt!" Romy's voice, cracked with stress and fear.

At the sound of his sister's name, Cobiah pushed himself up and scrambled toward the shanty door, the coins—and the beating—forgotten. His mother was less quick to respond, her liquor-addled mind struggling to grasp the meaning of the words. He could hear her behind him, still yelling, as Cobiah darted out onto the street.

The air held a bitter tang of fish and sea-stained nets, but the sky was still bright with morning. Cobiah spun about, fixing his eyes on Romy. The aged sailor was standing in the plaza, yelling as loud as his old lungs would allow. The man's face was white, his hands cupped around his mouth. "Cobiah, hurry! I only took my eyes off Bivy for a moment—just a moment, I swear it. She said she wanted to see a mermaid. I don't know what she meant, but she went a-running, and she's such a snippet of a girl, I couldn't keep up with her in the crowd—"

"Where is she?" Cobiah shoved passersby out of his way, clearing a path through the streets.

"On the shore, down under the pier!" Romy pointed with a shaking finger, his eyes wide with horror. Not wasting even a minute, Cobiah raced toward the planks where the great ships were docked. All the anger he'd felt, all the pain, was forgotten completely, channeled into a mad need to find his sister.

He skidded through the streets, grabbing hold of a pole to spin around a street corner, and took the stairs down to the ocean's edge three at a time. Cobiah's heart pounded in fear. Abandoning the stairs, he leapt down the rocky cliff from stone to stone, landing heavily in the wet sand below. He could hear the ships' bells tolling like a call to worship, mixed with the faraway catcalls of the street vendors, and he could see a small group of sailors clustered beneath one of the large pylons by the rocks. Cobiah shoved his way through them as he struggled to catch his breath. Reluctantly, they parted to allow him entrance. Just before he reached the center of the throng, a firm hand seized Cobiah's arm and dragged him to a halt.

"You don't want to go in there, son," a man with a full red beard said, reaching out with both hands to hold Cobiah steady.

Cobiah looked past him to the beach. He could see a sailor kneeling amid the rocks with an old green blanket in his hands. The sailor spread it out, and the blanket billowed but did not touch the ground, huddling instead over something that lay beneath it. Cobiah's mind balked, refusing to identify the outline. "Biv . . . no, Biv . . . I . . . I have to help my sister." He stumbled over the words. His tongue felt thick, like old gruel. Through the sailors, he could see a tiny black shoe peeking out beneath the edge of the blanket. Waves licked at it, foam teasing around the worn leather, a rusty silver buckle hanging from a mud-covered leather strap. A child's everyday shoe. Ordinary. Common.

"Your sister?" The man put his arm across the youth's chest. Cobiah hadn't even realized he'd tried to step forward. "You knew this girl?"

"Her name is Biviane. Biviane is my . . . my sister," Cobiah stammered, his blood cold. Why were they talking about her that way? "This girl"? Couldn't everyone see that Biviane needed him? That she was frightened and he had to protect her? Anger and shock flooded Cobiah, hot and cold and hot again, pounding through his veins. After a moment, he recognized that the old man was wearing the sky-blue robes of the goddess Dwayna. The bearded man was a priest, then. "She went to get breakfast. I gave her a coin. She'd be right back. She's coming right back." He glanced again at the blanket, trying to make his mind attach relevance to the shape beneath it. "She needs me . . ." Cobiah raised a shaking hand and pushed at the priest's shoulder, but the old man might as well have been made of stone.

The priest sighed grimly. "Your sister. I'm terribly sorry, son. She slipped from one of the dock pylons." As if this explained everything, the priest added, "It was quick."

Cobiah sank to his knees. The world around him spun, sickness rising in his throat. "I told her I saw a mermaid near the docks. I said . . . but it was just a story . . . just . . . Goddess Dwayna, no . . ."

"Don't blame yourself," the priest murmured, his hands on the young man's shoulders. "Those pylons are slick with ocean spray. No one saw her climb them. It happened too quickly for anyone to intervene. We must turn to Dwayna the Merciful, sweet and gentle comforter of the soul. Pray to her, young man. She will bring you peace."

In the midst of the priest's benediction, a piercing shriek split the air. Shoving the crowd aside with wild, drunken movements, Cobiah's mother lurched onto the rocky beach. "Biviane!" she howled insensibly. Hands clenching into fists, the woman shrieked in anger. "My little girl! She can't be . . . she can't be dead!

"Cobiah! You worthless, useless—Where were you?" she screeched, turning her anger toward her son. "*You* gave her money! I'll bet someone pushed Biviane off the dock to take her coin! This is your fault!" The priest turned to grapple with her as she kicked and struck at Cobiah's head and shoulders. "You foul piece of nothing! It's *your* fault she's dead! Your fault!"

Stunned, Cobiah couldn't even raise his hands to defend himself. She struck over and over again, jolting him from every angle, raining down sharp pain on his shoulders, arms, and face. The priest grabbed the harridan's wrists, forcing her to stop her attacks, but that did little to halt the abuse. "Foolish, worthless boy! Biviane was just a baby, she was an innocent child, and you've killed her!"

You've killed her!

His mother's words careened through Cobiah's mind. He couldn't force the sound from his ears, but his body reacted to expel it, vomiting bile onto the sand. Rage gripped Cobiah. Her abrupt, hypocritical turnaround felt like a punch in the stomach, and it took all the force of his will not to drive to his feet and strike his mother in return. Before he could move, sailors in the crowd dragged the woman off, her wails descending into screaming, incomprehensible accusations.

Cobiah drew a long, shuddering breath. He tried to focus his eyes and found himself staring at a rag doll floating in a tide pool. While everything around him was pandemonium and pain, the stitched burlap head with its cornflower-blue eyes still held for him a soft smile. Without thinking, Cobiah pulled the dolly from the tide.

Gently, the Dwaynan priest helped Cobiah stand. "Come, young man. I'll help you back to your house. There are preparations to be made . . ."

"No."

The old priest blinked. "What? No?"

"She needs . . . I can't pay for a funeral."

"I can arrange the funeral, son," the priest responded gently. "Your sister will have a safe place to sleep."

"Thanks," Cobiah murmured woodenly. "She'd like that." He squeezed the priest's hand and turned away, clutching the rag doll to his chest.

Numbly, Cobiah made his way back up onto the docks. He stumbled through the press of people, the calls of sailors and dockworkers echoing around him without any meaning registering in their words. He remembered Biviane's bright smile as he taught her how to read letters, forming them into words. She was so smart, so clever. The way she asked him questions when he told her tales, forcing him to elaborate further and further until she laughed. *She was the only good thing I had in this world.*

No job. No home: No sister to protect. He had nothing left except a sodden mother whose drunken binges would kill them both in time. Cobiah huddled in the cold, holding the limp doll to his chest. Her yarn hair was wet with seawater, but her stitched-on smile never wavered, frozen in a moment of time. Faintly, Cobiah realized that someone was calling his name. A familiar voice, rough and brutish like an old tree. Cobiah came to his senses and found himself standing at the base of a gangplank, staring past the end of the dock into the stormy sea. "Cobiah?" Bosun Vost's voice finally pulled Cobiah from his fugue. "What're you doing here, lad? We were about to raise the gangway. She's ready to sail." The old bosun eyed the youth with concern, taking in his bedraggled, pale appearance and the little bundle clenched in his hand. More soberly, the old bosun asked, "You doin' all right, laddie?"

"Were you serious, sir?" The words rushed out of Cobiah's chest, pushing down the tears and the sick feeling in his gut. "About my coming with you?"

Taken by surprise, Vost nodded. "Aye, we need a few more hands. You'll have to sign to a full tour of duty. Six months or more. What happened, Coby? Did you lose your girl?" The old sailor chuckled curiously, expecting the sad tale of a failed romance.

"Something like that." Cobiah didn't bother to correct him. "Sign me up, Vost. I'll take that berth." He lifted his chin, stuffing the rag doll beneath one arm and reaching for Vost's hand to pull him up the gangplank.

Something in the calmness of his words quieted the old man's protests and questions, and Vost simply nodded. "Come aboard, Cobiah of Lion's Arch. You're a mariner now."

Outside the city of Lion's Arch, the sun beat down on a vast and empty ocean. It twinkled on the foam of a thousand waves and shone warmly over the hulls and decks of massive ships that plunged into the sea spray. The galleon *Indomitable* heaved her bulk from the dock like a thick-shouldered bull, stiff and ungainly in the shallows. While her sailors called the chants and songs, she lowered her sails to catch an early wind, and they spread in wide white arches over the broad top deck. *Angel's wings.* Cobiah looked up at them as he gave a hand to the sailors slinging ropes from canvas to canvas across the lower boom of the mast. *Biviane's wings.*

Cobiah stared very hard at the *Indomitable*'s sails as the ship made her way into the open sea. He watched them as they caught the wind, putting the city of Lion's Arch—and the only life he'd ever known—far behind.

Cobiah woke in the cold, pale morning, his head spinning with illness and fatigue. Someone was shaking his hammock. He'd been conscious of it but too thick with sleep to rouse. As he struggled to focus, the pillow jerked out from under his head, and in a flash the whole hammock reeled and dumped him unceremoniously to the wooden boards of the deck.

"Five bells, Cobiah!" Vost, weathered bosun of the *Indomitable*, shouted down at Cobiah with the hammock still twisting in his hand. With a baleful glare, the leathery sailor grunted, "Up, fer Kryta's own sake! Wind's out of the west if'n our compass's boxed proper, and we've eased out of slack water and into sail. Time to heave the ropes, boy."

Cobiah lifted his head and scrambled to his feet despite the pitch and roll of the ship beneath him. "Aye, aye, sir," he gasped, trying to put a false energy into his words. "I'm ready." The tang of seawater, stronger than he'd ever smelled it, lingered all around him, and the dark brown boards sucked sunlight from the portholes as if jealous to see it roam free.

Vost snorted. "Yer ready all right. Ready as a dolyak calf fresh out'n its mother. Get on yer feet and try not to puke up yer dinner, green gills. And see that you do better next time, or I'll come with a bucket of seawater to dump over ye—wi' a crab in it to pinch off yer nose.

"Today's crew inspection, sailor. Be up-deck in five, or be tossed out to sea." The ship's bell rang like thunder on the main deck, its shrill clang cutting through the old sailor's snarls. With a grunt, Vost lost interest in Cobiah and stormed over to hound a man who'd been slow to find both boots.

Cobiah joined several other young sailors splashing water on their faces and scrubbing combs through their unruly hair. It was dark here in the berth, hot from the press of sailors and stinking of sweat and grime, but still cleaner than many an alley in Lion's Arch where Cobiah had slept on bad nights. Better food, too, and more of it— an entire apple to himself! He swiped one from the bowl and jammed it in his mouth.

More eager now, he jerked his shoes onto his feet as he hopped after the others. He'd have to earn enough money to buy boots at the next harbor; these city slippers didn't have enough traction for wet boards. Cobiah smiled around a bite of apple. Only seven days aboard the *Indomitable*, and he was thinking about a long-term future on the ship. He'd already worked harder than he'd ever done in Lion's Arch. The intense labor wasn't quite enough to make him forget, but it was enough to occupy his mind and keep him from thinking of—

"Up-deck!" Vost yelled. "Up-deck, ya scurvy lot! Now or never, and Grenth take you if you're slow!"

In quick succession, the mass of youths and men raced up two long ladders from the berth to the main deck of the ship. They grasped at ropes and pounded their feet on the rungs to draw them faster. Up above, Cobiah could hear the shrill call of a whistle blasting out a short rhythm of peculiar notes. Uncertain, he reached up to smooth his damp hair. "All call for inspection," one of the other youths said, smiling at him. "Don't worry, newbie. Cap'n Whiting won't even notice you. He never looks past the officers in the first row." Moving with an experienced roll to his footsteps, he scampered up the rungs toward the main deck.

Cobiah managed a shy smile of thanks. Was it that obvious? Although he'd never been to sea, he knew the ins and outs of ships from his time loading crates and wares. He'd cleaned them too, stem to stern, while they rested in the harbor. Lion's Arch was a seaport, after all, and most of the pickup labor was on the docks. He'd never been to sea, but he wasn't exactly a rube.

Just then the ship tossed under him, and Cobiah felt his stomach churn. The other boy grinned and clapped his shoulder. Cobiah sighed. *Fair enough.* His head crested the upper deck, and just as he'd done every day on board, Cobiah found himself staring out at the sea.

All around the galleon, the sea spread vast and deep blue. Touches of white flecked it here and there, but to the naked eye, no sign of land or harbor broke the smooth, even plane of the ocean. The sound of waves crashing against the wooden hull and the sharp crackling of wind in the broad sails of the galleon filled the air. Warm sunlight shone down upon the brown-and-gray deck, reflecting from polished iron small guns at either side. Huge white sails arched above him, their massive bulk speeding the ship across the water. It was a little bit creepy to a city boy who was used to the breakdown of streets and buildings, a horizon dotted with trees, meadows, and mountains high above. Here was the ship. Out there was nothing at all.

"What's wrong, you?" One of the sailors shoved him from below. "Keep going—we've all got to get up-deck!"

"Sorry," Cobiah said, abashed. Quickly, he stepped up his pace again and climbed out of the berth and onto the deck. He pushed forward with the others, seeking the end of the nearest row so that he could join the line.

The youth beside him grinned unevenly, his smile a dashed line broken by two missing teeth. He was only a little older than Cobiah, with dark brown hair pulled into a short ponytail at the back of his neck. "Don't worry about it," he whispered conspiratorially. "It seems like a lot of nothing would be boring after a while, but it takes a bit of getting used to, wotcher?"

"Yeah." Cobiah smiled in return.

The morning wind was steady and rippled the sail above him. He felt its cold fingers tug on the blond shag of his hair. Suddenly chilly, Cobiah pulled his sleeves down and wrapped his arms around his rib cage, trying not to shiver while the last of the sailors joined the lines on deck. Soon, the crew stood six rows deep in rough formation beneath the mainsail. They kept their backs to the forecastle and faced the quarterdeck, looking toward the stagelike balcony at the rear of the ship. "Her point's in the wind, sir!" came the call from the crow's nest. The bosun's whistle blew again, and the sailors stiffened. Not understanding, but willing to follow their example, Cobiah did the same.

On the high quarterdeck, three figures emerged from the shining oak doors of an interior cabin, stepping out onto the polished decks. Their yellow coats, set off at neck and knee with green striping, glittered brightly in the sunlight. Vost stepped forward and blew the bosun's whistle in a sharp, military pattern, snapping his arm down after the last blast of his signal. Cobiah stared. He'd never seen the rough-and-tumble bosun act with such formality, and he found it a little disconcerting.

On the balcony, an older man stepped forward, hemming and clearing his throat uncomfortably. In a long-winded, cheerily pompous sort of way, he introduced himself as Damran, the ship's pilot. With his black hair slicked over his forehead in a swoop from one side to the other, Cobiah thought he looked very much like a crow. Damran peered past a thick pair of spectacles to check names in a large book, which he read out one by one to be sure everyone was aboard and accounted for. Every time a sailor answered to his name, Damran would squint at him and scribble notes on the manuscript pages.

The second of the three officers on the balcony was a woman, stern-looking and hawkish, her brown mane tied back with a ribbon to keep the wind from mussing her near-immaculate curls. On her lapel she proudly wore the Krytan service medal that marked her as an official member of the king's military. She spoke for only a moment, demanding good behavior and condemning "scoundrelous activity" to punishment and the brig. As she spoke, her eyes raked each man below like a tiger sharpening its claws. When she stepped back, Cobiah breathed a sigh of relief. "Who was that?" he whispered to the youth beside him. "Is she the captain?"

"Naw, that's First Mate Chernock," the other sailor muttered, shushing him. "Don't let her catch you talking in line. She means what she said about the brig."

At last, the third man on the balcony stepped forward to address the sailors. He was square jawed and burly, though he stood at least a head shorter than his lanky first mate. His pale coat had cream-colored ruffles at the wrists and neck, and over that he wore a wide baldric of emerald green. The baldric shone with trinkets and military honors, markers of this sea crossing and that port, and the man's heavy black boots were shined to a mirror polish beneath his clattering spurs. The man walked with a stiff, self-conscious gait, furrowing his brow quite purposefully to show an attitude of intense concentration. Sweat touched the powdered forehead beneath his three-pointed green hat. He looked so pompous and so silly that it took effort for Cobiah not to laugh.

"Captain on deck! Full attention for Captain Whiting!" Vost called out. Cobiah stiffened a bit and looked around at the other sailors. This was as close as such a rabble ever came to full "attention." Interesting, but where was the—

Wait. Cobiah suddenly realized what Vost meant. *That prancing ninny's the captain?*

With a nervous gait, the squat little man approached the balcony rail, staring very fixedly over everyone's head toward the front of the ship. The captain glanced about idly, looking at the masts and the rigging, then the ocean all around them, until at last he turned to the side and murmured something indistinct to the first mate. Cobiah strained to hear the words, hoping that the captain would say something inspiring like the great sea captains he'd always heard about in sailors' tales.

Instead, Captain Whiting spoke quietly to his first mate and then to his pilot and seemed completely uninterested in everything else. After a moment, he stepped back from the railing, wiping his hand on his sleeve with a forgetful sort of sigh. Without even a word for the assembled sailors, the captain turned his back to the crew and strode through the rear door of the forecastle, heading back into his quarters.

"Dismissed!" cried Vost, lifting his whistle to his mouth again to blow the call to disperse. The two other officers congratulated themselves on a successful muster and followed the captain through the brass-studded door. Cobiah could feel the tension lift from the crowd, and sailors began to talk in too-loud voices, praising themselves or calling out for work to be done. Most of them didn't even look up toward the balcony again after Vost's whistle. Cobiah stared hard at the ornate door as it closed, wondering what was beyond it.

"That's all?" Cobiah couldn't help but blurt out. He colored slightly as others looked over in annoyance. It all seemed silly: the captain's preening strut on the quarter-deck, the sailors all in a row. What had been the purpose of it all?

"That's it. First-day assessment," said the youth in line beside him, nodding. His ponytail bounced with the movement. "They just need to count heads so they know how much money we're to have when we make landfall in Kaineng City. That, and warn us against 'scoundrelous behavior.' Just like they do every time."

Despite the world-weariness of his tone, the other fellow didn't seem much older than Cobiah's sixteen years. Eyeing him warily, Cobiah asked, "You've been through this a lot?"

"Three times." The other boy puffed out his chest and tried to look jaded. "I'm an experienced deckhand. Don't worry, you will be, too, once you get your sea legs. It's a good life here on ship, and despite what it looks like, the cap'n pays fair, and the bosun spares the whip even when we screw things up a bit. You'll see."

"But—Captain Whiting . . ." Cobiah glanced up at the balcony once more. "Doesn't he do anything?"

"Like what?" The young sailor laughed. "Cook our meals? Swab the decks? Sing shanties while we repair the sails? Grenth's imps, no! And we don't rightly want him to. An officer trying to do honest work on a ship's like a

monkey trying to paint the king's picture. Poop everywhere and a right mess to clean up after!" He laughed,
and despite himself, Cobiah joined in. Clapping Cobiah
on the shoulder, the youth continued. "Captain Whiting
doesn't care about us. He just cares about *paying* us. With
luck, we won't see him nor his officers again 'til the next
dock's in sight.

"See? That's why sailors call him 'the gull.' When you
catch a glimpse of the cap'n's fluttery white wings"—the
boy flapped his hands in the air to mimic the captain's
ruffled sleeve cuffs—"it's a sure tell we're close to landfall."

An older man interrupted their jocularity. "On with
you, Sethus." The sailor shoved both youths firmly, pushing them toward the fore of the *Indomitable*'s three masts.
"There's work to be done. You there, ya green stripling,
go with Sethus. Help him with the ropes."

"Sethus, huh?" Cobiah stuck out his hand. "My name's
Cobiah."

"Posh-sounding name for a scrub. You got any others,
bit more fit for a sailing man?" the dark-haired lad said,
looking skeptical.

Nodding, Cobiah answered, "Coby."

"Right, then—Coby it is. Let's get to work before Vost
hangs us by our heels on the yardarm."

The *Indomitable* was a hundred and a half feet long,
thirty-eight feet across the beam, and more than eighteen feet from the main deck to the bottom keel. She
had two lower decks resting beneath the main planking,
one for the sailor's berth and one below for ballast, cargo,
and stores. Three masts full of huge, square-rigged sails
fluttered boldly against the wind. She was armed with
thirty cannons below and twenty-six smaller carronades
above to each side, for a total of one hundred and twelve

guns—a solid ship of the line built in the proud ship-yards of Lion's Arch. As he worked, Cobiah explored, studying every hatch and timber and learning every line of the rigging from the massive topsails to the broad, tri-angular jibs that stretched out over the decks.

For the rest of a very long day, Cobiah followed Sethus through the ship. He caught a moment of rest whenever the work slowed, which wasn't often. Sethus taught him to wrap rough sharkskin straps around his palms and climb the rigging of the ship like a monkey, throwing down cast-off ropes as they were replaced with new ones. Below, less agile sailors picked up the ropes and twisted them along the length of their forearms to bundle them away. It was a struggle to keep up with Sethus, but Cobiah managed.

Before he knew it, Vost was blowing the bosun's whis-tle for change of shift. Arms aching, legs sore from keep-ing his balance, Cobiah headed gratefully down to the crew's berth. Sethus went with him, chattering about the things they could look forward to when they docked in Kaineng City. "We're carrying cotton bales to the Can-thans," Sethus said as he hopped ahead. "Like a cargo of gold, that is! There's a bit of extra pay in it for us if the ship makes port early. We always pray that Grenth keeps the pirates off our route and the wind on our course . . ." He slowed, and Cobiah pushed past to see what had got-ten his light-footed friend's attention.

Another sailor, a bit older than them but far more weathered, stood at Cobiah's cubby in the crew hold. In an instant, Cobiah could tell the man had been going through his things. "What's this, then?" sneered the older boy, pulling the worn rag doll from under Cobiah's blan-kets. As he spoke, the sailor shook the rag doll lightly. "You brought your *dolly* to sea?" A rough burst of laugher erupted from the assembled sailors, and Cobiah felt his face grow flushed.

Angry, Cobiah reached across the netting and grabbed the doll's legs. "Give me that. It's none of your concern." They tugged it back and forth for a moment before the sailor let go. With a flip of his hand, the other boy laughed.

Sethus chuckled good-naturedly. "Leave Cobiah be, Tosh. This is his first passage."

"It'll be his last if he's that much a sissy." Tosh had long, greasy hair pulled into a thin ponytail that snaked between muscular shoulders. His face was pockmarked and unpleasant. Although his clothing was worn, it had no patches, not even on the elbows of his belligerently crossed arms. As the other sailors laughed again, Tosh's brown eyes, narrow as a terrier's, mocked Cobiah's obvious embarrassment.

"C'mon, Cobiah." Sethus tugged at his sleeve. "Tosh's a big bully. Dinner'll be waiting in the mess hall . . ." Sethus tried to pull Cobiah away, but he ignored it and kept his eyes on Tosh's jeering grin.

"Dolly." Tosh considered, rubbing his chin. "Maybe that's what we'll call you, eh, new fish? Are you a little dolly, too?"

"Shut your mouth," Cobiah growled between gritted teeth. Quickly, he shoved the doll into his pillowcase. He rolled that into the hammock and tucked everything back into his small cubby. There were a few other things in there, mostly because of Bosun Vost's charity: another shirt, a spare pair of woolen socks, a fork, a bowl, and a thick wooden mug. "If Vost finds out you've gone through my things, you'll get a day without rations."

"Yeah, you just try and tell him that through a pair of swollen lips, Dolly." Tosh pushed, shoving Cobiah back.

Thick, ropy muscles stood out on his arms from years of labor aboard the ship. He grinned again, defying Cobiah to talk back.

By now, several of the other sailors had begun paying attention. "Dolly," singsonged the ponytailed youth, laughing. "You cry at night, Dolly? Maybe Mate Chernock'll be your mommy. Want me to ask her?"

Cobiah'd been in fights in Lion's Arch. When a new kid came to work on the docks, the others picked on him ruthlessly, like the packs of wild dogs around Lion's Arch testing to see if a new stray was strong enough to join their pack. The streets of Lion's Arch were tough on a kid alone. More so when your mother was a penniless drunk. He wasn't the best fighter, or the strongest. But he knew how this worked. The idea of a beating didn't bother Cobiah. He'd had worse at his mother's hands than they could ever give. But if these men thought he was weak, well, then the humiliation would never stop. There was nowhere to go, nowhere he could run or hide from the bullies, and portage to Cantha would take nearly eight weeks. What was he going to do, avoid Tosh? For months? On board a *ship*?

Staring at Tosh's smarmy face, Cobiah let his anger go for the first time. He was sick of losing. Sick of being picked on. Sick of fighting for the things he loved, only to see them taken away. He missed home. He missed Biviane, and that doll was all he had left of her. They weren't going to take it from him, and he wasn't going to hide it because he feared them. He wasn't going to be the stray. All the anger that he'd held back when his mother was taking things out on him, all the frustration of Biviane's death, suddenly rushed through Cobiah's veins, channeling itself into pure, cold rage.

"Dolly, Dolly," Tosh sang, still trying to grab Cobiah's bundled blankets.

Cobiah snarled sudden resoluteness. "My name is *Cobiah*, you stupid, prancing *sot*. Coby, if you're my friend, but you're not, so shut your stupid mouth and keep your filthy hands off my things." Then, as if announcing that he'd nothing at all to fear from Tosh, Cobiah reached out and shoved the pockmarked sailor as hard as he could, nearly knocking the surprised sailor over. "If you touch my stuff again," Cobiah threatened, "I'll toss you into the sea."

With that, Cobiah turned his back on Tosh and stuffed the bundle into the cubby marked with his initials. There was an echoed murmur from the other sailors when he turned away. They knew that Tosh couldn't allow that kind of brush-off and still keep his reputation. Sailors clustered closer, like vultures hoping to feed. "Oh, you got to ruffle 'im good now, Tosh. Don't let the greengill talk to you like that," called an eager voice in the crowd. "You best show Dolly 'is place!"

Snarling in embarrassment, Tosh spun Cobiah around and shoved back, forcing him to stagger into one of the hammock poles. A sharp burst of white sparks filled Cobiah's vision as his head cracked against the wood. He grabbed the pole and shook his head to clear it. All around, the rest of the sailors were gathering, cheering excitedly for a fight. Sethus tried to call them to reason, but nobody was listening. Like the dog packs in Lion's Arch, they were hoping for a fight.

"C'mon, Dolly," Tosh growled, eyes narrowing. "You're nothing but rag and stuffing."

"That doll belonged to my sister," Cobiah snarled. "She died back in Lion's Arch. Touch it again, and you'll be the one who gets ripped apart, I swear it on Grenth's knucklebones." Before Tosh could react, Cobiah hurled himself forward, burying his shoulder in the soft part of

Tosh's midsection. Shocked, the other youth choked. As the older boy bent in half from the blow, Cobiah straightened, bringing his fist up to crack Tosh in the jaw. Eager cheers and laughter rose from the other sailors.

"Cobiah," Sethus pleaded as he backed away from the crowd, "I'll go get Vost! Just hang in there." He turned to run, and Cobiah lost sight of him.

"Vost? Bah. I'll wipe the deck with you before Vost gets here, and no one'll tell the tale." Tosh wiped a bit of blood from his lip and squared off against Cobiah, this time ready for the pale boy to make a move. "You going to run away like your little friend, Dolly?"

But Cobiah had started this fight, and he was determined to end it.

Tosh cut loose with a jab as quick as a striking hawk. It caught Cobiah's cheek, snapping his head to the side. Cobiah stumbled but recovered in a flash, double-punching Tosh's gut again, taking advantage of his previous success. Tosh grunted in pain but didn't fall.

With a spin, Tosh responded with a heavy kick to Cobiah's knee. Even as he fell, Cobiah reached out and grabbed Tosh's ponytail, jerking the other boy to the floor as well. Together, they rolled about on the floor, legs kicking and flailing as the crowd shouted encouragement. Gaining the upper hand, Cobiah rolled onto Tosh and gouged his eyes with both thumbs. Still, Tosh was stronger, and before Cobiah could get a good push, Tosh rolled him over and started punching Cobiah in the face. Two blows, and blood spilled down Cobiah's cheek. A third, and he felt his eye start to swell. "Give up, Dolly," Tosh taunted. "You can't win." All around them, sailors were encouraging them to fight harder and passing silver back and forth with eager wagers. As he mopped at his eye with the back of his hand, Tosh leaned forward to laugh in Cobiah's face.

He could taste the coppery tang of blood in his mouth, feel the skin beginning to puff up and blur his vision. Ignoring the pain, Cobiah seized his chance and leaned forward to sink his teeth into the bully's ear. Tosh screeched and tried to pull away, but he couldn't get his ear out of Cobiah's grip. Raising his arms to either side, Tosh sent blow after blow into Cobiah's rib cage. Cobiah didn't care about the beating he was taking. He simply refused to give in.

Tosh howled, screaming and kicking, but Cobiah was relentless. Cobiah released his bite and hit him with a double strike of his fists. One of the other sailors tried to pull him back, lifting Cobiah bodily away from his foe. Cobiah pulled free and leapt back into the fray, going for the wounded ear again. "Help!" Tosh screamed. "He's gone mad-dog crazy! Get him off me!" Tosh rolled back and forth, trying desperately to throw Cobiah. At last, Cobiah let go of his opponent's ear and punched Tosh dead in the face. Blood spurted from Tosh's nose as Cobiah followed up by driving a knee into his groin.

Suddenly, hands grasped Cobiah's shoulders and jerked him away. Three brawny sailors held on to him, their faces pale. Eye swollen shut, lip split, and spitting blood out of his mouth, Cobiah twisted and nearly broke free again. "Let me go!" he snarled. "I'm not done!"

"To the Mists with you!" Tosh skittered backward across the floor in terror. Blood dripped from his broken nose as he gasped, "Keep that madman away from me!"

"Back away, you lot!" Bosun Vost shoved through the knot of sailors. He scowled in rage and put his hands on his hips. "What's going on here?" Glaring, he took in Tosh's hunched posture and torn cheeks as well as the rapidly growing bruise swelling on Cobiah's jaw. "You know the rules. No fighting aboard ship! Am I going to have to flog the both of you?"

Sethus, standing at Vost's side, was the first to speak up. "I told you, Bosun. Tosh tripped, and, um, Cobiah tried to catch him, then they both got tangled . . ." The crowd began to scatter and duck back to their own bunks, each sailor afraid of the bosun's wrath.

"Tripped?" Vost's eyes darkened. "Cobiah, is this true?"

"Yes, sir." Cobiah gulped, glancing from Sethus back to the injured Tosh.

Vost's withering glare turned colder. "Tosh?"

It felt like the pause lasted for hours, but eventually Tosh managed to say, "It's true."

The bosun looked back and forth between them with a grim nod. "You 'tripped' and broke your nose." Vost crossed his arms and fumed. "Fine. You two 'trippers' get swabbing duty tonight instead of dinner."

"But, sir—" Sethus began, and Vost rounded on him. "You, too, for bringing me down here over nothing." Sethus quailed and fell silent. The bosun looked between the three youths and scowled. "I'll let it slide this time, your 'tripping,' but the next time I catch any of you at it—or fibbing about it!—you'll be tripping at the end of my whip. Am I clear, you dogs?"

"Yes, sir!" all three chorused at once.

Vost grumbled and spun on one heel, pointing at Cobiah. "You and Sethus go up on deck. I want you to polish the brass up there until I can see Elona in it.

"As for you, Tosh . . ." The bosun leveled a stern glare at the other boy. "You head belowdecks to the bilge pumps. You'll check every pump for air holes, even if you have to drown yourself doing it. With the whole ship between you, you should have plenty of space to cool down.

"Do I make myself clear, gentlemen?" Vost shouted bracingly.

It wasn't a question. Stiffening his back, Cobiah bellowed, "Yes, sir!" with the rest.

"Now get going," Vost growled.

Cobiah and Sethus raced upstairs as Tosh slunk toward the ladder that led to the lower hold. Nearly tripping over their feet, the two youths clambered out of the berth and hurried through the press of sailors at work on the deck. Grateful to feel warm wind on his face even if his stomach was growling, Cobiah retrieved the brass polish from a small storage hold. Sethus grabbed a small pile of rags. With an overdramatic sigh, he said, "Let's start with the figurehead. The rest of the brass is on the forecastle, and I'd rather stay out of the bosun's way for a while."

The figurehead of the *Indomitable* hung at the fore of the ship just beneath the bowsprit. Masterfully formed and easily recognizable, the brass woman's glorious figure curved against the keel of the ship as if her back were arched in flight. Six arms rose from her curving torso: two reaching up to the sky, two more spread back against the ship in mute protection, and a third and lowest pair curled down like the graceful limbs of a belly dancer enticing her audience. She was beautiful but hellaciously difficult to keep from turning green.

Once they were polishing her, Sethus whispered, "Where did you learn to fight like that?"

Cobiah ran a hand through his hair, feeling the bruises where Tosh had knocked him around. "When you grow up on the streets of Lion's Arch, you learn to fight."

"So, you're a thief?"

Scowling, Cobiah retorted, "I don't steal things. I just learned how to take care of myself."

Sethus nodded, taking that in. After a moment, he blurted out, "You didn't have to fight Tosh. You could have walked away from the fight. We'd have gotten your old doll back sooner or later."

"What, have Vost step in on my account?" Cobiah snorted. "That would have only made it worse. In a week? Three weeks? Everyone would be helping Tosh pick on me. I'd be scum." He smeared polish roughly on one of the rags. "Terrible idea."

"I guess." Sethus paused. "Is that why you went crazy down there? You looked feral." Sethus shook his head in amazement. "You looked like a charr. You know, big teeth, claws, four ears, fuzzy killing machine?"

"I know what a charr is, Sethus."

"Seriously. I thought you were going to start foaming at the mouth. You were a wild thing!" He made snarling noises and sank his fingers like claws into the brass polish.

Cobiah chuckled. "I wasn't acting like a charr. I've just seen plenty of bullies in my time. I know what happens if they think they're in charge." Despite his sore jaw, it was nice to laugh again. He wiped the brass forehead with the rag, rubbing the polish in circles. "If you ignore a bully, he just gets worse. Soon everyone else joins in, and before long, you're in a hole you can't get out of.

"I could beat Tosh. But I knew I couldn't beat Tosh and his friends if they all attacked me together. A bully is one thing. A crowd . . ." His smile faded. "Anyway, I wasn't trying to win. I was trying to scare him. I wanted to show him—and everyone else—that picking a fight with me wasn't worth the cost of winning."

Sethus settled down on the other side of the figure-head and wrapped his rag around one of the woman's elegant arms. "Isn't that a little extreme?"

"Exactly." Cobiah nodded grimly. "It's all in the attitude. See, if you think a bully can beat you, then he'll *know* he can beat you. You have to make them think you're a difficult target, too dangerous to provoke." Frowning, he scrubbed at the brass. "If you want to stop a battle from turning into a war, you have to scare the other guy as fast and as hard as you can."

"Who taught you that?"

Cobiah paused. "My father. He was a soldier in Kryta before he came to Lion's Arch. He retired from duty after the war and became a sailor."

Perhaps hearing some sadness in Cobiah's tone, Sethus asked, "What happened to him?"

Shrugging, Cobiah answered, "He went out to sea . . . and didn't come back."

For a moment Sethus thought about that, rubbing the polish from the metal with the dry side of his rag. When it was bright and shining, he asked, "Cobiah? What would you have done if Tosh won?"

"Then at least it'd be over. Either way, he wouldn't pick on me anymore."

He studied the brass and worked to make it shine as brightly as it could, letting the conversation fall into silence.

"You're crazy, Coby," Sethus sighed at last, buffing the maiden's elegant shoulder.

"Maybe so." Cobiah grinned. "But now the bullies know it, too."

3

After ten months on board, Cobiah began to realize why sailors tended to look alike. The blazing sun and fierce winds of the sea weathered his skin, tanning it to a deep brown even as the labor tightened his muscles into cordwood. The food aboard the *Indomitable* was rough fare, mostly: hot coffee in the morning with oatmeal, and salted meat, boiled potatoes, or fish in the evening. It wasn't much, but it was more than Cobiah had gotten in his mother's house, and he never complained.

Tosh, for the most part, kept away from him. Even after the long marks on his cheeks healed, they left thin white lines from forehead to cheek, missing the curve of his eye socket by only a hair. Cobiah hadn't made any friends with the fight, but the toughs left him alone. More than once, he heard Tosh muttering curses while he played cards with the other men. Cobiah was never asked to join the poker game. He didn't mind.

They'd been twice to massive Kaineng City in Cantha, each time carrying a heavy cargo of cotton and returning with a load of silk and other goods. Cobiah loved exploring the twisted labyrinth of Kaineng City's streets and trying the strange Canthan food, but best of all was the pure freedom of being out to sea. Travel was glorious, opening his horizons to different cultures and perspectives. He relished life aboard the ship and being part of the *Indomitable*'s crew, despite the adversity of sailing and the difficult labor. He wanted to see the world.

But he never got off the ship when they docked in Lion's Arch.

Cobiah spent the better part of each day chatting with Sethus and the older sailors aboard the ship. If he saved part of his morning ration for them, the old-timers would share stories in exchange, and Cobiah loved their tales. They talked about heroes, like those who fought to save Kryta from the White Mantle as his grandfather had done, and about the men and women of Ascalon who struggled against the ferocious, man-eating charr. They told him about the wild plains of Kryta, the sunlit hills of Ascalon, the ghost tales of the Maguuma Jungle, and the soaring, snow-covered Shiverpeaks. But best of all, Cobiah loved when they told stories of the lost cities of ancient Orr.

"Why do you like Orr so much?" Sethus asked him one night when they were lying in their hammocks. He bunked below Cobiah, occasionally reaching up to poke him with one foot when he couldn't sleep . . . which was all the time. "Orr's boring, Cobiah. It's all sunk underwater now. There's nothing to see! It's not like you can ever go there, so what's the point? I'd rather hear about the heroes of the Searing in Ascalon. Taking out the charr." Sethus punched at the air as if fighting an enemy. "Winning the hand of the fair maiden Gwen! Those are good stories."

"Charr are just mindless monsters, Sethus." Cobiah yawned. "There's nothing interesting about a mindless eating machine. You might as well be scared of the dolyak that pull carts in the city. Orr is where magic comes from. The gods themselves lived there once. And now it's vanished beneath the ocean, never to be seen again. Think of all the riches it must contain—the wealth and ancient secrets! I'd take that over monsters any day."

"Orr sank because of the charr," Sethus said smugly. "They marched across Ascalon and then went to Orr next. And the wizards of Orr—"

"Viziers," Cobiah said, correcting him.

"Whatever. A vizier tried to use magic to stop the charr army but ended up sinking the whole peninsula. The gods themselves punished him; he got turned into a lich in penance for what he'd done. You know what a lich is? It's an undead creature, risen from the grave!" Sethus grinned ghoulishly. "He got punished, Orr was destroyed, and the charr conquered Ascalon instead. That means the charr won. See? Charr beats Orr." Sethus crossed his arms and swung back and forth in his hammock. Even though it was dark, Cobiah could *hear* the grin on his face.

Cobiah rolled his eyes and let the subject drop.

The next morning, Vost woke them up with his usual blustery yelling, rolling sailors out of their hammocks if they were slow to rouse. The ship's bell rang loudly. "What's going on?" Cobiah rubbed the sleep out of his eyes. "Corsairs on the horizon?"

"Captain's inspection," Vost grumbled as he stomped past. "Get on deck!"

Sethus punched Cobiah in the arm and raced toward the stairs. Not nearly as quick as the smaller boy, Cobiah called after him jovially as he trundled along with the press of sailors climbing up the ladders from the berth to the main deck.

The sailors arranged themselves in their rows. Some tugged their shirts down or straightened the bandannas at their necks in case Captain Whiting took notice. Most of them didn't bother, eyes wandering to ropes that needed to be coiled or sails that had mending to be done. An extra inspection was unusual, but it wasn't enough to cause concern. Most likely, the captain just wanted to double-check the ship's count before they reached port.

Heavy sighs and mutters escaped the bravest as the captain and his officers came out of the quarterdeck cabins. "Gah, get it over with," Cobiah grumped under his breath. Daylight was wasting. He saw Vost standing on tiptoe at the banister, speaking in low tones to Damran, the pilot. The conversation seemed sober, their voices grim, and a tension spread through the crowd. This was unusual. Even the cold sea wind felt somehow wrong.

"Can you hear what they're saying?" Cobiah whispered to Scthus, who was closer to the front ranks.

Sethus squinted and tried to put together the bits he could hear. "Sounds like a ship was sighted last night. The men on watch late said they saw something signaling. Flashing lights at us."

"A message? What did it say?" He got no answer. One of the older sailors in the front row hushed them with a hiss and a glare.

As Vost stepped back, Captain Whiting moved gingerly toward the banister. His emerald baldric shifted about his tubby belly, the medals of honor twinkling and clanking with each uncertain step. The captain paused to exchange a few words with his first mate and the old navigator, then ran one lace-cuffed hand through the sparse hair atop his forehead with a gesture that spoke volumes. Cobiah watched him interestedly, wondering what had the officers in such a strange state. Usually they spent only a few minutes on the quarterdeck, the thick brass banister separating the crew's world from the high heaven of the pampered officers.

But today, instead of tossing a glance over the crew and heading back inside, Captain Whiting sidled to the railing with obvious discomfort. He gripped the brass rail with both hands, cleared his throat, and began—hesitantly—to speak.

"Gentlemen and ladies," he said to the crew, staring out over their heads in awkward formality. Cobiah blinked. The captain's voice was thin, nasal, not at all what he'd have expected to come from the man's barrel chest. He'd thought it would have more gravity. Instead, the master of the *Indomitable* sounded like a sheepish schoolboy addressing the class. "King Baede has given us new orders. A creature has been sighted in these waters. It's wreaked havoc on two of his vessels, and now we're tasked with tracking down the monster and destroying it. Therefore, our normal voyage has been postponed.

"We are the only ship of the line in the area." Whiting shifted from foot to foot, gauging his words—or possibly, Cobiah guessed, trying to remember how he'd rehearsed them. "We're well armed and well crewed. Nothing will deter us from the king's duty." Captain Whiting lifted his hat and ran a hand through his thinning shock of hair. "Once we have ascertained the issue, we will return to Lion's Arch and bring word to the king at his palace. Only then will we resume our voyage to Cantha and deliver our cargo." He coughed. Lowering his eyes to stare down at his polished boots, Whiting finished lamely, "That is all."

Battle! Cobiah's heart leapt in his chest. He'd never seen a ship-to-ship fight, but he'd often imagined the *Indomitable*'s cannons thundering over the waves as the galleon nimbly danced through currents. He dreamed of sails stretched to their capacity, boards creaking with the force of a sudden turn. What an adventure!

Vost stepped in front of the ranks, shooting a concerned glance over his shoulder at the three officers on the quarterdeck. With a roar, he called out, "You louts heard the captain! Back to work, and twice as hard, or I'll flog your hides myself! Tack her rudder north by northwest, back toward Kryta, and make it fast!"

The sailors scrambled to obey, running for the sail ropes and the ship's rudder. Cobiah scrambled up the netting beside the galleon's mainsail, Sethus racing him to the top. "Vost's kidding, right?" Cobiah gasped, swinging aloft on a knotted rope. "We're halfway to Cantha on the Sea of Sorrows. The only thing north of us is—"

"The wreckage of Orr." Sethus looked distinctly less pleased. He pulled himself up onto the high yard, the upper crossbar of the main topsail.

"Why us? Sethus, why are we headed to Orr?"

Sethus shrugged. "Everyone knows our captain's a special favorite of King Baede; he's dining at the palace most of the time we're docked in Lion's Arch. My guess is that Cap'n Whiting talked up the *Indomitable*, and now that there's a problem, he's going to have to live up to his bragging."

"Well, we're on a good ship. We've got a lot of firepower and a full load of munitions. This'll be a breeze!" Cobiah swung out on the spar, tying a rope around his waist before he crawled out to cut free the sail. "The *Indomitable* can handle anything."

"Cobiah, we're talking about Orr. Those are dangerous waters. We'll be sailing through sharp corals and rock pillars. There are broken stone ruins under the sea capable of tearing open our hull if the tide's too shallow—and the tide there is completely unpredictable." Sethus looked pale. "I don't care what the tales say. No sane captain sails there. It's like asking to have your keel ripped open and your belly eaten by krait."

"Come on, Sethus. You're just angry we aren't sailing to Ascalon," Cobiah teased, pulling up the free-hanging ropes as he sat balanced on the crossbar.

"Ascalon doesn't have a coastline, you nitwit. It's land-locked." Sethus coiled the netting slowly in his hands. His dark hair fluffed out with the rippling breeze, brushing away from worried features. The ship was turning her bowsprit into the wind, and below them the ship rocked lightly to the side, altering her course with the movement of the rudder and recalibration of the galleon's tremendous white sails. "Nobody goes to Orr, Cobiah. It's a cursed land. A dead land. A drowned country that the gods themselves abandoned," Sethus murmured over the rush of the wind. "I don't care what the king thinks is important. We shouldn't be going there. If we get too close, that land will curse our ship, too."

A shiver ran down Cobiah's spine, but he laughed it off. He'd heard such rumors before. Sailors were notoriously superstitious and had an irrational trust in everything from the number of knots used on the sail ropes to coins thrown into stormy seas to appease the god of death before a voyage. A mere whisper of bad luck could make the swabs turn white and start muttering about curses and evil eyes. Nothing more than sailors' talk.

"Look there." One hand clutching the crossbar between his legs, Sethus raised his other to point toward the ship's bow. From their vantage at the top of the *Indomitable*'s mast, Cobiah could see a darkness on the horizon, a place where the waters turned into moving shadows beneath the storm. The sky there was green with sickly storms and black with clouds, and lightning flashed in the depths like twisting eels fighting in clouded waters. Where they reached down to touch the water, Cobiah could see shapes illuminated beneath the waves. At first he thought these were merely rocks, bits of island, or coral formations just below the white-foamed surface. As he peered longer, he began to pick out regular and oddly distinct edges, the features taking strangely familiar form.

Spires. Pointed stone rooftops, like the high pointed tops of churches and meeting halls in Lion's Arch, but standing beneath the surface of the sea. Startled, Cobiah narrowed his eyes and tried to see more. "What are those?"

"Those are the ruins of one of the great cathedrals of Orr. Legend doesn't say which one. Sailors call them Malchor's Fingertips." Sethus shivered, pulling himself back up onto the spar to stare out over the sea. "Ships don't cross that threshold. When the pilot sees those black spires, you turn back."

"Malchor?"

"An old legend," Sethus said. "Malchor was a great artist who carved statues of the gods. After he was done carving their statues, the gods shut themselves away from mankind. But Malchor had fallen in love with Dwayna. He couldn't stand thinking that he'd never see her again, so he threw himself into the ocean and drowned. Sailors say those steeples are Malchor's hands reaching out of the sea toward the heavens, trying to touch the gods that left him behind so long ago."

Cobiah looked at the faint pillars of stone at the edge of the horizon's curve. They did look a little like fingers. "That's where the seas of Orr begin?"

"Yeah. Right at that line of stones."

"What's beyond?"

"Orr itself. They say the water there is as black as night, like ink's been poured into the waves. It never gets lighter, and the sun never warms it. Sailors have used Orrian water to freeze things even in the Maguuma Jungle's heat. Just one drop turns meat into jerky. A canteen could ice over even the fires of Sorrow's Furnace!"

"Superstition," Cobiah snorted, but he didn't take his eyes off the sea. In his time as a sailor, Cobiah's stomach had never given him an inch of trouble. Come smooth seas or rolling winds, he'd never been seasick and he'd never offered a "sailor's prayer" over the side of the deck. Suddenly, thinking about sailing over the depths of a land abandoned by the gods and cursed by haunts, Cobiah felt his belly roll over. He'd been excited before, when Orr was a figment of his imagination. Now that he could see black stone fingers reaching up out of the ocean's murky depths, he suddenly felt the tang of fear.

"Do you think we'll find the monster that the king is looking for?" Cobiah whispered, coiling salt-roughed rope around his elbow and wrist. "Does it live in Orr?"

"I don't know," Sethus answered in a somber tone. "But I do know that no ship that sails beyond Malchor's Fingers"—Sethus gulped, suddenly looking down at his net—"ever comes back."

4

The next morning dawned crisp and cold, wintry enough to drive away the warmth of early autumn they'd known only the day before. Last night at sunset, the slender spines of Malchor's Fingers had been barely a jagged line against the horizon. In the soft gleam of morning, the spines were much closer, clawing their way up from the depths through rings of thick sea-foam.

"Eyes on the rocks, lads!" Vost shouted from the bow. The ship's bosun seemed ill at ease, one foot planted atop the bulwark near the *Indomitable*'s six-armed figurehead. He kept his bosun's whistle clenched in one hand, the other holding fast to a mainstay rope as wind buffeted his crisp white shirt. Captain Whiting and his first mate stood on the forecastle with him, staring past the cutting waves at the front of the ship toward the sea ahead where rocky stanchions loomed. The captain fidgeted with his sleeve cuffs as he stared into the wind, but the bosun and the first mate were as still as statues.

Ice-cold water splashed up onto the deck as the galleon made her way bravely forward. She barely rocked at all in the tow of the waves, cresting fluidly over each ripple and valley of the sea. Her topsail was wrapped against the crossbar; the jibs were lowered, and her long, pointed bowsprit was bare of white muslin sail. Only the two central wind catchers, the foresail to the front and the mainsail at the rear, remained aloft, shivering in the heavy winds that buffeted ocean froth around the tall jagged rocks.

"Were those stones really the top of an ancient church?" Cobiah whispered to one of the other sailors as they folded netting. He tucked the wrapped cords into wooden caskets below the railing of the forecastle.

"Who told you that old chestnut?" Urim scoffed, tightening the knot of a bright red bandanna wrapped about his neck in hopes of warmth. "They're just salt pillars. A rock somewhere below started breaking the water, and the salt of the sea's gathered up layer on layer 'til the whole thing sticks up above the waves. S'nothing to be afeared of."

Tosh snorted mockingly as he walked past, twisting a long skein of rope between his thumb and his elbow. "Church towers? Fell for that one, did you, whey face? I heard it when I was six—and I didn't believe it even then. You always fall for those toothless jawers' yapping. You should've been a priest, Cobiah. At least then you'd get paid to listen to fools." Although the jibes were rough, Tosh snorted and moved on without staying to pick a fight. That much, at least, had changed in the last half year.

"Cock of the walk, he is," Cobiah spat under his breath.

"Tosh's just ribbing you, as always. Don't pay him any mind," Sethus said as he trotted up with a grin. "And Urim's as glazed as Lyssa's mirror." Sethus pointed at the sailor and mimicked taking a swig of brandy. "Just salt rocks? What's under that salt, I ask you? Orrian church towers. Now c'mon, Coby, and help me shove this heavy lot after that gun." Sethus grabbed Cobiah's sleeve and dragged him toward the hatch nearby. Below, they could see four sailors dragging one of the ship's big guns to its firing post. The captain had given orders that the cannons as well as the smoothbore carronades were to be kept loaded and ready at all times. The top-deck carronades were bolted to the frame of the ship and were always in place, with firepower and shot nearby, but the cannons on the lower deck were too large to shot-pack without need. It was the first time that Cobiah had seen the big guns freed of their moorings, and he watched with great interest.

Sethus and Cobiah dropped down to the lower deck and moved to help the gunners, pushing pallets of cannonballs and small burlap bags of powder into place beside each cannon at its porthole. Although the work was hard, Cobiah couldn't help being pleased that he was helping with the gunnery while Tosh was saddled with the everyday task of gaffing ropes.

"Ho, there!" The voice was crisp, the vowels rounded, and the tone one of immutable authority. Aubrey Chernock leaned over to peer down through the hatch opening. The *Indomitable*'s first mate cut a fine figure, brown ponytail dancing against her shoulders, fists on her hips, golden coat flaring in the wind. "The captain left his astrolabe in the chart room." She pointed at Cobiah, hand striking out like a shark. "You there. Run back and retrieve it. Ask Pilot Damran—he'll know what I mean."

"Yes, ma'am!" Cobiah leapt up from the pallet he'd been loading and clambered back to the top deck, giving her a fumbling salute. He rushed toward the rear of the ship without a second thought, pausing only when he'd reached the mainsail. Damran? That was the pilot's name. Chart room? Astral *what*? Neither of those terms made any sense to him. Cobiah considered asking, but the first mate of the *Indomitable* had already turned and headed back to the captain's side on the forecastle. *Oh, well,* he thought. *I'll just have to figure it out on my own.* Cobiah ducked to avoid hanging shrouds of net as he jogged under the main boom. The captain's cabin was at the rear of the ship beneath the quarterdeck. That seemed like the best place to start looking for the pilot, and the captain's astral . . . laboratory . . . thing.

He climbed the stairs to the heavy oak doors of the captain's cabin, hesitantly pushing them open. "Hello?" Cobiah's voice wavered uncertainly. He slipped inside, hoping to be in and out before anyone noticed him there.

His eyes slowly adjusted to the dim light inside the cabin. The room inside felt as far away from the deck of the ship as Lion's Arch was from Cantha, and for a moment, Cobiah thought he'd been transported to the king's palace. Huge glass windows covered the rear wall, surrounded by velvet curtains the color of ripe tomatoes, spread wide to let in the sun. Gilding twinkled from the window frames, the ceiling, and even the chairs arrayed around a long oak table. The table itself was sturdily fastened to the floor with bolts through the clawed brass feet. On one side of the cabin, a soft down mattress was piled high with fluffy pillows in the same deep-red tone, each decorated with fine golden embroidery.

The wooden walls had been polished to a high shine. Small unlit candles hung in delicate ornate sconces every few feet. A rug in shades of blue and purple lay across the floor's open area, worth far more than the house Cobiah grew up in back at Lion's Arch. "Anyone here?" The sentence died on his lips as he noticed an old man sitting in a chair by the bay window, reading a thick leather-bound book. "Oh. You must be . . ." He struggled to remember the pilot's name. "Dargan . . . um . . . Darran?"

"Damran. Pilot Damran. And you are, boy?" Shifting his wire-rimmed spectacles down his thin nose, the old man stared at Cobiah with a disapproving smirk.

"Cobiah. Sir. I mean, I'm Cobiah, sir. I'm here because the mate—First Mate Chernock. She sent me."

The two men stared at one another for a long awkward moment before Damran finally snapped, "And?"

"Oh!" Cobiah blinked. "She wanted me to bring the captain his astro thing?"

Damran shut the book in his lap, blinking owlishly. "His what?"

"I'm not sure, sir." Cobiah faltered. "She only said it once, and she was talking really fast, but Chernock said the captain'd left something in his chart room, and I was to bring it to him right away."

"Did she, now?" Damran began to chuckle. "It's his astrolabe, of course. Captain Whiting wants his astrolabe."

"If you say so, sir."

"Come here, boy." Damran rose from his seat and stepped to the big table in the center of the room, lifting a metal instrument from a pile of papers there. It was a flat circle of metal within a thin frame. The frame was ornate, almost delicate, over the platterlike base. Much of it had been cut through to show the etching on the plate below. A second, smaller inner circle perched on top of the other one, both bolted through the center to the circular base plate. "You're new aboard ship, aren't you?" The old pilot raised an eyebrow at Cobiah's obvious interest.

"Not so new, sir. I've done three passages to Cantha."

"Barely got your sea legs under you, then. Now, look at this. The astrolabe is the most important instrument on the ship. Do you know what it does?"

"No, sir."

"It tells us what our eyes cannot. Namely . . ." Damran turned the brass frame, sending the circles spinning around and around over the etching of the under plate. "This little fellow can tell us where the ship is located even when it's on the open sea."

"It can?" Cobiah frowned. "But that's impossible. The sea is featureless. You can't tell where you are unless you can see the coast." Even as he said it, he realized that it couldn't be true. How did the ship find Kaineng City each time? It had to cross months of open ocean. The idea'd never occurred to Cobiah before, but now that he thought about it, he had no idea how the *Indomitable* found its way across the Sea of Sorrows.

"This instrument allows the captain to look at the stars and see our position—more or less."

Feeling brave, Cobiah ventured to say, "He can tell by the stars?"

The pilot pushed his glasses up on his nose. He took the instrument in both hands and raised the frame off the bottom plate. "This is the mater." He gestured to the solid brass platter, pronouncing the strange word "mayter." "Look at those etchings. Do they seem familiar?"

Cobiah stared down at it, trying to place the odd shapes. When he shook his head no, Damran harrumphed. "The sky, my boy. These are the constellations of the stars above us, you see? This one is the Vizier's Tower, and these are the four spokes of Grenth's Eye." Damran reached out and lightly rapped Cobiah's head. "Pay more attention to the things around you, and you'll solve half your problems.

"Now, this piece—it's called the rete—goes over the mater and spins. Like so." He placed the frame back on the mater and let it spin around.

"Why?"

"This lets you see how far apart the stars are, and how high over the horizon. With that, you can measure them against the height of the sun to tell your ship's *latitude*. Latitude," he said, noting Cobiah's confused stare, "is the measurement of how far north or south you are at sea. To use the astrolabe, you must look along this line"— he indicated a straight slice of brass that spun through the center—"and sight either the sun or Dwayna's Heart. That's the one star in the sky that never wavers or alters its place. By finding the altitude of that star—how high it is in the sky in relation to the horizon—you can tell if you are north or south of center. Center being Arah, you see?"

"Arah?" Cobiah asked.

"Arah is the city at the heart of ancient Orr. The city that the gods themselves created, at the center of the world. We judge everything's location by its distance north or south of Arah. When the astrolabe was invented, Arah was still alive and well, with a thriving society and a prominent armada of ships. The Orrian people were seafarers . . ." The old pilot cleared his throat and left off tale-telling to finish his thought. "Ahem, sorry, not important, not important.

"So, we find out how far north or south we are. We go to Cantha by heading steadily south and bearing west when we find the Canthan coast. We find Lion's Arch by heading north and bearing east when we see Kryta. North and south by the stars." Damran tapped the instrument proudly. "The captain will take our latitude at Malchor's Fingers so he knows how far into Orr we've gone. That way, he'll know how far we'll have to go to come back out. You see?"

This was a revelation to Cobiah. "That's amazing! How do we use it to tell if the ship has gone too far east or west?"

Damran sighed, brows knitting together over his wire-framed spectacles. "I'm afraid we can't. The sun only goes in one direction, and thus, so does the astrolabe. There's no marker to tell how far east or west we've gone. Perhaps one day, some enterprising young sailor will discover a way to tell." Damran patted the astrolabe and laid it down on a soft cloth from the table. Gently, he wrapped the brass instrument inside.

"That's fascinating. Thank you, Pilot."

Damran smiled. "It's not often that an old man like me gets to share his craft. Now hurry along and take the astrolabe to the captain. Shoo, pup." The old pilot settled down in his chair again and nodded toward the cabin door.

Cobiah managed a shuffling bow, making the pilot smile. He crossed the cabin and then the main deck toward the forecastle. He cradled the little bundle against his chest, fearing he might break the precious instrument.

He was halfway across the deck when the ship jolted beneath his feet. Caught by surprise, Cobiah fell toward the gunwale and skidded precariously toward the *Indomitable*'s edge. With one arm wrapped around the bundle, he grabbed desperately for the central mast. The ship was shuddering violently, boards protesting in high-pitched shrieks, and there was a horrible crunching sound from the rudder at her stern.

The ship pitched again, and Cobiah's hand slipped on the damp wood. Toppling down across the deck, Cobiah crashed painfully into the butt of one of the massive cannons. He desperately grabbed its iron cap, wrapping his legs around the gun and holding on for dear life. Other sailors, not so lucky, were cast into the icy sea. Cobiah could hear men screaming beyond the gunwale.

With a lurch and a groan of her arched keel, the *Indomitable* righted herself in the waves. Water splashed onto the deck in huge swells, toppling over the sides of the ship as the galleon settled into the ocean once more. Cobiah lifted his head and tried to ascertain what had happened. Had the ship hit the rocks? Was the bottom of the ship torn, taking on water that would drown them all?

Fingers of stone towered above the ship to either side, pointed tips clawing toward a gray, boiling sky. Yet they were still distant. The ship couldn't have struck one. Cobiah glanced over the lip of the deck and saw deep blue ocean—no sign of reef or coral. That left only one answer.

If they hadn't hit anything, then something— something *big*—must have hit *them*.

A shudder raked the *Indomitable* from stem to stern. There was a resounding crash of wood, the sound of splintering keel and hull, and the screams of wounded men echoed across the writhing face of the sea—and still, Cobiah could see nothing beneath the dark waves.

"Did you see it?" a sailor roared at the edge of the deck. "Where did the beast go?"

"What hit us?" another shouted amid the clamor.

"A sea monster! It was fifty feet long," the first answered. "With a maw the size of the *Indomitable*'s main anchor!" Before he could say more, a clear, sharp command cut through their yells.

"Stand your posts!" Chernock yelled sternly into the wind. The ship rolled farther to one side, the masts wavering uncertainly with the change of gravity. "Clear for action!"

The sailors rushed to obey, leaping to close the hatches as the ship's bell clamored the general alarm. Something that sounded like a broadside battered the *Indomitable*'s bow, and there was a heady sound of creaking wood. The foremost of the three masts tipped to the side with the severity of the jolt, a thunderous crack heralding its demise. With a twist, the broad shaft of the mast swung to an awkward angle above the main deck. There it hung, tangled in the rigging of the mainsail and tethered to the shards of its broken stump by jib and spar ropes. Each time it slipped down a bit more, the weight of the mast pulled the galleon farther and farther to its side—and closer to the sea below.

"The Maw!" one of the sailors cried out. "Beast of the sea! They said it was just a legend!"

"Legend or no," Chernock said through gritted teeth, "if it's flesh and it bleeds, it can die. Man the cannon and fire at will!"

"Watch out for those mast spars!" Vost yelled. Cobiah saw that several long ropes had broken away from the wildly flapping sheets. They whipped about like shooting stars, and where they touched flesh, they cut through to the bone.

Cobiah lunged to his feet. He scrabbled toward the mast but froze as his hand reached the smooth facing of his belt. His knife was down among his bedding. If he was to be of any help cutting loose those lashing ropes, he'd have to grab it before he made his way into the rigging. Cursing, Cobiah reversed course and dove down the stairs past a cracked and battered hatch.

The crew's berth was ravaged, and rocking hammocks had dumped sleeping sailors, bedding and all, onto the lopsided floor of the hold. Several shouted for help, while others dug to find them, lifting comrades to their feet as the boat fought to right itself. Cobiah made his way to his cubby as one of the men shouted, "Are we taking on water?"

An answer came from farther down, in the hold. "Cracked but holding, sir! Aye, we are!"

"Draw out the bilge pumps! Get them ready to draw

water!" One of the older sailors quickly took control, ordering others down into the dim belly of the ship. The fury of the unknown sea creature's assault hadn't cracked the keel, but the ship was suffering. If the creature returned and they couldn't fire the ship's cannons, the *Indomitable* would be split open by the next blow to the ship's hull.

Kneeling by the crew cubbies, Cobiah jerked bedding out, dumping everything on the floor in his haste to get to the knife. As his hand drew it out by the white hilt, his sister's rag doll tumbled from his pillowcase onto the floor.

Cobiah stared at the rag doll. Was it a sign from the gods? *Goddess Dwayna, protect our ship,* Cobiah thought, sweeping up the doll. *Biviane, if you're an angel now, keep a weather eye out for me.* He began to stuff the doll into his vest but realized quickly that it wouldn't fit beside the captain's astrolabe. Instead, he tied Polla to his belt with the scabbarded knife and dashed back onto the main deck.

The first mate, Chernock, stood near the rear of the ship. She drew a leather tawse from her belt and shouted orders that cut through the pandemonium. She called for the men to bring hoses and water, thumping stunned sailors with the heavy, knotted leather if she caught them standing still. Her expression was as hard and cold as ice.

Something to the rear of the ship was smoking, black wisps trickling out from beneath the quarterdeck. Cobiah grimaced; fire on a ship was more dangerous than sinking. Fire would eat you faster than the sea would swallow you, and if those flames reached the black cannon powder . . . they'd all be done for.

"Cobiah!" Sethus waved to catch his attention. The young sailor was standing by the tottering foremast, sawing desperately at a thick sheet of sail. "If we don't cut this free, the canvas will take on water. The weight will tip us over!" He hacked at the ropes and tarpaulin with great sweeps of his long knife. "Grenth's mercy, help me!"

There was so much going on all around him that for a moment, Cobiah froze. But in that moment, his anger rose, and he felt the same stubborn rush that had come over him when he was fighting Tosh on his first day aboard. Cobiah set his feet against the planks and ran forward through the sloshing water, hurling himself past lashing ropes and over slick boards with a lack of care that bordered on the suicidal. His friend needed him.

Everyone else was dealing with the fire in the rear or the bilges belowdecks. A few stood at the side of the ship, trying to pull their fellows back aboard before they vanished into the black waters of the Sea of Sorrows. Vost was below. The first mate was concentrating on the flames. Captain Whiting clung to the ship's wheel on the forecastle, his face as pale as the sail that dragged, heavy and drawing water, against the side of the *Indomitable*. His lips moved, but the sound emanating was too soft to distinguish between prayers or orders. Whimpering and wide eyed, the captain tightened his arms about the many-spoked rudder wheel and did nothing at all.

The mast wavered and the ship shuddered again. "If we can cut the rigging free," Sethus panted, "the mast will carry away the sail." Spray and panicked sweat plastered brown hair to his forehead as he chopped wildly at billowing yards of loose canvas. "I'll cut this part. Can you climb to the yardarm at the top of the mast and slice the cross ropes free?"

Nodding grimly, Cobiah slithered beneath the sail. He gripped the unsteady trunk of the mast and studied the damage. The trunk hadn't come entirely free of its base, but it hung half-shattered, rippling with its weight. It was definitely unsafe to climb, but if he didn't try, the sail fabric would take on water and the ship would capsize. Forget the fire and the bilges, even the awful sea creature that threatened them from below—if the ship rolled, the crew would die to a man in the icy sea.

Cobiah wrapped his hands with sharkskin and pressed the palms to the wooden beam. There was still tension on the mast from the thick ropes twined about its yardarms, interlaced with the other masts of the great galleon. As he'd done a hundred times before, Cobiah shimmied up the trunk, grasping rope and netting and pushing his wrapped hands against the slick wet wood to get some faint purchase. The ship tossed beneath him like a horse testing its reins, and the thick smell of smoke clogged his nostrils.

He could hear the shouts below on the deck. Captain Whiting seemed to have found his voice at last—if not his sanity—and was yelling orders to fire into the waves. The heavy guns roared. Sparks flew, and to the starboard side of the galleon, a plume of white sea-foam sprayed up from the charge.

"Gun crew!" Cobiah heard the captain shriek. "Raise the level! Fire again! We're consigned to bloody that beast by the king of Kryta himself, and by Balthazar's dogs, we'll do it even if it sinks us!" Some of the sailors struggled to obey the captain's command on both decks, manning the upper carronades and the lower main guns. Others jumped to ready a new fuse, pushing the black rope into the cannon's small touch hole. After powder and a heavy ball had been rolled down the barrel, one of the sailors brushed a handheld torch to the fuse, and within seconds, the mighty cannon thundered its massive bellow of deadly flame.

Now Cobiah could hear the picket fire of the smaller guns, carronade blasts pounding out a martial rhythm. He risked a bit of balance to glance down at the deck below. The fire in the rear cabin had been put out, but smoke still trailed up from the windows. Sailors clustered about the guns, heaving powder and shot into the glowing-hot mouths of long barrels. Sethus was nearly finished cutting the ropes to one side of the great mast. Unable to stop himself, Cobiah looked out to sea.

From his vantage near the top of the tilting foremast, he could see black water quilted with white foam. The sea stones that had frightened him with their nearness were now far to the side, well out of reach of the beleaguered *Indomitable*. No sign of the underwater beast. Breathing out a breath he hadn't realized he'd been holding, Cobiah reached for the tethers that tangled the foremast with the forward jib sails and began to saw at them with his knife.

He'd cut through two of them when something in the water caught his eye. At first it was a purplish blur beneath the surface, a shadow within shadows, notable only by the speed and direction in which it flowed— counter to the ocean's tide. The knife slowed in Cobiah's hand. He watched the oily patch of color pass beneath the ship, trying to mark its true size and shape. Could the gunners see it? Grasping a rope, Cobiah leaned and shouted down to the deckhands, "Look aft, boys! The creature is—"

Just then the beast rose from the depths. Sharp teeth, each nearly the size of a man, broke through the glassy surface of the ocean, pouring water in flowing gouts down its massive throat. Cobiah could hardly believe the scale of the creature. Its maw was vast and cavernous, capable of engulfing half the ship's stern in a single bite. Beady eyes flickered behind thick, coiled lips. From his high vantage, Cobiah could see fins the size of lifeboats propelling the monster forward and, far below, a tail that thrashed so hard it formed its own mighty current beneath the sea. One of the cannonballs had struck the monster in the cheek, rending a bloody hole in sensitive flesh, and the pain must have driven the monster to strike again. Cobiah barely had time to wrap his arms tightly about the mast before the monster slammed into the rear of the ship. Everything pitched forward, and he slipped precariously, his body twisting into the very rigging he'd been working to cut away.

The planks of the stern began to crack and complain as the Maw's great teeth fastened upon it. Windows in the ornate rear cabin shattered as it bit down, and heavy shards of broken glass slashed the creature's lips and gums. The pain only infuriated the creature further.

Its roar shook the sails, stinking of brine and rot. There was a horrible, crashing impact as the creature bit into the rear of the *Indomitable*, tugging the ship backward into the water. Teeth sank into thick wooden panels, and the vessel lurched in the water like a wounded animal. A splintering of boards was followed by a sickening yaw, and with a jolt, the entire mast began to slip toward the sea, carrying Cobiah along with it.

The trunk toppled, crashing through line and spar, and caught with a listing stagger in the netting between the two main masts. It spun about, wrapping Cobiah in rope and the canvas of the sea-damp sail hanging more than seventy feet above the deck. He choked back a scream and clung to the swaying lanyards. In his desperation to hold on, the long knife slipped from his hand. He lost sight of it as the blade vanished into the ocean's dark waves.

Somewhere in the pandemonium below, Vost was

howling orders. If they could only get it to release its grip before the Maw crushed the ship's hull, the *Indomitable* might just survive the encounter. To push it off, they'd taken up the ship's fishing harpoons, jabbing at the monster's eyes with all their strength.

Tosh's spear struck flesh, and the Maw roared again. As it did, its teeth slipped from the stern of the galleon, and the monster fell back into the sea. Slowly, it sank into the ocean, dark fins circling in massive watery drafts, the tail lashing up waves that swept the top deck. The ship shuddered with the effort of shaking off the beast, but she bobbed back to her full height once its weight dropped away. The hull wasn't punctured. The *Indomitable* still held.

That didn't help Cobiah. He stretched to grab the sail canvas as the deck swung sickeningly below him. The mast tilted from side to side as the wind and the violent rocking motion of the ship tossed the heavy timber back and forth in its stays. He wrapped the ropes around his fists, struggling to pull himself upright, but the effort was barely worth it. There was no way he was going to disentangle himself from the netting without a knife.

Along the southern horizon, a dark line swelled against the gray-green clouds. It rose up from the sea, first a thread, then a rope, then a hand's breadth of thickness, and then, impossibly, reaching higher than the forecastle—higher, even, than the ship's yardarms on her great masts, all while it was still too far away to ripple the sea around the *Indomitable*'s bow.

It was a massive wave, a tsunami. Cobiah had seen storm billows in Lion's Arch. One year when he was a child, there had been a great storm in Lion's Arch. When the sun went down, a little cluster of sturdy houses stood along the sandy strip near the docks. When it came up the next morning, after the storm had blown itself out, the sand was clear, clean, and empty. The houses, families and all, had simply ceased to exist. Later, sailors said those waves stood more than twelve feet high when they hit shore. Those storms were nothing compared to the wall of water filling the sky on the *Indomitable*'s starboard side. Because of his awkward vantage point high amid the topsails, Cobiah was the first to see the wave coming. It crested more than twice as high as the ship's great mast, and it was still growing. Cobiah struggled to understand—there wasn't even a storm on the horizon. Something must have happened past Malchor's Fingers, deep in the heart of the ocean of Orr.

Desperately, Cobiah struggled to be free of the twisting ropes and tangled netting. He screamed for aid, but his voice was swallowed by the cheering on the deck below. The sailors had driven off the sea monster, and now they were celebrating. Tosh was lifted on the shoulders of the older sailors, thrusting the harpoon over his head in glee. Vost thumped his shoulder and yelled his name with pride.

They were cheering far too loudly to hear Cobiah. Only Sethus remained below the broken mast, chopping desperately at stays and ropes to separate the sinking canvas from the galleon's rigging. He looked up at Cobiah, white faced. "Hold on, Cobiah! Don't let go of the mast!" Seconds were passing, but they felt like hours. The sailors never even saw the wave until it was too late.

It rolled across the ocean's surface as fast as flickering lightning, closing the distance in breaths. The wall of water was curved at the top, snarling with white foam, sweeping aside everything in its path. The ocean dropped beneath them as the tsunami pulled close, and the *Indomitable* groaned and settled in the water. Cheers turned into shouts of fear as the sailors finally saw the wave. Cobiah's stomach whirled, sickened by the motion of the great galleon in the ragged swell of water. The tsunami bore the ship aloft in slow motion, pitching her inexorably forward. For one horrible breath of time, the *Indomitable* stood on her stern, nearly perpendicular to the ocean floor.

From his perspective at the top of the mast's rigging, Cobiah felt the graceful rise and tilt, the sway of rope and the twist of the galleon in the current of the wave. It felt as though he were riding some kind of wind beast, lifted into the air on graceful, weightless wings.

The wave crested with maddening slowness. If there were screams on the deck below, they were muffled by the sound of rushing water, and Cobiah couldn't hear them. If the sailors prayed to the Six Gods, their cries were lost in the crash of the crest against wood. Everything seemed overwhelmingly bright, and loud, and terrifying. Cobiah was pitched higher and higher still as the galleon rolled, until for just a moment, he saw over the peak of the massive wave. There, in the center of the darkest, deepest ocean in the world, at the very heart of the Sea of Sorrows, Cobiah saw something that should not have existed.

He saw land, where there was nothing but ocean.

Dark, tattered wings, as if something long dead was rising from the grave.

Ancient cathedrals of coral-crusted stone. Torn flesh and ice-white bone against a storm-laden sky. Corpses, crawling from the waterlogged earth like maggots; bodies by the thousands, roiling like waves themselves over sodden ground.

As Cobiah stared in shock, the wave fully crested. The *Indomitable* teetered in the curl of blizzard-white water, then pitched violently downward, rolling onto her back with a horrible crashing yaw. Foam shattered timbers and masts beneath the massive weight of the wave. With a low, deathly groan, the mighty galleon rolled over beneath a thousand tons of sea.

The *Indomitable* was lost.

6

A sailor's life's filled with toil and strife
The sea's both boon and bane, O
We're Kryta bound on a northern tide.
Through the lightning and the rain
We'll sail through all these stormy nights
'Til we're safe at home again, O.
                    —"Weather the Storm"

I can't think. I should think of something. What? What was I doing? Something important. I need to think. How do I make my mind focus?

"Draw the bilge-rat up!"

A lurch rolled through Cobiah's stomach, and he felt himself purge its contents. The effort didn't stop the motion that rocked him back and forth, and he tightened his hands on the sheets wrapped about his body, unsure if he was clinging to them or struggling to push them away. Where was he? What had happened? Opening his eyes brought a painful flash of white-hot light. Cobiah whimpered in distress. Wherever he was, he wasn't dead.

"Lookit 'im puke!" a too close voice roared. "This little mouse is still fighting to live!"

"Cut its throat, like any other gaping fish," snarled another with a ringing laugh, "then throw it back into the sea." There were shouts of agreement all around.

Hesitantly, Cobiah forced his eyes to focus, making himself ignore the pain that wracked every muscle and bone of his body. He lay on the deck of an unfamiliar ship, fouled in the knots of rigging still attached to a chunk of the *Indomitable*'s foremast. Someone was using a sharp knife to cut the ropes. With a groan, Cobiah tried to roll over but found himself too tightly tangled in the cords that held him to the thick spar of wood.

Memories twisted confusedly in Cobiah's mind. Tosh, laughing and grabbing for the rag doll. The officers standing on the forecastle. The shine of a polished glow on brass arms. The billowing of white sails. Sethus grinning like a monkey as he swung from spar to spar. A dark land beyond the edge of the storm . . .

"Keep it alive—for now," another voice grated, and there was a *thump-thump-thump* echoing closer across the boards of the deck. Cobiah tried to focus his eyes on the motion, hoping to see a familiar face, or at least the recognizable colors of a Krytan officer's coat.

Instead, the face that leaned close to study him wasn't human at all.

The horrible features were feline, the skin covered with thick white patterned fur. A black nose sniffed distastefully, and the mouth parted to show a row of long, sharp teeth in the jaws of a predator. The creature moved with eerie grace, its paw-like hands sure on the ropes, tremendous claws sliding out of their sheaths to slice through the bonds tangled all around Cobiah. Cobiah stared in horror as two ears cocked forward curiously at the base of the long skull, and two more swept back with disgust. Long black horns, and braids wrapped in leather thongs and straps of sharkskin, lay amid the heavy mane that rippled down the curve of the beast's thick neck. *Claws . . . horns . . . four ears . . .* Cobiah struggled with an uncertain, quickly rising sense of alarm. *That thing called me a mouse!*

"You're sure it's worth bothering with, Engineer?" Cobiah could barely believe he was hearing understandable words from the monster's fanged muzzle. "Seems like we're just searching for drake eggs in the forest here. Complete waste of time." The white-furred brute leaned closer, his eye glinting with feral cruelty as it looked Cobiah up and down.

"I'm certain, Centurion. It coughed up enough water to flood a small village, but give it a little rest, and you'll see." The first voice had more humor, less threat. Hoping to see a friendly face, Cobiah placed it amid the blurry shapes, marking a big, rust-colored beast standing a short distance behind the other.

Fighting down the bile that rose in his throat, Cobiah refocused his attention on the tawny yellow eyes that glared into his own, struck by the cruel intelligence he saw there. The beast noticed and grunted, poking Cobiah with a sharp black claw. A speck of blood rose where the needle-sharp point scratched the flesh of his cheek, and Cobiah flinched away. Suddenly, he realized what they were, and his stomach revolted again—this time, in fear.

These were *charr.*

"Fine." The word curled out of the charr centurion's lips, as much a curse as a confirmation. "Your responsibility, then. Take the mouse below, but keep it on a leash. When your pet's done puking, you can put it to work in the engine room singing you pretty songs and worshipping anything that stands still." There was a cacophony of howls at the jibe, the mocking, terrible laughter of hyenas closing in for the kill. The awful sound swelled and filled Cobiah's mind as blackness claimed him once more.

Cobiah wasn't sure how long he had been asleep. He could feel the rhythmic rise and fall of the sea surrounding him, but this was not the ship he knew. The bed was far too large, a thin shelf hanging from the wall rather than a hammock cradled between two poles. Glancing around to get his bearings, Cobiah recognized that he was in a berth, surrounded by similar sleeping shelves, each with a thin mattress and a worn wool cover. This was definitely a ship, but it wasn't like anything he'd ever been on before. He could feel that she was a sizable craft, but not as large as the *Indomitable*. Maybe a small galleon or a brig? Cobiah could see the ribs of the hull holding up the curved wall. They weren't made of wood but of iron, and forged U-shaped brackets solidified the ship's frame. The beams were heavier, the doors wider, and the beds far more solid than those on a human ship. Curious, Cobiah sat up in bed, surveying the room more carefully. There had to be other crew quarters. The number of beds here would barely man a sloop, much less a large ship like a galleon.

On a shelf at the foot of the bed lay his clothing— relatively clean and folded—as well as the pilot's astrolabe and the small rag doll he'd had tied to his belt. Although his knife sheath was there, it was empty, and only one of his boots had made it out of the sea. Cobiah tugged the clothing on over his head and felt the ache of sore muscles stretching through his frame. Rope burns marked his chest, legs, and arms where he had been tangled. He considered the boot but decided not to wear it—two bare feet would be better for keeping his footing on board a pitching ship.

Cautiously, Cobiah touched his fingers to his wounds. They'd been treated with some kind of strange-smelling greenish goop that had dried upon his skin. Suspiciously, he scraped a bit of it away with his fingernail. It smelled of fish oil and pungent herb.

Heavy, booted footfalls stomped down the stairwell outside the sleeping area. Cobiah scrambled back. The charr were coming! Cobiah glanced around in panic. The arched doorway was the only way out of the room. He was trapped. Quickly, he looked around for a weapon, a board, or anything to fight with, but the biggest thing in the room was a pillow. Left with no choice, he grabbed it and spun to face the door.

Out of the dark passage came a charr. He was a bulky fellow, wide shouldered, standing more than a head taller than the slender human youth. The monster's thick fur was the color of rust, touched here and there with scalloped, leopardlike spots of darker brown and black on his arms and legs. He had a paler muzzle, more of a rusty white, and the lighter shade spread across his chest and down the insides of his arms. Massive ram's horns spread out on either side of his head, and four slender ears flicked back and forth below them. Cobiah recognized the creature—this was the charr that had rescued him from the sea. The one they'd called "Engineer."

The monster moved like water over glass, each padding stride cushioned by catlike paws. Before he entered the room, he paused, sniffing at the air, black lips curling back from curved, meat-ripping teeth. "Huh." The charr tilted his head, four ears flicking forward and back. "Awake already, are we, mouse?" Growling faintly to himself, the beast took another step into the doorway and his golden eyes searched the semidarkness until he found Cobiah. For a long moment the two stared at one another. The charr's dark eyes flicked from Cobiah's hastily raised pillow to the tray that he carried in his clawed hands. At last, the beast broke the silence, saying wryly, "I know the grub's not good, but I don't consider soup to be a killing offense."

Cobiah couldn't help it. The stress of his ordeal, coupled with the entirely ridiculous situation, overcame him. He started snickering. The charr, seemingly amused by his own joke, quickly joined in; the chuckling became guffaws, and those soon turned into howls of laughter. Sitting down on the bed, the burly charr put the tray on the floor between them and wiped tears from his eyes with the back of his hand. Cobiah lowered the pillow and gathered enough breath to ask, "You're not going to kill me?"

"Kill you?" answered the charr. "If I was going to kill you, I wouldn't have hauled you up onto the deck in the first place, you moon-headed idiot." Despite his reassuring words, the charr's muzzle seemed perpetually drawn into a snarl, and the claws on his paws were as sharp as daggers. The charr sniffed the air again, and his long auburn tail twitched on the bunk. "Smells like your wound's healing, too. No infection. Would I go to that kind of trouble just to cut you open again for jollies?"

"I don't know. You're a charr." Cobiah struggled with his fear. "You did save me, but I don't know why. You had to have a reason." Still, he slowly lowered the pillow, the rich, warm smell of the soup nearly overcoming him.

"I'm the one who saw you floating out there, spar and all. Been out there since the wave hit, I'd wager, and that was three days before we found you. We saw no sign of your ship or your crew." The rust-colored charr watched Cobiah out of the corners of his eyes. "Lost, I'd imagine?"

Cobiah managed a nod. "Last thing I remember, the *Indomitable* turned on her side in the water. The wave . . . swallowed her whole." He gulped, the adrenaline beginning to run cold in his veins. He shook off the feeling and faced the charr. "What happens now?"

"Now you put down the pillow, human, and you work a charr ship."

"I . . . what?" Stunned, Cobiah sank down to a seat on the floorboards, leaning back against the shelf-bed with the pillow limp in his hand. "Work? With charr? What, until you eat me?"

"Eat you?" The charr snorted, shaking his four ears disdainfully. "Arrogant mouse! I saved your *life*!"

Suspicious, Cobiah pressed him. "You're a charr. I'm a human. You had to have a reason."

The big leopard-spotted charr threw up his clawed hands in frustration. "Pish. The wave's tossed more fish to the surface than I've ever seen before. What do you think that is in front of you? We've got plenty of food. We need workers to keep this tub floating long enough to get us safely to shore."

"So it's slavery, then," Cobiah said grimly.

"Consider it indentured service. Once the ship finds landfall, we'll go our way, and you can go yours. We're not a slave ship. When that wave hit us, we lost half our crew—and we were running shorthanded as it was. Now we barely have enough sailors on board to trim the sails and heft the rudder.

"More, the ship's damaged. She'll never make a southern port, so we'll have to find a closer one and hope for the best. Which is going to be hard, considering how far that wave tossed us off course. To be honest, I don't think the centurion has any idea where we are." The charr's words were gruff but not unkind. "Your fate's tied with ours, human. The sooner you get used to that fact, the sooner we all get out of this mess." The charr gave Cobiah a long look, his catlike eyes unreadable. With a raspy cough, the creature changed the subject. He flexed his fist, and the claws disappeared under the fur. "My name's Sykox. Sykox Steamshroud." The charr held out one paw in an unexpected gesture of camaraderie.

Cobiah stared at the extended paw, noting the sharpness of the claws, the thick fur that covered fingers and wrist. Then, with a sigh, he took the proffered paw and shook it, stumbling over the creature's strange name. "Sick ox?"

"Close enough, close enough. Sykox. I'm the engineer on this brig."

"I'm Cobiah Marriner, lately of the crew of the *Indomitable*. Friends call me Coby . . . or they used to." The words hung heavily in the air. Sethus. Vost. Even bullying Tosh and pompous, self-important Captain Whiting . . . dead. It was hard to believe that he was the only one who had survived.

"Titan's blood, human, you're white with hunger. If you don't eat that soup right now, one of your flower-headed gods is going to show up and take you home, and put all my effort to waste." The charr's tail twitched higher, though whether out of amusement or annoyance, Cobiah couldn't tell. "Eat. I'll talk."

Against his better judgment, Cobiah reached out and grabbed the soup bowl, scooting away from the charr to sit on the berth across from him. The soup was thin, but the fish was fresh, and it tasted of strange spices that burned against his tongue.

"Our ship is the *Havoc*, an Iron Legion tub sailing out of the coastal fort south of the Shiverpeaks. My warband, the Steam warband, is one of two assigned to sail her.

We used to be a crew of seventeen," Sykox said. "But now we're a crew of seven." He sighed and lashed his tail. "The Iron Legion's original goal was to create a naval unit that could challenge Kryta for control of the Sea of Sorrows. Maybe make an assault on Lion's Arch." As Cobiah began to bristle, Sykox chuckled ruefully. "What do you expect? We're at war, human! Oh, c'mon, it's no use getting your dander up. I bet the whole damn fort's gone now, town and all, wiped clean by the wave. We've been pushed so far north by that wave there's nowhere else to dock. We're limping for the shallows around Lion's Arch and just hoping we can make it that far."

"Lion's Arch? Are you mad? That's the capital of Kryta! If a charr ship shows up there, the crew'll be hung on the gallows before you can drop anchor."

Sykox shrugged. "Maybe so, but we've no choice. The only other dock that might have survived is Port Stalwart, and that harbor's too shallow for our ship. What else can we do? Our hull's damaged, and the mast steps are cracked. Our sails are torn, the engine's laboring, and we can't trust the keel to hold if this ol' brig finds another storm."

Confused, Cobiah spluttered into the dwindling remains of his soup. "Engine?"

"Yes, boss." Sykox crossed his furry arms over his massive chest. "That's my design. The imperator of the Iron Legion wanted us to push the boundaries, so I did. Took one of the experimental engines we've been working on and built her into the brig. Coal-foddered pistons propel a turbine beneath her stern, pushing us forward. With that, plus the wind in her jibs, she'll go half again as fast as one of your human galleons. We can turn ninety degrees and not lose speed. Doesn't matter what direction the wind's coming from—we can strike out with it or against it and still make ground." The big charr's smile faded. "Unfortunately, the *Havoc*'s the only one of her kind. We were out of harbor on a test run for the engine when the wave hit; that's the only reason we survived at all."

"What made it?" asked Cobiah. "The wave, I mean."

The big charr shook his furry head. "Nobody knows. One minute the ocean was quiet, and the next, we were sweeping before a sheet of water higher than the Great Northern Wall!"

Taking a long breath, Cobiah ran one hand through his hair and tried to remember. "We'd just passed Malchor's Fingers, headed toward Orr. Our ship was in combat with some sort of creature. It wasn't going well. I was in the rigging, trying to free the broken mast, and I got tangled. When the ship went down—" He halted, wiping his sweating face with a torn sleeve. "I saw beyond the wave as it caught us. I thought . . . I thought I saw land."

"Land? Out there? There're no islands that deep in the Sea of Sorrows." Sykox furrowed his brow. "You didn't imagine it? A fever dream, maybe, while you were ship-wrecked?"

"It wasn't a dream," Cobiah said firmly. "I saw mountains. A black plain and high peaks beyond. Ruins and . . ." He paused. "People. Things that looked like people, at least."

"Now I know it was a fever dream." The charr shook his head. "Hurry up and finish your soup, mouse. I'm ordered to bring you on deck to meet Centurion Harrow, and that's the last thing you want to do on an empty stomach."

After the soup was gone, Cobiah followed Sykox out of the berth. It was clear from the moment he set foot on deck that the *Havoc* wasn't like any other galleon Cobiah'd seen. To start with, it was smaller from stem to stern than human galleons, but wider through the middeck and the rear. Two masts stood side by side on the ship's open deck rather than stretching stem to stern. Their sails were triangular and oddly rigged, ropes running to the fore rather than square-blocked to the mast. A strange musky odor hung in the air—not that of wild animals or feral cats, as he would have guessed, but rather a thick sulfurous smoke. None of the furred sailors seemed distressed at the smell, and he assumed they knew their ship better than he did, so Cobiah tried to put it out of his mind. It must have been the scent of the *Havoc*'s engine.

The ship's main deck was crewed by seven sailors— a pitifully small number, even with Sykox's brag that they needed fewer to run the ship. There was a high forecastle and a rear quarterdeck, but no captain's quarters and no decorative brass. It seemed the centurion— whoever he was—slept with the men, somewhere in the main berth. Above the rear of the ship rose two short cylindrical chimneys of iron that chuffed out streams of grayish smoke. A thumping, uneven rhythm emanated from the area below the quarterdeck, matching the ship's strangely jolting movement forward against the sea.

Worse, it was filled with charr. White-furred ones, as well as brown, black, and tawny, many marked with stripes or spots amid their tufted fur. They moved about the deck with ease, claws sinking into the wooden floor to hold them steady in a swell, and clawed, pawlike hands working rigging as deftly as any human sailor. Just like Sykox, they all had horns, four ears, and long waving tails, but each was nevertheless distinctive. Some were brawny, some slender; one had shaved most of his mane away, leaving only a stiff crest, while another had waxed braids woven through his, giving the charr a fierce, bristling appearance. A slender charr, one that Cobiah guessed might be a female, sat on her haunches near the ship's bow, playing a low, mournful rhythm on a drum. Others repaired injury done to the hull by the mighty wave. Even though few of the beasts turned to look at Cobiah, he could feel their attention riveted on him, the way he'd seen stalking felines in Lion's Arch pretending not to notice an injured bird before they pounced. Cobiah took a deep breath to settle his nerves, then immediately regretted it. The whole ship smelled like wet cat.

Sykox took Cobiah to the forecastle, ignoring their pointed gazes and low snarls. Cobiah felt his hackles rise at their stares and thought immediately of Tosh. If he picked a fight with these bullies, it wouldn't matter if Cobiah got in a few good hits. He'd be dead. The thought chilled Cobiah's usual daredevil nature, and he stayed close to Sykox. They passed a black-furred beast with narrow yellow eyes sharpening a long, wicked-looking knife against a leather strap, the *swish-swish* echoing in time with Cobiah's steps. Another, his fur streaked with gray and his body slightly bowed from age, lowered his head and growled a warning as the human walked past.

"Hail, Centurion Harrow!" Sykox's bellow almost made Cobiah leap out of his skin. An even larger charr at the bow of the ship turned his head to regard them thoughtfully. His title might have been centurion, but Cobiah recognized the stern aura of a captain without any need for explanation. This soldier was in charge.

This was the pale-furred beast who had threatened him when he'd first come aboard. Harrow was shorter than Sykox but even more muscular, with white fur marked by gray and a sharp, fierce cast to his muzzle. He had many scars lacing his fur and face, and his left leg below the knee had been replaced by a thick peg of iron.

He wore clothes like a human, but far less than most sailors Cobiah'd known: leather straps to hold his weapon to his side, and a simple pair of breeches; no hat, no shirt, and no shoes.

Cobiah's knees shook, but he locked them together, conscious of his pounding heart and the expectant silence that fell over the rest of the animals. As he struggled to show no fear, Cobiah found himself wondering if the charr's leg was strapped on or if some awful surgeon had fused the metal directly to the stump of the centurion's bone. However it was on there, the leader of the charr clearly considered it a wound worthy of pride, for as he came closer, he made no effort to hide his sullen limp. Suddenly, Cobiah was glad he hadn't worn the single boot.

The centurion tapped the fingers of one clawed hand against a piece of parchment tucked into his belt. He waved away the other charr clustered about, and they obediently backed off a few steps so that the centurion could take a good look at Cobiah.

"The human's awake, sir." Sykox spoke altogether too cheerfully for Cobiah's comfort.

"So I see," growled the centurion, unamused.

Another charr, this one a thick-limbed, tawny beast, gave an indignant snarl. "What is this foolishness, sir? We're not a menagerie! I told you, the human's useless . . . unless we're planning to toss him over the side as bait to catch our dinner." A soft rumble of eager laughter coursed through the other sailors on the deck. Cobiah gulped nervously, acutely aware that he was the only one without claws. One of the centurion's paws shot up, fist clenched in an unspoken command, and the crew fell into instant, obedient silence. Lowering his hand, the leader gestured to Cobiah's escort.

"Cobiah Marriner, this is Centurion Harrow Shroud-weather, leader of the Shroud warband and captain of the *Havoc*." Sykox stiffened into a salute. "Sir, this is the human who washed up on our hull. He tried to attack me with a pillow, but he settled in well enough once I told him what's what."

Unflattering, Cobiah thought with a wince, *but true.*

Centurion Harrow rocked back and forth on his peg leg. Rather than being offended by Cobiah's apparent show of defiance, the captain looked vaguely pleased. "Going to take on an entire charr crew with a pillow, were you, mouse?" A titter went through the troops, and Harrow silenced them with a glare.

"Yes, sir." Cobiah lifted his chin and met the centurion's tawny eyes. "I recommend you all surrender now. You have no idea the things I can do with a handful of chicken feathers."

A loud burst of laughter erupted from the gathered charr. Surprised, Centurion Harrow's eyebrows shot up into his mane, and he snapped his teeth together with amusement. "You're a bold one, you are!" He chuckled, the sound rumbling through the centurion's broad chest. His lips curled back from his sharp white canines, and Cobiah realized that Harrow was smiling. "Good. I like a little spirit.

"Sykox argues that my ship's better off with you on it, and alive. *You're* certainly a sight better off in that case, so it's to your advantage that you prove your worth. Understood?" The last words were barked with a curt, military precision.

Cobiah jumped. He stood at attention and stammered, "Y-yes, sir."

"Good." The centurion raised an eyebrow. His lips curled into a faint, wicked smile. "While you are here, you are a soldier on this ship, a gladium, with no warband at your side and the lowest rank aboard. You have two duties on this ship, Gladium Cobiah. The first is to do any job you're told, and the second is to obey any order you're given. We're shorthanded, by the claw, and you'll pull your weight or you'll be ballast!"

"Y-yes, sir," Cobiah managed to say. He had no idea what a "gladium" was, but he wasn't going to ask questions. Not when all the charr around him were staring like hungry cats over a roasted haunch of dolyak.

"And here I was hoping he'd make a mess of things." Grist Fellsteam, the oldest of the charr, chuckled, wheezing slightly. "Ah, well. He's skinny. Probably wouldn't make a meal anyway."

"So we might as well work 'im hard, eh, Grist?" The charr leader nodded his head in agreement, ears flicking back and forth beneath his coiled horns. Turning back to Cobiah, Harrow raised one clawed hand and rubbed the fur on his chin. "When we arrive in Lion's Arch, you and Sykox will take one of the lifeboats and row to the docks. Tell them we come in peace. If you don't convince the Lionguard to let us dock and make repairs, Sykox kills you. Then the humans at the port will kill him.

"If that happens, our ship won't dock, and as we can't make it to another port without repairs, the *Havoc* sinks. We drown." Harrow narrowed his eyes like a feral creature, his sharp claw raking through his rough whiskers. "In this scenario, everybody dies. *Including you.* Understood, soldier?"

"Agreed," Cobiah pledged. "I'd say that's a fair trade for my life."

"Understood, Engineer?" Centurion Harrow rounded on Sykox, his voice taking on a bellow of command.

"Yes, sir!" Sykox's yell rang out on instinct. Realizing what he'd agreed to, the rust-furred charr nodded as well, all four ears drooping in worry beneath his heavy horns. He managed a salute, eyes forward, back stiff, tail up. Cobiah did his best to imitate Sykox's gesture, but without a tail, it fell a little flat.

"Until then, you work in the engine with Sykox. *Dismissed*." Centurion Harrow bit out the word between gleaming fangs.

Sykox and Cobiah backed away cautiously. When they reached the edge of the forecastle and jumped down onto the main deck, Sykox sighed. "Not what you expected, I gather?" Cobiah muttered.

"Well, er, not exactly. I was expecting the part about murdering *you*."

"Nice. Glad to know something went the way you planned." Cobiah met the eye of the black-furred charr sailor, and a chill went down his spine. Despite the centurion's orders, the soldier looked as if he'd rather have been gutting Cobiah than working with him. Cobiah murmured, "They'll kill me, won't they, if they catch me alone?"

"Yeah. Probably. The hatred of humans is part of our blood. You worship false gods, you betray your promises, and you smell kind of like a wallowing murellow. There are old wounds. Deep ones that go back generations, like the war in Ascalon."

"What about the humans? The charr stole our homeland." Stung, Cobiah nevertheless was careful to keep his voice down. "If your people hadn't tried to conquer Ascalon, King Adelbern wouldn't have cursed the kingdom, and humans would still live there."

"I say 'forecastle,' you say 'fo'c'sle.' If the humans hadn't stolen Ascalon from us a few hundred years before, we wouldn't have had to fight to get it back," Sykox retorted. "At least the charr had the good grace not to shatter a city and enslave the souls of the populace as a fare-thee-well. Your King Adelbern, whoo, howdy. He was a stinker."

Cobiah steamed a bit, at a loss for words. "I can already tell I'm going to hate arguing with you."

"Arguments are like battles. If you don't have superior firepower, don't engage." Sykox grinned.

"How about you? Why don't you hate humans as much as they do?"

Sykox looked down at him appraisingly. With a shrug, he said, "I recognized what was left of the pennon tangled up with you and that mast. See, I was raised in a fahrar—that's like a cub training school—near the border of Kryta. We spent a lot of time studying the people who lived in Lion's Arch. Guess I always wanted to meet one." He lifted one paw and licked it, rubbing the damp pads over his tangled mane to smooth the fur. "Don't worry about the other sailors, mouse. You'll be working in the engine room, and I'll be there with you. After the wave hit us, the bellows blew, and most of the charr who worked down there with me died in the explosion. I managed to save the ship, but I couldn't save them." Sykox turned his head and pretended to smooth down another patch of fur, but Cobiah could see pain echoed in the bestial soldier's eyes.

"Your crew means that much to you?" he asked more gently.

"They're my warband. I grew up with some of these lowlifes. That's what 'warband' means to a charr. 'Family.' It's the only family a charr ever knows. Only family they ever need."

Cobiah had never thought he'd have a meaningful conversation with a charr. If anyone had asked, he'd have said the murderous, bestial charr couldn't even string sentences together, much less express the kind of regret and pain he heard in Sykox's tone. Shaking his head, the rust-furred charr growled deep within his throat and changed the subject. "Follow me, human. I'll take you down to the bellows and let you see our ship's beating heart." Cobiah grinned and followed his strange companion toward the lower hold.

The *Havoc* had a strange quality to it, a sort of stilted chugging that Cobiah'd never felt aboard any other ship. As they walked down a curled stairwell, he could feel the air growing heavier, thicker with the stench of acrid smoke. On the *Indomitable*, the rear quarterdeck had housed the captain and his officers. Here, the *Havoc*'s quarterdeck had been entirely opened up from the keel to the roof of the highest deck, so that the room itself was twice as high. Instead of stained-glass windows and polished candelabra, the room was dark and muggy, as hot as hell and twice as cavernous.

A strange contraption made of steel and bronze had been built at the rear of the *Havoc*. It looked like a squatting toad with a flickering tongue of orange flame that darted out between its iron teeth. Piles of coal lay in a massive metal bin to one side, with two large shovels sticking out of the top like headstones in a graveyard. To each side of the engine was a great circular crank, ticking in unison with some inner working of the engine. Chains clanked and shivered, leashing the contraption to a massive cog at the rear. As it clicked in circles, the motion turned a rotary paddle wheel beneath the ship's hull and propelled the *Havoc* forward.

"You built this?" Cobiah stared in amazement.

"I built it, and I run it." Sykox grabbed one of the shovels and yanked it out of the coal bin. Shoving the handle against Cobiah's chest, Sykox added, "Now you run it, too."

"How does this thing work?" Cobiah rolled up his sleeves, struggling to hold the shovel in one hand and wipe the smoke from his face with the other.

"The 'how' isn't your concern, mouse." Sykox smiled. "Just keep shoveling coal 'til we make port."

"And when we make port, what then?" a new voice cut in. It had a nasal tone, and condescension hung on every syllable. "We get blown out of the water by the Lionguard? You're an optimistic fur bucket, Sykox. Making for Lion's Arch is a stupid plan."

"I thought you said there weren't any other charr down here, Sykox," Cobiah said. A shadow stepped out of the smoke near the engine's main cog. It was small, topping out barely higher than Cobiah's waist, and it definitely didn't move like a charr.

"How did you know we were making for Lion's Arch?" Sykox blurted challengingly, shaking a clawed paw. "I talked Centurion Harrow into that plan only yesterday!"

"I hear everything that happens aboard this blasted ship, you loudmouthed blunderbuss. So, tell me, when we reach this aforementioned port, what do we do then?" The figure walked into the light of the engine fire, and Cobiah could finally see it clearly. It was a woman—well, at least it was female, as far as he could tell. She marched forward and stuck her hands on her hips with a ferocious attitude and a toss of her head, making her long ears flap against her shoulders. A thickly braided loop of leather on the top of her head held back dyed braids that cascaded down her back and over one shoulder in a cacophony of rampant color—none of which looked the least bit natural. Orange, green, blue, and pink vied for dominance against the little creature's pale skin. Wide eyes glinted like obsidian chips, and her bowed mouth was set in a frown of disapproval.

She wore an embroidered blue smock with a magical-looking bird's-eye pattern stitched on the chest, and blue-black feathers hung from gold cuffs above her elbows. As she talked, her hands flapped, and the motion reminded Cobiah of a bird struggling to fly. Although Cobiah was already sweating, and poor Sykox looked to be broiling under his thick coat of fur, the interloper seemed perfectly comfortable despite the engine's intense heat.

Sykox jerked a thumb toward Cobiah with a rough chuckle. "Cobiah, meet Macha, our asuran stowaway. Macha, this is Cobiah, the mouse I netted out of the sea."

"Stowaway?" The creature's eyes flashed. "Slanderous, libelous, extraplunderous accusations, Steamshroud! How dare you show such tooth to me!" Macha stomped forward and shook an accusatory finger at Sykox's belly, pointing up toward the big charr's nose. "I was invited to be part of this crew, fuzz wad! Invited, I say!"

"'Invited.'" Sykox snorted, amused. "'Blackmailed your way aboard' is more like it, Macha."

"You say 'firefly,' I say 'bioelectric pharmaceutical neonyte.'" The asura brushed imaginary dust motes from her ornamented robe. "A few of my harsher critics may have discovered certain anatomical difficulties upon rising one morning, yes, and perhaps those issues caused me to seek a vacation outside the camp, I suppose, yes, but to be quite honest, your ship has more than benefited from my presence. I consider the utilization of my genius to be more than repayment for a meager berth."

"What's she talking about?" Cobiah asked in a whisper.

"Some of the other asura said Macha's latest experiment was too dangerous," Sykox murmured. "They woke up dead."

"If they'd altered their tangents to the proper coefficient and redone the math like I told them to, they'd

never have experienced that particular side effect."
Macha lifted her nose imperiously. "I left their successors
to deal with the ramifications of their unfortunate lack of
forethought."

"Meaning," Sykox said, rolling his eyes, "she stowed
aboard the *Havoc* to escape a lynch mob."

"Oversimplified. Distinctly distorted. A multifarious
misstatement." Macha sniffed and crossed her feather-
ornamented arms. "The truth is that I negotiated a profit-
able exchange: my security aboard this ship in return for
an investment of my brilliance during the voyage."

"Negotiated *after* we put to sea, but she'll say that's
'equally irrelevant.' In any case, Macha's been tinkering
with the engines since we left shore."

"What . . . is she?" Cobiah managed to ask, trying not
to move or get the little creature's attention.

"'What is she?'" Macha turned her waggling finger on
him. "She is an asura! What are you, you ignoramus, that
you don't know an asura when you see one?"

"Asura?" Cobiah knew the word, but he'd never seen
one. All he knew about asura was that they were odd,
underground creatures that lived in the deep Maguuma
Jungle.

"Yes, asura. Not very good with words, is he?" Macha
raised an eyebrow.

"Doesn't have to be, so long as he can shovel coal."
Sykox thumped Cobiah on the back of his shoulder,
shoving him forward. "Say hello, Cobiah."

Cobiah grinned sheepishly. "I've never met an asura.
It's a pleasure." He held out his hand, unsure if asura
greeted one another like humans did. To his relief,
Macha took it.

"I'd say 'it's a pleasure' back, but I have met humans."
The diminutive woman tossed her head, ears flapping to

either side, and fixed him with an appraising stare. "So, Cobiah. Can you do anything useful?"

With a smile, Cobiah answered, "I can read an astrolabe." He pulled the brass device out of his vest and saw the asura's eyes light up like furnace flames.

"Well, well, well!" Macha grinned, rubbing her hands together. "An educated human. How abnormal. How unexpected. Between that device and this engine, we might just make it to Lion's Arch after all."

Sykox smiled. "I told you, Macha. Everything will work out just fine." With a bark of laughter, the charr shoved them both toward the coal pile. "With the three of us working together, nothing could *possibly* go wrong. You'll see!"

C obiah had sailed for nearly a year with the *Indomi-table*, and he knew every rock formation and major island in the northern bay of the Sea of Sorrows—yet not one of them broke the horizon, even after six days of sail. No seagulls hovered beneath the low-hanging, dark clouds, and the sea was littered with wreckage. Severed masts and shattered keels tossed on the waves, and fouled white sails clung to rolling waves like funeral cloths. Thick kelp floated in massive drifts, and even the roll and swell of the waves seemed labored. The sea itself was filthy with sand and churned grit, and—horribly—here and there Cobiah could see something floating that may have once been part of a house.

"We should have seen *something* by now," he muttered to Sykox as they leaned out over the *Havoc*'s rail. "You can spy the lighthouse at Lion's Gate a day before you see the port." But there'd been no lighthouse. No Lion's Gate. Most sickeningly, there'd been no sign that any other ship had survived the wave. As they followed in the wake of the catastrophe, even the bullying charr were quiet and subdued. The *Havoc* felt like a funeral.

From the crow's nest came the sound of a signal

whistle. Sykox perked up, his four ears shifting forward with interest. "The scout's spotted land!"

"Claw Island, maybe," Cobiah guessed. "Or the harbor cliffs?"

"We'll see for ourselves soon enough." Macha looked up from scribbling sketches of the astrolabe onto a dirty scrap of torn canvas. She handed the brass disc back to Cobiah, stuffing her designs into a hidden pocket of her blue robe. "I just hope the modifications we made to the rudder won't flummox the whole thing and run the ship aground."

The three of them stood at the port railing with the others, watching as land slowly came into sight. Cobiah recognized it first—the harbor cliffs. His smile faded as soon as he saw the cliffs. Something was wrong. There was no sign of the city's lighthouse. No indication of the skyline of roofs, nor of the watchtowers, nor of the islands that should have ringed the city's harbor. The wave had washed them full away, covering everything in a blanket of deep water.

The feeling on deck wasn't one of celebration or even tense battle readiness. Silently, the *Havoc* sailed between the high cliffs that once stood guard over the city's harbor. They were half as tall now, mere circles of stone peering over the high line of the sea. Around them, the remains of waterlogged masts jutted up through the waves. Cobiah peered over the side of the *Havoc*, staring down into the water. Silt and earth swirled around the wreckage of houses, shipyards, and even cobbledstoned roads. There was nothing left of the white towers that had ringed the central keep or of the lion statue that stood guard over the city walls. There was nothing left of the home he'd known, the city where he'd been raised. Everything was drowned, buried in the massive surge of water.

No one had survived.

So many dead. And why? Where had the wave come from? What magic had overturned the sea? Had the nature goddess Melandru struck out in wrath, or had some darker force cast a horrible spell? Stories claimed that the entire kingdom of Orr had been destroyed by such a spell, cast by an ancient vizier. Cobiah remembered the land he'd seen beyond the great wave. Among those strange mountains and the wide black plain, he'd seen buildings. Tall ones, with spires like Malchor's Fingers—but far more elaborate and delicate than those jutting stones. Could it have been Orr itself, risen from below the ocean's depths? The fabled city of Arah? Was such a thing even *possible*?

Was King Baede alive? Had the royal family escaped the devastation? Who ruled Kryta, and where had they gone now that Lion's Arch was destroyed? Cobiah sank to his knees, clinging to the *Havoc*'s railing. "The ships. The city. Thousands of people . . . Gone." His thoughts briefly flickered to his mother. Even though he'd hated the woman, he wouldn't have wished this kind of death on her. On anyone. The vastness of the realization sank in with a rush.

The city was gone. The *Indomitable* was lost. Everyone he knew was dead.

Macha put her arm around Cobiah's shoulders and tugged at him. "Stand up, you idiot," she hissed with uncharacteristic gentleness. "The charr are watching." She helped him to his feet, letting Cobiah lean his elbow on her shoulder.

Centurion Harrow stood at the forecastle rail, scowling out at the water-filled basin that had once been a city. "May your filthy gods take you all," he snarled under his breath. "Even the shore's wasted. Silt-packed, slippery, and shifting. There's no docks, not even a rock to rest our bow on. Nowhere solid enough to disembark for repairs. We can't land." Harrow raised his voice to a growl. It echoed over the still water, the sound bouncing from sheer cliff walls. The rest of the crew tensed, clenching their fists and snarling in disappointment.

Although the charr's casual blasphemy sent a shudder down Cobiah's spine, he understood the captain's anger. Getting to Lion's Arch had been a treacherous journey. They had plenty of fish but very little fresh water, and the *Havoc* wouldn't survive if the waters turned rough. More-over, now the charr had no reason to keep Cobiah alive. He could feel them all around, feral with anger and disap-pointment, looking for someone on whom to visit their wrath. "We have to sail for Port Stalwart," Cobiah said quickly. "Your plan still works, Centurion. If Lion's Arch is flooded, then Stalwart's overflowing as well. That means the storm's deepened their bay enough for us to make harbor. The *Havoc* can sail into their bay." Cobiah tried to keep his voice steady. By now, he knew the charr well enough to realize what they'd do if they heard weakness.

The centurion's eyebrow lifted. He turned and fixed an unblinking stare on the human. "A fair point, mouse," Harrow conceded at last. "But what if the wave's destroyed Stalwart as well?" A skeptical rumble thundered through the crew.

"Stalwart's on high ground. That's why their harbor's shallow. The town'll be there." The centurion still looked dubious, and Cobiah repeated firmly, "It'll be there."

With a bored noise, Macha yawned. "What the human's *not* telling you, Centurion, is that the nations of Orr and Kryta were at war when Lion's Arch was built. That's why they put it behind the natural fortifications of those stone escarpments.

"Stalwart's newer, designed generations after the Orrian peninsula was destroyed. Despite its doughty name, Port Stalwart is a vacation town, not a fortress. It's built to have an oh-so-pretty view." Macha tugged on her multicolored braids, tightening the leather strap that held the thick coil atop her skull. "Unless the tide rose higher than one would surmise by looking at this soggy rubble, Stalwart's fine. The human's right." When Cobiah and Sykox stared at her, the asura tossed her head and had the gall to look annoyed.

"How did you know all that?" Cobiah whispered. "I never heard that story."

"Yes, well," Macha sniffed. "Some of us can *read*."

The charr crew muttered, arguing back and forth as they chewed on the information, while their centurion considered. Cobiah looked him in the eye and tried not to let his nerves show. One of the charr in the throng laughed darkly. The captain shot him a snarl.

Sykox cleared his throat, and the centurion's glare focused on him. "As I see it, sir, the only other choice is to scuttle the *Havoc* and swim ashore. If we do that, we're committed to marching through Kryta, over the Shiver-peaks, and all the way across Ascalon to get back to the Black Citadel. That's eight weeks' march, sir. Six, if we're lucky. Ten, if we have to fight our way through a host of Krytan soldiers coming to see what happened to their capital city." The centurion didn't seem convinced, and Sykox added, "Most importantly, we'd lose the prototype engine, and it'll take years to build again. The tribune said—"

"I know what the tribune said!" Displeased, the centurion clenched his clawed hands around the deck rail. "The engine's our priority. I am aware of my orders, Engineer. I don't need you to remind me." At the rebuke, Sykox stiffened to attention and stepped back.

Centurion Harrow considered his options in silence. His eyes flicked over the broken masts sticking out of the water, the rough edges of the muddy sea, and the ruins of the city both above and below the tide. There were plenty of reasons to make shore. The strain of the voyage was beginning to tell on the soldiers, and the tides around Lion's Arch were difficult to navigate—especially so in the massive overflow of water from the giant wave.

Cobiah tried to stay calm and let no indication of fear show on his face.

"We sail for Stalwart," Centurion Harrow announced. "Sykox, the engineers will need to shovel low to save on coal. We'll use wind power as best we can until the mastheads give way, and then we'll limp the last portion—"

"Centurion!" The bosun in the high crow's nest blew his signal whistle imperiously, drawing attention to his cries. "Sail ahoy! Sail, sir!" yelled the watch. "A ship to south, sir!"

All eyes turned toward the mouth of the ruined harbor. Indeed, there among the waterlogged tops of ravaged houses, between the trunks of shattered masts, sailed a narrow brigantine. She was smaller than the *Havoc* but quick in her turns, with two tall, square-sailed masts festooned with mismatched canvas sails. To her fore, two long jib sails stretched to the end of a long bowsprit, and along her side, one word had been crudely painted: *Disenmaedel.*

Cobiah could see that the six cannon ports along the *Disenmaedel*'s starboard side were already open, the black noses of cannons nudging out from within. Along her upper deck, five small carronades perched over the deck railing. At the brigantine's quarterdeck, a massive garrison gun had been fixed; turned at any angle, it could destroy an enemy with a single shot. Cobiah stared at it in disbelief, recognizing the weapon. It was a bombard, one of the guns stationed on the wall surrounding Lion's Arch . . . or it had been, before the city was destroyed. The brigantine's crew must have prized it from its place on the stone and bolted it to their ship. That gun had the firepower to open a four-foot hole straight through the *Havoc* and out the other side.

"What are their colors, Bosun?" said Centurion Harrow.

"They're not flying colors, sir. No flag a'tall."

Cobiah frowned. "If that ship was Krytan, they'd be flying the king's flag. I don't think they're a chartered ship, not with their sails in that condition."

"Pirates." Harrow reached the same conclusion. "Vultures taking advantage of the damage caused by the storm. Plenty of refuse here for them to pick through." Cobiah nodded, and the centurion continued. "Doesn't matter if they're chartered or not, mouse. They're human. We're charr. Our ship is obviously wounded.

"They'll attack." The centurion shook his head knowingly, furry mane settling about his shoulders. "It's what I would do in their place." Indeed, the little ship tacked toward them, and Cobiah could hear echoes of the sailors on board. Turning away from them, the centurion started barking out orders to his men.

"Is the *Havoc* armed?" Cobiah grabbed Sykox's shoulder.

Sykox sighed. "Nah. We were just out to test the engines; we weren't on a combat mission. She's set sail with barely anything to speak of." The engineer rubbed his cheek thoughtfully, his rusty whiskers sticking out at all angles between his claws. "Fifteen carronades, six cannons, and four firemauls."

Cobiah blinked. "You call that unarmed?"

Sykox crossed his arms stubbornly. "You do if you're

a charr." Seeing Cobiah's eyes light up, the engineer sighed. "I said we sailed with that. I didn't say we still had it. The wave messed up the *Havoc* right bad, and we had to dump the heavy load, or her keel'd have given out long before now. Those cannons are at the bottom of the sea. All we have left are the firemauls." Seeing Cobiah's blank stare, Sykox explained, "Firemauls shoot balls of fire, not iron, so while they might set that brig alight, they won't do much to sink her. They're slow falling, too—the shot's made of goose dung and powder instead of weighted metal. The brig'll dance right out from under 'em."

"How many shots do we have?"

"That's the other problem." Sykox fell silent. The wind swept through the charr's fur in ripples, and Cobiah could hear the human sailors on the other ship yelling as they loaded their guns.

"Can the firemauls win this battle?"

"No," Sykox sighed. "Almost certainly not."

"Then we have to find something else." Cobiah found himself desperately wishing he had a pistol. A sword. Something! He snatched up a belaying pin, willing to chuck it at the brigantine if there was any chance it would help. "We're done for, aren't we?"

"Don't be so overdramatic, mouse. This ship has all the weapons it needs." Macha narrowed her eyes. "It has me."

"That's right! You're a mesmer! I forgot. Hey, does that mean you can blast them?" the charr asked eagerly, his four ears flicking forward with delight.

Macha snorted. "Don't be stupid."

"Can you make a big wind to push them away from us?" Cobiah asked hopefully.

"Of course not. That's not how my spells work."

"Then what help are you?" Sykox tugged at his horns in frustration.

Macha tossed her head smugly. "I'm smarter than they are."

The first volley from the brigantine fell just short of the *Havoc*'s bow, splashing huge gouts of water across the deck. The echo of guns roared like thunder over the ruined harbor, an earsplitting bang coupled with the acrid smell of powder smoke. The charr were already in their battle positions, but Cobiah was aware how pitifully few they were, and how poorly armed. If they'd been aboard the proud *Indomitable*, they would have had a chance—a many-gunned ship of the line against the quick brigantine might have been a good fight, but there was no way the *Disenmaedel* could bring down a well-prepared galleon.

Against the *Havoc*, in her battered shape? Cobiah had little hope they would survive.

The crew pulled out the firemauls: short-barreled guns that looked like crouching lions, their mouths opened wide and their claws clenched around stiff brass wheels. The charr crew quickly loaded the guns with strange, sticky ammunition that looked for all the world like gooey balls of twine. Cobiah caught the scent of lamp oil and a strange, sickly-sweet tang. The black-furred helmsman roared a command, and *Havoc*'s firemauls boomed in response.

Four balls of flame exploded into the air. Long fiery tails stretched out behind them like comets as they arched toward the *Disenmaedel* in long languid curves, drifting almost in slow motion. Cobiah could see what Sykox meant about the brigantine dancing out from under the firemauls' attack—the balls of flame fell far more slowly than cannonballs and were easier to see, even during the day. As soon as their flight began to curve and the pirates saw where the balls of flame would land, they let their sails swell and darted out from beneath the attack. Each of the four comets splashed into the water, unraveling in great, greasy splotches across the bay. Fire spread across each floating oily mass but no farther, making the patches easy to avoid.

The wind swept smoke from the firemauls across the ship, clouds of it billowing in dark waves around Cobiah. He leaned out across the railing to keep clear of it. He could see the tide tugging on the oily patches, carrying some of the flame to ignite the thin masts of wreckage that thrust up from below like the skeletal bones of Malchor's Fingers. The *Disenmaedel* darted between them and turned her port side toward the *Havoc* to launch another volley of heavy shot at the *Havoc*'s hull.

The ship rolled in the heavy surf as the centurion howled for a turn. "Hard to lee, Fassur!" Harrow's long tail cracked like a whip as he strode over the deck. The helmsman called his assent and spun the wheel at the rear of the quarterdeck. In a breath, the ship tilted dangerously away from the gale. The rudder beneath the *Havoc*'s stern shifted to the side, and wind leached out of the high sails.

Sykox spun on his heel and raced toward the stairs that led below. "The engine!" he declared. "I've got to keep her fired, or we'll stall. We need to head against the wind, or they'll catch . . ." The last words were lost beneath the increasing whistle of more incoming shot. The sheets and braces of the *Havoc*'s sails creaked against the mast as they tried to catch the wind once more. Macha and Cobiah grabbed the railing as the *Havoc* tilted, and were rewarded by huge guffs of water exploding from the sea below as the *Disenmaedel*'s cannonballs landed only a few feet short of the charr ship's wooden side.

"One more like that, and they'll cave us in!" the helmsman roared, his sharp teeth glinting.

"Ram them!" Cobiah screamed, stumbling to his feet. He lurched toward the centurion and grabbed the charr's arm, not caring for his own safety. "Sir! Head toward them! Not away!"

"What in the mists are you rambling about, mouse?" bellowed the centurion. "Are you mad? Their guns—"

"I know how those carronades work, sir! We have just a few minutes while they water down the guns and reload. If we charge them now, we can board them!"

"Board them?" the helmsman choked. "Their crew's three times the size of ours."

"Yeah." Cobiah gave him a thin smile. "But if I remember the stories right—and if your engineer's bragging has any substance—a charr's worth four humans in hand-to-hand combat. You don't have guns," Cobiah gasped. "But you do have claws."

The centurion paused, whiskers twitching. "It's a trick. You're trying to get us closer to that ship so you can bolt and join your kind."

"Grenth take me if I do!" Cobiah pointed at the other ship with his belaying pin. "One more man on their side wouldn't make any difference either way. There's no time, Captain. Point us at the *Disenmaedel* and argue with me after!"

The old charr rubbed his white-furred chin. "We could catch them," he finally agreed reluctantly. "They're with the wind, and we have the use of our engine—something they won't expect. We can catch them." Convinced, the centurion nodded sharply and turned to roar at his crew. "Turn the ship 'cross the wind, full-bore the engine, and run them down!"

A cheer went up from the sailors. "Aye, sir!" Grist, the gray-furred old charr, saluted. "I'll set 'er bow for the rush!" With a groan of wood and creak of sail, the

Havoc turned back toward its enemy. Cobiah watched the humans labor desperately aboard the *Disenmaedel.* Wadding, shot, and gunpowder were being tossed back and forth as the crew hurried to ready their guns once more.

"Prepare to board the enemy!" Centurion Harrow snarled. He turned on Cobiah with a fierce red glint in his eyes. "You'll be at the fore, mouse. And if you waver, you'll die by my claws before you can draw breath."

He strode away, ordering the other charr into boarding positions. Cobiah leapt to the deck railing, trying to gauge whether they would draw alongside the *Disenmaedel* before her guns were ready to fire again. Every second was an agony.

"What's your plan, human?" said a quiet voice at his elbow. "Are you really going to help the charr against your own people?"

Cobiah glanced down at Macha. "Not you, too."

"Humans and charr have been at war for generations. They've done you a service saving your life, but it's been forced labor since you set foot aboard the *Havoc.*"

He shook his head. "Even if I was the kind to do such a thing, that brigantine over there's probably filled with valuables picked from the bones of the city I called home. It's crewed by scavengers. It attacked us, unprovoked, because they saw that we were wounded and looking for aid."

"So?" Macha's wide mouth tilted into a skeptical smile.

"When the wave came, it took the *Indomitable.* It took Lion's Arch. It took everything I had left, after—" His voice broke, thinking of blue eyes and bouncing yellow curls. Gritting his teeth, he reached down and put his hand around the rag doll at his belt. "I don't have a home, or a job, or a family. All I have is a ship. *This* ship." Cobiah set his feet against the motion of the *Havoc* tossing in the waves. "This crew's been good to me, whatever their reasons. That one's picking clean the bones of everything I ever loved."

"Hmmph." The asura nodded curtly. She looked out to sea, the stiff wind tossing her multicolored braids about her shoulders. "So when we reach the *Disenmaedel*, your plan's basically: 'Gah! Getum!' You expect to survive that?"

"Always worked for me before." Cobiah leaned forward on the rail, trying not to focus on the past. "You have a better idea?"

"As a matter of fact, I do." Macha grinned, showing a smile made of sharp little teeth. "Head for the battery gun at the back of their ship. Whatever else happens, no matter what you have to do, get to that gun." She gestured toward the brig's quarterdeck with both hands as if she were unfurling a flag. "Get over there and 'gah getum' in *that* direction."

"And then what?"

Macha stared at him as if his head were filled with feathers. "Fire the gun, idiot."

"Fire the—?" Cobiah choked. "Are you kidding me?"

"Use your anemic human eyes and look at their ship, mouse. *They've bolted a bombard to their deck.* That thing's not meant to be fixed to a hull, it's meant to be attached to a massive hunk of stone, and there's a reason for that! Even your simplistic human mind should be able to understand that it's a matter of applied force." Macha leaned closer and broke her sentence into small words. "They've never fired that gun. If they do, it'll twist their keel, and the *Disenmaedel* will flounder in the water like a chicken off a cliff."

Cobiah considered this. "They've probably reinforced the main deck. Or set a brace from the mast step."

Macha snorted. "We're talking about pirates, not mathematicians. Unless they have an asura aboard, I doubt they've thought beyond, 'Ooh, cool, a really *big* cannon!'" She swatted at him chastisingly. "Just get on that ship and fire the bombard—preferably not at *us*—and then get back here before that mad cat Sykox runs out of coal and throws me into the furnace." She snorted and then winked up at him. "Fire the gun, Cobiah.

"Physics will do the rest."

8

The thunder of guns echoed from the cliffs surrounding the bay. The brigantine's sails flushed with wind as she tried to cut away from the charr galleon, but Sykox had been right—even with the gale at their back, the *Disenmaedel* couldn't escape the *Havoc* under full steam.

Cobiah stood among tense, crouched charr, their tails lashing with eagerness, bright swords or cocked pistols grasped in their clawed fists. Battle ready, tension thick in the air, they waited. Centurion Harrow had a grin on his furred face, fangs bared behind curled red lips. Some of the other charr spoke in low tones, voices muffled by the wind of the ship's passage and the rumble of the sea against her hull. Cobiah couldn't hear them. He wasn't even sure he wanted to know what they were saying. Every eye was fixed on their enemy. Every muscle was tensed to leap the moment their ship struck hull.

"Hold our course!" Harrow snarled. The cry was taken up by the charr standing closer to the engine room, carrying the call throughout the ship.

The hull of the *Disenmaedel* surged closer with each swell of water. Cobiah could see the frantic hands on board, stuffing the carronades, aware that every second brought them closer to impact with the oncoming charr vessel. One man stared at the *Havoc* as she closed, and Cobiah could read naked fear on the man's features. The *Havoc* closed to pistol range—twenty yards. Half pistol range. Small-arms fire exploded from the human ship, and the charr crouched in preparedness.

Cobiah imagined what it must be like to see a ship full of ferocious charr bearing down on you, only a few feet of water separating you from claws and teeth. The *Havoc* grew closer, and closer still, and the humans desperately fired their pistols and tried to load their carronades. But they weren't fast enough with the ship's guns, and the *Disenmaedel* had run out of time.

The charr helmsman let out a mighty bellow as the *Havoc* plowed bow-first into the brigantine's side. Although Cobiah was braced for impact, the collision knocked his feet out from under him, slamming him forward into the guardrail. He grunted, trying to right himself, and realized he was the only one lying down. Each of the charr had their claws sunk deep into the oak. As Cobiah scrabbled to rise, the sailors of the *Havoc* leapt over the rail in massive leonine pounces and landed on the deck of the *Disenmaedel.*

The gun crew of the brigantine flung themselves at the charr in response, drawing swords and knives from their belts. Battle cries rose above the clash of steel on steel. Even old Grist, who was not as fast as the others, fought with a fury that Cobiah had never seen before in war. If this was what charr brought to the field of battle, it was little wonder that Ascalon had been lost. At their furious charge, the deck of the *Disenmaedel* erupted in confusion. Huge furred charr swept down upon their enemy, swords flashing viciously. Claws slashed here and there, cutting through the human ship's ropes, tearing down their sails. Pistols fired, puffs of smoke erupting into the air, and, once empty, were shoved back into their holsters—there was no time to pack and reload.

The *Havoc* struck her enemy relentlessly, driving the thick limb of her bow into the *Disenmaedel's* hull. Both ships had suffered damage. The *Havoc's* hull was cracked, the sturdy boards separated in small breaches. They could be tarred back together, the water in her berth eased out by bilge pumps. The *Disenmaedel* had not been so lucky. Her side was caved, her sleek curve wrenched apart, and water was pouring into her berth. She'd survive, but only if she could dislodge her unwanted suitor and plug the rent he'd made in her corseted hull.

Cobiah pulled himself to his feet and climbed over the rail. With a gulp, he steeled himself and stared across the divide between the *Havoc* and the enemy brigantine. Gripping the belaying pin tightly in his hand, he leapt. Three . . . two . . . one—then he slammed into the brigantine's deck, rolling across the slippery surface with the force of his impact.

Within seconds of his feet striking the wood of the *Disenmaedel's* deck, someone attacked him. A fist drove into his cheekbone, knocking him sideways over a carronade. A sword swept over his head, clipping his hair and drawing blood from the edge of his ear. Spinning in his crouch, he plowed the belaying pin into the side of the other man's knee and saw him fall forward with a stiff crack of bone. The sailor swung again, but Cobiah parried his sword with the thick oak of the pin. He returned the blow and drove his belaying pin into the man's gut. The *Disenmaedel* sailor dropped his sword, howling with pain as Cobiah cracked him across the face and kicked him over, watching as the sailor collapsed into unconsciousness. Just then one of the charr stormed past, burying a heavy-bladed axe into the sailor's back.

"Well done," snarled the helmsman. "And here I'd bet three gold you weren't really on our side." He laughed, and the sound was bloodthirsty. "Perhaps you're worthwhile after all, mouse."

"You didn't have to kill him, Fassur!" Cobiah choked. "He was out of the fight!"

Pulling his weapon free and sighting his next prey across the ship, Fassur shrugged. "Now he's out of the world." Without another word, the burly charr sprang across the ship toward another human sailor. Galled, Cobiah faltered and ventured to the rear of the ship, avoiding fights wherever he could. All around him, charr and humans were locked in vicious struggles, and the charr didn't fight fair. They took no prisoners. They exploited weakness and ground it into dust. Although badly outnumbered, they were clearly the more seasoned warriors, fighting in small clusters of two or three against groups twice, even three times, their size. Cobiah had never seen such glee in the eyes of combatants. It sickened him. Even charr who had shown him common courtesy on board the *Havoc* now fought with joyous abandon, seemingly unaware—or uncaring—that their prey were terrified and overwhelmed. The sailors, convinced that the charr would never surrender, returned hate with fury, killing any charr they found alone. The longer the conflict progressed, the more people on both sides would die.

The only way to stop the killing was to end the fight as quickly as possible.

Cobiah hurdled a hatch to reach the brigantine's quarterdeck, dodging through two shouting sailors as he broke into a run. The deck was slippery with blood and salt water, but he did have one advantage—for the most part, the pirates of the *Disenmaedel* ignored anything furless.

On the quarterdeck, four burly sailors manned the bombard. One hefted a pair of burlap gunpowder sacks into the barrel, and two more were working to lift a massive iron cannonball. The fourth stood at the top of the stairs to the deck, a loaded pistol in each hand, two more stuffed through his belt, and a cutlass in a sheath at his side. Right now, the armed thug was watching the strife with a patient, ready eye, weighting the pistols in his hands. His forehead wrinkled in a frown as he watched Cobiah approach. Clearly, he couldn't place the youth among the crew.

Using that to his advantage, Cobiah pretended to stumble on his way up the last few stairs. "Sir!" he said. "The cap'n says . . ." Then, at the last moment, instead of straightening, Cobiah charged forward and buried his shoulder in the thug's midsection. To Cobiah's surprise, the big man didn't go down. Although Cobiah's shoulder hit him solidly, eliciting a meager grunt, the man stood his ground at the top of the stairs as if he were a brick wall. Cobiah looked up over his shoulder at the immense man's broad, pielike face and managed a halfhearted smile.

The pistol in the sailor's right hand slammed down onto Cobiah's back with terrific force, missing his temple by inches. A second motion, and the handle of the other pistol crashed into his collarbone with enough force to knock Cobiah to his knees. As Cobiah lay there, his head spinning, the big thug raised his pistols and cocked the hammers back in slow motion. Staring down twin columns of doom, Cobiah tried to murmur a prayer to the god of death. He couldn't finish it. Instead, he whispered his sister's name.

The roar that followed wasn't one of flame and gunpowder, or the crashing impact of iron ball against bone. Instead, something fuzzy smacked Cobiah's cheek—a tail?—as a large rust-colored mountain of muscle tore up the stairs and launched itself at the sailor.

"Sykox?" Cobiah said, marveling.

One of the thug's guns went off as Sykox plowed into him. An iron ball whizzed past, sinking deep into the oak deck a few inches from Cobiah's feet. Unlike the slender Cobiah, Sykox had more than twice the mass of the thug, and the two toppled and rolled onto the deck like a cat with a ball of yarn. "Get the others, Coby!" Sykox roared. "Stop them before they point that thrice-burned thing at our ship!"

Startled, Cobiah pushed himself to his feet, looking past the brawlers. The other sailors on the quarterdeck were rushing about in a panic, trying to get the gun readied. They shoved a watermelon-sized cannonball into the gun's barrel, and one tamped it down with a long, padded stick while another unscrewed the cover of the vent tube and frantically shoved a friction primer down into the hole. One tug on the lanyard sticking out of the thin hole in the breech of the cannon, and the heavy gun would fire.

As Cobiah watched, the third man drew a cutlass from his belt and strode murderously toward him. Still holding the belaying pin, Cobiah stepped forward to fight. The *Disenmaedel*'s sailor took the first swing. His blade swished forward and Cobiah dodged nimbly. With a shrug of his shoulders, the youth returned the favor, swinging the belaying pin widely in the hopes of ending the fight in a single shot. The sailor ducked easily and grinned, revealing four gold teeth. With a snatch of his free hand, he gripped Cobiah's wrist as it passed, twisting viciously. Pain wracked Cobiah's arm as the belaying pin slid through numb fingers. When it struck the deck, the sailor kicked it away, laughing at Cobiah's grimace of pain.

Cobiah tried a shallow kick at his enemy's leg, but the other man dodged it, keeping hold of Cobiah's arm. Cobiah rolled closer, under sword range, pressing his back against the sailor's chest. Recklessly, he drove his free elbow into the sailor's rib cage and was rewarded by a whoosh of air and the soldier's grasp loosening on Cobiah's wrist. Tilting his forearm back, Cobiah slammed his fist upward. Bone cracked as his knuckles creased the man's lower jaw.

Nearby, Sykox fought far more warily. "You're big," he said, circling the massive thug who had guarded the stairwell. The mountainous sailor turned slowly, keeping his eyes on the canny charr. His hands spread wide, he waited for the inevitable rush . . . but Sykox only smiled and stepped again to the side.

"You'll find no opening, kitty!" the big human bellowed. "I've fought your kind before. I was raised in Ascalon! I use charr hides as hearth rugs!" He drew a deep breath, bald pate shining in the sunlight. "I'll tear out your claws and carve 'em into scrimshaw!"

Sykox lashed his tail, feinting left and right. He'd already gotten several blows in, marking his burly opponent with bloody streaks down chest and arms. But it hadn't been enough to slow the sailor's motions. The charr managed to turn the sailor away from the stairs. Narrowing his eyes, Sykox measured his opponent with a snarl. The thug was nearly as tall as the tawny charr, and even wider through the chest.

"Do you think I'm weak?" the thug taunted. "Stop stalling. I'm ready for you, charr!"

"You may be ready for him." A reedy voice piped up from over the side of the ship. Macha stood on the railing of the *Havoc*, her feathered armbands and embroidered blue robe whipping in the strong wind. "But you're definitely not ready for *me*."

A brilliant spell flowed from the asura's fingertips, leaping through the air in fractal twists and unpredictable patterns. In one hand she held a short scepter, and from the other poured a wild burst of magic. Serpents formed of brilliant, glittering points of light swarmed forward, writhing one over the other as each fought to reach their target first.

"Pain!" the asura shouted. Her twisting barrage pummeled into the sailor's broad chest. "Anguish!" Macha pointed again, and the snakes lashed out around his body, their glittering, viperous heads striking the sailor again and again. "Ruin!" The final word of her spell hissed out between the asura's gritted teeth.

Overwhelmed by agony, the *Disenmaedel* thug toppled to the ground with a shriek of pain. He thrashed violently as spectral serpents coiled about his torso, piercing his flesh repeatedly with their poisonous, sparkling fangs. Cobiah had never seen the like.

"I thought you said you couldn't blast them with magic!" Sykox yelped, smacking at his arm where a spark of passing starlight had set fire to the fur.

Macha tossed her head, rainbow braids flying. "No, I *said* it was a stupid question."

Across the deck, Cobiah's assailant staggered back as the youth planted another uppercut beneath his jaw. Bewildered by the concussion, the sailor shook his head and tried to clear his thoughts—only to have Cobiah slip out of his grasp. He shook his pale hair out of his eyes and launched two quick punches. They landed with rock-hard thuds, and the staggering pirate tumbled to the deck.

"Arrgh! Is it out? Is the fire out?" Panicked, Sykox smacked desperately at the singed area on his arm. Cobiah grabbed him, smothering the last of the flame with the sleeve of his shirt. He couldn't help laughing at the agitation on the powerful creature's face. "What?" Sykox moaned. "Fur is flammable!" Laughing, Cobiah clapped him on the shoulder with a wide grin.

"Get to the weapon, you idiots!" From the railing of the *Havoc*, Macha thrust her finger demandingly toward the other sailors on the quarterdeck. "Stop fooling around!"

Sykox rolled his eyes. "The woman sets me alight and then accuses me of wasting time! Completely unfair."

Five yards away, the last two sailors worked frantically to maneuver the now-loaded battery gun into place. One spun a wheel at its base, turning the cannon on its harness, while the other desperately shoved at the barrel with all his strength. They'd turned it almost a full ninety degrees. Now, the swell of its huge muzzle pointed toward the *Havoc*'s hull.

On the main deck, charr and human sailors fought viciously. Several on both sides had fallen, and the deck was stained red with blood. A few of the humans had broken free of their catlike foes and now struggled over the side of the *Disenmaedel*, using heavy crowbars and thick oak staves in an attempt to dislodge the charr vessel. They hacked at the *Havoc*'s hull in a reckless frenzy. As they did, a few of the charr remaining on the *Havoc* shot pistols at them, glad to join in the fight. Madness everywhere.

Cobiah could see Centurion Harrow fighting back-to-back with a wounded Fassur near the *Disenmaedel*'s central mast. The captain's white fur was stained with oil and gunpowder, and one arm hung limply by his side. Leaning wearily against the mast, he kicked an adversary in the knee with his heavy peg leg, unloading his pistol at the human at the same time. Fassur was doing less well. Labored breathing aggravated a long, deep gash on his chest where his pelt was matted with blood. Yet the charr was not giving up; with each gasp of air, he swung his sword again, driving back the mass of humans that threatened to overwhelm the captain and his loyal second.

"Sykox!" Cobiah yelled. "I'll man the cannon if you handle the sailors." Pausing, he added, "But don't kill them!"

"Don't kill? Pish. You humans are so binary," growled the charr, but his snarl twisted into a smile. "I should have left you in the ocean!" With a bound, he lunged toward the frantic humans. Claws outstretched, mouth open, fangs wide and threatening, the engineer vented his fury on the two humans with gleeful abandon. He was as fast as a jungle cat and more than their match. In moments, they'd both been knocked senseless. Long claw marks on their faces and chests offered tribute to the tawny charr's precision.

While Sykox was handling the threat, Cobiah raced to the rear of the massive bombard. The vent was open but unlit, and down the narrow channel he could smell gunpowder and oil. Cotton fiber hung limply from the chamber, a thread that drove down the vent into the darkness where the charge had been packed inside the bowl of the barrel's deepest recess. One flame, even one small spark, and the vent's wick would catch. If that happened, the bombard would suck a breath of fire into the depths of its belly, where sacks of black powder were waiting for just such a kiss.

After that, all hell would break loose.

What are you waiting for? A whisper, high-pitched and snarky, resounded magically in Cobiah's ear. Startled, he blinked and looked around. Macha stood on the *Havoc's* railing, across the divide between the ships. She glowered at him, activating her vocal illusion again. *Turn the gun and fire!*

Cobiah reached down and cranked the handle that turned the bombard. Rolling it in its tight circle, he swung the barrel away from the charr ship and rocked it sharply to the right. A piece of tarred wood rested in a metal bucket beside the bombard, sparks popping and flames flickering along its end. One touch of that flame, and the cannon would fire. He planned to clear the *Disenmaedel's* deck, point the weapon into the open waters of Lion's Arch's bay. Perhaps he would have—if the path of the barrel hadn't crossed over the brigantine's deck.

Staring out over the battle, Cobiah took stock of it. The charr captain had fallen. He lay unmoving on the *Disenmaedel's* scarlet-washed deck, surrounded by his conquered foes. Fassur was still fighting despite his terrible wound. If anything, the dark-furred charr's energy had been renewed with the fall of his centurion. Roaring in grief and anger, he lashed out at anything that came too close. Beyond him, a small knot of bloodied humans readied themselves for an assault. They might have been planning to murder the charr and take their ship, or simply drive the enemy from their decks and push back the *Havoc's* prow; they might have been planning to die in battle, throwing themselves on their foe until one or both were eradicated. And suddenly, with a fire that rivaled the *Havoc's* massive furnace, Cobiah realized he was *angry.*

The charr were killing his countrymen.

The humans were killing his crew.

With a wave of possessiveness, Cobiah realized that he had to protect them. All of them.

He hadn't foreseen his next actions; he didn't plan them. Some slight shift in thinking altered his course, changing his intentions as fluidly as the wind altered the canvas of a ship's sail. With the bombard pointed at the center of the *Disenmaedel*'s deck, Cobiah raised his voice and bellowed.

"No more killing!" Cobiah shouted the words so loudly that the hair on the back of his arms stood up. Even Sykox, guarding the stairwell between the main deck and the foredeck, bristled and stood still. Even with that, the two crews probably wouldn't have stopped fighting if they hadn't suddenly realized they were staring down the muzzle of a bombast cannon. As it was, the freeze crept over the ship like a winter frost whispering along the shoreline. Both charr and human alike turned to stare up at the youth angling the cannon's mouth directly into the belly of the *Disenmaedel*. Yet again, Cobiah was leaping into action without thinking of the consequences, just as he had with Tosh—but this time, there was a lot more on the line than just pride.

"Wake up, you fools! Look at what you're doing!" Cobiah roared. "You're killing each other for no reason. Why? For glory? For gold? For the legions? Out of loyalty to a king who might not even exist anymore? Or because that's what the charr and the humans have always done?" With a snarl worthy of a charr, Cobiah roared, "To Grenth's realms of torment with the past! The past is dead! Ten thousand gallons of ocean just wiped it from the shoreline, along with the greatest city in Kryta—and all you want to do is kill each other?" Cobiah felt his face grow hot, his eyes filling with acrid tears in the wake of his anger. "Put your weapons down!"

Across the *Disenmaedel*, realization dawned over the combatants. The huge cannon was pointed down at them, primed and ready to fire. None of them—charr or human—could reach Cobiah before he could ignite the weapon. Uncertain and unwilling to let go of their weapons, the warring crews nevertheless stepped back from one another in slow realization of their situation. The brigantine was badly damaged, her hull pierced by the nose of the charr galleon. The *Havoc* was also in danger; despite the efforts of the human sailors, its nose remained firmly lodged. If the *Disenmaedel* sank into the waves, she would take her charr suitor as well.

"You have three minutes to abandon this ship and get on board the *Havoc*," Cobiah yelled. "We're bound for Port Stalwart. The charr won't hurt you—they've lost enough sailors in the storm, and this fight, that they can't even crew their own ship anymore."

"What?" Fassur yelled. "Take these pirates on board?"

"We're not pirates," one of the human sailors shouted resoundingly. "We were two days out of Lion's Arch when the wave threw us back and crashed us against the cliffs. We fixed 'er as best we could and were trying to guard the wreckage—to look for survivors. When we saw your vessel, we thought you'd come to attack. That maybe the wave was caused by charr weaponry . . ." His voice faltered in a chorus of muttered agreement from the sailors of the *Disenmaedel*. The charr crewmen snarled disapprovingly, but none raised a challenge in the face of Cobiah's bombast.

"None of us are responsible for the wave," Cobiah said. "I can promise you that. It came from Orr. I can tell you this wasn't some new charr weapon. It also wasn't an accident, or a storm, or a natural disaster. I was there . . . when it happened." Cobiah struggled with his memories as he spoke, trying to force the jumbled recollection into something resembling a sane account of the images he'd seen. "I saw beyond the wave. I saw land in the middle of the Sea of Sorrows. A drowned city, erupting from the waves. Not just buildings, but mountains, shorelines, plains of rock and coral, they'd all been ripped up from the depths. I saw Orr rise—and I saw the thing that did it."

Cobiah gripped the cannon with white-knuckled hands as both crews stared at him, aghast. "I don't know what kind of creature it was, but it was big. Bigger than any ship—like a mountain of rotted flesh and shattered bone. When that thing out there raised its wings, the very earth trembled and rose beneath it. The sea parted, and the wave of its awakening swept over us." Cobiah paused to wipe the tears from his eyes.

"Now, you listen, and listen good. We are going to work together. We're going to sail together, and we're going to survive together. Otherwise, we're all going to die." He took a deep breath and growled down at them, as fierce as one of the charr. "Neither of these ships will make it on their own, so we're going to do it as one crew, like it or not. Everyone get aboard the *Havoc*. We're headed for Port Stalwart. Once there, you can stay or go as you like, and may Dwayna keep your sorry hides." Both crews looked back and forth at one another, swords still drawn and pistols ready, only a breath away from falling back into the fight.

"Are you sure about this?" Sykox muttered up at him. He crouched on the stairs, ears back, arms wide, and claws extended in a ferocious pose.

"Don't look at me." Cobiah gave him a thin-lipped smile. "This was your idea."

"Mine?" The charr glared.

"You started this when you saved me." Cobiah gripped

the torch over the cannon's back so that everyone could see it. "Now I've got to save them." A thin veneer of fire trickled over the tip, illuminating the dark tar there with eager, hungry flame. Holding it a few inches above the vent at the cannon's breech, Cobiah fixed them all with a cold stare.

"You're killing each other because *this* is the enemy you know," Cobiah bellowed. "But the enemy you *don't* know just wiped out the city of Lion's Arch without even trying! It raised an entire city from the ocean floor, and that's just for starters! Are you going to waste your time tearing each other apart just for old times' sake?"

"Why should we believe you?" asked the helmsman of the *Havoc*, his black fur tinged with blood.

Uncompromising, Cobiah met Fassur's skeptical stare. "Believe me or not, but something made that wave. Whatever it was, it destroyed the charr harbor to the south and killed all your friends there as well as the humans in Lion's Arch." Cobiah faced the human sailors with the same defiance. "Clearly, it doesn't care if you're charr, or human, or asura, or anything else. Do you think you can fight it alone? *Do you?*"

The two crews stared at him in shock. Cobiah continued. "Now, I don't know what that creature was, but I'm going to give you the same choice it did." Cobiah positioned the torch within an inch of the bombard's fuse vent.

"Work together," Cobiah said, challenging them, "or die together."

The ocean lapped hungrily against the ship's side, echoing in the silence that followed Cobiah's speech. He watched many sets of eyes flicker toward the line of dark storm clouds hovering on the distant southern horizon. Even the brash Fassur quietly lowered his sword.

"I'm glad you understand me. Now get moving." Slowly, Cobiah moved the flame toward the bombast's wick. "You've got three seconds."

Roused to motion, the sailors of both ships scattered, racing from the deck of the *Disenmaedel.* Fassur and Sykox snapped orders to human and charr alike, commanding them to grab anything that could be scavenged from the failing brigantine. Cobiah smiled, one hand slipping to touch the rag doll at his belt. "I'm going to save them, Bivy," he whispered. "All of them."

Bold move. The asura's illusory words hummed in Cobiah's ear, startling him. *But what makes you think any of them will listen once the bombard's gone?*

"It's six days to Port Stalwart, if the *Havoc* can weather it. She's damaged, and she needs a full crew. This is the only way for any of them to survive." Cobiah wasn't sure Macha's spell let her hear as well as speak, but it didn't matter. "I'll make them listen. I won't let anything happen to these sailors. Not while they're under my watch.

"Trust me." Cobiah smiled, and lit the fuse.

ACT TWO

1229 AE
(AFTER THE EXODUS OF THE GODS)

Open sea, and we're homeward bound
Fair or foul the weather, O
The cap'n swears we'll make our port
Though the sun's burned to an ember
If the Dead Ships come and the darkness falls
Then we'll all go down together, O.
                    —"Weather the Storm"

9

Captain Cobiah Marriner trod the boards of the main deck, hands clasped behind the back of his long dark green coat. Defying convention, he wore a common sailor's shirt instead of a formal blouse, and a gold-striped kerchief tied in a knot about his throat. He kept his blond hair tied in a ponytail at the nape of his neck nowadays, but his bright eyes were as blue and clear as the day he first set to sea. If time had tempered the reckless boy, it had also granted him confidence. Cobiah strode across the deck with the certainty of a man who'd been through fire—and beyond.

"Avast, there, you at the stay tackles!" he called to one of the newer sailors. "Belay that lift. Mister Fassur, keep an eye on what your men are doing."

"Aye, sir!" the dark-furred charr rumbled. A long white scar marked the old wound across his chest, but his yellow eyes had lost none of their spark. He turned on the errant sailor with a roar. "Aft, I said, you shiftless layabouts! Get that netting to the aft bay, or I'll tan your hides before you can say, 'I'm sorry, First Mate'!" The sailors scrambled to obey the command, though the older hands aboard the ship smiled in confidence at the youths' terror. In a wink, Fassur rounded on the others. "What are you looking at, you bilge rats?" he roared. "You're not paid to be ballast, you're paid to work! Put your backs into it!"

"Aye, sir!" The sailors—human, charr, and asura alike—scrambled to comply.

Cobiah smiled. Although Fassur Steamreaver seemed ill-tempered, he had proven to be fair handed and, beneath Marriner's command, a good officer. "Keep a grin on your muzzle, mate," Cobiah said, winking at him as he passed. "We'll be in harbor soon, and maybe that minx you fancy will still be in port. We wouldn't want her seeing that scowl of yours. Might scare her off."

"She's Blood Legion, sir. If I'm not scowling, she won't think I'm interested!" Fassur grinned ferociously.

In the years since the destruction of Lion's Arch, Cobiah had won more bets than he'd lost. Many of the crew of the *Havoc* remained under his command, along with more than a few from the *Disenmaedel*, as well as a handful of asura willing to exchange labor for a chance to test experiments out at sea. The crew had made their name sailing the Krytan coast, living the life of a for-hire mercenary trade ship or privateer—or in lean years, a brigand on the open seas. They were unorthodox at best, a mix of races, but they respected the captain's courage and daring. He was the key that kept them together when old habits might have driven them apart—Cobiah, and the gold they made sailing under his command. The companionship and camaraderie that had sprung up between them gave the ship her strength, but it had also made them more than a few enemies. Still, there were plenty of merchants in Tyria looking for sea passage with an experienced captain and a crew that would ask no questions.

The Krytan military considered the *Pride* a threat

simply by virtue of its strange makeup. In the new capital city of Divinity's Reach, some of King Baede's advisers called Cobiah a traitor to his country. After the fall of Lion's Arch, Cobiah no longer considered himself a resident of Kryta. He was a citizen of the open sea, as free as the wind itself.

Their ship was the *Pride*, a lightweight pinnace best suited for shipping and smuggling. Although she had plenty of cargo space, she was thinner than the larger galleons. Though she had only two masts, she was quick in the waves and easy to pilot with just a small crew. She wasn't the prettiest ship at sea, but she was stalwart: a rough, rugged-looking thing with many varieties of wood patched into her smooth hull. The portholes had no covers, and water splashed in when the waves were high. Worn brass fittings and rows of mismatched guns dotted her side. Designed to sail but rigged to fight, the *Pride* was more than one might take her for at first glance.

The foremast carried a conventional square course and topsail, but her mainmast was lateen rigged, carrying a massive triangular sail set on a long yardarm mounted at an angle from the mast. Converting the triangular sail rig typically seen on smaller fishing vessels to a larger pinnace had been Macha's idea, and it was one of two things that set the *Pride* apart. Her other advantage was even more unusual, and the crew of the *Pride* did their best to keep it a well-guarded secret. Beneath her cobbled-together exterior and patchwork sails, the *Pride* had the brave, beating heart of a lion. The *Havoc*'s engine had been redesigned to be smaller and more efficient than the original. Although the ship couldn't carry enough fuel to run it nonstop, the engine got them through the doldrums and was a massive advantage in a fight.

With engine roaring and sails to the wind, no pirate

could catch her at sea; the *Pride* could outmaneuver any brigantine. She could turn on a gold coin, with or without the wind, and bring her broadside armaments to strike a blow wherever she chose. Though she wasn't much to look at, her decks were scrubbed sparkling from quarter-deck to forecastle with the diligence of a dedicated crew, and the eager glint in each sailor's eye spoke of a deeper devotion—both to the ship and to her master.

The *Pride* had made good time plunging across the high tides of the southern sea. She carried a legal cargo—as she did on occasion—from the asuran docks in lower Maguuma bound for Kryta via Port Stalwart. Like all ships these days, she stayed close to the coast, giving a wide berth to the storm that hovered, always present, past the distant curl of Malchor's Fingers. The Orrian Veil, it was called: dark and deep in shadow even when the sun rose to its zenith. A few brave souls had tried to sail into the waters beyond Malchor's Fingers in the years just after the great wave, but none had returned. Not the sailors, not the ships, not even a whisper. Most recently, there'd been legends of phantoms: "Dead Ships" with rotting sails, silhouettes glimpsed past the veil. Others claimed they'd seen witch lights in the fog, colored like the stained glass windows of cathedral towers. Unlike other captains, Cobiah never dismissed the tales.

The sea breeze picked up as the *Pride* sailed closer to Port Stalwart's docks. Cobiah heard the sailors shout greetings to old friends as the port's tugboats pushed against their ship's sides. Sailors, both charr and human, threw lines down to the workers on the smaller boats and those walking out on the jetties. Slowly, the port's workers pulled on the lines, helping to guide the pinnace into her moorings.

"Engineer!" Cobiah leaned over the gunwale of the

Pride, his voice echoing through the portholes below. "Sykox! Come up on deck. We're docking!"

"He can't hear you." Macha rocked back and forth on her heels, the hem of her brilliant blue robe tossing in the wind. "He's wrapped up in that new 'cog's breath' he's been inventing. Some kind of doodad that'll take pressure off the rudder . . . I don't know anymore." She twirled her brightly colored braids through quick fingers, tumbling two loose feathers from her hair. "He hasn't slept in three nights, and he's been drinking for four."

"Slacker. He should be up here." Cobiah laughed. "He's missing a hell of a view!"

Port Stalwart shone like a pale jewel above the glistening turquoise lagoon. Built on a hillside that rose sharply above the water, the little village had swelled in the last ten years. The clean white masonry of new buildings rose like gulls' wings, hovering above the tidy rows of small houses that dotted the crisp, snowy beaches. Two waterfalls poured out of the forest, one above the other, leaping down from threaded boulders through heavy greenery, and pouring at last with a burbling roar into the bay. After the great tidal wave hit the Krytan shore and devastated Lion's Arch, Port Stalwart's harbor had swelled well beyond its banks. Now it was home to bustling docks, a massive wharf, and the most active trade community on the coast. The asura traded through Stalwart; on occasion a norn or charr vessel would dock there, risking the ire of the humans in the name of profit. While not welcomed, exactly, such vessels had little choice if they wanted to berth after a storm.

Yet as idyllic as Port Stalwart was, neither the buildings nor the jewel-like waters held Cobiah Marriner's attention. At the end of the busy wharf, past galleons and trade sloops, far from the bustle of the guide dinghies, his eye was fixed on a ship still docked in the shipyard. The shipwrights of Port Stalwart worked on the beach at the far end of the harbor, where the water rippled low against pale sand. When the *Pride* had left Port Stalwart several months ago, their newest construction entailed little more than a few long curve-ended keel ribs rising against an exterior frame in the center of the beach. Now she was a thing of beauty.

A great black-hulled clipper ship rested in the far cove of Port Stalwart's bay, sheltered by the protective shipyard docks. Three great masts rose above her, with crossbars six high on the main. The black ship was square-sailed, with massive triangular jibs reaching out to the end of her long bowsprit, and small rectangular canvases hung on the top yardarms. If there was even a faint breath of wind, this ship would catch it and use it for her own. Her stem was sharply raked, and her narrow body would surely cut through the waves like a knife through warm butter. The black ship's figurehead took the unique form of a sea goat, horns curling and legs striking out as it coiled a long fish tail beneath the bowsprit. In golden letters on the ship's stern shone her name: *Capricorn.*

"She's too long in the belly." Sykox had come up behind Cobiah while he stared at the clipper. Sighing, the charr leaned on the gunwale of the *Pride* and looked across the bay at the newly crafted vessel. "I like them with a wider berth, myself."

"Her narrowness makes her fast. Twice as fast as a caravel, they say. Faster than our pinnace—even with her engine running full bore." Cobiah pounded a fist on the rail of the deck. "I have to have that ship."

Long accustomed to this argument, Sykox put his chin in his hands and stared morosely out at the ship. "There's nothing wrong with the *Pride*. She's solid. Every inch of her . . . except maybe that rotting boom on the foresail, but we were going to replace that in port. Oh, and the torn topsails, but they'll get by on a few more patches. Maybe the rudder, too, after that last crack in her wood . . ."

"They say the *Capricorn*'s magical," Cobiah went on, ignoring Sykox's complaints. "They say her shipwright freed an Istani djinn from captivity, and in return, it cast powerful enchantments on the ship."

Before Sykox could pooh-pooh Cobiah's excitement, Macha interrupted. "I've heard that as well." She strutted past them, treading lightly on the rail, lifting her feet delicately to step over their hands. Cobiah dodged her, unwilling to lose even a few seconds of gazing at the *Capricorn*, but Sykox sighed and allowed the asura to take her time as she meandered past. Smugly, Macha continued. "A Maelstrom djinn, in fact, one of the most powerful kinds. They say she'll make three times any other ship's speed, with or without the wind. She'll be keener, hardier, and sweeter-sailing than anything crafted by mortal hands. No ship will ever defeat her in battle. None will outsail her. They say the *Capricorn*'s a spirit of the waves."

"Yeah, yeah, even better than an enchanted Orrian xebec, and for the record, those are fairy tales, too." Sykox yawned. "Why do I always get outvoted on these ideas?"

"Maybe because I always agree with him." Macha grinned at Cobiah.

Cobiah took his eyes from the *Capricorn*. "Don't say that word."

"What, 'Orrian'?" Sykox raised a lazy eyebrow. "Cobiah, how many times have I told you? You're too bound to superstition. We're at harbor! There's no ghost, specter, or phantom ship can hear us at port, right? They're out there." He waved a tawny paw toward the south. "Even if there are Dead Ships, they don't venture beyond Malchor's Fingers. We're safe here at Stalwart."

Still uneasy, Cobiah turned back toward the *Capricorn*. The sight of the black clipper eased him, and he gazed upon her hungrily, taking in the magnificence of the ship's tall masts and perfect sail. Even the sea goat decorating her bow was a work of art. "The captain of that ship will go down in legend," he murmured. "It's done, then. We'll have her for our own." Cobiah grinned, clapping Sykox on the back. "We're going to board her, we're going to steal her, and we're going to keep her. I've already got a plan. She's set to sail in three days, on the morning tide. I just think a ship that lovely should be set free a little earlier. Don't you?"

"Do you even have a plan?" Sykox groaned.

"Do I *ever* have a plan?" Cobiah laughed. "The plan will come with the doing. Just like it always does."

"He's obsessed." Macha's high-pitched chortle warbled like some kind of seabird. "You know we can't talk Cobiah out of anything once he's fallen in love with the idea."

"And we'll help him, of course. Rot you both to Hell's Precipice." Sykox put his forehead to the deck rail and pressed giant paws to either side of his furred forehead. "It's not possible. The security alone's going to be massive, plus spells, getting the ship out of harbor, and doing it all without anyone on the docks raising a fuss. Impossible! I should never have pulled you out of the sea, you stubborn, codswalloped, storm-tossed . . . *human!*"

Cobiah knew better than anyone that beneath those rusty paws, Sykox was already turning his mind to the task. There was nothing his friend loved more than a puzzle.

The thin streets of Port Stalwart twisted in serpentine coils beneath the pale night sky. Moonlight shone brilliantly over the lagoon, the straight line of its gaze far wider and clearer than any roadway in the village. Macha was all but invisible in the darkness, her tiny figure hiding easily against every wall and behind every rain barrel. Cobiah had to struggle more, darting from shadow to shadow and freezing whenever the city guard passed too close to the back alleys.

Sykox, however, had a different problem. Though he could be as silent as a cat, his bulk was a hindrance. Unless there was a building between the burly charr and the light of the street torches, it would be fairly obvious he was wandering through the town. Especially if he was trying to look inconspicuous. Therefore, he didn't bother to try.

"*Oh, broadside, hey, broadsi-i-i-de,*" the tawny-furred engineer yowled at the top of his lungs. Alone on the main street of the port, Sykox wandered aimlessly, as if he were a drunken sailor on shore leave. He rolled, he staggered, he sung, and he swung a bottle of Black Citadel whiskey in wild curves, lifting it to punctuate particularly ribald lines. "*I heard the first mate cry!*"

The charr's yowling quickly drew the attention of the watchmen, but they were used to such displays. So long as Sykox wasn't causing any trouble or breaking into any of the shops, he could wander to his heart's content. And while the guards kept an eye on Sykox, Cobiah and Macha crept past them, into the shipyard.

"You're certain it wouldn't have been better for me to make him look like something that wouldn't attract attention?" Macha grumped. "A beached whale, maybe?"

"Save your magic, my friend. We'll be needing it soon enough." Cobiah winked at the mesmer as they crept toward the mooring lines. Cobiah's heart pounded in his chest as they grew ever closer to the clipper ship docked close against the shore. At last, he paused, ankle-deep in soft, wet sand. "There she is."

The *Capricorn's* tall, slender masts rose over the water, her sleek hull riding so close to the waves that a man could almost reach up and pull himself inside. She was even more beautiful than she'd seemed from the harbor. Cobiah ran his hand along her boards, feeling the smooth, even grain. His hand shook, a tingle creeping up his fingers. The hair on the back of his arm stood up straight, but whether from excitement or some legendary magic, he wasn't sure.

"Magnificent. Can we sail her alone?" For once, Macha's voice was soft.

"Three of us? No, but we won't have to. We can rig and set her lower sails to catch the breeze and then drift with the last of the outgoing tide. The *Pride* is stationed at the mouth of the lagoon, ready to cast lines and tow the clipper out to sea. Once the *Capricorn* is free," Cobiah murmured eagerly, "she's ours."

"Yup," Macha teased. "And as soon as ol' Baede shows up and hands over his pointy crown, I'll be queen of Kryta."

Cobiah ignored the jibe. He waded into the water, reaching out to grip one of the mooring lines that held the *Capricorn* still. With a few quick saws of his broad-bladed knife, Cobiah cut through the hemp. Macha shimmied up one of the others, slipping aboard the *Capricorn* with an easy vault. "She's perfect." Cobiah ran his hand over her smooth black hull. "Not a mark, not a splinter out of place." It was now or never, and Cobiah had always hated the word *never*.

Sykox's singing echoed with gusto across the harbor. "*Oh, broadside, broadsi-i-i-ide! Haul 'em high and let 'em dry!*"

"I think that gear-braincd charr pretends a little too well." The asura wrinkled her nose.

"Uh . . . at this point, I'm not entirely sure he's pretending." Cobiah frowned. "Sykox'd better hurry and lose whoever's following him, or we'll miss the tide."

"Don't worry. Any minute now, Watch Commander Pierandra will rally a pile of guards and toss him tail-first into the puddle! She's tough as an ettin, that one. Never gives anyone a second chance. If she gets hold of us, we're as good as dead."

"Shhh. Don't tempt fate." Cobiah made the sign of Dwayna in the air.

"Fate can't be tempted. It's part of the Eternal Alchemy, just like everything else. Days pass, the cogs turn, the future comes." Macha chuckled at his superstition. "Don't worry. Everything's in place. Sykox will sneak back, and we'll cut the last of the stays and use the mooring poles to push off from the sand. After that, the breeze and the tide will sweep us out to meet the *Pride.* I'll even use an illusion to darken the *Capricorn.* She'll be nearly invisible against the water at night. Once Sykox gets here, that is."

"*Catch 'em at sea, set them alight, burn 'em all the day and night, we'll give 'em a broadsi-i-i-de . . .*"

"*If* Sykox gets here, that is."

"He'll be here." Macha pushed a sandbag over the side, letting it sink into the water with a soft *flumph* of the waves.

"That fur-brain didn't like this idea," Cobiah fretted. "Maybe he's changed his mind."

"He hasn't. Sykox'd never abandon you," Macha said. When Cobiah raised an eyebrow inquisitively, the asura pinned him with a glare, the way one might fix a bug to a piece of corkboard. "Sykox considers you part of his warband."

A warm feeling swelled in Cobiah's chest at the asura's words. Part of a warband? That was like being a member of a charr's family. With a wide grin, he slashed all but the last few tethers and pulled himself aboard the dark shadow of the ship. Cobiah wrung the water from his clothing onto the smooth boards of the deck, shivering in the chilly night. Wriggling up the central mast, Cobiah began to untie the sail lacings. The bowlines spun out in his hand, dropping stealthily to the ground as the canvas began to unfurl. It wouldn't take much to start the ship moving once the sails could catch the soft night breeze. Already, he could feel the *Capricorn* tugging gently against her last moorings. Amid the sound of the ship moving . . .

"Did you hear that?" His hands froze on the mast lines. "That sounded like music."

Macha pushed another sandbag over the side. "Sykox bellows like a foghorn. I'd hardly call it music."

"No, not that. Listen." Wind rippled the *Capricorn*'s sails. In the quiet, Cobiah could hear water lapping against the hull, echoing as it rolled onto the sandy shore. Laughter trickled across the water from Port Stalwart's bars and inns, lights drifting over the water as late-night patrons and sailors moved about on the dock. The sound of violins and drums pulsed in some distant tavern, and farther along the city streets, Cobiah could hear faint shouts, as if from some mild argument or fight.

None of that had caught his attention. There was something beneath the noise of Port Stalwart and the sea. He could hear a soft chiming, like a string of silver bells twisting about a slender ankle. "There it is again. Did you hear it?"

"You don't have to repeat yourself, Coby. Asura have far better hearing than humans, you know." Macha's oversized ears rose slightly. "You're right. I do hear something. But who would be playing an asuran xaphoon in Kryta?"

"A what?"

Before she could answer, something splashed against the side of the ship. Cobiah spun, fingers leaping to the hilt of his sword. To his relief, the hand that clambered over the gunwale was covered in orangey fur, the claws neatly trimmed and shortened. In a moment, Sykox's bushy head poked up between the railings. "Help," he whimpered, water dripping in rivulets down his shoulders. "Had to . . . swim . . . from the docks." Sykox shuddered. "I almost drowned."

Macha and Cobiah grabbed the big charr's arms and pulled him aboard.

"Did the watch see you?" Macha whispered. "Do they know we're here?"

"Nope. The watch commander and her guard were up on Docker's Row, handling some kind of disturbance there. It looked like someone set fire to a row of blackpowder bangers inside a rain barrel. The whole pub was in an uproar." Sykox pulled himself into a crouch on the deck. Instinctively and without warning, the charr shuddered, twisting from side to side in animalistic joy before Cobiah and Macha could react. Water flew everywhere, his leopard-marked fur fluffed out, and Sykox let out a long, low moan of joy. "By the Claw of the Khan-Ur, I *hate* water."

"You crazy . . . shortsighted . . . half-witted . . ." Macha spluttered. She and Cobiah stood in shock on either side of Sykox, drenched from head to toe in the cast-off water from the sodden charr.

"It's not my fault!" the burly charr whispered sheepishly. "I can't help it. When a charr gets wet, we *have* to shake it off. It's an involuntary reflex. Like human sneezing."

"I'll involuntary you, you ridiculous hairball!"

While they laughed, a shadow swept up behind Cobiah, taking advantage of their distraction. A hand grabbed his neck as a warm body pressed against him from behind. In an instant, a bright blade flashed to his throat. A voice cut through their amusement with icy command. "Freeze. All of you. One move, and I swear by Balthazar's twin hounds, I'll leave you dead."

They had been surrounded, albeit by a small group. A second black-garbed figure stood warily behind Macha, the point of a short spear blade crowded against her ribs. A third readied himself a few feet away, pistol aloft, pointed at Sykox's furry head.

"I thought you said you ditched the watch!" Macha protested fiercely.

"I *did*! I swear I did!" Quick as lightning, the charr shifted out of his crouch and launched onto Macha's opponent. Their attackers thought the threat of a fight would deter them; they'd clearly never fought charr. The gunman missed his shot by a mile.

Cobiah saw his opponent's hand loosen a fraction of an

inch on the hilt of the dagger. Seizing the opportunity, Cobiah drove his elbow into the ribs behind him with all of his might and felt the body behind him buckle. As the knife blade fell away from his throat, Cobiah spun eagerly and drove his fist into the belly of his foe. He turned to crack his fist against his foe's skull—

It was a woman. Cobiah froze.

He'd punched women before; there were as many female pirates as there were males, and plenty of the roughest sailors in his crew were women. But this one . . . this one was glorious. Almost as tall as he, and willowy, her hair was a dark mahogany and pulled into a thick ponytail that poured over her shoulder like a banner. She wore leather pants, a gray blouse, and a vest that buckled tightly beneath her breasts. Dark boots, soft and flexible, gripped the deck of the *Capricorn* with a sailor's easy grace. Her face was strong featured, with wide lips and a long aquiline nose, and her full lips were curled into a snarl of pain and fury.

Nevertheless, she was definitely not a member of the watch.

"I'm sor—" Cobiah started to say, reaching instinctively to help her up. She repaid his kindness with an uppercut that sent Cobiah spinning.

On the far side of the ship, the man with the spear tried to impale Macha, but she caught his weapon in a fold of her thick blue robe. Eyes flashing with anger, the asura turned and whispered a few words of magic through gritted teeth. Purple sparks erupted across his face and eyes. Before he could regain his sight, Sykox was upon him, and the man found himself flung over the side of the vessel and into the sea.

"Isaye! Are you all right?" Dropping his pistol, the gunman drew two long blades from his belt and strode toward them. He was a rough-looking sort, with greasy black hair and old scars crisscrossing his forearms and shoulders. Claw scars.

"I'm fine, Henst," the woman declared. "Throw them overboard and cut the last of the stays. These goons were trying to do our work for us—but we'll finish the job."

"You—you're not watchmen!" Cobiah stammered. "You're trying to steal the *Capricorn!*"

"What we're doing is none of your business." Henst's eyes moved to Sykox with a twisted delight as he readied his swords. "How exciting. A charr. Hey, mongrel! My grandfather was a member of the Ascalonian nobility. He taught me how to deal with flea-bitten strays like you."

The woman—Isaye—made a quick gesture toward the shadows of the ship's quarterdeck, and more figures stepped out of them, all tough-looking sailors carrying knives, bosun's pins, and other short weapons. Cobiah counted seven in all, including the one swimming for his life in the tide. The man with two swords faced off against Sykox, but with a flick of his tail, the charr leapt up to the spar over the deck, cutting the stays with his claws. Unbound, the sail fell from the yardarm and poured down over the black-haired man in a massive tangle of canvas. "Anyone who says they know how to fight charr," Sykox said scathingly, "doesn't deserve the chance to prove it."

Cobiah and the woman spun in circles, striking back and forth to test each other's resolve. "Just the three of you?" the woman laughed. She flicked back her dark ponytail and tossed the dagger back and forth between her hands. "By the king's shaggy red beard, how were you expecting to get the ship away?"

"The same way you were. We're going to use the tide." Cobiah grabbed a yardarm and swung on it, kicking as

hard as he could. The bottom of his boots collided with
the woman's shoulders, knocking her back—but only
half a step, and she was swinging her dagger at him even
before Cobiah landed on the deck once more.

By Grenth, was this woman a stone golem?

"Fool. *We* bet on more than the tide." Isaye's blade
swished close to Cobiah's chest, rending his shirt and
leaving a shallow, bloody slash on his skin. Cobiah
ducked her second stroke and leapt back from the third,
trying to lead her away from the others. Unfortunately,
it seemed she was ready for that ploy. Nearby, Sykox and
Macha were holding their own against the other sailors,
but even with the charr's ferocity and the asura's magic,
they would soon be overcome by the numbers.

"Verahd!" She raised her voice and issued a command.
"Take care of these trespassers."

"As you please, my lady," said an unexpected voice
close by. Cobiah glanced around, trying to figure out
who had spoken.

An elementalist stood on the surface of the water at the
ship's side, staff in hand, his eyes alight with glee. The man
was thin to the point of fragility, tall, with long fingers that
resembled a bird's talons, and wore a pair of wire-rimmed
glasses perched on his nose. Red-streaked brown hair
hung in thin strands around his head and shoulders, half-
covering the man's narrow face. He did not wear a bright
robe, but instead wrapped himself from head to toe in
strange, bandage-like strips of black and green fabric, each
strip embroidered with magical sigils of power. As Cobiah
watched, the elementalist lifted his hands and whispered,
and a strong breeze swept through the chaos, filling the
half-furled sails. In its wake, the ship's mast made a soft
creak of protest, and once again, Cobiah thought he heard
the sound of silver bells.

Suddenly, a brilliant flash of light exploded nearby and Cobiah smelled the acrid scent of burning ozone. Before he could move, a white-hot bolt of chain lightning ripped from the elementalist's hand and seared the air, arcing into the main group of combatants. It crashed through them indiscriminately, burning flesh and fur alike. As it crackled and faded, two of the humans had fallen unconscious and a third staggered in shock. Sykox withstood the blow better than the rest, merely sagging to his knees with a dazed, pained expression.

"Verahd!" Isaye admonished. "Those are *our* sailors!"

"Theirs, too," the elementalist said breezily. He gave her a lopsided, lunatic grin and walked across the water toward the *Capricorn.* "Magic isn't always predictable, Captain." The man's voice was a soft, breathy whisper. "We must accept the thunder along with the rain."

"Brilliant." Isaye shook her head in resignation. Before she could say more, a piercing whistle split the air. On the beach, men and women dressed in the blue tabards of Port Stalwart's guard raced down the narrow streets. Among them was a stocky older woman with honey-colored hair tucked beneath a blue-studded chaplet. Cobiah saw her lift the whistle to her lips again for another earsplitting note, summoning the rest of the militia to her side.

"Watch Commander Pierandra." Cobiah blanched. "She'll have us dancing on the gallows if she catches us."

"That's a problem," Isaye agreed, narrowing her eyes.

"Truce?" Cobiah offered tensely.

Mercurial as the sea, Isaye quirked her lips in a wry smile. "Done!" She tossed back her dark ponytail and lowered her dagger, impulsively reaching out to shake his hand. Cobiah wondered if she regretted that gesture afterward; he found it difficult to let go. Isaye spun on her heel and jammed her dagger into a belt sheath. "Cut the stays!" she called out, no longer caring if her voice carried. "We'll finish this fight later. Set sail toward the open sea!"

"Aye, Captain!" Sailors put away their weapons, scrambling to obey her command.

Eager to do his part, Cobiah looked toward his friends. "Sykox! Sykox, get off him!" Cobiah rushed to pull Sykox away from a man he'd been choking. The charr, still disoriented from the lightning, tried to focus his eyes on his friend's face.

"I'll get off 'im when 'e stops wriggling!" Sykox panted, smacking his dazed captive on the face with one sloppy paw. The blow was enough to knock the man senseless, and he slumped in the charr's grasp.

Cobiah shook him roughly. "Sykox! I need you to man the poles. Push the ship off the sand. The guard's coming!"

"Guard?" Sykox's eyebrows knitted together in a frown. "Commander Pierandra? Here?" Dropping the unconscious sailor, the tawny charr roared to his feet in terror. Around them, sailors rushed to unfurl the sails— but as they reached for the stays, the sound of bells grew stronger, changing from tinkling amusement to a throatier chime of warning.

"Pierandra will be here any minute, you lunk. We— have—to—move!" Punctuating his words with shoves, Cobiah half pushed, half guided the charr toward the stern of the ship. "Macha, hide the *Capricorn*! Do it now!"

"Um, Cobiah . . ." The asura's voice came from the forecastle. "I don't think our plan's going to work. There's a problem—"

"Macha, stop arguing with me!"

The watch commander and her guard raced up the shore, anger radiating from her with every step she took toward them. The soldiers rushed into the water, eager to reach their quarry even as the *Capricorn*'s sails swelled and snapped the last ropes of her mooring.

Desperate to help the ship leave shore, Cobiah snatched up a ten-foot length of pole lying by the ship's railing. He dropped one end into the water, feeling it thump solidly against the sand below the waves. "Sykox! Help me push."

The charr and the human leaned into their task, shoving the pole hard into the sand. Isaye grasped the pole as well, her hands above Cobiah's, and added her slender weight. The warmth of her body pressed against his made the task seem less arduous, and even in their dire straits, Cobiah couldn't stifle his grin.

"I'd advise you to stop doing that, Captain." Macha's voice was sharp, almost brittle.

"What? We've almost—"

"I said *stop*," Macha keened, her voice breaking with panic on the high pitch. Again, Cobiah heard the ringing sound of bells, but they were no longer soft or delicate. Instead, they intensified, erupting into angry peals.

"Cobiah?" Macha yelled, and his eyes were drawn to the front of the ship. Hovering over the *Capricorn*'s forecastle was a wraithlike image whose regal demeanor spoke of ancient days. It was human from the waist up, though blue-skinned and transparent, as if made of wind and smoke. The creature's legs were entirely mist, rising from the ship's prow as smoke and fog cascaded over the water. "Remember that story about the Istani djinn? Turns out it's . . . kinda . . . true."

The mist crept over the *Capricorn*, rolling like morning fog from the djinn's ethereal body. It stretched a hand toward Macha with a stern glower. Before the fingers touched her, the asura scampered back and summoned magic of her own. Chains of light wove from her scepter and struck out toward the djinn, trying to capture it in their embrace. With a faint, wry smile, the creature shifted in the air. Macha's chains passed through its transparent form like a net through water.

Isaye's mad elementalist, Verahd, hissed in menace. Keeping his bright eyes fixed on the djinn, he lifted a clawed hand from his staff and whispered an invocation of air. More lightning crackled about Verahd's outstretched fingers, playing hide-and-seek through the strips of black bandage woven around each of the mage's arms. At his call, whirling gusts of wind swirled through the mist, attempting to force it either to dissipate or to coalesce and be tangled in Macha's writhing chains.

In response, light flowed through the djinn's ethereal form. There was a flash like the sun through clear water. The sea around the *Capricorn* swelled, rising in great waves against the ship's hull, and with each crashing wave, the boom and toll of chapel bells reverberated through the deck. Cobiah felt them echo deep in his body, shaking his bones with each furious peal. All around him, Isaye's sailors were knocked into the water as the sound swept the ship's deck clean. As they screamed, the djinn's smile grew.

"What is it?" Cobiah howled, grabbing a yardarm rope to keep his balance. The peals continued, so loud he thought he would be deafened. The sail tossed madly above them, torn between Verahd's gale and the buffeting swell of the djinn's magic. "Macha! Make it stop!"

"It's the ship!" Macha shouted, her voice barely carrying through the music and the wind. "The djinn *is* the *Capricorn*. The ship's alive—and it doesn't *want* to be stolen!"

The ringing of the mighty bell rose even farther, and

as the sound rippled over the ship, Macha's chains shattered into thin motes of spinning light. Verahd's tornado of wind dissolved as well, delicate wisps of smoke collapsing into nothingness. The djinn gestured with a flick of its hand, and as it did, both magic-users were tossed over the side as if they were made of straw.

Isaye held on to the last. Silhouetted by magic, her grip on the mast slipped, and she was flung into the air by the pulse of the djinn's bells. Without thinking, Cobiah reached to catch her. Their fingers wrapped tightly together, and he clenched his other hand about the yardarm rope. Isaye's ponytail snapped in the gale-force wind, and Cobiah heard the masts creak and groan with the weight of the *Capricorn*'s ire.

Turning to face the djinn, Cobiah ignored the rope biting savagely into his palm. Blood ran down his wrist, and his pale hair lashed at his eyes, nearly blinding him, but Cobiah stubbornly refused to yield. He raised his voice above the din and yelled, "As captain of this vessel, I *order* you—" In that instant, the mast line snapped.

Cobiah and Isaye tumbled, end over end, into the ocean.

The next few moments were a chaotic jumble. Seawater splashed everywhere, churned white by the forces that whipped it into a frenzy. Terror gripped Cobiah. Old memories stirred in him: another ship, a great wave, and a hundred sailors lost beneath the waves. He hadn't realized how clearly he remembered that day until it was echoed, and he was once more flung into the sea by a storm-wind. Unable to control his rising panic, Cobiah thrashed wildly, fear choking him as certainly as the ocean could.

A gentle hand gripped Cobiah's arm. He tried not to struggle as it dragged him upward. As his head broke the surface, there was another grip, this time on his shoulder. With monumental strength, a massive paw hauled him out of the undertow and dropped him unceremoniously onto the sand. Isaye waded out of the water beside him, managing a smile.

Cobiah pulled himself to his hands and knees, coughing up water through a raw, salt-rough throat. Forcing open his stinging eyes, he looked out at the lagoon and saw the sleek shadow of the *Capricorn* sailing—without wind or crew—back to her harbor in the shipyard. "I couldn't get to you, Cap'n," Sykox lamented. "Lucky thing that girl grabbed hold and pulled you up. She's a real scrapper, isn't she?"

Isaye lay on the beach beside him, panting in exhaustion. Her sailors were scattered up and down the beach, crawling out of the tide or collapsed on the dunes. Cobiah could hear the two magic-users spluttering and arguing somewhere nearby. It seemed that they'd all survived their humiliating withdrawal from the *Capricorn*.

Sykox slumped down onto the sand. The charr was waterlogged again, his fur sticking out like a half-drowned bilge rat's. All four ears hung limply, and a long strand of seaweed was tangled about his horns. The expression on his bestial features was somewhere between exasperation and despair. He looked up at the approaching watch guard. "No use running, I suppose."

"None at all," Cobiah agreed.

Watch Commander Pierandra marched up to them, sword in hand. From the tip of her jet-black boots to the top of the tabard over her glittering metal armor, Pierandra radiated fury. Her honey-colored hair was damp, and her skin was flushed with anger. Without hesitation, she lowered her sword and pointed the sharp edge into Cobiah's face.

"Good morning, Watch Commander Pierandra." Cobiah tried not to move, lest her sword waver and cut off his nose.

"You're all under arrest for grand larceny, piracy, and illegal commandeering. Surrender yourself to the guard for immediate execution of justice." She bit off the words angrily, her breath heaving from the effort of the run. Ten more guards moved to surround them, and more were headed toward them from the town. Cobiah held up his hands in surrender and watched the others do the same.

"I . . . aaah . . . eeeerk . . . can't stop . . . have . . . to . . ." Sykox shuddered. Before anyone could move, he started to shake violently, unable to control his instincts any longer. Water flew off the charr in thick splatters, drenching Cobiah, Isaye, the watch commander, and most of the others. When the urge finally left him, Sykox let out an aggrieved sigh.

Cobiah hadn't thought it was possible for Pierandra to appear less amused, but he'd been wrong. Dripping from head to toe, the watch commander clenched her hand on the hilt of her sword. "*That is enough.* By the authority given to me as watch commander of Port Stalwart, you are all found guilty of piracy. You will be hanged from the gallows until you are dead."

11

"Not many spellcasters have the intellectual fortitude for a spell of that magnitude. The cosmogony of the sigil matrix has to be incredibly precise. Are you quite sure it works?"

"Extremely. I've done it on numerous occasions. You can rely on symmetry to stabilize it so long as the structure is etherically ideal."

"Ideal?" The asura blinked. "How do you make that kind of a matrix conform to an ideal? By definition, its points of light are randomized—"

"Not randomized," Verahd corrected Macha gently. "Not arbitrary or accidental, either. Only inconsistent. Subjective. Once you take into account the factors that misalign the sigil's plane, you can predict the pattern."

Macha clamped her palms to her head. "But your theory precludes thousands of potential algorithms!"

"It's daunting at first, yes, but you get a feel for it." Verahd shrugged, pushing his reddish hair behind his ears. It didn't stay there long, fluttering down around his face again the moment his hand fell to the drawing. "If only I had my staff. It's really quite relaxing to do once you know how. A pity magic can't be done without weapon-focuses. This really is much easier to understand if you simply see it done."

"I'm sure if you ask, Pierandra will gladly give you back your staff so you can teach. Maybe she'll give me back my pistols, too. I'm in the mood to hand some 'education' of my own to those guards," Cobiah grumped.

Exchanging a wearied look with his friend, Sykox leaned against the cold stone wall and rubbed a paw through the salt-clumped fur at the back of his neck. "Well, at least *someone's* having a good time." In another cell, the dark-haired sailor, Henst, sharpened a loose stone against the wall and grunted in bored agreement.

Their prison was underground, beneath the watch commander's station house. The walls were made of hewn earth reinforced with thick oak beams. Iron bars separated four large cells, with a small central hallway where prisoners were led down from above. There were two wooden cots in each cell, as well as a chamber pot with a lid. Thin windows, only six inches tall, allowed a fillet of morning light to illuminate each cell. The floors were hard-packed earth with a light covering of straw. *Comfortable and humane, really, for a prison,* thought Cobiah. They'd been here only a couple days while the guard readied the gallows. He'd stayed far longer in far worse.

The prisoners from the *Capricorn* debacle had been separated into three cells. Macha, Cobiah, Isaye, and two of her crew were in one of them. Verahd, Henst, and the other sailors were in the second, and Sykox was alone in the third. None of the thin cots could hold the charr, so he sat on the ground amid the hay and mourned his fate.

Two days. They'd been rotting in this cell for two days, with no sign of escape or release. Cobiah stood on the cot in his cell, leaning morosely against the shelf of his narrow, barred window. Yesterday had been sunny, and he'd been able to glimpse the *Capricorn* under full sail. All hands on board were waving and yelling during the casting-off celebration on the docks. Today, on the other hand, was dawning gray and cold.

"It's not so bad, Sykox," Cobiah said, trying to cheer him up. "At least they're feeding us."

"Human food." The charr slumped, and his tail smacked rhythmically against the floor. "What I wouldn't give to eat something that kicks when I bite it."

". . . You could apply the same aspect-ratio ideology to astronomical calculations, too," Macha was saying excitedly. She and the elementalist Verahd sat at the shared bars between their cells, heads bowed together as they drew in the dirt with bits of hay.

"I suppose you could," Verahd agreed. "Take the sigil plane and apply it to Tyria's horizon. Then find two points to triangulate instead of simply measuring the singular aspect of the sun's verticality . . ." Macha stared, utterly absorbed by the patterns he'd drawn in the earth.

Upstairs, the thick oak door to the dungeon cells creaked on its hinges. Heavy boots lumbered down the stairs. Four burly guardsmen carrying lengths of rope tromped down to stand in the central hallway. Behind them came Watch Commander Pierandra, thin lips twisted into a satisfied smile. "Tie everyone securely before you take them from the cells. As for the charr . . ." She drew a large pair of iron manacles from her belt and tossed them onto the ground in front of Sykox's cage. "He's too big to hang. Clap his arms and legs in irons, and throw him into the sea."

It was a relatively simple task to hold the human crew and Macha at swordpoint and tie their hands—simple, that is, when compared with the effort required to manacle a charr. By the time the guards were finished, their tabards were torn, their armor dented, and their faces bloodied by swipes of Sykox's claws. One had a concussion; another's head was wedged tightly between the cell bars; a third cursed energetically and hobbled on a twisted ankle. Though he fought valiantly, Sykox was finally cuffed and chained.

The prisoners were attached to a long strand of rope and then paraded out of the prison and through the town of Port Stalwart. Cobiah counted ten guards in all, including the two still nursing their wounds back at the watch commander's headquarters. Eleven, if you counted Pierandra. Taking a moment to size up the watch commander's graceful step and thickly muscled arms, Cobiah decided to round the number up to twelve.

Twelve. There were almost as many prisoners— if Isaye and her crew were willing to take the risk . . . Cobiah glanced toward the tall woman, admiring how her dark hair shone with a soft reddish undertone in the morning light.

Blinking, he snapped his head down again. Twelve guards. Their numbers were close enough. The guards were carrying weapons. They had armor, and their hands were free. The prisoners, on the other hand . . . *What we have,* Cobiah thought, *is . . . is . . .*

Two exhausted magic-users and a very annoyed charr.

Cobiah sighed under his breath. "We're doomed."

A rough gallows had been erected at the end of the dock closest to the guardhouse. A dozen tall beams stood like scarecrows at the edge of the jetty, each bearing a short crossbar from which hung a length of rope. A man stood at the gallows, tying the ropes into thirteen-coiled hoop knots that sailors called the devil's window. Several locals gathered on the docks: fishermen and laborers, fellow sailors and local farmhands, all eager to see the show. Henst spat on them from his place in line, returning their jeers with taunts of his own. The rest of the prisoners marched quietly and kept their thoughts to themselves.

A knot caught in Cobiah's throat as they marched ever closer. He scanned the vessels in the harbor as they walked past each one, but the *Pride* was not among them. She must have been still waiting, hidden in their false cove near the harbor mouth. *Good,* Cobiah thought. *My crew won't have to see this. More, they won't be fools and risk their lives trying to save us before we hang.*

One by one, the prisoners were detached and moved to the individual gallows. Cobiah took his turn among them without complaint. Isaye was placed beside him, the noose sliding over her head and tucked beneath the thick mane of her hair.

She caught him looking and scowled. "If you hadn't gotten in our way—"

"In your way? We were there first."

"Your plan was stupid. Ours was better."

"So we should have just left? Excuse me, but I had a knife at my throat. I wasn't thinking about 'ladies first.' Especially not for one engaged in committing piracy."

"*Successful* piracy." She stressed the word. "I had a plan. We'd worked everything out, every detail. We had enough sailors to man the sails and an elementalist to create wind enough to blow us ahead of any pursuit. And you—what were you doing? Jumping and hoping there'd be a net to catch you?"

Stung, Cobiah protested, "It's always worked in the past."

"You are so shortsighted. How did you ever get to be a captain?" Isaye grumbled.

"By being shortsighted, of course," Cobiah retorted.

The guard checking the knots hushed them as he moved past, but Cobiah ignored it. This might be his last few moments on Tyria, and Cobiah'd be damned if he'd let this woman go out with the last word. "I've sailed from here to Cantha. I know every cove from Rata Sum to the Splintered Coast, every shipping route from Port Stalwart to Port Noble. I—"

"All that," Isaye said, shifting grumpily in her noose, "and you didn't take into account that the tide won't help you if you don't have the wind on your side as well? If we hadn't been there, you three would never have been able to get the sails down in time. I may not know your secret coves, but I know how to tell the exact minute the tide will turn. After Lion's Arch fell, I studied the new currents in the Sea of Sorrows until I knew them by heart."

This woman was absolutely infuriating! "We only needed the tide for a few minutes. Our ship was waiting at the harbor mouth to tow us out to sea. We had a chance . . . until the djinn came," Cobiah said mournfully.

"Yeah." Isaye's hazel eyes softened. "Until the djinn came." They shared a long moment, silently cursing luck, timing, and Istani djinn.

Watch Commander Pierandra blew a long, somber note on a hunting horn. The chilly sound echoed over the gray cove as the morning mist thickened. As the note faded away, Cobiah's sharp ears caught the sound of waves lapping against ships' hulls, splashing on rocks, and rolling up the shore. In half an hour, the sun would rise and burn away the fog. The town would rouse from slumber. Sailors would report to their ships and dockhands would begin the day's labor. Just a morning, like every other. Just another day.

Goose bumps rose on Cobiah's arms as he realized it would be a day he'd never see. Guards stepped up from behind them, tightening the nooses. "The prisoners are ready, Commander!" one yelled.

Watch Commander Pierandra marched solemnly along the row, gazing at each prisoner in turn. Verahd muttered something under his breath as she passed, and the watch commander snarled. "If you have a problem with your situation, pirate," she said, goading him, "all you have to do is jump. Maybe you can swim away."

Frowning, Verahd twisted his hands in the ropes and did not reply.

Reaching the end, the watch commander turned to face her prisoners. With a nod to the hangman, she prepared to blow a third and final note. When it sounded, the guards would push the prisoners from the edge of the dock, and it would all be over.

"Cobiah!" Sykox shouted in desperation. Twisting his head to the side, he could see the valiant charr being forced toward the water by three stalwart-looking guardsmen with spears. "I don't want to drown! I'd rather die fighting!" The charr roared again, slashing at his enemies with manacled hands and hobbled feet, but he was little match for the long reach of their spears. Tears welled in Cobiah's eyes as he fought helplessly against his bonds.

"You really care about that charr, don't you?" Isaye murmured softly.

"Of course I care about him." Cobiah bit back something sharper. "He's in my crew. Would you feel any different if they were going to drown Henst?"

Isaye bit her lip and shook her head in silent understanding.

At the shore end of the dock, Watch Commander Pierandra raised the hunting horn, and Cobiah felt the sword against his side press in more deeply. Sykox's snarls and the clank of his chains filled the morning air, but

Cobiah couldn't watch. He felt frozen, without breath, every muscle tensed as if for battle.

But the sound that pierced the slowly dissolving mist wasn't a hunting horn. Nor was it the massive splash that Cobiah expected to hear at any moment from the end of the pier where Sykox was being pushed farther and farther toward the sea. Instead, Cobiah heard the sound of a mighty naval bell echoing across the water as a galleon burst out of the fog. Cobiah's heart leapt into his throat. He imagined the *Pride* coming to their rescue, or one of Macha's illusions, fooling their captors into giving them an opening for escape. But what he saw coming through the fog was none of those things.

Instead, the mist was shredded by a rotted black prow.

The ship was massive. Her gunwale rose eighteen feet above the water, and her keel was sleek and sharp. Three huge masts, broken and splintered along their length, nevertheless rose like bristling wires from the center of a barnacle-covered deck. Magic held them aloft as wind caught in her festering sails. The galleon wallowed in the water, but her heading was true, and as she tilted to bring her broadside about, Cobiah could see the sickly green-gold of a brass figurehead guiding her over the murky waves.

Six arms rose from a woman's torso, two reaching up to the sky, two spread back against the ship in mute protection, and the lowest pair curling down at her sides. The smile on the figurehead's face may once have been lovely, but beneath the green tarnish and the blackened cracks in the brass, it had become the visage of a demon.

The ship in the fog was the *Indomitable.*

"Dead Ship!" one of the guards on the dock screamed. He fell back, dropping his sword with a clatter onto the planking. "*Dead Ship ahoy!*"

The first bloody red rays of morning crept through the mist, and Cobiah could see a second keel, then a third, then more bursting out of the fog: frigates and bilanders, scows and carracks, with the mighty galleon at the fore. It was a nightmare armada. The ships were ruined, their hulls cracked and weathered, yet still they sailed on. The sailors on their riggings were blue with water, flesh sloughing away from still-moving bone. Hideous creatures swept past on spectral wings, tattered skin flapping in a twisted imitation of seabirds—but far more massive in scale.

The undead armada bombarded the docked ships of Port Stalwart with ferocious enthusiasm. The galleon's broadside pealed out like thunder. Heavy black cannonballs launched through thick tufts of smoke obscuring her open portholes. Cobiah had little time to react, and even if he'd had the presence of mind to yell, the sound of whistling flight would have drowned out any orders he'd have given.

The shot roared into thunder as it struck, shredding holes in the moored ships, the wharves, and the long dock on which they stood. Some went farther, crashing into buildings by the shore and tearing into the city. Where the heavy iron struck wood, it exploded, casting chunks of timber and broken brick in every direction. The dock tilted to the side as several of the pylons holding it above water shattered out from under its boards. Cobiah heard the guards at the end of the wharf scream as creatures with tattered wings and fetid claws swooped down and snatched them away. Several of the guards broke and ran, dropping their weapons in a panic to reach the shore before the dock capsized into the sea.

"Isaye!" Cobiah called. "The sword by your foot. Kick it to me!"

She looked down and discovered the weapon. Without hesitation, Isaye tucked the toe of her boot beneath it, flipping the sword into his hands.

Cobiah turned and let the weapon slap against his back, trapping it with his tied arms as it slid down his body. "Back up against me. Cut your hands loose on the blade," he said in a rush. "Hurry. It'll take them nineteen seconds to reload." She spun, bending as far forward as her noose would allow so that she could reach back with her tied hands. There was a sharp exclamation as Isaye blindly found the sword's edge. Drawing the ropes across the blade, she was free.

Isaye wrenched the noose from her neck. "How do you know how long it takes that galleon to reload? Every ship's timing is different," she gasped, reaching to help Cobiah get free.

"I know that ship," Cobiah said grimly.

Isaye cut him free, and as she did, a second peal of gunfire sounded from the galleon. This time, there were echoing booms from several of the smaller ships in the harbor. The sailors of Port Stalwart were beginning to fight back. Still, looking at the size and number of their enemy, they wouldn't be fighting for long.

The dock trembled warningly beneath his feet. Through the screams of people fleeing the collapsing wharf and the war cries of sailors on ships being attacked, Cobiah heard a charr's enraged bellow of pain.

"Get Macha," Cobiah said determinedly. "Take her to the shore with your crew."

"The asura?" Isaye asked, baffled. "But—"

Cobiah cut her off, pushing the sword into Isaye's hands. "Take this. Tell Macha that I'm giving her an order to go with you. Take your men and get out of here, Isaye. Sykox and I will meet you afterward."

"Meet—do you even have a plan?" Isaye snorted. "Of course not. You're Cobiah Marriner. Shortsighted as hell—and too damn brave for your own good." She started to say something else, but instead impulsively leaned in and kissed his cheek. "Don't worry about us. Just rescue your Six-cursed charr and get out of here." With that, Isaye turned and ran toward the other gallows, cutting captives free one by one as the guards fled toward the shore.

The sound of clanking chains and another terrible howl broke through the chaos, dragging Cobiah's attention away from the dark-haired woman. "Sykox!" he gasped. With alacrity, Cobiah spun toward the end of the pier and raced toward his engineer.

The guards were scattering, fleeing from the collapsing dock as rotted sailors dropped from the fleet into the sea, making their way toward the town. Some swam above the water; others walked below the waves, leaving a thickening trail of mold and decaying flesh. They carried all manner of weapons, from knives and cutlasses to long shards of broken bone and clubs of shattered coral. Cobiah saw the last guard pulled down into the waves by undead swimming beneath the collapsing boards of the dock. There were battles up and down the shore, undead shuffling on the sand toward those living beings who stayed to fight. If Isaye didn't move it and get to the shoreline soon, they'd be trapped on the docks.

He didn't have time to worry about the others. Sykox, still chained, stood with his back to one of the pylons, staring in horror as revenants with pasteboard skin clambered up the shattered planks. Cobiah reached him just as the *Indomitable* released her third volley. Two of the ships in the harbor, their crews trying desperately to get them under sail, were destroyed by the battering of the Dead Ship's broadside.

Tugging at the manacles that bound his friend, Cobiah struggled to find some way to get them to open. They were solid steel, heavy and sealed with a lock, and the chains that bound them to the set on Sykox's feet were equally stalwart. "Don't panic," Cobiah said, cursing. "I can get a knife, jimmy this lock—" Even as he said it, an explosion rocked one of the ships in the dock nearby. Their powder room must have caught fire, and the concussion shuddered the dock's already-weak foundation.

In a voice far too soft for their surroundings, Sykox whispered, "There's a spear . . . one of the guards dropped it when the flying creatures took him. Use it to kill me."

"No, Sykox. I can get through these locks."

"Not before the undead get up here. Then what? We outrun those things up there and swim the Sea of Sorrows to get away?" The charr shook his head dejectedly, his rusty mane shagging over broad shoulders. "You might make it, but me? But you can give me a better death than to be torn apart with my hands bound."

"You didn't give up on me when you fished me half-dead out of the ocean. Don't give up on me now." Stung, Cobiah tugged at the manacles, trying to find any weakness in the steel. Bony hands scrabbled at the dock as the zombies pulled themselves up, gathering their footing as they hissed through barnacle-encrusted cheeks. Cobiah's stomach turned at the sight of them, and he focused on Sykox's bonds, hoping desperately that he wouldn't see anyone he knew . . . or had known.

"What in the Four Legions are you good for, then, human?" Sykox roared back. "Help me die like a charr, don't let me go out like some kind of . . . uh . . . flopping . . .

wet . . . *fish*! Toughen up! You're nothing but a spineless pudding!"

"A pudding? Really? That's the best insult you've got?"

"I'm under pressure here!" Sykox snapped.

Out of nowhere came the crack of a pistol and the sharp whiz of shot flying past. Cobiah spun, grabbing for the spear, while Sykox roared and instinctively raised his claws. Both stared, awestruck, as the manacles fell away from his wrists. There was a second shot, the ringing of metal on metal, and the shackles on his feet sprang open.

"Magic?" Sykox said, mystified.

"Accuracy, you idiot." Standing back at the gallows with Isaye, Macha raised a stolen flintlock pistol to her lips and blew a puff of smoke from the barrels. "Have you ever known me to obey an order?" she asked with a self-satisfied purr of scorn. "Anyway, the shore's covered with zombies. We can't go that way." Aggrieved and annoyed, Macha stuck out her tongue at them both.

Cobiah threw up his hands in exasperation, but there was no time to argue.

The undead were upon them.

"The dock's disintegrating! If we don't stay together, the zombies will tear us into chum!" Isaye yelled to the gathered sailors, trying to herd them into a smaller group at the end of the dock.

Hideous wights scrabbled across the undersides of the boards. They crawled through broken planking to swing at them with vicious, eager swipes. Cobiah blocked with the broken haft of the spear, kicking one undead creature in the belly hard enough to send it tumbling back into the sea. Already, the way back to the shore was blocked by zombies. There was nowhere else to go. "Follow Isaye!" he called to the others. "Gather at the end of the dock!"

Isaye began their retreat, hacking at withered arms reaching up through the boards to foul their feet. Two of the guards who had been cut down at the shore end of the dock shuffled and rose, given hideous unlife by the power of Orr. As Cobiah watched in horror, they turned upon the still-living soldiers in their group—men and women who had been friends and shield mates only a moment before—and tore out their throats. They, too, were limp for only a few minutes before rising to shamble hungrily with the others. Every person killed by the

Dead Ships or their minions became another soldier for their cause. There was no winning this battle. As the number of living grew smaller, the undead force grew larger and larger still.

Cobiah saw townsfolk fighting on the sand, screaming in terror as the undead slouched out of the sea in seemingly never-ending numbers. The survivors rallied, only to be devastated by a fresh volley of cannon fire. As the undead climbed up the sides of the moored ships or lumbered onto the white-sand beach, the rotting ships fired round after round of detonations. The harbor's mist had been replaced by the acrid smoke of black powder, and the waves were covered with sludge, tar, and wooden shrapnel from sinking ships. Villagers ran through the streets of Port Stalwart, some fighting, others grabbing what they could and fleeing for their lives into the Krytan hills.

Cobiah, Isaye, and her sailors stood in a cluster on the docks. Isaye still carried the sword she'd used to cut them free; Cobiah held the broken-hafted spear. Verahd had torn off a narrow length of wood from one of the gallows to use as a makeshift staff. Macha had a pistol, and a few of the others gripped broken bottles or other scavenged weapons. It wasn't much of a defense.

The cannon barrage had destroyed the harbor end of the dock, knocking out pylons and dragging the remnants of the planks into the shallow water. Newly animated creatures shuffled over the damaged dock between them and the shore. There was no way they could swim to safety—not with the dead crawling through the water. Nor could they remain on the crumbling fragments of the wharf. With each pounding wave, the dock wobbled and rotated on its shattered foundations, threatening to collapse.

A few of the scabrous dead pulled themselves from the water onto the timbers and scuttled toward them with greedy, grasping hands. The stench was palpable, a cross between rotted flesh and waterlogged, moldering plant life. Some were dressed in modern clothing. Others wore little more than rags. But a few—notably those debarking from a ship called the *Harbinger*, a strange-looking pilot clipper with wide, triangular scarlet sails—wore armor made of articulated metal that reminded Cobiah of ornately worked and fitted lobster carapaces. It was damascene, but streaked with red, as if blood itself was worked into the steel. He'd never seen anything like it in all his days traveling the sea.

"We can't fight them!" one of the sailors screamed. "They're already dead; they can't be destroyed! We have to make the hillside—run for your lives!" The guards stumbled back, many of them dropping their weapons as they raced toward the shore, hoping to find a way through the undead gathered there. Cobiah didn't blame them. If you cut off a zombie's head, it still fought. If you chopped away its limbs, it barely slowed them. No one had ever defeated a Dead Ship before, nor done anything but flee from their undead crewmen. The only saving grace had been that the Dead Ships stayed in Orrian waters, far out at sea . . . but that, it seemed, was no longer true. He watched those who ran, but they didn't make it very far.

"Cobiah!" Sykox pointed out into the harbor. "Look!" Out in the fetid water, a living ship darted through the bitter fog of gunfire. Her hull was patched and weathered, but the bow was pristine; her sailors leapt with the fire of life, and her cross-rigged sails were whole and as white as a gull's wings. More important, a low, rhythmic sound resonated from the ship, pulsing beneath the cannon fire like a bravely beating heart. It was the deep-throated pulse of an engine.

"The *Pride!*" Cobiah cheered, relief washing over him. "She's still whole!"

"Don't get too excited," Macha grumped. "The ship's out there. We're stuck here."

"It's a chance, Macha. If we can get to the ship, we can sail out of here before the Dead Ships block the harbor. They've cut down the ships at dock, but the *Pride's* already mobile. Once we're away, they'll never catch us."

"My poor little pinnace," Sykox moaned as he gauged the waves. "She can't reach the dock without slowing down, and if she slows, their cannons will chew her to pieces. It's too shallow for maneuvers here. She'd be sluggish, unable to tack quickly to avoid their fire, and it'd take time to gather speed again. But she's still a sight to see." Sykox waved toward the ship, and on board, dark-furred Fassur lifted a cutlass in the air. "At least they've seen us."

"She's close enough." Cobiah turned and grabbed Sykox's arm. "How far can you jump, Sykox?"

"Farther than you, mouse," Sykox blustered. Sobering, he followed up with, "Oh, no. I see where you're going with this." Eyeing the distance to the *Pride*, Sykox shook his head. "I could get close. Swim the rest of the way, maybe, before they got ahold of me. But there's no way you'd get anywhere near the ship before the ones in the water ate you alive. Your legs are too short."

"Then you'll have to go alone." Firmly, Cobiah pushed the big charr toward the edge of the crumbling dock. "Get aboard and keep those engines running. We'll need them full speed to get away." Before the charr could argue, Cobiah said, "You weigh three times as much as any of us. The dock'll hold longer if it's not bearing your weight."

The dark leopard spots on Sykox's tawny shoulders rippled as he shrugged in resignation. "Fine. But I'm not going alone. A little extra weight won't hurt me." With a smooth motion, Sykox grabbed Macha by the back of her neck, the way a cat would carry a kitten. He lifted the shocked asura and set her on his shoulders, grabbing her legs tight to his chest. Nodding to Cobiah, the charr crouched, lunged forward—and leapt with all his strength. Sykox soared heavily through the air—three times as far as any human could have jumped.

"There's no way I'm doing that," Isaye breathed.

"You're telling me." Cobiah grinned, feeling the faint lift of hope within his chest.

The engineer landed just short of the *Pride*, crashing into the waves with a mighty splash. Within moments, pikes and boards pushed out from the ship's deck, offering Sykox something to grab on to. Eager to get out of the sea before the undead swarmed him, the charr sank his claws into the offered leverage and climbed on board. Even from the dock, Cobiah could hear Macha complaining, a sound somewhere between glee and terror, as she pointed back at the dock and took Sykox to task. Cobiah smiled despite the tenseness of his own situation.

"I've got an idea." Turning to her men, Isaye yelled, "We have to chop out the pylons. Use your weapons, cut the stays, and chop through what's left of the main planking. Keep this area of the dock together as long as you can, but cut it free of the foundation."

"What? That'll sink us!" Cobiah grabbed her arm.

"C'mon, you're the brash one. I'd thought you'd love this plan." Isaye winked. "We won't sink right away."

"And in the meantime?"

"The meantime is all we'll need. Trust me, Cobiah!"

Despite himself, he did. The sailors around the dock

used their makeshift weapons and knives to cut into the ropes that held the planking to the main dock. They stabbed at grasping hands below, fighting to obey their captain's orders.

Suddenly, Cobiah understood. "Verahd, tell me you can cast a wind spell."

With a wicked little smile, Verahd murmured, "So long as I have a staff, Cobiah, I can do anything." He tamped the length of wood in his hand onto the dock boards and shook thin lengths of reddish hair out of his eyes. "It may take a moment, though. This weapon isn't exactly what one would call outstanding for the task."

The boards suddenly shifted and began to float away from the closest foundational pylons. Cobiah reached out to steady Isaye. She leaned against him, and he kept his hand on her arm as the elementalist stepped into the center of the group. Black strips dangling from his arms and legs, the madman stretched out his arms and began to chant. Verahd bent forward like a marionette on loose strings, leaning lightly on the thin rail of wood between his hands. He began to whisper, calling forth the magic of air, channeling the elements through his staff and through his spirit. As Verahd chanted, two of the deck boards beneath their feet collapsed, and one of the sailors was grasped by the undead, dragged down screaming into the sea.

"Hurry!" Cobiah urged.

"He can't hurry." Isaye balanced on the edge of the planking. "If the spell misfires, it could kill us." She chopped at a rotting sailor trying to claw their ankles through the floating boards. Cobiah drove the butt of the spear against it, trying to shove it away from the plank, hoping to salvage some time. There was a tremendous creak as part of the raft broke away beneath the wight's hand, disintegrating under their feet. Sheepishly, Isaye said, "You heard him, Verahd! Hurry up!"

Verahd's words resonated with power, shuddering through the broken boards and rippling the waves. His long, thin fingers stretched out in strange patterns, moved by the flow of power. He lifted the staff. Black straps fluttered, shining with eerie green sigils as the wind rose in a whirlwind of force and movement around their shattering raft. The energy stiffened Verahd's body, puppeting his arms up, up, above his shoulders, over his head, lifting him in the wind. Caught in the ecstasy of his spell, the elementalist's voice grew stronger and surer until it resonated with the ring of absolute command.

An uncanny wind swept against the remains of the dock, swirling around them with such force that Cobiah felt himself falling forward into the thrust of it. Like a leaf swirling in the eddies of a fast-moving stream, the raft skittered across the water, pushed by Verahd's magical wind. The small crew grasped the boards, clinging to their tattered island of wood with desperate fingers. Only Verahd, his eyes glowing the same sickly green as the mystic sigils, seemed calm. His thin reddish hair swaying back and forth over his shoulders, he chanted, hovering over the center of the floating boards.

"Wait! Wait for me!" Watch Commander Pierandra raced up the last of the dock, trying to catch the raft before the wind swept it out of reach. She and three of her guards gathered at the edge of the crumpling dock pylons, weapons still clutched in their hands. "You can't leave us to die!" But there was no helping them; the raft was already far beyond their grasp, and there was no way to return to the dock before the boards fell apart completely.

From his place in the center of the floating debris, Verahd fixed the watch commander with a crooked, marionette smile. "All you have to do is jump, Commander," he crooned softly. "Maybe you can swim away."

Unable to aid the soldiers on the dock but unwilling to watch them die, Cobiah turned his face away. He could hear the planks collapsing, exploding under the concussion of another cannon volley from the Dead Ships. Pierandra's scream of terror reverberated across the waves along with the din of shattering lumber. Better that, Cobiah thought, than the sound of zombies rending her flesh from her bones. He struggled not to think about the watch commander's fate as the wind brought them ever closer to the *Pride*.

Without warning, the wind spell ended. The flurry and giddy whirl of air around Cobiah's body slowed and ended, and water began to splash coldly against his ankles. Something slammed into his shoulder. They'd struck the hull of the *Pride.*

"Get aboard!" Cobiah knitted his hands and offered them to Isaye. She stepped into his palm and he lifted her up to the ship's rail. Hands reached out from above, grasping the survivors and drawing them aboard even as the little raft gave way for good. The undead beneath the waves closed in upon the debris, ripping it apart in violent frenzy, seeking flesh amid the boards.

"Officer on deck!" the call went out. Cobiah pulled himself over the railing, feeling hands thump his back and shoulders in welcome relief. The sailors parted, and Fassur stepped forward. "I stand relieved." A knife-edged grin slid across the first mate's muzzle. "Welcome aboard, sir. Care to call all hands to inspection, maybe tour the decks, or are you of a mind to get the hell out of here?"

Laughing, Cobiah reached out and grasped Fassur's arm like a brother. "As you were, Mister Fassur," he declared. "Full speed ahead."

"Aye, Cap'n." Straightening, Fassur bellowed to the assembled sailors of the *Pride*, "You heard 'im, boys! Set the rudder and make for the open sea. Don't worry about those Dead Ships killing you"—the massive charr presented his claws, squaring his shoulders with a roar—"because if they catch us, I'll bloody well kill you first!

"Move!"

The sailors rushed to fulfill their orders, scrambling up the rigging and unfurling every square inch of sail. Cobiah looked at Isaye with a wide smile. "We made it."

"We're not out of the roughs yet, Cobiah." Isaye pulled out the strap of leather holding her ponytail, running her hands through the mane of dark hair. Her voice was low and quiet, meant just for him. "I told you. I know the tide . . . and by this time of morning, the current's turned. Whoever's in command of those Dead Ships had a plan. They attacked during the outgoing tide and held the harbor locked down while it changed. Now the tide's drawing in to the shore; ships can't leave.

"There's no current, and there's no wind." Isaye's voice quavered, but her chin lifted in quiet defiance. "We're trapped. We'll die like the rest."

"Underestimate me all you want, Isaye." Cobiah took her hand with a teasing grin. "But never underestimate my ship.

"Engineer!"

"Sir!" Sykox's voice boomed up from below. "Engine's running full. Ready to bore for the open sea!"

"Engine . . . ?" Isaye asked, wide-eyed.

"Give the ship her head, Engineer, and make all the distance you can before nightfall." Cobiah turned back to Isaye. "We'll leave the tide to confound the Dead Ships." And indeed, two of the vessels in the Orrian armada had turned to follow them. One was the great galleon

Indomitable, her dark bow splitting the water like a blade. The second was the strange scarlet-sailed clipper, *Harbinger*. The *Pride*'s engine beat in steady rhythm, pulling the little pinnace ahead of her pursuers even as a light wind stretched taut her white sails.

Isaye shook her head in wonder, dark hair flying about her shoulders. "I'll give you this, Captain Marriner. You may be a shortsighted fool, but you know how to throw a party."

Cobiah looked back at Port Stalwart, watching buildings burn in the wake of the devastating attack. Brilliant flames licked the sails and masts in the harbor; the hulls of the ships at dock were sinking, their smoking, ruined timber filling slowly with the sea.

Isaye frowned. "I wish we could have saved some of the townsfolk," she lamented.

Cobiah shrugged. "My crew and my ship are safe. The rest isn't my problem."

They stood in silence for a while, watching as the Dead Ships fell farther and farther behind. The *Harbinger* was clearly the fastest among them, by far. Something about her odd, triangular sail structure gave the lightweight clipper a significant advantage. Still, of the two, it was the *Indomitable* that Cobiah feared most. If anyone had asked, he'd have said it was because of her mighty guns, but in truth, the ship's unexpected return had shaken him to the core.

How many of his friends were enslaved in death by foul Orrian magic? Did Sethus still climb in her ruined rigging? Did Vost blow his bosun's whistle through rotting lips?

On the deck of the *Pride*, the charr and human crew rushed about their work, eager to put danger behind them. Macha came to stand at the stern, staring darkly at the ocean—and at the two Dead Ships valiantly following them. Her hair back in its binding leather tie, Isaye lowered her hands and slipped her fingers between his. Cobiah smiled.

"You're sure they won't catch us?" Isaye asked at last.

"They won't catch us." Cobiah turned away from the great black ship in their wake. "But they'll try."

She's a restless sloop with a six-armed maid
A-dancing on her prow, O
Her brassy cannons crease the sea
But the weather's chased her down
Her compass spins, and her captain screams
And the crew's all dead and drown'd, O.
  —*"Weather the Storm"*

"**W**e're almost out of coal for the engine, our water supplies are low, and the men are beginning to rumble about pay. We unloaded our cargo at Port Stalwart but never had time to pick up the gold, what with that hanging-gallows-thing going on." Sykox sat with his back to the *Pride*'s mast, dealing cards from a worn deck. He swept up a share in his paw and laid the deck down between the players. "We also need to do something about . . ." He jerked one clawed thumb toward their passengers. "*Them.*"

Isaye, Verahd, and Henst sat together on the quarter-deck. Throughout the voyage, the three had kept their distance from the men and women working on the *Pride*. They'd pitched in where they could, but without relish, and several small arguments had cropped up between Isaye's sword-wielding companion and members of Cobiah's crew. Although few involved spoke about the reason for such scuffles, Cobiah could guess what was causing them. Henst made no secret of his Ascalonian lineage— or his hatred of the charr.

Cobiah rested in the narrow shade of the *Pride*'s mainsail. They were nearly a week out of Port Stalwart, with no sign of the Dead Ships since the *Harbinger*'s red sails had faded into the distance three days before. "Where do we take them?" Cobiah drew a card from the deck and shuffled it into his hand. "Port Stalwart is gone. Port Noble's still standing, but King Baede of Kryta closed it off to profiteers and turned it into a military harbor. Lion's Arch is a ruined lump of waterlogged rocks."

"We can't exactly ask them to swim to shore. And anyway, they could be useful."

"Useful?" Sykox snorted rudely. An ocean wind ruffled his tawny fur about his shoulders. "She's pretty, more like."

Stung, Cobiah flattened a card into the pile with a snap. "Considering our engine's near dead, having a wind elementalist on board is *useful.* And I certainly wouldn't say Verahd is 'pretty.'"

"Did you mean to play that one?" Macha asked curiously, reaching to snatch Cobiah's discard into her own hand. The captain stared down at the pile, then at his hand, and blanched as Macha laid out a full set of cards one by one with a smirk. "Ha! I've got an ackle. That's fifteen points!" She tittered in delight, rainbow braids flicking back and forth like striking serpents. Sykox and Cobiah groaned.

"Again," Cobiah muttered. "You make up the rules as we go along, don't you, Macha?"

"I'll have you know that Ackle-Denth is an old and established asuran diversion played by my people for more than seven hundred years. Just because you don't understand the rules doesn't mean they don't exist. Now, mark down my score." She poked Sykox in the ribs. The engineer sighed and wrote the number on the deck with a bit of charcoal.

"We need provisions. Supplies. Fuel for the engine. We used most of our coal getting out of Port Stalwart. If they catch up to us now, we're at the mercy of the wind." The charr shuddered as if this were a nearly unthinkable prospect.

"Yeah, but to get any of that, we need gold. We can't just send lifeboats to the shore and tell the men to chop up some wood." Cobiah made a sweeping gesture toward the distant shore. "That's the Maguuma Jungle out there. It'd eat them alive! It's full of skale. Harpies, too."

"You're being unimaginative, Coby." Macha's black eyes glittered. "My people live in that jungle. It's got mantid, trolls, giant spiders, wild devourers, and worst of all, skritt. I hope anyone who goes ashore knows which plants are flesh eaters."

"Flesh-eating plants?" Sykox stared at Macha with new respect. "That sounds like a good fight."

Cobiah elbowed the charr. "Stop thinking about how much fun it would be and play a card already." Sykox did, with a grumble, and the captain continued. "We can't send the crew into the Maguuma. So what are our other options?"

"Well," Macha said thoughtfully, "we could go to Rata Sum and buy what we need. Might be able to put the passengers ashore there, too . . ."

"But?" Cobiah could hear the hesitation in her voice.

"Nothing in Rata Sum is free. If you don't have silver

and gold, you might as well not even bother docking. You'll find yourself in debt up to your eyeballs faster than you can say 'wharfmaster.' But if you've got money . . ." She peered at him thoughtfully, and he found himself covering his cards. "You could use the asura gates to go anywhere in the world. Anywhere there's a gate, of course. But the gates go to the Black Citadel—not that Henst would go to the charr capital—and even Divinity's Reach, so I've heard."

"Divinity's Reach?" Sykox cocked his head. "Where's that?"

"It's a new human city." Isaye's voice startled them. She had approached from the other side of the mast. As she spoke, she leaned against it and watched their game progress. "I'm surprised you've heard of it, little one. The project's only a few years old, and still only half-built. King Baede moved to Shaemoor after Lion's Arch was lost, and now they're designing a city on the cliffs near Lake Regent. When they finish, it'll be the new capital of Kryta."

Macha's ears twitched warningly, but amazingly, the asura kept a civil tongue. "Baede commissioned an asura gate for his city, which is how I know. He's planning to make it a hub of trade. Makes sense. The sea's crawling with undead, and Lion's Arch is full of water—how else are you going to get trade through? But anyway, if we can get you three to Rata Sum . . . we can get you home." She squinted up at Isaye and gave a little smile. "If that is your home?"

"It's not," the human woman replied tersely. "But until I have a ship of my own, it'll do."

Sykox played a card, exchanging it for another. Cobiah's turn was next, and he carefully placed a card on the pile, setting four more in front of him in a duplication of Macha's play. "I have an ackle, right?"

The asura inspected his sequence. "No, you have a half ackle. It's only worth six. See how two of your cards are red, and all of mine are black? That's the difference between a full ackle and a half. Still, it's not a bad play for a beginner. Six points for you." She tapped Sykox's arm. "Write it down."

The charr scribbled on the deck again, looking pleased with himself. "So, we need to find gold and silver. We don't have the money to dock, much less to send Isaye and her men anywhere. Where are we going to get that kind of coin?"

"Well . . ." Macha paused, twirling her next card in her hand thoughtfully. "King Baede could give it to us."

Isaye laughed out loud. "The king of Kryta? Pay for my passage? Either you underestimate the size of the human race, Macha, or you overestimate my political clout. I'm loyal to the Krytan throne, but the king doesn't know me from a stone in his shoe."

"Baede doesn't have to know you, and we don't have to know him. The only thing we have to know is the shipping route he's using."

Cobiah raised an eyebrow. "You're getting at something, Macha. Out with it."

"Remember how I said he commissioned a magical gate for that new city?" Macha looked smug. As she talked, Verahd and Henst approached from the bow of the ship, curious as to the nature of the conversation. "My brother's wife's old college friend's roommate was on the krewe that built the gate in Divinity's Reach, and I saw him while we were in Port Stalwart. He said that the gate won't be ready for a few months yet, but the asura wanted a down payment. King Baede's sending a hunk of gold to the Colleges of Rata Sum via a ship out of Port Noble."

"Out of Port Noble?" Cobiah did some quick figuring

in his head. "That means they'll be traveling down the Maguuma shore."

"Right past where we're sailing now." Isaye looked skeptical, but Henst brightened.

"Sack the king's ship?" he said, rolling his shoulders as if in anticipation of a fight. "I'm all for that."

"At last," Sykox rumbled grumpily. "Something we agree on."

Isaye fixed her gaze on Henst with a chuckle. "I'd thought you'd refuse, since you're such a stalwart 'son of Ascalon.'"

Henst chuckled smugly. "I'm of the noble lineage of Ascalon, not Kryta, Cap'n. You folk may consider them the same, but I certainly do not. Kryta refused to send troops to help King Adelbern when the charr beasts attacked my homeland. I've nothing against taking gold from Kryta. Unless he's helping me retake my country, the king of Kryta can kiss Grenth's boots for all I care. *To the fore, O sons of As-ca-lon*," he sang patriotically.

Isaye looked thoughtful, but Sykox refused to be silent. "'Beasts'?" he growled, all four ears flicking back behind his curled horns. "Watch your words, Ascalonian, or you'll be eating them with a spoon."

With a dark chuckle, Henst crossed his arms and leaned against the mast. "It's not my words you should be watchful of, charr." One hand fell casually to the hilt of the sword at his waist.

Before the argument could escalate, Cobiah broke in. "This ship bearing the king's gold. Do we know anything about it?"

"I bet she does," Macha said, gesturing at Isaye with a handful of cards.

"I can make an educated guess," Isaye said with a frown. "King Baede would use the *Salma's Grace*. It's his largest and most well-armed ship of the line. Not to disparage your pinnace, but I doubt the *Pride* could match her in a fight, even if we had the speed to overtake her."

"Won't even be able to do that without the engine." Sykox drew a card from the deck, grumbling under his breath before he played another on the discard pile. Macha squealed happily, snatching it up, and the tawny charr sighed. "We'd have to be in the ship's path before she saw us, and even then we'd only catch her if we could cut off her wind."

"I can bring the wind . . . or take it away." Verahd tilted his head thoughtfully. "But I am no oracle. I cannot predict where the *Salma's Grace* will be."

"That's how Baede protects his vessels." Isaye looked frustrated. "This is a terrible idea. The king's ships don't sail along the coastline. They sail to the wreckage of the Ring of Fire Islands and use an astrolabe to make their way north from there. We'd never find them."

Macha played another row of cards. "Ackle again."

"Right, right. Fifteen points." Sykox began to scribble.

"Eighteen point seven five, actually." The charr huffed in surprise as Macha preened. "The second one's worth twenty-five percent more. If I had a denth as well, it would have been an additional five times the inceptor of the highest card on the table."

The charr's claws tightened around the charcoal stick, cracking it between his fingers. Glaring at her, he growled, "I think I'm starting to figure out how your little game works, asura. How many points do I get if I stab you?"

Macha ignored him. "You know, Cobiah . . ." She drew enough cards to fill her hand before passing the turn. "The fact that an astrolabe can direct us only north and south of the sun's rising is terribly inefficient."

"Inefficient?" Henst sneered. "I suppose you can just wave away more than six hundred years of sailors' wisdom in an instant and come up with something better?"

Macha stiffened at the challenge, snapping her cards together in her hand and glaring at the dark-haired sailor. "I'm a genius-ranked member of the esteemed College of Dynamics," she retorted. "*Of course I can.*"

Cobiah stopped shuffling, looking up from the brightly painted cards. Even quick-witted Isaye took a second glance at the asura, doubt written across her face. Henst was the first to speak. "Oh?" he asked mockingly. "Next you'll tell us that you're the queen of Rata Sum!"

"Rata Sum is far too enlightened to practice primitive lineage-based feudalism, you rot-witted skelk. The Colleges of Rata Sum are the premier educational facilities in Tyria. An asura works all her young life to create an invention good enough to be *accepted* to one of the colleges, much less graduate with genius-ranked honors! This is exactly what I'm talking about." She smoothed down her braids and sniffed disparagingly. "The reason humans have lost every significant battle with the charr in the last hundred years isn't because they're tougher than you. It's because they're *smarter* than you. They have training. Education. Murder drills and combat instruction. They keep learning while you stupid humans sit on your butts and pray." Before Henst could respond, Macha pressed on, her voice as vibrant and sharp as the feathers woven into her multicolored braids. "Consider this: Tyria has one sun and one moon, you monolithic moron. We measure latitude, or the distance north and south, by measuring the point of the sun's rise on the horizon with an astrolabe. So, you addlepated, mouth-breathing digestive tract on legs, it stands to reason that we should be able to determine our east-west position by the movement of the moon—if we can find the right measuring stick." The asura's smirk contained as much pleasure as anger, and her black eyes flashed in joy.

Sykox frowned. "That doesn't make sense. They move the same dir—"

"Shhh." Cobiah elbowed him into silence. "Don't interrupt her. She's on a roll."

Putting down her cards, the asura rose to face Henst, jamming her hands onto her hips as if she were a colossus straddling the sea. "I have to admit that it was a human who gave me the idea. Though, clearly, a human with more brain cells to rub together than the ones you have inhabiting the cavernous, lonely space between your obviously vestigial ears. He told me something elementary that changed my perspective." She turned to Verahd. "Isn't that right? Once we take into account the factors that misalign the sigil's plane, we can predict a pattern along that plane."

Verahd nodded absently.

"So, shut your festering blister of a mouth, you earless, witless, clay-brained blowhard!" Hands on her hips, she glared at Henst as if defying him to prove her wrong. Infuriated at the asura's mocking tone, Henst clenched his sword hilts, drawing them free of their scabbards with a ringing tone . . .

. . . As Sykox leveled a flintlock pistol inches from Henst's left cheek. "That's my friend you're threatening, mouse," the charr growled blackly. "Now, I recommend you put your weapons down and let the little lady finish. Or didn't your Ascalonian grandfather teach you how to be polite?" Outmaneuvered, Henst let his weapons slide back into their scabbards and lowered his hands. Sykox nodded for Macha to continue.

"Time." The asura narrowed her eyes like a preening

cat. Blue sleeves fluttered as she crossed her arms over her chest, and her hair swayed with the rocking movement of the *Pride.*

The wind rippled in the sails, and the ocean lapped playfully against the side of the clipper.

Clearly unhappy with Henst's treatment, Isaye nevertheless prodded Macha with, "Time?"

"Time! Time! Time!" Macha leapt into the air, arms raised above her head and braids flying. "That's the secret, don't you get it? *That* was the clue I needed to revolutionize navigational theory. As simple as that. See, once you've chosen a central meridian—Rata Sum, of course—the rest is just a matter of counting the ticking clock back and forth from that cardinal point.

"Observation of altitude of celestial bodies is useful only if it is measurable. As we chase the moon across the sky, east to west, we alter our own time scale on Tyria. All I had to do was discover a way to measure time irregardless of the sun."

"That's not a real wo—" Henst began.

The hammer of Sykox's gun clicked back. Isaye bristled.

"Er . . . go on. Do go on," the Ascalonian said through gritted teeth.

Cobiah stepped to Sykox's shoulder, slowly placing his hand on the charr's outstretched weapon. Gently, Cobiah pushed the gun's muzzle toward the floor. "Tell us what you've figured out, Macha." Sykox sighed in resignation and pushed the pistol back into his belt.

"It's probably too complex for your limited minds, but I'll explain anyway." Macha feigned annoyance. "Between my amazing scientific discovery and Isaye's knowledge of the tides, I believe that I can plot the singular course of the *Salma's Grace* through the shoals of the Ring of Fire Islands."

A smile lit up Cobiah's face. "You're a genius, Macha."

"Council certified," she said, preening.

"Do we know when the *Salma's Grace* left Port Noble?" Cobiah asked, tossing his handful of cards into the discard pile.

"Six days ago. Or so said my brother's wife's old college friend's roommate," she mused sorrowfully. "Right before the zombies ate him."

"Then we make for the Ring of Fire Islands and lay a trap for the *Salma's Grace*." Cobiah reached for Macha's shoulders, nearly lifting her from the deck. "You're sure you can do this?"

She grinned in delight. "I can. The question is whether *she* can." The asura jerked her thumb at Isaye. "Even with my invention, we need to know the tides, or the reefs and wreckage of the Ring of Fire Islands will impale the *Pride* long before we see the *Salma's Grace*. That's another reason they sail there."

All eyes turned to Isaye.

The dark-haired pirate woman stood near her crewman, unable to stop the argument between Henst and Sykox, but clearly displeased by its tone. Now that everyone was staring at her, she narrowed her eyes and set her shoulders as if going into battle. Cobiah set Macha down. "What's wrong, Isaye?"

"It's the *king's* ship."

Cobiah scoffed in amusement. "Oh, come on. Baede has enough money to build a city and buy an asura gate. He can afford to lose one ship full of gold. C'mon, Isaye. You said you knew the tides," he coaxed her with a smile. "Here's your chance to prove it." Cobiah's smile faded as Isaye shook her head and looked down.

"I don't think I can do this," she sighed.

"What?" Cobiah frowned. "Don't doubt yourself. Of course you can."

"I don't doubt anything, Cobiah." Isaye fiercely raised her eyes to meet his. "I can't attack the king of Kryta. I'm Krytan. It's my nation! The people have been through enough already, and I can't add to their suffering by stealing from them."

"'The people' won't miss that gold, Miss High-and-Mighty," Macha grumbled. "It's been in the king's vaults for years."

"Macha's right. And, technically, we're stealing it from the asura, not from King Baede."

"It's taxed from the people, and it'll be the people who get taxed again to replace it."

"Look, Isaye." Cobiah stepped closer. He didn't like the pain in her eyes, but she had to see this was the only way. "We can find—"

Before he could take her hand, Henst shoved himself between them. "Don't touch her," he said darkly. Still angry from the asura's upbraiding, he growled, "Isaye said she doesn't want to do it, so back off!"

Cobiah stepped back, anger lighting in his blue eyes. Isaye shoved Henst away with a flash of anger. "I can defend myself, thanks." The black-haired Ascalonian didn't step back, but instead continued to stare daggers at Cobiah.

Half turning, Cobiah shrugged as if the offense was of no importance, but instead of stepping away, he rocked on the balls of his feet and shot back like a recoiling wave. He lashed out fiercely, cracking the Ascalonian's cheek with a blow that knocked the sailor full to the ground. Henst landed hard, cursing, swords clattering to the deck. A trickle of blood ran from a split along his cheekbone.

"Attaboy, Coby," Sykox chortled.

"*Never* tell me what to do on my own ship, Henst."

Cobiah's voice was as cold as the waters of Orr. "Next time you won't survive it."

Glowering, Isaye bent down and took Henst's arm. He shook her off, snatching up his swords and glaring at Cobiah. She whispered something, low and urgent, and Henst's movements slowed. He nodded, allowing her to help him stand as he shoved his swords back into their scabbards with a sullen thrust. With a sigh, Verahd moved to join them, steepling his fingers and whispering quietly to Isaye.

Angry that she'd sided with Henst, Cobiah crossed his arms and glared at all of them. "You want off this ship? Then you do what I tell you. I don't care two figs about the king of Kryta, his people, or the asura in Rata Sum. I care about this ship and this crew, and while you're aboard, you're going to put them in front of any other loyalties. While you're on the *Pride*, you take orders, and you do as you're told.

"If you don't like it, you can swim home." He met Henst's murderous stare unflinchingly. Turning to Isaye, Cobiah's tone softened. "We get the money, you get your freedom." She kept her hand on Henst's arm and didn't meet Cobiah's eyes. Hurt, Cobiah lost his patience and snapped, "Fine. You heard me.

"Now get to work."

"Shift the cords!" cried Fassur, leaning over the banister of the quarterdeck. The sailors below saluted and ran to their posts, altering the rigging of the clipper as it slipped between two massive rocks. Fassur yelled, "One—two—hoist!"

Cobiah watched from his post near the ship's wheel as his sailors climbed the high netting. The creaking took on a different tone as the sails shifted, letting the wind escape. It blew through the crevices of the ruined islands, lifting the ship over low coral reefs. For the first time in three days, Macha wasn't at his side. Instead, she sat on the bowsprit like a strange, multicolored imp. She held an odd little telescope to her eye and a notebook in her lap, scribbling and muttering as the *Pride* drifted through shattered islets. Here and there, bubbles rose in foamy, sulfurous-smelling wafts where heat from underground volcanoes welled up beneath the ocean. These made the tides even more dangerous as warm waters rose to collide with the cold currents of the open sea.

Isaye held the ship's wheel tightly, keeping her eyes forward and counting beneath her breath. She and Cobiah hadn't spoken in days. Nor had Henst left her side, which was part of the reason. The Ascalonian stuck closer to Isaye than her own shadow.

The weight of the sails shifted as the yardarms settled into a new position. Fassur called to the men in the sails, "Belay your pull! That's far enough." The dark-furred charr turned back toward the quarterdeck and yelled toward Isaye, "Pilot? What's our heading?"

"Our position's twenty-one minutes from the north latitude line," Macha piped up. Fassur stared at her, and she began to explain her odd time-distance north-south conversion. The moment she slowed her incomprehensible gibberish to take a breath, the first mate cut her off in desperation.

"Hush, you crazy asura. I don't care what the damn latsnood is, I need to know our heading." The charr turned toward Isaye. "Pilot!"

Isaye answered soberly, "North by northeast. Wind's from the west at six knots."

Macha shot Isaye an evil look. She hopped down from the bowsprit and tucked her notebook into a pocket of her robe. "How soon can we get that woman off the ship?" she growled to Cobiah. "Can't we just put her in a cannon and fire her at Divinity's Reach?"

"Macha," Cobiah scolded gently. "We need her."

"Yeah. Like a trephination patient needs a head cold."

Cobiah shot the asura an irritated glare. Macha'd been moody lately, up and down, ranging from happy to snarky—sometimes within minutes. She'd refused to talk about whatever was bothering her. Between the asura and Isaye, Cobiah felt as if he were walking on glass. "We should be sighting the *Salma's Grace* soon, Captain," Verahd murmured at Cobiah's elbow. Macha was unpredictable, Isaye was angry, Henst was worse, and Sykox stayed below to keep the engines running—meaning that the creepy elementalist was the only one talking to Cobiah. That didn't make Cobiah feel better. If anything, it made him feel worse.

"Any time now," Cobiah sighed. "It'll be dangerous, fighting in these shifting tides, but at least the *Grace* will be at a disadvantage. She's larger than the *Pride*, and these islets are narrow. Hard to navigate."

"Reefs," Verahd mused. "If she strays from her path through the maze, the Krytan ship could tear out the bottom of her hull." He didn't seem either happy or sad about it, simply acknowledging a random truth. As he talked, Verahd toyed with the wrappings that bound his arms, tugging them tight and then loosening them again in bored preparation. Cobiah caught glimpses of strange tattoos hidden beneath the black cloth strips.

"She likes you, you know," Verahd observed. "But *he's* going to cut your throat."

Blinking in shock, Cobiah blurted, "What?"

Before the elementalist could respond, the sailor in the crow's nest waved a bright red kerchief. That was the signal! All eyes turned toward the bow of the *Pride*.

"There she is!" Victory flashed in the asura's black eyes as she lowered the telescope. "I did it!"

The *Salma's Grace* came into view. It was a massive galleon in the Krytan style, but fatter through the belly and lower in the water than any ship Cobiah'd seen before. Her hull was shaped of rich old wood, a mahogany brown striped with golden whorls, and on her sails flew the strutting golden griffon of Divinity's Reach: the symbol of the royal family.

Cobiah counted three tall masts with two great sails each. A triangular jib hung so far at the stern that it lapped the rear of the ship and hung out over the waves. To the front, leaning out past the bowsprit was a fourth mast, cocked at an angle and rigged to the foremast by a spider's web of rope. The rigging swung down on either side of her hull, making the ship seem for all the world as if she'd been draped in a cat's cradle of string. Ten guns were rolled out below the top deck, the portholes latched open as if they remained so at all times. But for all her beauty and all her more than two hundred crew members—the standard on a galleon, and four times the number of sailors on the *Pride*—the *Salma's Grace* moved like a wallowing pig. She was sluggish on her turns through the islet channels, and her sails were half-stowed to prevent strong winds from accidentally running her aground.

"Is it the gold that makes her ride so low in the waves?" suggested Fassur, greed dripping from his tone.

"Gold"—Cobiah drew the cutlass from his belt—"and guns." He turned to face the rest of the crew and raised his voice above the wind. "There's our prey! Let's take her for our own!" His cry was met with a resounding cheer, and the *Pride* turned slightly to her port and let her six-pounders roar.

Bursts of flame flashed along the side of the pinnace, and the thunder of cannon fire ricocheted off the chasm walls. The *Salma's Grace* was taken by surprise, with nowhere to turn and the very rocks that had sheltered her now hemming her in. Holes tore through her hull just above the waterline. One of the *Pride*'s gunmen was so accurate that a ball crashed directly through a porthole and destroyed one of the *Salma's Grace*'s cannons in a single shot. Cobiah whooped with glee.

The *Pride* was prepared for battle, but the *Salma's Grace* was a sturdy ship; a few cannonballs wouldn't sink her outright. Cobiah ordered the charr warband forward to the bow. "Ready, Verahd?" The elementalist was standing by the gunwale with an absent smile. He nodded, and Cobiah grinned even more widely.

"Now!" Cobiah yelled as the guns on the Krytan galleon sounded a return barrage. Her cannons were larger, broader, and more numerous, and their cannonballs were ten pounds of iron shot—nearly twice the size of those from the *Pride*. But the *Pride* had something the Krytan ship didn't have.

An elementalist.

Verahd raised his voice to summon a mighty wind spell as cannonballs burst through the cushion of smoke. As it had at Port Stalwart, the gale rushed forward to answer Verahd's command. The spell served two purposes. First, it raised a wall of air before the armament of the *Salma's Grace*, shoving her cannonballs back down her throat. Second, the wind lifted the *Pride*'s warband as they leapt from its bow. The charr arced up through the gunnery smoke like hunting hawks stooping upon their quarry.

The sailors on the *Salma's Grace* had been trained in combat tactics. Each and every one of them was a member of the military, their captain was a Krytan officer, and his personal guards were battle-hardened Seraph. They'd drawn weapons, manned the guns, and responded to the threat with exacting discipline and obvious training. But they could not possibly have been prepared for six gigantic armored charr leaping from the smaller ship. The king's sailors fell back in shock and horror as Fassur, Sykox, and the rest of the *Pride*'s warband burst through the smoke, landing with heavy thuds on the deck of the *Salma's Grace*.

To their credit, only a few of the Krytan sailors broke ranks and outright fled. The rest stood their ground, courage shaken but unbroken. Sykox landed before the others of his warband, the engineer's impressive bulk pulling him to the deck first. A pistol in each hand, he unloaded a double shot of small-arms fire into his foes, blazing a trail for the rest of the charr to follow. When the guns were empty, Sykox cast them aside and bared his claws.

Fassur alighted immediately after the engineer. His longsword flashed through the ranks of men defending the *Salma's Grace*, dropping one of them before any could react. The warrior charr rocked on the balls of his feet, haunches bunching, and leapt to knock one of the deck guns aside. As Fassur's shoulder struck it with massive force, the carronade erupted into flame. The gun spun sideways. The shot misfired and blasted through the *Salma's Grace*'s quarterdeck.

The rest of the warband landed at last, claws extended, weapons ready. The youngest of them, golden-maned Aysom Steamhawk, let out a battle cry and raced forward, tearing into the crew of the Krytan ship with abandon. Filled with bloodlust and battle fury, the charr laughed and called out to one another with vicious glee as they waded through their enemy. Henst fought among them, for once ignoring the charr. His blades flashed like quicksilver. Two of the Krytan sailors fell to his advance before they could draw their weapons. Even clustered together four-to-one against them, Krytan sailors were no match for the battle-hardened charr. But humans were not the only sailors on board.

"What in the Mists happened to the ceiling?" someone bellowed from the mid-deck as two figures shoved their way up through the ruined boards. Massive by human standards, the men stood head and shoulders above even the charr. Salt-gold hair capped broad, identical faces. Although those faces were the same, one wide jaw sported a long, braided beard, and the other had muttonchops and a thick mustache.

"Oh no," Sykox groaned. "They hired norn!"

"Looks like twins, even. Are the ships close enough for the rest of the boarding party to get over here?" Fassur looked back over his shoulder.

Shaking his head, the engineer answered, "Not yet." With a sigh, he crouched and readied his claws. This was going to be a much harder fight than anyone on the *Pride* had anticipated.

"What—charr? A battle? Ha! That's a far better use of our time than guarding a rock-boring storeroom door," the bearded figure bellowed enthusiastically. "Bronn, my brother, remind me to thank King Baede for providing entertainment for our voyage."

The second one soberly drew a massive two-handed sword from his back, shifting it from one hand to the other as if it were no more than an oversized dagger. "I don't think the Krytan king had anything to do with it, Grymm. These are pirates."

Laughing, his companion replied, "Then remind me to thank the pirates!"

Grymm, the norn with the braided beard, strode forward and grabbed young Aysom in his hands, grappling with the catlike warrior without a trace of fear. Bronn paused to bellow a battle prayer: "May the Spirits of the Wild have mercy on your souls!" He lowered his sword like a horseman's lance and charged Sykox with fire in his eyes.

Sykox dodged the greatsword thrust with a quick sideways leap. As the mustached norn passed, Sykox clawed him, landing a fierce blow that raked down Bronn's shoulder and left arm. The norn roared in pain and returned the blow, lifting one hand from the sword and burying the fist in the side of Sykox's muzzle. Meanwhile, the bearded Grymm lifted Aysom entirely off the ground, wrapping his arms around the charr's arms and rib cage to give him a mighty squeeze. Aysom cried out in pain, and Sykox heard a rib crack.

Bronn tried to bring his sword across Sykox's belly, but the charr kicked the weapon aside. As the norn lunged to retrieve it, the engineer called out to the other norn. "Hey! Fur face! You're picking on a cub?" Sykox snarled mockingly. "And here I thought norn preferred a fair fight."

Grymm paused and looked carefully at the charr wriggling in his grip. "That's a fair argument," he said musingly. Smiling, he loosened his grip on young Aysom. As the young warrior fell to the deck with a gasp, the norn paused to pat the golden-furred charr's shoulder and give him a smile. "Sorry 'bout that, mate. Didn't notice you were a bit overmatched. Been shut up too long—you know how it is." Aysom didn't respond, unable to do anything but desperately draw breath back into his lungs. The norn laughed. "I'll go pick on one of yer larger friends." Spying Grist, the norn nodded in eager anticipation and strode away.

"Leave it to Sykox to fight with his mouth instead of his claws," Macha grumbled. She peered through her little spyglass, watching the fight through the smoke of a second cannon volley. Her ears flicked, and she perked up, pausing her sweep of the other ship's deck. "Well, hello, pretty . . . Cobiah?" she called out. "I think I found their captain."

She pointed, and soon Cobiah could see the man as well. He was older, stocky and graying, wearing a sharply pressed frock coat of Krytan gold and green. The officer's coat reminded Cobiah of Captain Whiting—but the cold competency that radiated from him was nothing like the whining steward of the *Indomitable*'s living days. This man showed no fear of battle. He strode into the fray and called on the sailors to rally—and rally they did. Cobiah noted a long scar down the right side of the captain's jaw; this man was no stranger to a fight. As he watched, the sailors on the vessel rallied around their captain, drawing strength from his mere presence. Indeed, there was something about the man, a strangely calm aura that bolstered his crew even against cannon fire, wind magic, and six furry murder machines.

The captain of the *Salma's Grace* strode down the stairway onto the main deck, pulling loose a heavy spiked mace from its holster. His eyes narrowed as a charr crewman tossed one of the Krytan sailors over the ship's side. Although Cobiah couldn't make out what he was saying, the look of disdain and anger on the Krytan captain's face spoke his thoughts as clearly as words. Fassur spun to face him, shifting his longsword in a figure eight before him as he prepared for battle. The weapon never finished its maneuver.

The captain of the Krytan ship swung his mace, calling out in a stentorian tone. As he did so, a brilliant orb of lightning crackled from his weapon, flying out from the end of his heavy mace and launching itself toward the charr. The crackling sphere struck Fassur so hard that the quick-footed charr was flung backward. He slammed into the mast with a painful yelp and slid to the deck, stunned. The Krytan captain raised his weapon and called out to the heavens. He brought it down with a loud rumble of thunder, and as he did, thick manacles of energy coalesced around Fassur's wrists.

"What's he doing? What kind of magic is that?" Cobiah stared, snatching away Macha's telescope to get a better look. "Is he a mesmer like you? Is that an illusion?"

"Stop that! Hey!" Macha leapt at him, trying to grab back her sighting glass. "Let me see!"

"That's got to be an illusion! Right? Right, Macha?"

One of the other charr hurdled past the row of sailors trying to fend him off and dove between the captain and Fassur. It was Aysom, young, wounded, and stubborn, his lionlike features shifting from battle courage to concern as the captain did not waver but stood in the path of his charge. Roaring, Aysom shook out his pale mane and clawed the Krytan with all his strength. "Aysom! No!" yelled Fassur, but the charr youth was angry from his treatment at the hands of the norn and eager to redeem himself against a smaller, human opponent.

The captain pressed his mace to his chest and murmured softly. As Aysom's claws tore toward him, a glittering golden shield surrounded the captain of the *Salma's Grace* in a protective shell. Aysom struck the glowing light with his full weight, but the blow merely ricocheted away. He struck again, claws out, but he could not shatter or penetrate the magical defense. The Krytan captain smiled and continued to chant.

"That's no illusion." Cobiah frowned.

Macha managed to wrest the spyglass away from him and thrust it to her own eye. With a frown, she considered the spectacle occurring on the far deck. "It's a pile of Elonian protection magic, mixed with a little monk training, wrapped up in some crazy ritualist hoo-ha from Cantha. A real grab bag of 'you can't hurt me.' They're called guardians, and simply put"—Macha lowered the little telescope—"they mean trouble. I don't think the warband can handle that guy. What do you think we should do, Cobiah?"

There was no answer. Macha looked to either side, confused, but she was standing alone on the bow of the *Pride*. "Cobiah?"

The captain of the *Pride* was already grabbing his

ship's rigging, climbing so fast he seemed nearly a blur against the knotted rope. When he reached the top of the *Pride*'s forward mast, Cobiah drew his knife and cut free one of the long ropes that tied the masts together. Before anyone could stop him, Cobiah leapt out and swung away. He spun over the pinnace, her white sails rippling beneath his feet as the world tilted dizzyingly. The canyon wall careened toward him, and Cobiah slammed into it with both feet, using the leverage to push himself toward the *Salma's Grace*. Where the charr warriors knew how to use their bulk in battle, Cobiah's training as a child had taught him how to act quickly, with no waste of movement and an impeccable sense of balance. It was a skill that served him well aboard the *Pride.*

The rope skidded through his hands, chafing the callused skin, and when he reached the end, he shoved his legs against the stone, pushed off, and jumped for all he was worth. Everything spun as the weight of gravity took hold. Knife still in his hand, Cobiah plummeted into the galleon's mainsail. Deftly, he buried the blade into the white silks and rode the ripping sail down toward the *Salma's Grace.*

Across the deck, he could see Sykox and old Grist fighting tenaciously against the twin norn. They circled like hunting animals, feinting and striking with quick, sharp blows, while the norn bellowed and laughed. Occasionally, Bronn's greatsword lashed out in a circle, keeping them back while Grymm taunted them good-naturedly. Cobiah couldn't help admiring the brothers' sense of strategy. If the charr stayed at sword range, Bronn's greatsword would cut them to pieces. If they came too close, Grymm would grab and hold them, punching them with his titanic strength. These norn might have been playing around, but they knew how to fight as a team.

Cobiah slid down the sail, both hands desperately clutching the hilt of his knife. He could see scattered fighting all around, blurred by the smoke drifting in gray clouds from the ruined quarterdeck. Overall, the *Pride*'s forces were winning. Several of the Krytan sailors were on the verge of surrender, dropping their weapons before the fury of the charr. The *Pride*'s weaponry had caused damage, crashing holes through the outer hull and causing panic in the lower decks.

Directly below, Cobiah watched as the Krytan captain swung his mace and knocked Aysom to the ground. Weary and wounded, the young charr still struggled to rise, but with another swipe, the captain's weapon cracked against Aysom's skull. The golden-maned charr fell limply to the deck.

Fassur roared in fury. The grizzled old captain glanced down at the unconscious stripling and stepped over Aysom, lifting the mace as though to level another blow at Fassur's snarling muzzle. Cobiah saw Henst charging toward the captain, but the human was not close enough—or, perhaps, wasn't motivated enough—to get there in time to save the charr. There was only one thing he could do. With a yell, Cobiah let go of the knife and dropped the last several feet, landing squarely on the Krytan's shoulders. As they tumbled onto the deck, Cobiah managed to wrest away the man's mace, sending it skittering across the dark boards. Henst kicked the weapon through the open hatch toward the hold.

The two captains grappled, rolling together across the deck. Cobiah's fist cracked against the Krytan's jaw. The man threw Cobiah off and shook his head to clear it, reaching for another weapon. Cobiah attacked furiously, forcing the captain to defend himself rather than prepare for his own attack. Grasping the man's wrists as he struggled to stand, Cobiah brutally kicked the other man in the shins. The Krytan cursed a blue streak, falling to his face on the deck once more. Cobiah jumped on him, launching a quick one-two series of jabs to the man's face, but the older man wasn't finished yet. A strong right hook thumped into Cobiah's cheekbone with a shock of pain.

Suddenly, the Krytan froze in Cobiah's grasp. A sharp length of steel slid past Cobiah's shoulder, its finely honed point pausing a mere breath above the Krytan captain's throat. With a rabid grin, Henst snarled, "Can I kill him?"

The Krytan captain glared and raised his hands in surrender.

"No." Cobiah let go of his enemy and leaned back. "There's no reason to kill anyone, so long as the captain surrenders his vessel. We aren't here for blood." To the Krytan, he said more soberly, "You have my word on that. None of your crew will be injured."

Slowly, the gray-haired Krytan nodded, and the tension eased from his body. "On my word of honor, I and my ship yield to you. But I tell you this, pirate—if you go back on that promise, we'll fight 'til every last one of us has cut his name in your sorry hide."

"I'd expect no less." Cobiah rose victoriously. "Henst, go free Fassur and make sure Aysom's all right. Then go tell those overeager norn that the battle's over. We've gotten a formal surrender from Cap'n . . . ?" He reached down to offer the Krytan a hand up.

"Moran. Captain Osh Moran." A sour look on his face, the older man took Cobiah's hand and allowed himself to be pulled to his feet. "Ten years younger, and I'd have had you."

"Ten years younger, and you'd have been fighting a stripling kid with no sea legs at all." Cobiah smiled, but the image of himself so many years ago brought back a painful memory. As he always did after a victory, Cobiah touched the old rag doll that was now tucked into the pocket of his vest. *Biviane,* he mused inwardly. *Has it really been ten years?*

"Cobiah!" Macha called from the *Pride,* interrupting his reverie. She waved her arms and augmented her voice with magic so that he could hear her clearly. "We have another problem." She flapped her arms, half dancing on the bowsprit. When she saw him looking, the asura began to jab her fist to the north as if trying to shake something horrible off her sleeve. Staring at her curiously, Cobiah turned to look where Macha was pointing.

A third ship was approaching through the tall, jagged rocks of the ruined island chain. It was easy for Cobiah to recognize, despite the weariness of battle and the reflection of sunlight from the waves. He'd seen this vessel only once, but there was no other like it on the open sea.

An ancient pilot clipper with scarlet sails.

"It's one of the Dead Ships." The blood drained from Cobiah's face. "They found us."

Although the sailors on the *Salma's Grace* did not recognize the ship with scarlet sails, the men and women aboard the *Pride* certainly did. Isaye spun the tiller, boldly calling out commands to the sailors aboard the pinnace. With their captain and first mate on the deck of the *Salma's Grace*, the crew of the *Pride* could have fallen to pandemonium had Isaye not taken a firm hand. Although they had little reason to listen to her, Isaye was used to command. Her orders were sharp with the ring of authority—and with Verahd at her side to assist, the well-trained sailors of the *Pride* were quickly responding. Cobiah could see his distant crew shouting and racing along the deck. As he watched, the pinnace adjusted her sails and turned her broadside away from the crippled Krytan vessel, pointing her guns toward the newcomer.

Would that the *Salma's Grace* could do the same.

"Captain Moran!" When the Krytan captain stared at him in befuddlement, Cobiah jerked the man by the shoulders and spun him toward the west. "Do you see that ship?"

"Aye." Moran looked hopeful. "Bad luck for you, pirate, if that's a Krytan vessel. Once they've freed us,

King Baede will hang you on the gallows in Divinity's Reach."

"I've been hanged before," Cobiah said offhandedly. "It didn't take." Pointing at the incoming vessel, Cobiah traced the shape of its odd sails in the air. "Ever seen a Krytan ship with sails like that, Captain Moran?" Knowing the man's answer before he spoke, Cobiah pressed on. "I'll bet all the platinum in your hold that you haven't— not unless you've sailed beyond the Orrian Veil.

"It's a Dead Ship, Cap'n, and she's called the *Harbinger*. I saw her strike Port Stalwart as part of an armada crewed by walking corpses. They left Stalwart in wreckage and now they've come after us. It's your bad luck they caught up to us right now . . . or maybe good luck. If that ship'd found yours alone at sea, I assure you, *they'd* make no promise to spare your crew."

"Dead Ship?" Moran squinted. Suddenly sober, he stiffened in fear. "By the Six Gods. If that's true, they'll sink us both, pirate—"

"Cobiah."

"—and raise our flesh as rotting husks once we've been drowned!"

"That's no good for me, Moran, and I'm betting it's not your favorite idea, either." Cobiah released the man's jacket, and Moran stumbled backward. He was caught by a sturdy paw. Blood matted the fur at Fassur's wrists as the black-furred charr helped the captain to stand. The grizzled captain flinched as he realized he was leaning against a charr, but to his credit, Moran said nothing. He nodded a simple thank-you and turned his attention back to the Dead Ship.

"Damn it, we have to go back!" Henst cursed, every muscle taut as he watched the *Pride* readying to engage the *Harbinger*. "Isaye's on that ship!"

Cobiah knew exactly how the Ascalonian felt, but he didn't have the luxury of panic. Instead, he kept the Krytan captain's attention and kept his voice even and firm. "We have to work together, Captain Moran. The *Pride* can't handle that vessel alone, and in these narrow corridors, we can't outrun her. That's why we attacked your ship among these rocks."

"No matter where we are, son, we can't defeat it." Moran's voice shook despite the gruff old man's militant bearing. "I'm a servant of the church and a captain of the Krytan navy. I have faith in the gods." He made the sign of Dwayna in the air. "But that ship's anathema to all things sacred. It can't be defeated, and it can't be destroyed. Nobody's ever beaten one! There's only one sane thing we can do—turn the *Grace* while that ship's fighting them and leave the *Pride* to die. I don't like leaving men and women to their deaths, but there's no other choice. Their sacrifice will be remembered in the halls of the Zaishen."

Cobiah's face darkened. "Leave my crew behind? Not today, not tomorrow, and damn well not *ever*. We're going to fight, Captain Moran—and we're going to win. You've got to believe me." Moran met his eye dubiously, and Cobiah lowered his voice. "That pinnace is our home. It's all we've got. The *Pride*'s not defenseless, either—it's got an astonishingly powerful elementalist, a mesmer with a brain the size of Mount Maelstrom, and the finest pilot on this whole shade-spawned sea. More than that, it's got *me*." Cobiah let go of the Krytan and turned to point at the four charr.

"Sykox! Check belowdecks and make sure this crate is still seaworthy.

"Fassur! Ready the cannons and deck guns and give me a full accounting of our firepower."

"We're fighting?" Sykox's four ears shot up in delight and horror. Fassur looked impressed as well. Behind them, old Grist was holding up the still-woozy Aysom. All four of the charr stared at Cobiah.

"Of course we're fighting." He nodded curtly. "We're charr." As the others broke into wide grins, Cobiah started giving orders. "Grist! Get Aysom belowdecks and find him a berth; then get back up here and help Fassur and the others."

"Yes, sir!" A sharp grin creased old Grist's muzzle. "Get us close enough, and we'll tear that blood-covered ship apart with our bare claws."

Shaking his head, Cobiah contradicted the gray-maned elder charr. "Don't be so sure. Orrian wights fight better than sailors, I assure you, and they're far less afraid of guns and swords. We can't fight them one-on-one and hope to survive. We need to get to work and—"

"You can give all the orders you want, pirate," Moran interjected. "There's more of us than you, and without your ship firing on us, my sailors can sure as Grenth's frozen underworld overcome you lot. If I give the command to turn this ship, we're turning."

"You gave your word." Cobiah's tone was sharp. Silence fell between the two, and you could have heard a pin drop on the deck of the *Salma's Grace*.

Moran looked as if he were being forced to eat glass. "Balthazar break your bones, you wretched thing." Setting his shoulders stubbornly, the Krytan captain asked, "Do you really think we can do this?"

Cobiah swallowed the lump in his throat and answered boldly, "I know we can."

"Fine. Nicola!" Moran roared, glancing across the deck toward a female sailor whose formal military coat had the epaulets of a first mate. Hesitant to approach the charr, she nevertheless stepped forward and saluted. "Ready the ship for another assault. Turn her broadside to that red-sailed scum." Under his breath, Moran grumbled, "If that Orrian ship sinks us, at least we're saved the indignity of explaining to King Baede that we were boarded by pirates."

Cobiah grinned.

"Nicola, help them take that injured beast down to the hold and get him bandaged. Show the dark one where the guns are and bring out as much extra ammunition as we have left aboard. Get ready to shoot the ballast out of the cannon, if we have to, but keep those guns loaded."

"Yes, sir!" she said. Fassur, Grist, and Aysom followed her down through the open hatch. Henst put away his swords to help Captain Moran call together the human crew—from both the *Pride* and the *Salma's Grace* alike—and set them to task.

Sykox clapped him on the shoulder. As the others scattered to their duties, he paused. "Reminds me of the time we rammed the *Disenmaedel*," the engineer said fondly. "One minute we're two crews fighting, and the next, we're one big dysfunctional family all looking to you to keep us alive."

"I don't know if I can do it this time, Sykox," Cobiah said softly.

"But you said . . ." The charr's smile waned. "Ah. I get it. You're slipperier than a greased grawl, Coby. Must be how you did so well at Ackle-Denth." He nodded, placing one big paw on Cobiah's shoulder. "C'mon, Coby. Who raided the Xunlai warehouses near Lake Bounty? Who bluffed our way out of the Splintered Coast with three broken bottles and a handful of flash powder?" Sykox crossed his arms and flicked his ears back. "Whose idea was it to sail right into the middle of a krait deeps just to rescue a cook?"

"In my defense, his chicken pie was *amazing*."

"You," the engineer said. "You've turned crazy, reckless courage into a career. You've got a gift, Cobiah. A gift for bringing people together even against their better judgment. If anyone can defeat a Dead Ship, it's you. Even if we die, I'm proud to have had you as my captain . . . and as my friend." Sykox shrugged nonchalantly, making the leopard spots ripple in his tawny fur.

"Same here, fuzz face." Touched, Cobiah thumped Sykox's shoulder. "Keep the bilges going," he said. "If we sink before they blow us to the heavens, I'm blaming you."

"Aye, sir." Sykox winked. "Off I go to see what's beneath *Salma's* skirts!" With that, he ambled toward the hatch, sliding rapidly down the ladder toward the galleon's lower decks.

From a distance, the boom of cannon fire thundered in the air. Cobiah's skin crawled, and he looked instinctively toward the *Pride*. Smoke rose from the pinnace's guns as she fired on the Orrian vessel with reckless abandon. Isaye and the others were fighting for their lives— and he was stuck here, without any way to help them.

Magical fire swelled from the Orrian vessel like a twisting serpent of flame. As cannonballs passed through it, they melted into liquid, falling harmlessly into the sea. The shimmering inferno flickered and swayed, flowing in protective circles around the Orrian ship. Cobiah thought he heard a chanting aboard the *Pride*. The wind rose, swirling through white foam and whipping the waves into a frenzy. The rush of air approached the *Harbinger*, tamping down the flame, pressing the Orrian fire closer and closer to the ocean in an attempt to quench it with the waves.

"Fine work, your elementalist." Moran had recovered

his mace from below, holding it tightly in one hand. "You might have noticed, we've no offensive magic aboard the *Grace*. All we've got here is me."

"It'll be enough," Cobiah assured him. Moran gave orders to the crew in gruff tones, and slowly, the *Salma's Grace* began to turn. Cobiah leaned on the ship's gunwale, staring at the combat unfolding on the sea.

"Cap'n Marriner!" Startled, Cobiah looked over the gunwale and saw Fassur's dark head peering out from a hole between the boards of the ship. "Her hull's compromised, but it's all above water. As long as she doesn't hit roughs, the ribs'll hold. But . . . that's not the problem."

"What, then?"

"Some jackass got a lucky shot during the *Pride*'s volley. Landed straight in the main hold. The twice-blasted thing set fire to the dry stores and nearly lit up the ammunition. Sykox turned the bilges on the armory so it wouldn't blow us all to the Mists . . . but now the gunpowder's swimming in brine."

Sighing, Cobiah rubbed his temples, trying to think clearly. "Can we fire the guns?"

"Aye . . . some. Whatever's out there already is the last of the powder. Two, maybe three shots each? The rest won't be dry for hours."

"Great," Cobiah groused. "So what *can* we do?"

Fassur grinned up at him hopefully. "Board them and fight one-on-one?"

"See?" Grist wheezed enthusiastically somewhere inside the lower hold. "That's what I told him!"

Cobiah slapped his hands to the sides of his head. "Who *taught* you guys this stuff?"

As one, the charr answered, "You did!"

Cobiah groaned and raised his palms to his forehead. Another voice rang out across the deck. "You're going aboard that Dead Ship?" Raising his head from his hands, Cobiah saw the two norn standing behind him, listening to the argument between him and the charr. Their wide grins were a matched pair. "I like your gumption, pirate," Bronn said, leaning on his broadsword.

Behind his brother, Grymm tugged his hard-leather sap gloves tighter around his knuckles. "Looks like we've got some real fighting to do, eh, brother?" Grymm beamed.

"About time," Bronn agreed. "I was starting to get bored with the warm-up."

"Goddess Dwayna, forgive whatever I did to deserve this." Cobiah gazed up at the heavens in exasperation. With a sigh, he lowered his eyes and surveyed the sea before them. The *Salma's Grace* was barely moving, sailors shifting her sails to try to catch the wind once more. Over the waves, he could hear Isaye giving orders, the *Pride* working valiantly to obey as it engaged the red-sailed *Harbinger*. Longing struck him, and fear. That was *his* ship fighting out there.

Without him.

"Just keep her alive," Cobiah whispered, looking down once more.

Fassur, whose ears were far better than any human's, peeped out through the hole below. "You mean the *Pride*?"

"Yeah," Cobiah replied, turning away from the rail. "The *Pride*."

The *Salma's Grace* rode low in the water, a wallowing dolyak when compared to the nimble *Pride*. The rocky lumps of island surrounding them proved a blessing, for the *Salma's Grace* would never have caught the other two ships had they been on the open sea. Even with the rocks hemming them in, she had a hard time keeping up with the lighter, more mobile crafts.

The Orrian xebec was nimbler than the *Pride*, easier to turn, but the pinnace's engine made her faster in the straightaway. Each time the *Harbinger* tried to close in for an attack, the smaller ship warded her away with volleys of booming cannon fire. Over and over, the two vessels swooped and passed one another like bristling fighting fish. Guns roared, and wind and flame struggled over the water, a testament to the magic at work on either side. At one point, the *Harbinger* expended a full broadside, only to have it blown into empty waters a few yards from the *Pride*'s bow, and Cobiah saw Verahd's willowy form hovering above the pinnace's deck with a pleased little smile.

Despite Verahd's efforts, the *Harbinger*'s fiery shield maintained a near-constant protection around the xebec. Verahd tried to use the wind to dispel it in pieces, pushing it aside so volleys from the *Pride* or the *Salma's Grace* could make it through to their enemy on the far side of the flame. Cannonballs tore through the Orrian ship's red sails and impacted the xebec's deck with explosive force, but in return the *Harbinger*'s guns did significant damage of their own, roaring easily out of their fire shield and impacting on the smaller ship with massive concussions. The booming of cannon fire from both ships shook the tall stones throughout the narrow island straits.

"Captain!" the female first mate, Nicola, shouted as she reloaded one of the deck guns. "We're reaching the last of our powder!"

Moran yelled back, "Ready the guns and hold your fire!" The old captain grimly set his jaw and clenched a hand around his heavy mace. To Cobiah, he said, "Our guns are twice as powerful as those on the *Pride*; that's why you pirates chose to board us. If we can just get one solid hit on that red-sailed blighter's hull . . ."

Watching avidly, Captain Moran waited for the *Pride* to swoop past, cutting off the *Harbinger*'s wind so the Orrian ship would be an easy target. Instead, the faster *Harbinger* turned her scarlet sails to port, staying between the *Salma's Grace* and her companion. Moran cursed. "Clever bastards. They've seen what your elementalist can do, and they don't like it. We need Verahd's gale to get through that flame shield, but so long as we're on the opposite side of the *Harbinger*, the wind's always pushing us away!"

"And stopping our shot from getting anywhere near that Dead Ship," Fassur added, helping Nicola load a heavy cannonball into the muzzle of the gun.

Verahd's wind flared again, pushing down the flames on the far side of the *Harbinger*. Waving his arms broadly above his head, Cobiah managed to catch the elementalist's attention. Frowning and pushing his reddish hair behind his ears, Verahd released the spell, and the Orrian flames roared back to life again. Cobiah could see him speaking to Isaye, pointing curiously across the waves at the *Salma's Grace*. "All right. The *Pride* can't bring that shield down for us, so we'll have to do it ourselves." No longer pushed away by the gale, the *Salma's Grace*'s punctured sail swelled and the galleon began to gain speed. Cobiah leaned over the side once more, shouting belowdecks. "Engineer Sykox!"

"Aye, sir?"

"I need you to turn on every bilge pump we have. Work them as hard as you can down there; I want 'em pumping full bore."

"But, Cap'n, the deck's near dry down here," Sykox said.

"Then put the ends into the sea!" Before the charr could ask any other questions, Cobiah yelled, "Just do it!"

Sykox relayed the order to the crew in the ship's hold. Long rubber hoses slid out the holes in the deck, sinking into the ocean at the ship's side. Within minutes, the sound of chugging water redoubled itself as more sailors grabbed the pumps and labored to move the levers that worked the bilge. Seawater flowed up from the ocean, through the hoses, and out the other end—back into the sea. "Water's flowing, sir," the tawny charr assured him confusedly. "I don't know what your plan is, but I don't think we're going to drain the sea out from under them."

"We won't have to." Cobiah waved to Nicola and Fassur and pointed toward the *Harbinger*. "Ready the cannons, and send a team of sailors down to hold the bilge hoses. We're going to need them." They quickly did as they were told, and soon the crew on the guns were awaiting the order to fire. Leaning on the gunwale, Cobiah waited with bated breath until the *Salma's Grace* was within forty yards of her enemy. Thirty . . . twenty . . . He could feel the heat of the *Harbinger*'s flame shield scorching the galleon's hull. "Now, Sykox! Point the bilges to our starboard side and spray for your lives!"

Up went the hoses, and the pounding bilge pumps shot massive arcs of water toward the *Harbinger*. The shower struck the fire shield, hissing and steaming as the flame was doused.

"Give 'em hell!" Cobiah commanded.

The galleon's cannons thundered a full broadside, pounding out their ammo so violently that the great ship shuddered with animosity. Cobiah saw more than half of their shot make it through the superheated steam, crashing heavily into the *Harbinger*. At this close range, and without a magical shield to protect them, the Orrian vessel was brutally damaged.

The crew of the *Salma's Grace* let out a great cheer as they saw the red-sailed clipper twist and shudder. The *Harbinger*'s protective flame shriveled away, and on the far side of the Orrian ship, the *Pride* unleashed another blast of cannon intended to seal their enemy's fate. Their assault crashed through the xebec's hull, magnifying the damage done by the *Salma's Grace*, and a great flood of water rushed into the *Harbinger*'s shattering hulk. The volley had gone through the ship's boards and destroyed the mast step. The foremast tipped forward with a mighty crack of timber. As it fell, the keel of the xebec splintered beneath the twisting weight, and the ship's deck split open like rotten fruit.

"We did it!" Captain Moran said disbelievingly. "We sank them! It's over!"

Cheers rose from the sailors aboard both living vessels. Cobiah stared grimly, saying nothing as the *Harbinger*'s red sails stained the water like pools of blood. While the others celebrated, he watched a shadow spread beneath the Dead Ship's decayed and shattered husk, moving toward the other vessels with malicious purpose.

"We may have sunk them," Cobiah said, staring intently at the waves, "but it's not over." Raising his voice, he yelled loudly enough to be heard even aboard the *Pride*. "The undead are moving under the waves. Make sail before they board us!"

16

A bitter wind swept fiercely over the open sea, driving the waves beneath it. The gale chased them through the broken shards of islands, over washed-thin beaches and high coral reefs, giving the tide no quarter. Between the rocky fragments, two ships hove into view. One was small, a lightweight pinnace with rippling, strangely rigged sails. The other was larger, damaged, lumbering like an old and weary man.

The *Pride*, and the *Salma's Grace*.

They left behind the waterways that threaded amid towering lumps of stone, sailing with desperate speed through narrow straits. A shadow spread through the wreckage in their wake, but too slowly to catch the ships once they reached the open sea. Some of the wights made it aboard, but between the eager norn and the vicious charr, none survived long enough to impede the ships' escape.

"Too bad we didn't get to go aboard," Bronn grumped to his brother as he cleaned rotten flesh from the edge of his sword. Grymm nodded in agreement, and the bearded norn continued. "Could've learned a lot from poking about on that Orrian tub."

"Learned . . . ?" Old Grist cocked his head, his yellowy

eyes glittering with suspicion. "What are you, some kind of scholars or somethin'?"

"You could say that," Grymm answered the gray-furred charr. "My name's Grymm Svaard. This is my brother, Bronn. We're explorers for the Priory. We wanted passage on the Sea of Sorrows, and King Baede offered to pay if we'd keep an eye on his gold. Learning all we can about these Orrians—that's our real mission."

"The Durmand Priory?" grumped Grist. "I've heard of you lot. Refugees from Lion's Arch, hiding up there in the mountains with salvaged books and things. Odds and ends. What are you out here to learn?"

Bronn sheathed his greatsword in a scabbard across his back. "How to kill them all."

"That's one thing we can agree on," said the rugged old charr with a smile.

Both ships remained under full sail as anxious sailors watched the Ring of Fire Islands fall back against the horizon—and, long before nightfall, vanish from view. Once the ships were out of danger, they slowed and pulled side by side. Sails were furled, ropes were thrown between them, and the planks were placed to allow free passage from one ship to the other. Sailors shook hands and congratulated one another on their victory, relishing the fact that they'd lived through a hard-won battle. Cobiah paused once again to touch the little doll in his pocket, thanking the gods—and his watchful angel—that his life had once again been spared. Through all the horrors he had witnessed and all the dangers he had faced, it was more than his crew that stood with him. He could feel Biviane's presence as well.

"So, Cobiah." Captain Moran interrupted his reverie, reaching to shake his hand. "I suppose this is goodbye."

"Good-bye to you, sir." Cobiah winked and clasped the old captain's hand. "But not to that Krytan gold."

The grizzled old captain grimaced stubbornly, but after a moment, the frown faded, and he sighed. "You're right. We made a deal, and I won't shine you out of it after you and yours saved our lives. You could have left us for dead, and fighting with us is more than most would have done in your place." He ran a hand through his short gray hair and sighed again. "I'll tell King Baede you held me at swordpoint and spirited away the fortune. He's already got his asura gate. It's the Colleges of Rata Sum who are out a pretty penny."

"Don't underestimate the asuran capacity to pass the buck, Captain," Macha said. She stood on the board between the ships, waiting to greet Cobiah. "Your king's in for an earful."

Moran laughed. "I suppose you're right, little one."

"'Little'?" she huffed. "I may be little, but I'll have you know I'm the one who tracked your ship. I conjectured the mathematics of your speed and the latitude of Rata Sum versus the longitude of your port of origin at Port Noble. If it hadn't been for *me*—"

"Ah, so we *can* blame the asura!" Moran interrupted, eyes twinkling.

Her eyes bulging with annoyance, Macha protested, "That's not what I said!" But her words were drowned out by the laughter of the crew. "Fine." She put her hands on her hips in defiant pride. "But if you pass that on, be sure to tell them that my invention will revolutionize—sailing—forever!" She hopped up and down on the board for emphasis, and it creaked dangerously. Sykox quickly scooped the asura up and hoisted her aboard the galleon before the plank could break and dump her into the sea.

Cobiah's eyes were irresistibly drawn to the figure

standing at the rear of his cheering crew. Isaye. The wind blew her dark hair in loose strands about her face and shoulders as her hazel eyes found his. Before Cobiah could call out to her, Henst thumped his way across the planks and strode to Isaye's side. The Ascalonian hugged Isaye closely, thumping her back in relief and telling her of their side of the battle in loud, too-eager tones. Cobiah was relieved to see that her greeting in return was significantly less enthusiastic. They were friends, then. Not . . .

Cobiah suddenly noted a dried stain of blood on Isaye's shirt. "You're injured?" Cobiah strode across the planks to her side.

"One of the *Harbinger*'s deck guns hit our rear quarter. It splintered the wood, and a piece of flying board caught my side." Stepping closer to Cobiah, Isaye lifted the edge of her shirt to show him the wound. It had already been wrapped in a thin bandage of canvas and showed no sign of seepage. Lowering her shirt, Isaye reached out and put her arms around Cobiah's neck and hugged him in a gesture much warmer than the one she'd given Henst. Cobiah grinned smugly at the Ascalonian's surly glare.

"I'm glad you're all right, Coby," Isaye said quietly. "I tried not to let them shoot up your ship. We just weren't fast enough."

Cobiah breathed in the scent of her hair and felt her warmth against him. "It's all right. The *Pride* will manage. Scars give her character." He looked down and placed his forehead against hers in a gentle gesture. "I'm sorry."

"Me too." Isaye gave him a smile of relief. When she slid out of his arms, she kept her hand on his, twining Cobiah's fingers with her own.

Laughter bellowed among the burly charr transferring four chests of coin from one ship to the other. Cobiah saw Aysom and Fassur struggling to carry one across the planking, arguing about how much weight the board would bear. Fassur had taken the Krytan flag from the *Salma's Grace,* draping it over his shoulders like a king's cloak. "Look at all this gold!" he announced, thumping the side of the chest. They set it down on the *Pride's* deck and pulled open the lid to show a wealth of shining gold. Fassur raked his claw through the coins covetously. "How do we split it up, Cap'n?"

"That's Krytan gold." Isaye sobered, staring darkly at the four iron-banded chests.

"First," Cobiah said, "a share to Isaye and her crew. Enough that they can buy a ship of their own—and get the heck off ours." He chuckled lightheartedly. Verahd studied his staff as if it contained something more interesting than gold. Henst frowned and looked toward Isaye.

"No, I can't," Isaye protested. "I won't make a profit on Krytan gold."

"Isaye," Cobiah said to her before she could go on. "When the *Harbinger* attacked, you and your friends risked their lives to save ours. You could have left us on the *Grace,* but you stayed to fight. I know you weren't in favor of robbing King Baede's vessel, but I want to reward you for that courage, at least. Take a share of the money and give it to the people of Kryta. That way, if the king taxes them again, they'll have plenty of extra to give him without hurting themselves."

Isaye brightened, her eyes widening. "You mean it?" He nodded, and she hugged him again in gratitude. "I'll do just that."

"If you're headed to Kryta, we can take you there, miss." Captain Moran gave her a stiff sort of bow, prompting Isaye to manage an awkward curtsey in return. "Assuming Captain Cobiah permits the *Grace* to sail home after he's finished looting our hold." Moran's tone was sober, but his gray eyes twinkled with mild amusement. "If . . ."

"I'm keeping the flag, snub nose." Fassur's tone seethed with suspicion.

"Wasn't the flag I was after," Moran said evenly. "Marriner, I'm looking to allow any sailors who want to, to disembark from the *Grace* and sail to another port with you. Once the tale gets out in Divinity's Reach that we've been fighting beside pirates and charr, some of them won't be welcome home again, no matter what the reasons. Me, I'm a mad old coot; I can get away with anything. But some of these boys are mighty young to have the stain of it on their reputations."

"It's more of a stain to fight beside charr than it is to be sunk by a Dead Ship?" Grist shook his grizzled head. Scornfully, he snorted, "Ridiculous humans."

"I'm sure Captain Marriner will make them welcome on the *Pride*." Isaye smiled, ignoring the charr's jibe. Cobiah gave the gray-haired Krytan a solemn nod. "As for your other offer," she said, "thank you, Captain Moran, but no. Henst and the others might take you up on the ride, but as for me . . ." She looked up at Cobiah. "Once I've finished distributing the gold, I'd like to remain aboard the *Pride* . . . if they'll have me. This ship could use a good pilot."

"Indeed, we could." Joy swelled Cobiah's heart. "You're welcome to stay among us, Isaye." In the background, Cobiah heard Macha's snort of derision and Fassur's sly snicker, and ignored them both.

"I'll stay as well," Verahd murmured, pushing a curtain of reddish hair out of his eyes. "Isaye's been a good friend to me. I prefer to work in her company."

Cobiah met the elementalist's eyes and nodded gratefully.

"Me too, I guess," Henst added with a surly grimace. Although Cobiah knew the man was nothing but trouble, Henst had pulled his weight aboard the *Grace* when he was needed most. Cobiah nodded again . . . perhaps a bit less gratefully.

"So what about the gold?" Fassur belligerently crossed his arms. "That still doesn't tell us what the split's going to be. There's enough money here to pay for five vessels the size of the *Pride*—or to carve your grinning face on a mountain if you wanted."

"We could buy an asura gate," Aysom teased.

"Or acquire a laboratory the size of a palace and build a gate of our own." Macha managed a grumpy smile, and Sykox thumped her shoulder, nearly knocking the little asura over in amusement.

"We could buy gold-plated pistols and swords with diamond-studded hilts!" Fassur guffawed. Old Grist whistled at the thought.

"Or we could build a city," Cobiah added.

"Exactly! Well, a town, maybe. We could call it 'Port Cobiah'!" Sykox's laughter died as he noticed the solemn look on his captain's face. "You're not kidding."

"No. I'm not."

Cobiah leapt onto the high step of the quarterdeck and called the crew to attention. "Sailors of the *Pride*!" he shouted over their enthusiastic banter. "Today you not only bested King Baede's finest ship of the line, you also made history. Together with the fine men and women of the *Salma's Grace*, we achieved something never done before. We sank an Orrian ship." The celebration shouts from the crew drowned out his voice as they roared in approval.

Cobiah raised his hands, calming them again. "Everyone said it was impossible. They said the Dead Ships are unbeatable, that the plague of undead assaulting us was as unstoppable as the tsunami that brought them to our shores. That the only thing we could do was run away.

"Well, no more." He looked down at his crew proudly. Eager faces shouted and called his name, but he felt the most pride simply looking into a single pair of hazel eyes. "Our ship stood against every one of the *Harbinger*'s weapons—guns, magic, and more—and we didn't just survive. *We won.*" A great cheer went up among the assembled crew. Some of the charr shot their pistols into the air, roaring their approval, and even Macha smiled. "Settle down, settle down." Cobiah chuckled. "It's a victory—and a big one. But it's not enough.

"They call the beast in Orr a 'dragon.' A big one, like the tales of Primordus from my grandfather's time. When that monster rose from the sea, it took Lion's Arch from us. Since then it's ravaged a dozen other towns along the shore. What's next? Rata Sum? Port Noble? The Tarnished Coast or the eastern shores? Well, I say Orr's tyranny stops today. We draw the line with the fall of Port Stalwart.

"First Mate Fassur's right. We could use this money to live comfortable lives for a year or more. Maybe even longer. But I have a better idea. I say . . ." Cobiah took a deep breath and plunged onward. "I say we build a port of our own. We build it, and we defend it against Orr. We make it a free port, not beholden to any nation, open to anyone who sails the sea. We'll teach others how to fight against the Dead Ships, using charr weaponry, asuran innovation, and human courage."

"All that, eh?" someone bellowed from the crowd. "What about the norn?" Bronn stepped forward with a teasing grin. "Sounds like you're building a place of adventure. Is there some reason you'd keep our people out of this mercenary utopia you're proposing?"

"Not at all," Cobiah laughed. "The norn would be welcome. *You*," he said, "would be welcome."

"We promised King Baede that we'd stick close to his gold. You won it from Moran fair and square, but that doesn't release us from our promise." Grymm shook his armored fist at Cobiah. "You'd not be asking us to break an oath, now, *would you*?"

"No, no!" Cobiah pretended to fend him off as the gathered sailors laughed uproariously. "The port would be open to any and all, so long as they'll fight against Orr and help to keep our waters clear." Bronn and Grymm smiled, nodding to each other in satisfaction.

When the cheering died down a bit, a surly voice shouted, "Where will you build this mythical 'free city,' Cobiah? On the king's land? Or are you planning to conquer part of the asuran coast?"

"No, Henst." Cobiah guessed the speaker without seeing him. "We'll build it in a place nobody else wanted. A site that's been abandoned, left as wreckage; a place that's just waiting for us to return and give it life again." Enjoying the drama of the moment, Cobiah pointed to the northeast. "We'll build our port on the ruins of Lion's Arch."

"Lion's Arch?" Fassur blinked. "That city's drowned. Covered in water!"

"As Isaye can tell you, the tide's been going down over the last few years," Cobiah explained. "If we built farther back and used the cliffs as protection for the town, the ruins in the harbor could even be part of our defense against the Dead Ships."

Isaye considered Cobiah's words seriously, running a hand through her dark hair as she spoke. "The tides in that harbor are still unpredictable. Ships would have to go very slowly sailing in and out, or they'd break their keels on the stone remains below the waterline."

"That's exactly what I mean," he agreed. "That would slow down any Orrian vessel that tried to sail there, just like the corridors of the Ring of Fire Islands gave us an advantage here. That slow approach would be to our favor. We could put bulwark guns back on the cliffside, maybe even outfit the island at the harbor mouth with a defensive barricade of some sort. The port could employ tugboats to guide bigger vessels through the ruins. It's the perfect place to make a stand against the ships of Orr—and most of all, it would give people hope. Not just the hope that we can survive the Dead Ships, but that we can come back from all this destruction and thrive."

Cobiah called to them, "I know it sounds like a lot of work. I know it'd be easier to just take the money and enjoy ourselves. But that's short-term thinking. We can defeat the Dead Ships, and we can show the horrors of Orr that we're done hiding from them. But to do that, we need a safe harbor. We need Lion's Arch. Tyria," he said more quietly, "needs Lion's Arch."

Isaye beamed up at him with pride. "I'm with you," she said firmly. He smiled and pulled her close, looking toward the gathered crew.

"Me too," Sykox said brightly. "It sounds fun." One by one, the other charr of the warband nodded, adding their voices to the throng.

"I guess we can't be pirates forever," Fassur sighed.

"Even if we want to be?" grumped Macha in return. But underneath her knitted brows, the corners of her lips twisted into a smile.

Cobiah breathed a sigh of relief. "So . . . are we agreed? All those in favor of rebuilding Lion's Arch?"

The cheers erupting from the crew were all the answer he required.

ACT THREE

1237 AE
(AFTER THE EXODUS OF THE GODS)

The sails are rent, and the engine's blown
The keel is split to stern, O
We lost the rudder to the tide
And the mizzenmast is burning
The rain's like nails, and our harbor's lost
And the compass spins and turns, O.
—"Weather the Storm"

17

"I don't understand why the man can't see reason!" Cobiah strode up the large cobblestone steps in the town's main plaza. Walking beside him, Sykox laughed and shifted a heavy bundle of cogs and gears he carried over his shoulder. A dolyak cart clattered past in the roadway, carrying a wide load of lumber from the nearby forests. Merchants hawked their wares throughout the streets, and citizens ate, shopped, and moved about in the casual errands of everyday life.

Lion's Arch had been reborn.

"You've been saying that for five years, Coby. If you dislike Captain Nodobe so much, why don't you throw him off the council? Or kill him? That works in the citadel. A nice, clean killing always makes me feel better." Sykox's smile split his tawny muzzle, and the black leopard spots along his shoulders rippled with the effort of carrying a hundred pounds of iron.

Cobiah ran his hands through his hair, mussing up the ribbon that held it. He jerked the thing out, annoyed, and smoothed the hair back behind his ears. "You know I can't do that. The Captain's Council doesn't work that way."

"Well, maybe it should!" Sykox shrugged—an impressive feat, given the circumstances.

A hot sun beat down on the stones of the plaza, blazing on merchants and sailors alike. In the seven years since the area had been cleared and the first docks built, the newly reconstituted town of Lion's Arch had prospered and thrived. Merchants had been desperate for a place to ship their trade rather than porting it by dolyak caravan through the dangers of the Maguuma Jungle. The response had been overwhelming, once the harbor was considered "safe." It'd taken only four years, through three attacks by Orrian raiders, to prove Cobiah right. Now the port held a populace of over five thousand, of many different races from all areas of Tyria. The primary rule: leave your bigotry and bias at the gate of the city. Everyone was welcome here. Thus far, it'd worked well.

Now the docks were bustling with trade ships, and though they weren't always the most reputable businessmen, they always paid their portage fees. Ships of every size and structure came through the Arch: shady dealers from Rata Sum, mercenaries from Ascalon, norn from the far north, and pirates of every stripe from cutthroats to vagabonds. The best of them, the wealthiest, had been offered a chance to invest in the port and join the Captain's Council, of which Cobiah was the head.

It was a tenuous situation at best. Money changed hands frequently, keeping the wheels of commerce turning, and the city had a thriving underbelly of illegal trade. The only person who'd stepped up to take the position of guard captain was a roaring drunkard named Mort Duserm, and the keeper of the biggest store in the city was a strutting, self-centered asura named Yomm. Each captain was expected to keep their crew in line, and they did, for the most part, but the disposition of the city was only as stable as the ships in the harbor—and every captain had his own idea of how "strict" he wanted to be in observance of the laws.

When something needed to be decided in Lion's Arch, the captains who had purchased a seat on the council were contacted. Those already in the port, or who could make it to the city within a week's sail, would gather to discuss and address the problem. Other than that, and arranging for the small roster of guards to be paid, there was little in the way of bureaucracy governing the settlement. The system had worked when Lion's Arch was little more than a handful of structures clustered around two long docks. But the town had grown.

In the last year or so, the friendly little port had become larger as more ships started using it. Before, it had been a loose confederation of rogues, pirates, and misfits. Now that it was clearly holding its own against the incursions of the Dead Ships, it was becoming practically respectable—and ironically, that meant there was a lot more crime. Furthermore, the friction was starting to show, and profiteers circled like vultures, waiting to see how they could gain wealth by taking a side in the arguments. Yomm and Nodobe were only two of many.

"I can't kill Nodobe," Cobiah said at last. "It'd cause too much trouble."

The charr engineer bellowed in laughter, clapping his friend's shoulder. "Good old Coby. You had to take a while to think about it!"

Grinning, Cobiah chuckled. "I did. And if we were back on the *Pride*, maybe I'd have come to a different conclusion. If there was ever a man who could use a good keelhauling, that'd be Nodobe." Striding through the streets of the little town, he continued. "But I have to consider the fact that Captain Nodobe's paid his due, just like the rest of us. Man's got the right to argue his point."

"Pity. I was hoping you'd give him the old 'Gah! Getum!'" Sykox extended his claws and made a silly-looking murder face. Cobiah laughed, and Sykox settled back into their walk. "I don't like Nodobe, either. He wants the council to allocate an additional twenty percent of the town's revenue to building new docks. We can barely defend the five we have now! Bah, the man can argue his point from here to the Orrian deeps for all I care. It's not going to change *facts*."

They reached the top of the wide stone staircase that led up the cliffside. Below them, the town spread out like a blanket, with some fourteen buildings catering to five long docks. There was an inn, a general market, and a plaza full of carts tended by wandering traders selling odds and ends. Most of the buildings were built on the wreckage of the original stone houses left behind when the floodwaters receded. One or two captains, their ships irrevocably ruined by Orrian assaults, simply dragged the hulls up onto the beach and built them onto permanent foundations. The ship-buildings were as good as anything else, and Cobiah had to admit it gave the village a certain nautical charm.

"Look, Sykox." Cobiah pointed up toward the cliffs. "They've nearly finished the ramparts on the east face. We'll have those last two bombards installed as soon as the architects say the foundation is stable."

The engineer chuckled. "If they're using the architectural columns from the old temple of Balthazar, they'll be stable."

"Well, of course they a— How can you know that?" Cobiah stared at him. "That temple was washed away by the tsunami. You said you hadn't been to Lion's Arch before the wave hit. How did you know where the temple of Balthazar used to be?"

Sykox looked uncomfortable. "Er . . . thought I'd mentioned this before. We studied the architectural plans of Lion's Arch in the fahrar, when I was a child. The imperator of the Iron Legion was planning for our generation to assault and seize the city. You know . . . when the charr were done conquering Ascalon." A sheepish smile. "Nothing personal."

"Really? Huh. I grew up begging on the steps of that temple," Cobiah responded with good humor. "It's probably a good thing the charr never got very far along with that plan. We had this one priest named Brother Bilshan. I swear, the man must have been seven feet tall. He fought with a giant war hammer—in each hand. I don't think the fight would have gone well for the charr."

"Maybe so, Coby." Sykox smiled. "Maybe so. I'll give you this—we weren't exactly eager for the duty, that's for sure." The big charr narrowed his eyes to stare past the stone pillars. "Ah . . . and there's the *Nomad*. As usual, the last to arrive."

Cobiah's smile grew twice as broad. He looked out to sea, where a big galleon was being towed into the harbor by Lion's Arch tugboats. The ship's sails were half-furled upon the yardarms of her two large masts. The flag waving upon her highest point was colored with the gold and green of Kryta, yet this was not a military vessel. It was the *Nomad*, a merchant ship and occasional privateer with a letter of marque from King Baede himself, signed in Divinity's Reach.

Few Krytan ships came to Lion's Arch these days. King Baede considered the city a pirate haven: lawless, filled with anarchy and criminals hiding from Krytan justice. To some extent that was true—most of the human ships that came to the city were there to avoid Krytan ports— but by no means was Lion's Arch completely without laws.

Rambunctious, perhaps, and chaotic, but it was ruled by the Captain's Council. Those who threatened the safety of the town met harsh punishment.

But this ship was well known to the citizens of the Arch, and Cobiah felt his heart leap to see her colors. The *Nomad*'s captain was a supporter of their rugged little town, one of the members of the Captain's Council, and known to be the best pilot in the Sea of Sorrows. *Isaye's back,* Cobiah thought, wishing he could catch sight of a dark-haired form on the *Nomad*'s deck.

The ship moved slowly past Claw Island, a stony curve near the harbor's mouth. A small defensive fortification was being built there, designed to keep enemies from sailing close enough to bombard the docks. Cranes lifted stone deliveries to a rudimentary dock, placing them carefully on foundations that would one day become walls. It was the crowning jewel of the protection Sykox planned for Lion's Arch, and the charr was understandably proud of it. The fortress would take years to complete, but when it was done, it would guard the mouth of the harbor, providing gunnery posts and defenses as well as early warning if the Dead Ships came in force, as they'd done at Port Stalwart years ago. Still, for now the fortress was little more than a pile of rough-hewn stones and foundation ditches along a rocky stretch of shore.

"Glad to see Isaye could make the council meeting." Sykox hefted his load higher on his shoulder and started down the thoroughfare that ran along the cliff.

"I specifically held it off until she could make it. Her last letter—"

"Her last *love* letter, you mean, Coby?" Sykox grinned wickedly. "Aw, c'mon, I'm surprised she's not living here with you. When are you going to pop the question and make an honest woman of that pilot, eh?"

Cobiah rolled his eyes. "I'm busy here in town. Isaye wanted to help keep the sea safe for Krytan traders. Our relationship works better when we don't see each other all the time." He ran a hand through his hair, mussing it unconsciously. "I just hope Grimjaw doesn't give her a hard time when she docks."

"Oh, he would if he could, I assure you. Grimjaw can't stand Isaye. Still, I doubt the black-hearted gunrunner will give her any trouble on the docks . . . since he's right over there." Sykox grunted and jutted his muzzle toward the building ahead of them.

In the wide doorway of the town's main store, four charr clustered around a burly, square-shouldered asura. The asura's arms were crossed, and a glower was smeared on his features, belligerence positively dripping from his long sloping ears. Opposite him, the charr sailors were clenching their fists and growling in low tones. Their legionnaire—the captain of their vessel—snarled down at the asura in warlike defiance.

"What's the problem, shopkeep?" Cobiah pushed his way through the charr nonchalantly. Though he managed to sound at ease, he was glad Sykox was by his side. "Is there some kind of disagreement?"

Xeres Grimjaw was the charr captain, a surly fellow with dark tiger-striped fur, a thick muzzle, and two long snaggled canines. "It's a scam. Nodobe said that his crew gets twenty percent off at the store. I want my crew to have the same. He gives preferential treatment to humans." Grimjaw said the word scathingly. "This wretched, miserly asura's the problem, and I'm the solution."

"I'll admit one thing, you surly stinkball. I *do* give Nodobe's crew preferential treatment," Yomm sneered haughtily. "But I do it because I prefer customers who pay their tabs. You and your crew skipped town with seven gold on your ledger. Seven gold!" The asura wrinkled his nose as if he smelled something rancid. Jade-green eyes as hard as stone chips glared at Grimjaw. "You're a dirty cheat!"

"You copper-counting cutthroat! We'd pay if the prices were fair!" Grimjaw roared, the furor of his breath blowing back the little asura's ears. "You'll get that gold from us over our blood and bone!"

"Blood, bone. Whatever," Yomm taunted, revealing long rows of teeth. "You're still not getting the rum."

Two of the charr reached for their weapons, jerking them half clear of their sheaths. Cobiah stepped between them quickly, shouting, "Enough! All of you!" Sykox flinched, ready to fight. Among the crowd, Cobiah saw Aysom, the youngest of the charr in the *Pride*'s warband. The golden-maned warrior moved up behind the others, looking to Cobiah for a signal to attack. Since the death of old Grist a few years back, Aysom had taken the post of bosun aboard the *Havoc* and had grown into a massive specimen of his race, each muscular arm as thick as a human thigh. Aysom shook his mane with a growl and looked intimidating.

Sykox shifted the bag of machine parts onto his shoulder like a club. Although Cobiah couldn't see Fassur, he was certain that the black-furred charr was somewhere nearby, just waiting for an opportunity to strike. Heartened, Cobiah squared his shoulders and met Grimjaw's eyes. "The Captain's Council meets today. If you think Yomm's prices are unfair, you can make a complaint at the meeting, Grimjaw. Now, take this out of the street."

Frustrated, the charr knocked it aside. "You're damn right I will. And that's not the only complaint I'll be making," he snarled. "I stored four bags of goods in his shop, and he says he's lost them!"

"I didn't lose them." Yomm shook his head, ears flopping smugly. "I *sold* them, and all the belongings inside them, to pay part of your debts."

"What!" Grimjaw roared even louder. "You skelk-stinking, ooze-chasing gold monger! Those were my dress uniforms!"

"Really?" Yomm lifted his eyebrows in mock surprise. "With all those spikes? I'd hate to see what the charr consider 'dressing down.'" Pompous to the end, the green-eyed asura tossed his head. "I'll tell you the same thing I tell everyone who uses my storage services: pay your tab or lose your deposit."

"This isn't over, Yomm. Not by a long shot." His whiskers bristling in anger, the striped charr glared at Cobiah. "C'mon, boys." Gesturing for his warband to follow, Grimjaw stormed away. One of the other charr spat on the hearth of the general store before he turned away. Yomm reached for a pistol at his belt, but Cobiah stepped in front of him and caught the asura's arm. As Grimjaw and his warband strode off, the shopkeep redirected his anger toward Cobiah. "I demand the right to speak before the council!" Yomm said imperiously. "I have a right to refute these ridiculous claims and demand repayment."

"We've had this discussion before, Yomm." Cobiah shook his head. "What you do with your store is your own business, so long as it's legal." Cobiah's eyes darkened. "You've got the right to refuse them service, but the council can't force Grimjaw to pay you if he says he doesn't owe anything. He's a captain of the council. Unless you have evidence, we have to trust his word."

"That charr's a liar and a cheat. I've caught his sailors stealing more than once. My 'evidence' is the ledger of debt he owes. I tell you, Marriner, that thieving charr shouldn't be allowed to get away with this." Yomm crossed his arms belligerently. "I'll pack up and leave, that's what I'll do. Without my store to get your goods into Kryta, this town's just a glorified pit stop."

Cobiah sighed and exchanged a glance with Sykox. "I'll bring up your side of the story, Yomm, but you can't come to the meeting unless you're on the council. It just confuses the issue. If everyone in the town showed up and kept interrupting us, we'd never get anything done." More sternly, he added, "You're no captain, Yomm. You abide by the laws we set, or you take your business elsewhere. Don't worry about the town. We'll build another store and make another shopkeep rich."

"Macha will hear about this." Yomm's scowl was as fierce as any charr's.

"Go ahead and tell her. Tell whomever you like." Cobiah stepped down from the shop stairs. "If you think you'll get further with her than with me, you go right ahead and try."

When they were out of earshot, Sykox cracked a smile. "You're a mean cuss, Cobiah Marriner. You realize Macha will eat him alive if that little rat tries to get between the two of you, right?"

"Realize it?" Coby winked devilishly. "I'm counting on it, my friend. I'm absolutely *counting* on it."

18

The central building of Lion's Arch was a long well-built pavilion on the eastern cliffs with a magnificent view of the harbor. It was sturdy, built from the hull of a large galleon and constructed to weather even the coldest of severe winter storms. Since the flooding, the tides and the weather in Lion's Arch had never been quite the same. Meaner, some said. "More protective," Cobiah would reply. The storms made the winter harbor even more difficult to navigate without the tugboats. That kept the Dead Ships away and gave the city a season of relative rest. To Cobiah, it felt as if the goddess Dwayna were watching over them in the wintertime. Of course, he'd never say that to the charr.

After escorting Cobiah to the council building, Sykox had returned to the *Pride* to take his bundle of tools and equipment aboard. Each captain was allowed to bring one crew member as aide to the council meetings. Cobiah had learned from experience that bringing any of the charr—even Fassur or Sykox—only caused trouble. Neither had the patience for long meetings. "Too many brunches, not enough fighting," Sykox would grumble. Macha, on the other hand, actually enjoyed going with him.

She was already inside the foyer of the pavilion,

waiting for him, tapping her foot in sullen annoyance. Macha's braids were still dyed all the colors of the rainbow, but in recent years, she'd exchanged her blue feather robe for a plainer set of clothing. She wore a turquoise bracelet around the top of one arm, a mark of her advancement in the asuran colleges—genius first grade. Its inscriptions matched the markings of Macha's invention, a navigational tool she had titled "the sextant." The first norn who laughed at the name found himself unable to speak properly for a week. Regardless of that, the instrument had so revolutionized navigation that the city had named a section of the docks after her: Macha's Landing.

Macha glared at him. "You're late," she said grumpily. "I got stuck talking to Nodobe for ten minutes. Ten minutes with that pompous, self-absorbed nincompoop is worse than three days in the doldrums with no wind. How could you do that to me?"

"Sorry. I had a little problem with Yomm." Cobiah paused outside the big pavilion, lowering his voice so passersby wouldn't overhear. "By the way, he might come talk to you."

"Is this about Grimjaw and his warband?" She raised an eyebrow inquisitively. "I've heard rumors they're running up tabs and then leaving town. Sometimes it takes months for them to come back, and when they do, they argue the charges before they settle up for the minimum possible. Now, I'm sure Yomm's charging them an arm and a leg above everyone else, but I don't blame him for being angry."

"Angry's one thing, but Yomm's threatening to shut down the store."

Macha paused at that, cocking an eyebrow. "Is he now? Hm. He might do it if he's mad enough."

"Can we stop him?"

"Is it going to go that badly?" she replied.

Cobiah sighed. "Worse, I think. Yomm wants to set prices according to each ship, so he can charge Grimjaw's crew more. Grimjaw wants standard prices for everyone. Most of the other captains will vote with Grimjaw. Yomm won't like it, but we'll just have to find a way to deal with him."

Macha's expression darkened like a small thunder cloud. "Don't underestimate Yomm. He's dangerous, Coby."

"So's a ship full of charr. Do you want to tell Grimjaw that we're going to let Yomm gouge the captains?"

Macha's ears twitched as she spun the issue around in her head. At last, the asura tossed her rainbow hair and sighed. "Nothing we can do about it out here. Best get inside, Coby, before the other captains vote to hang us while we're not there."

Cobiah chuckled and started walking again, Macha toddling along at his side. "Always practical. How late are we?"

"*We* are not late." Macha smirked. "*You* are late. I've already been inside, so they know I'm here."

They walked into the main chamber of the building, where a single long table stretched the length of the room. It could have easily seated thirty people. Today, there were only seven, plus an equal number of aides: seven of the fifteen ships whose captains had invested in the city. Cobiah's contribution had been the largest, but these captains had each bought a seat on the council so that they could have a say in the city's management. When the beacons were lit, they made their way to Lion's Arch. Today, these captains would set the law.

Four captains were already seated at the table. One

was the elegant Captain Nodobe, his dark skin shining in the sunlight that streamed through the pavilion's high windows. Grimjaw reclined in a chair farther down the table, speaking to his first officer in low growls. Cobiah recognized the other charr as the burliest of those escorting the legionnaire that morning.

Captain Hedda was also at the table: a broad norn woman whose flabby arms disguised her well-known strength. She was renowned for lifting the entire prow of her ship from the shore and shoving it into the sea during an unexpected low tide. Although the rumor was greater than the truth, it wasn't much of an exaggeration.

The last of the four at the table was old Captain Moran, previously of the *Salma's Grace*. After retiring from the Krytan military, he'd used his severance to purchase a small clipper of his own, which he'd named the *Valor*. He'd stayed on good terms with Cobiah and the others over the years and spent more time than not in Lion's Arch. Moran was the only captain who smiled when Cobiah entered the room.

A small cluster of other individuals stood at the far end of the room. One was an asura, bigger and more muscular than most of his people, carrying a heavy war hammer across his back. His name was Captain Tarb, a relative newcomer to the council. His first mate was with him: a petite human woman named Gamina, only slightly taller than the burly asura. Gamina was slender, with a snub nose and honey-colored hair. Cobiah didn't know much about either of them other than their ship's name, the *Priority Divide*. It was an odd name for a vessel, and Cobiah didn't get it, but Macha assured him that the name was extremely meaningful to the asura of Rata Sum.

Neither of them held Cobiah's attention once his eyes

fell on the final captain in the room. She was a human woman, tall and athletic, with her dark mane pulled back in a simple ponytail. Hazel eyes caught the sun as she turned her head, and her lips turned up into a charming smile. Clearly, she was as happy to see him as he was to lay eyes on her.

"Oh, great," Macha groaned, ruining the moment. "Isaye brought the bookah."

Indeed, Henst was standing beside Isaye, wearing his typical gear: two swords and a scowl. He placed his traveling rucksack in a corner of the room and took his place standing behind Isaye's chair. It was as if Henst's presence sucked all the joy out of the room, dimming even the sunlight. Henst had served on the *Pride* for a short time, but difficulties with the charr and a dislike for being thrown overboard made him leave the ship for other work. Yet he stayed in touch with Isaye, and when she commissioned the *Nomad*, he joined her aboard as first mate. "Predictable. When Isaye's had a good journey, she brings Verahd." Macha hopped into the main chamber, keeping her voice low so that only Cobiah could hear her speaking. "She has a bad one . . ."

"And we get stuck with the squall," Cobiah said, finishing Macha's sentence with a sigh. Ignoring Henst's scowl, Cobiah crossed the room to greet Isaye, but he'd made it only halfway there when a resounding voice boomed out from the big table.

"Ah, there you are, Captain Marriner." Sidubo Nodobe spoke without rising from his chair, but his thundering basso voice rumbled in the pavilion. "We feared you were forced to abandon the meeting." There was no other voice like that in all of Lion's Arch—possibly in all of Kryta. Nodobe was Elonian by birth, and when he spoke, it was with a flair for oratory and the distinct, ringing timbre of the people of Vabbi. It was too bad that the warm color of his skin and the generous tone of his voice didn't reach the man's features. Nodobe's smile was brilliant, but his eyes were cold and sharp.

"I wouldn't miss the meeting, Captain Nodobe," Cobiah replied formally. "I, and the *Pride*, are here to serve Lion's Arch." Cobiah curved his path toward the table, trying not to let his voice reveal his annoyance. Isaye nodded and strode toward the table as well. Their hellos would just have to wait.

"Then we are fortunate, for today, Lion's Arch needs you. And here you are, ready to face the many problems plaguing our town." Nodobe spread his hands in welcome. Cobiah stopped himself from obviously looking between the man's fingers for a hidden knife. Nodobe smoothly took control of the meeting, directing everyone's attention as if he were wholly, smilingly in charge. Although it rankled, Cobiah wasn't going to let the man see his irritation. He smiled and took a seat, waiting for the others to gather around the table.

Once the last of the captains was seated, Cobiah spoke up before Nodobe could get started. "Lion's Arch is growing more rapidly than we expected. The larger the city becomes, the more we will be a target of Dead Ships, pirates, and other predators. Raiders already patrol the roads from here to the Shiverpeaks, seeking to take out easy prey. We need to capitalize on the natural defenses of our location, and build more. We need to put those guns on the north cliff. Finish the fortress in the bay—"

"Claw Island?" Nodobe's laugh was condescending. "A doomed undertaking. The sooner we abandon it in favor of realistic improvements, the more certain it is that our little town"—he spread his ebony hands, revealing dusky palms—"will grow into something mighty."

"Mighty?" Macha's eyebrows shot up like hovering seagulls. "What do you mean, 'mighty'?"

"A force to be reckoned with." Nodobe lowered his hands and pressed the palms against the table. "Prosperous. Strong. Independent. Isn't that what we all want?"

"Point of order." Tarb, the burly asura with the war hammer, rapped his knuckles on the table. "Seconds are not allowed to contribute unless directly requested. Macha, be quiet or leave the room." He fixed Macha with an icy gaze, and she returned it in kind. Behind Tarb, Gamina gulped and stared at the floor, shifting from foot to foot in a nervous sort of dance.

"Agreed." Cobiah made no apology for Macha's outburst. He kept his eyes on Nodobe and said, "The simple fact of the matter is that unless we defend the port, it won't matter how 'prosperous' the businesses are in Lion's Arch. They'll be rubble."

Nodobe shook his head. "Cobiah, you're overestimating the threat. The town has survived several attacks in the last six years. We can easily survive more. Our defenses are already adequate."

"Is there such a thing as an adequate defense against the dragons?" Hedda, the heavyset norn woman, tapped long fingernails on the table. She'd painted them red, possibly with the blood of her enemies, but more likely with a bucket of ship's primer.

Farther down the table, Moran sounded unconvinced. "The town's been attacked, all right, but by small groups of ships. Not a full-on assault like the one that destroyed Port Stalwart."

"No one's been to Orr and returned. We don't know what they might throw against us. There's no proof the Dead Ships are the worst thing Orr can bring to bear." Hedda frowned.

"They're puny, rotten wrecks." Grimjaw ran his claws through the fur on his forearm in an idle gesture. "You're scared of ships that barely sail and gunnery that barely fires. The Orrians are about as efficient as a devourer with a torch between its tails."

"Perhaps," Nodobe said. "We know that nothing we do will stop them from raiding. But we've also seen that Orrian ships seek out locations they can overwhelm. They'll choose an easier target than Lion's Arch. Hylek villages along the coast. The smaller, private docks at the edge of the Maguuma Jungle. Perhaps the Krytans' new dock at Port Noble. We won't be their first choice—"

"That's your argument? Let them kill somebody other than us?" Cobiah said, mocking him. "These are walking corpses; they're not ogres or grawl. They don't get weaker with every attack; they get stronger. With each battle, they add more undead to their ranks—and more fire-power to their armada." An awkward silence settled over the table as each captain pondered this point of view.

"I don't agree with either of you. Make more money? Pfaugh! Build more walls to hide behind? Bah! I say we buy enough ships to storm Orr and destroy the dragon that lives there once and for all. Anything else is just wasting our time." Grimjaw snarled, his long canines glinting hungrily. "Cowards, both of you." He glared at Cobiah and Nodobe. "You humans have got to get your fingers out of your noses and try to find your spines."

"That's uncalled for!" Isaye's voice was loudest among the chorus of captains shouting Grimjaw down. The table erupted into catcalls and shreds of arguments. Captain Tarb finally pounded his fist on the table and raised his bellow over the others, shouting them into silence so he could speak.

"In my three years' docking at Lion's Arch," Tarb

barked loudly, "I've heard nothing but 'island fortress' this and 'ultimate protection' that. Cobiah, you say these defenses are critically important, but you also say they'll take years to finish. How long can we sit around waiting for stone and lumber, construction and shoring, before we turn our attention to a better market plaza? Or hire more guards to keep our ships and cargo safe? I'm all for keeping those monsters out of our harbor, but I'm not willing to wait ten years to build a bank."

Nodobe leaned back in his wicker chair. "A bank is extremely necessary to the town's growth, Tarb. You're quite correct. Port Noble doesn't have a bank, so we'd be solidifying our place as a preferred port for neutral shipping concerns. Traders interested in dealing with bulk goods, or large sums, would be more likely to come to Lion's Arch."

Cobiah grabbed the table's attention, not wanting to give the smooth-spoken Elonian an opportunity to sway the audience. "Moran," he tossed in quickly. "You're quiet. What are your thoughts?"

"I'm thinking that most of you are blind idiots, to tell the truth." Ever blunt, old Moran sighed and scratched his scalp beneath his thick shock of gray hair. "All plans and no foundation. Where's the money to pay for the defenses, or the bank, or the attack ships . . . or, by the Mists, your furless Aunt Maybell's parlor house, if that's what the town needs! Every one of you is snapping jaw about how you're going to spend money, but nobody's said word one about how we're going to *get* it."

"I believe I can help with that." A smarmy voice from the doorway made Cobiah turn sharply in his chair. The voice came from Yomm, the asuran merchant. With a smug tilt to his chin, Yomm trotted toward the long table. He wasn't alone, either; a norn was with him, walking slowly so as to keep pace with the merchant. With a start, Cobiah recognized the norn as Bronn Svaard. Further, Bronn was carrying a sack over his shoulder, much like the one Sykox had been carrying earlier that morning. But this sack was not filled with machine parts and engine tools. Bronn dropped it on the table at an insistent wave of Yomm's hand, and the entire group heard the unmistakable *clink-clink* of coins.

"I'm here to buy a seat at the table." Yomm's long ears flicked back determinedly. He met each captain's eye with unflinching resoluteness, defying them to say no. Everyone froze for a moment, shocked by the shopkeep's brass. This was unheard of.

"Yomm, you blithering idiot," Grimjaw snorted. "You're no captain. You've no ship! Don't waste our time with this skale-headed bilge."

Shooting the arrogant charr a black look, Cobiah tried to soften the blow. "I know you're worried about the discussion on fixed prices, Yomm, but he's right. The law says you must be an established captain before you can pay the regency fee and join the council."

"You think I don't know that?" The asura's green eyes narrowed haughtily. He rounded on Grimjaw without fear. "It so happens that I've purchased a ship, you slack-jawed mouth-breather. Her name is the *Nadir Shill*. And, before you insult my intelligence any further, I've hired a crew as well."

"He has," Bronn added blithely. "He's hired me and my brother, Grymm."

"Only two?" Grimjaw guffawed. "Smallest crew ever! What're you sailing, Yomm? A cork with a toothpick mast?"

"That's no business of yours, mongrel." Stiffening at the charr's laughter, Yomm nevertheless waved the argument away. "I've obeyed the law in letter and spirit. I've brought the entire regency fee, in cash, and my first mate to boot. You can't keep me out any longer."

"Not entirely true, Yomm." Isaye's voice was serenely neutral. Cobiah was grateful for her ability to stay calm; it was a rarity among the captains of Lion's Arch. She continued. "There's one more thing. You also need the approval of a majority of the council in session."

"Well, by the Mists, he's got mine." Moran stared at the bulging sack of money. "That coin will go far toward any of the plans you lot have proposed, so I'm all for it." The old captain was clearly amused by the discomfort around the table. "He's got my vote."

Nodobe thoughtfully rubbed his clean-shaven jaw. "The laws of the town are clear, and the shopkeep has obeyed them. Even if we don't like his methods, we cannot deny that Yomm already has a great deal of investment in the city. I suppose . . . very well. I accept him in our number."

Dubious, Cobiah frowned. "Well, I don't." He glared at Yomm angrily. "Look, Yomm. If we allow anyone with coin and a seaworthy bathtub to buy their way onto the council, the city's going to be overrun by greedy profiteers. Maybe King Baede will send a hundred captains to buy seats and then vote to annex Lion's Arch back into Kryta." The idea spawned several uncertain grumbles around the table, and he added, "Yomm, you're only doing this to get back at Grimjaw. You don't care about the city. You just want power. I find that unacceptable. My vote is no."

"By the Khan-Ur's metal claws, I actually agree with a human." Grimjaw snorted, his dark stripes rippling with amusement. Leaning back, he thumped one boot and then the other onto the table's surface, tail flicking in annoyance. "I vote we don't let the little gouger make idiots of us all. And I *still* say we go attack Orr!"

Cobiah wasn't sure he enjoyed being on the same side as the arrogant charr. With a sigh, he looked toward Hedda and Tarb and tried to predict their reactions. Hedda looked thoughtful, eyes lingering on the money satchel with obvious interest. Tarb, on the other hand, never stopped staring at Yomm. His expression was difficult to read, but his ears flicked back and forth against his shoulders as if twitching away a wasp.

"I suppose," Hedda said at last, "we could see our way clear to accepting his regency and allowing Yomm on the council." She shrugged, the motion rippling down her fleshy arms. "What harm can a little thing like him cause? It's not like he's buying the whole city. The rest of us can disagree with him in council."

"That's two nos and three yeses," Cobiah tallied. "Tarb? Isaye?"

Tarb sat in silence, arms crossed over his chest. When he realized all eyes were on him, the asura captain grumbled under his breath and shifted belligerently in his seat. At last, he proclaimed simply, "I vote no." His lips twisted in sour disapproval.

"Tarb's Dynamics, like me," Macha whispered conspiratorially into Cobiah's ear. "Yomm's Statics."

Cobiah turned and gave her a blank stare.

"Colleges," she prompted. When Cobiah's face remained expressionless, Macha clenched her fists to her ears in frustration. "Asuran colleges? They have fierce rivalries. It's a well-established fact in asuran society that we sabotage each other whenever given the opportunity . . . Coby, don't you ever *listen* to my stories when we're at sea?"

"I listen to the ones where stuff blows up." He grinned

unhelpfully. Macha squeezed her eyes shut and muttered something under her breath. He turned toward Isaye and asked, "Three and three. Your vote will decide, Isaye."

Isaye ignored their whispers. Thoughtfully, she stated, "You aren't a sailor, Yomm. I understand your dissatisfaction with the process, but it doesn't change the reasons we chose captains to run it and not the townsfolk. Captains are capable of commanding a crew in life-threatening situations. Lion's Arch is under threat from Orrian attack. Only those who can—and have—put their lives on the line against the Dead Ships have the right to make decisions for this port. We pay for that right in more than gold. Many of us have paid for it with the blood of our sailors."

"I could be useful against the Dead Ships!" Yomm blustered. Angrily, he rushed on. "Sailing isn't everything. I could import weaponry for the townsfolk—"

"That doesn't help us," Isaye repeated gently, shaking her head. "Orrians come from the sea. We need ships in the harbor to defend the village. Invested captains who can and will fight for the town where we need it the most. Villagers flailing about with swords aren't going to stop a Dead Ship's attack. Yomm, you don't sail. You're not a real captain."

"I don't sail, hmm?" Yomm crossed his arms and his tone turned nasty. "I . . . well—" Suddenly struck with inspiration, Yomm jabbed a finger toward Cobiah. "Ha! Neither does he! When was the last time anyone saw the *Pride* leave the harbor? Half of her crew's out on other ships or looking for work. Like you, Isaye, with that Krytan tub of yours. Or this big bookah." Yomm jerked a thumb toward Bronn, ignoring the norn's snort of surprise. "Cobiah Marriner spends all his time in the city. Everyone knows his engineer's insane, his crew's disbanded, and his first mate's a murderous scallywag who's been in more fights than a drunken skritt. If Cobiah's your idea of a 'real captain,' then by the sparks and atherions of the Eternal Alchemy, I'm one, too." Yomm tossed his head and dared the council to disagree.

A mutter ran through the group, and at the head of the table, Nodobe laughed out loud. Heat flushed Cobiah's face. Before he could stammer an indignant reply, Tarb sighed with annoyance and sat back in his chair. "Yomm's got a point," the asura said grudgingly. The captains erupted into shouts, yelling opinions one over the other.

Hedda banged a fist on the table, shutting them all up. "Captain Isaye hasn't voted yet. Let her speak. The rest of you, shove it in your brig and let her talk." She placed her hands on the table, red-painted nails scraping like claws against the hard wood. "Well, Isaye?"

The room fell silent, staring at Isaye. The dark-haired woman steepled her fingers before her lips in thoughtful concentration. Cobiah could tell she was weighing the arguments that had been given. In frustration, he clenched his fists beneath the table and struggled to remain silent. At last, Isaye met Cobiah's eyes and then Nodobe's, finally settling on Yomm. "All right, Yomm," she said at last. "The council has never set guidelines on how often a captain has to be at sea if they're to be considered master of their ship. I have to admit that you meet all the other requirements. We'll have to clarify the rules . . . but we can't hold you accountable to laws that haven't been made yet. For now, you're acceptable by all the standards we have in place for Lion's Arch. Welcome to the council." However well reasoned, her words felt like a slap in the face.

Angry, Cobiah pushed away from the table and stood. "I think that's enough business for today." At his side, Macha's dark glower matched his tone perfectly. "Council is in session for a week. We can meet tomorrow to talk about how we spend Yomm's . . ." Cobiah waved at the bag of money on the table. "Regency." The word was bitter.

"Captain Yomm," the shopkeep said, gloating.

"Don't push it, you sniveling rat," hissed Macha, her hand falling to the hilt of a pistol at her belt. The two glared at each other for a moment, and then Yomm tossed his head and looked away.

"Cobiah," Isaye protested.

"Fine. You made your choice. The vote's done." Pretending not to see Isaye's hurt look, Cobiah turned on his heel and ignored the sputtered arguments behind him. He heard Isaye rise from the table. Even Bronn reached to stop him. "Sorry, Coby," the norn said pensively. "Times are hard. I need the job to support my children. You understand, yes, my friend?"

Shoving the norn's hand from his shoulder, Cobiah marched on. He could hear Macha trotting along behind him, multicolored braids flapping across her shoulders as she hurried to keep up. Once they were outside the gate, she grumbled, "Was that really necessary? The tantrumy-storming-out part? They still have a quorum. They could continue the meeting and you won't be there—"

"They won't continue the meeting." Cobiah took the wide steps of the pavilion two at a time and didn't care who was in his path.

"How can you be so sure?"

"Yomm just joined the council. He's not going to want to vote on anything until he's knows what's going on, and that means he's going to want exhaustive argument on every issue. That'll take a while." Cobiah's tone lightened a bit but lost none of its sharpness. "Trust me."

"Fair." Macha grunted. "Poor Bronn."

"Poor Bronn?" Cobiah rounded on her, his last nerve frayed raw. "That traitorous braggart. I'd like to see him keelhauled!"

"For what? Not wanting to starve?"

"He's a member of my crew! He works *my* ship!"

With an unkind laugh, Macha snapped, "He *was* a member of your crew, but he's not now. He has to make money somehow, Coby. Yomm's right about one thing: the *Pride*'s always at port. We don't go raiding, or adventuring, or even pirating. Most of us have jobs on the side. Half the *Havoc*'s old warband work as night guards on the dock, and Sykox spends his time repairing busted-up ships to be used as buildings. He hasn't worked on the *Pride*'s engine in months, but you wouldn't know that. You're always on land, pandering to merchants and planning out the town."

Her words stung. "What about you, Macha? Have you started taking jobs, too?"

"No." She stiffened brusquely. "The only thing I want to do, Coby, is sail with the *Pride*. But you've got to wake up and look around." Macha tugged awkwardly on her bright braids as she rushed to keep up. "Tell me something. I heard Sykox say this morning that you were going to ask Isaye to marry you. Is that true?"

"I've thought about it," he answered, puzzled. "Why?"

"Is that what's making you so invested in this city? Get married, settle down . . . I mean, the way you light up when she comes into port. That big house you're building on the north shore. You know, the one with the high bedroom and the view of the harbor?" Macha's eyes twinkled. "You built it for her, didn't you? Love is positively smeared all over your face."

"I have to sleep somewhere!"

"You used to sleep on the *Pride*," Macha teased. "C'mon." He still didn't answer, and Macha's smile faded into genuine curiosity. "What if she says no?"

Cobiah reddened. "I don't know. I hadn't really thought about what I'd do then." Cobiah paused to look around, taking in the pleasant streets and freshly painted buildings. "Look at this wonderful town we've made, Macha. Isaye was a big part of that. Without her, I don't know if I could even live in Lion's Arch. Seeing the city, every day, without her? It'd remind me too much of . . . what we had."

"Yeah." Macha nodded, patting his hand. "I understand that. Don't worry, Cobiah. I'm sure she'll say yes. What's there to say no about? You're scoundrelous, violent, unpredictable, and utterly incorrigible."

He laughed out loud. "Thanks, Macha."

"You wouldn't be able to make it without me, and you know it. We're a team." Narrowing her eyes, she rushed on, changing the subject abruptly. "So, Yomm has a council seat. What will happen now?"

Somewhat abashed, Cobiah answered, "I guess I should apologize to Isaye."

Macha rolled her eyes. "That's not what I'm asking, loverboy. Sheesh, you have a mind like a dolyak following a carrot. I'm *asking* what's going to happen to the city."

Cobiah sighed and looked out at the docks. He could see blue water through the jagged spiderwebs of open alleyways, and he could hear the shouts of sailors on the tugs, bringing a clipper into its mooring. "Yomm's on the council. He gets a vote. Most likely, he'll quell any argument about standardizing prices in the town—or bringing in a bank or other shops. He'll fight against anything that could jeopardize his control of trade. He's got enough money to pay off some of the other captains, or at least to promise funding for their pet projects if they go along with his ideas."

"That's bad." Macha worked the figures in her head. "If Yomm manages to get his way with shipping and sales tariffs, he'll control trade through Lion's Arch. Captains will have to go through him to unload their wares or load new stores aboard their ships. He'll eventually rule Lion's Arch de facto, no matter what the council says."

She grabbed Cobiah's sleeve, jerking him around to face her. "What then, Coby?" The little mesmer's eyes were dark pools of shadow.

"He'll get greedy, like he always does, and he'll raise prices. Captains won't want to pay his fees. Ships will stop using our port." Cobiah looked down at the bustling docks. "Lion's Arch will die."

19

Twilight crept over the harbor, bringing with it the sweet scent of open flame and meals cooking in homes and taverns. The lapping of water against the ships on the docks matched the rhythm of drums and violins in the ale houses where sailors spent their pay on a night of drinking and debauchery. A light from the windows of the captain's cabin aboard the *Nomad* shimmered on the waves.

Cobiah marched stiffly down the dock toward the clipper. He heard a distant bell ringing the hour in the town and paused at the gangplank to hear it toll. On the deck of the *Nomad*, the few sailors still on board called out to one another, saying their good-nights and walking the rounds before they turned in below. Cobiah twisted the cuffs of his blue frock coat and straightened the collar at his neck. He wished the walk had taken longer. Now that he was here, he had no idea what to say. Taking a deep breath, he considered turning on his heel and going back to the *Pride*, but even as he tried to convince himself to leave, Cobiah stepped out onto the gangplank, and he found himself striding up the walkway onto the *Nomad*'s deck.

"Ahoy!" a voice called from the deck. The soft glow of

a lantern moved closer as someone approached the gun-wale. "Who goes there?"

"Hail, aboard," he answered, waving awkwardly. "I'm here to . . . I mean . . ."

"Is there some problem?"

"No, no problem. It's Captain Marriner. I'd like to speak to . . . um . . ."

"Cobiah?" As the figure approached, Cobiah caught the shadow of gently fluttering black wraps on the wrist holding the lantern. "Dwayna bless my soul."

Recognizing both the voice and the odd, bandage-like strips of fabric, Cobiah relaxed. "Verahd. Good to see you."

Lifting the lantern higher, the elementalist pushed back his wire-rimmed glasses and studied Cobiah intently. "You look like a fop," he said bluntly. "Where did you get that terrible coat?"

"Macha gave it to me. You don't like it?" Cobiah looked down at the frock coat in distress.

"I can lie if you want, and say it's very fashionable. Isaye, on the other hand, will tell you the truth. Probably through a lot of laughter."

Grumbling, Cobiah took off the coat and tossed it to hang on one of the dock pegs. He walked up onto the deck and shook Verahd's hand. "Thanks." Verahd nod-ded with a sound that was half chuckle and half sigh and gestured for Cobiah to follow.

"Lucky for you, Henst's at the tavern with most of the crew; you'd have never gotten aboard. She's a bit miffed at you. What did you do?"

"Me?" Cobiah raised his hands in a gesture of surren-der. "I didn't do anything."

Verahd snorted. When they reached the big oak doors of the captain's cabin, the elementalist stared at him appraisingly and then shrugged and knocked three times. "Cap'n?" the elementalist announced with resignation. "You've a visitor."

"At this hour? Who in the Mists . . . ?" Cobiah heard the scrape of a chair, followed by the sound of bare feet on deck boards. Isaye opened the door.

She wore her leather pants and white shirt, as she had in the council chambers, but now her hair was unbound, spilling down past her shoulders in dark mahogany waves. Isaye wrinkled her nose and narrowed her green-gold eyes. "Cobiah? Forgot where you docked your ship, did you?" Crossing her arms, she leaned against the arch of the doorway and looked him up and down.

"No. I . . . Look, Isaye . . ." Suddenly awkward, Cobiah glanced over at Verahd.

The slender elementalist raised an eyebrow, tapping his long, birdlike fingers atop the lantern's hood. "Oh, *fine*." Verahd sighed again and tucked long strands of reddish hair behind his ear. "I'll check on the forecastle. You two behave, or I'll turn into a tornado and hurl you both into the sea." He eyed Cobiah with skepticism and lowered the lantern, muttering as he walked away.

Isaye was still staring at him, a bemused quirk twisting her full lips. "Well?" she said blankly. "You didn't come all this way just to stare at me, did you?"

"No." Cobiah blinked, rubbing his eyes. "Look, Isaye, I wanted to talk to you about the council meeting today."

"Talk to me?"

"Apologize," he added smoothly. "I want to apologize."

"Hmph." She stepped to the side and walked back into the cabin, leaving the door open for him to follow. "Come in out of the wind, Cobiah Marriner."

The main room of the captain's quarters on the *Nomad* was spacious, not unlike his aboard the *Pride*, with well-scrubbed floors and shining brass ornaments. But that was where the likeness ended. Cobiah's quarters were rambunctious, filled with the trinkets and trophies of a life raiding ships at sea. Isaye's were sparse and business-like. They were tidy, if lavish, with colored window glass in diamonds of yellow, red, and blue. Light came from covered wall sconces that smelled of burning oil. There was a table with a stack of maps and charts, a desk that had been bolted to the floor, and several chairs shod in heavy lead to keep them standing when the ship tossed on the waves. A tall, three-part Canthan screen blocked Cobiah's view of the bed, but he caught a glimpse of tightly tucked sheets beneath a scarlet-and-gold coverlet. A wardrobe stood in the same area, its doors closed and latched to keep its contents safe even in a storm. Cobiah smiled to see his hat and a book he'd been reading still on her nightstand, right where he'd forgotten them before she left port three weeks ago.

Isaye crossed to the captain's desk and poured two glasses of whiskey. She kept one in her hand and set the other on the table with a thump. Choosing the large padded chair near the desk, Isaye settled down, pulling her bare feet underneath her legs. She gazed curiously at her visitor. "If you're here to start an argument, it's going to be a short one." Isaye tapped the side of her glass with her fingers. "I'm tired, Cobiah, and I don't have enough whiskey to entertain myself while you rant."

"I'm not going to rant. I told you, I'm here to apologize." He took the whiskey gratefully, turning one of the hard wooden chairs around to straddle the seat. "Thanks."

"All right, then get to it." She eyed him.

Cobiah phrased his thoughts carefully. Something about Isaye's manner always made him think twice before he acted—something he wasn't at all used to doing. It was uncomfortable, but he liked the results. Simply put, she was good for him. "I'm sorry I got angry at you during the council meeting. You had the right to vote your conscience, and I shouldn't act like that's wrong. Even when I don't agree with you." He managed a sheepish smile.

He went on. "Yomm was right. I don't take the *Pride* out as often as I'd like, and maybe that makes me 'a bad captain. But Yomm's a terrible one. He doesn't bring anything to the defense of the city, and despite his platitudes, he's not planning on being helpful. You know as well as I do that he hasn't joined the council to protect Lion's Arch. He joined it to keep his power—and his profits—intact."

Isaye nodded. "I know."

"You . . ." Cobiah blinked. "That's terrible!"

"Yup." She took a sip of her whiskey. "It's damn lousy of him. Yomm's a skunk, and there's no doubt about it."

He stared at her, restraint forgotten. "Then why the hell did you vote for him?"

Isaye set down her whiskey glass and answered, "I voted to uphold the rules of the city, Cobiah. I didn't vote *for* Yomm."

"Are you kidding me?" Cobiah exploded. "The city's in jeopardy. You know that asura's trying to rook the council, and you don't feel any kind of responsibility to keep him out?" Shaking, Cobiah took a gulp of the whiskey and felt it burn against the back of his throat. Choking slightly, he said, "Did they pay you?"

Isaye's eyes flashed—the first sign of genuine anger he'd seen. "You think I was bribed? You know me better than that."

"Then what were you doing?"

"Not that I owe you any kind of explanation, Coby, but Yomm followed the laws. Laws *we* made, and laws we have to obey. If we don't, nobody else will, and then this city really will be everything King Baede says: chaotic, anarchic, and lawless."

"Oh, so now it's all about what Baede's going to think of us."

"Yes. I mean, no. I mean—" Isaye thumped her whiskey glass onto the desk. "Kryta used to rule Lion's Arch. We're lucky King Baede's got his hands full with the war in Ascalon and the building of his new city, but that won't last forever. If he thinks Lion's Arch is a problem, he'll allocate Seraph from his army to conquer us. Then what do we do? We don't have the manpower to fight trained military.

"The only reason we've managed to keep operating independently is because we're not a thorn in the king's side. We're too small to give him reason to take us over, and despite our reputation, Lion's Arch does have laws, and we live by them." Isaye leaned forward and met his eyes. "The minute those two things change, King Baede will take an interest. I assure you."

Cobiah took another sip of his whiskey. "Fine," he said through gritted teeth.

More gently, Isaye continued. "Laws are important, and we need some new ones. We can't kick Grimjaw off the council for not paying his bills. Or Nodobe for running a slaver. And maybe we should." She pointed at him with the hand that held her glass. "If this sets a fire under the council's ass to make those laws, then I'm willing to be the one to do it."

"And then what? We turn into Kryta? Next we'll start making laws against norn in taverns because they brawl too much. Or outlawing asuran laboratories inside the city limits."

"The ones that research on skritt, yes," Isaye countered. "Those poor little rats." She rolled her glass between her hands in concern. At last, she said, "Cobiah . . . this city needs better morals. And so do you."

Cobiah thumped the glass onto the table. "I've got plenty of morals." He frowned.

"No, Coby. You don't. You've got a conscience, and that's different. Remember the time you sacked that norn vessel carrying settlers—women and children—south of the Shiverpeaks?"

Stung, Cobiah raised his voice. "I put them all ashore!"

"But you kept their money," Isaye replied. "And the charr freighter carrying Ascalonian relics?"

"I had no idea they were carrying holy artifacts. Even if I had known, how was I to guess that they were a peace gesture bound for Port Noble? You were as surprised as I was to see those statues of Dwayna."

"It's true, I was. But you sold them to a private collector for quite a bit of money, and that sank any hope of a treaty between Kryta and the charr," Isaye scolded. She stood up, pushing her chair aside and moving to sit on the fore of the desk closer to him. In a gentler tone, she continued. "You'll do what you want, Cobiah Marriner. Usually, I like that about you—but in this case, it's hurting the city."

Cobiah gritted his teeth. "You're blaming this whole thing on me?"

"Of course not, but you are the leader of the council, and this is hardly a surprise. Lion's Arch isn't a cluster of buildings and landed ships anymore. It's a town, and someday soon, it's going to be a city. But you're not mad at me over supporting the law. This is a personal issue for you, Coby, and you know it."

"Personal?" Cobiah leaned forward and placed his hand on her knee. "What do you mean?"

"You weren't half this mad before Yomm accused you of being a bad captain."

A pause. "All right, you've got me there," he said grudgingly. With a smile, he added, "How about this: I'll grant you that we need better laws, if you admit that Yomm's captaincy's bad for Lion's Arch."

"Granted," Isaye replied. She lifted his hand to her lips and kissed it gently. "So, what are we going to do about it?"

Grinning, Cobiah held up his empty glass. "I like the 'we' part of that question. How about 'we' pour another round of drinks?"

She laughed and shook her head knowingly. "Scamp." Emptying her glass in a single swallow, she let go of his hand and walked back to the table. Isaye uncorked the crystal bottle and refreshed their glasses. "I'm worried, Coby. It's clear that Yomm's not working alone. That bag of money? It wasn't his. He couldn't pay for the cargo I brought out of Rata Sum, so I know he didn't come up with that much cash on the spot. Yomm's finances aren't good. He must have had a backer."

"Interesting. Who?" Cobiah took the proffered glass.

With a smile, Isaye sat on the edge of the desk, taking his hand in hers. She smiled contentedly and intertwined their fingers. "I don't know. But they already know that you're their enemy, Cobiah. Based on the way you argued against Yomm in council, they know you won't let his shenanigans go on without a fight. I swear, if that asura had had a knife in his hand during the council meeting, you'd be a dead man."

"If Yomm wants a shot at me, he can stand in line." Cobiah winked.

They laughed together, voices lifting in camaraderie.

A knock on the door drew their attention. Isaye set down her glass and rose, chuckling as she crossed the room. "I swear, Coby. You're incorrigible."

"According to Sykox"—he smiled and leaned back comfortably—"I've made a career out of it."

Isaye opened the door. The deck outside was empty. Frowning, she glanced in both directions, trying to spot the watch lantern. "Verahd?" After a moment, she called again. "Verahd?" There was no answer. Isaye took a step onto the deck, hair blowing in the sea breeze, and Coby noticed a small package resting at her feet.

"What's that?" Getting up from the chair, he walked toward her, pointing at the brown-wrapped parcel. As Isaye bent to pick it up, Cobiah caught sight of a small figure hurtling down the dock toward the *Nomad*. Multicolored braids bounced wildly in its wake as a familiar voice shouted into the darkness.

"Coby! Get off the ship! That package, it's a—"

Questioningly, Isaye reached for the bundle. Something sparked along the edges of the paper as she did. Before Macha could finish her sentence, the spark blazed into a flicker of scintillating yellow light. Flame leapt across the surface of the package. In the same instant, Cobiah leapt toward Isaye.

A massive explosion rocked the *Nomad*, roaring over the deck in a wave of hungry flame.

20

The boom of the detonation echoed across the harbor with the impact of a thunderclap. The quarterdeck of the *Nomad* splintered from the concussion. Fire caught the timbers and spread through the back of the clipper with the speed of a racing centaur. On the dock, Macha screamed and called for aid, calling sailors on the docks and guards from the town with shouts of "Fire! Fire on the wharf!"

Aboard the *Nomad*, sailors dove into the ocean, choosing the cold darkness of waves over the scorching heat of flame. Only one remained on the upper deck, his steely blue eyes flashing with impenetrable surety. Verahd raised his hands in the motions of magic, holding his staff high to summon wind. As flame trickled up the wrappings around his wrists, Verahd stood fast and directed the steadily rising gale, pressing it into service against the fire.

Macha made it to the top of the gangplank, raising one hand to shield her eyes from the glare. "What are you doing? We have to get off the ship before the munitions catch fire!"

"I'm not leaving my captain." Verahd's voice was barely audible above the inferno.

"Isaye's dead!" Macha grabbed for him, but her fingers were singed by the burning straps that wrapped around the elementalist's wrist. "We have to go!"

"I'm not leaving my captain!" The wizard's voice cracked like glass. Renewing his efforts, Verahd pounded his staff against the deck of the ship. Magic thundered around him, pouring over Verahd's body, churning wind and flame into a storm across his skin. Macha was thrust back by the power of it. The elementalist continued to chant, his eyes wide, and with a roar of energy, his body transformed into a tornado of swirling wind.

"Verahd! No! You can't—" Macha raised a hand before her eyes to shield them from the overwhelming gusts, but if the elementalist could still hear her, the tornado didn't change its path. She stumbled backward. With a curse, Macha clawed her way back to the gangplank and made her way down it to the dock, unwilling to lose her own life to the blaze.

The tornado-bound Verahd showed no such self-interest. Amid the flame and thick clouds of smoke, he spun unwaveringly, fire lacing each sweep of massive wind as he pounded the ship with gusts. The tornado drew spray and water from the sea around the clipper, drenching the deck as well as blowing the fire out. As the tornado slowed, Verahd could again be seen walking across the *Nomad*'s deck. Clothing alight, hair greasy with sweat, and skin pink from the heat, Verahd took step after step toward the rear of the ship, pushing the flame apart with wind and storm despite his own injuries.

There, amid the wreckage of the cabin, lay two bodies. Protected from the initial blast by the solid oak wall, they now huddled in the center of the room. Cobiah had managed to wrap a blanket about them, dumping water from the washbasin over it to slow the fire. Even with that, the smoke had overcome them, and Isaye lay huddled in Cobiah's arms, both of them unconscious from the heat.

Verahd's anger was like the tempest of storm winds. He pushed through the blaze, tamping out the fire, fighting his way toward them. The elementalist's wrappings roasted, and his flesh seared, but no pain, no suffering, no injury would make him abandon his loyalties. At last, Verahd knelt beside the sodden, roasting blanket pile. They were alive. He tucked the blanket tightly around them, like a father putting his children to rest.

"I only have strength enough for two, Captain," Verahd whispered to the unconscious Isaye, not caring if she could hear him. "You'll be all right." With a great effort of will, he summoned the wind once more. This time, he commanded the gale to lift the sodden burden, raising it high above the leaping flames. As the cabin began to collapse around him, Verahd's final spell swept Isaye and Cobiah out the shattered windows and into the night.

On the dock, a bucket brigade had started. Sailors and workmen, guards and villagers struggled to dump water on the flames before the blaze could spread. Macha stood at the forefront. As the wind lowered its bundle to the boards, Macha raced toward it, tears streaking the ash on her cheeks. "Coby!" she shouted, dragging away the smoking blanket. "Are you all right? By the Alchemy, say something. Please!" She shook him, splashing seawater on his face until he roused. "Blessings on the etheric equation," the asura breathed gratefully. "You're alive."

"Macha?" he asked groggily. She smiled and nodded, squeezing his hand in hers.

Just at that moment, the munitions room on the *Nomad* caught fire. There was a roar of flame and a thundering boom as the stern of the ship detonated in a massive explosion of spraying gunpowder and shot.

Dawn was rising, pink stripes lightening the horizon and giving them a clear view of the damage. The fore of the *Nomad* was in fair shape, but the rear—the quarterdeck, the captain's cabin, and the lower berths—were seared, blackened, and torn open. "Who would *do* this?" Isaye asked quietly, standing on the end of the dock. "Verahd . . . my brave, loyal friend . . ." Tears overwhelmed her, and she bent her head as they slid down ash-stained cheeks. Cobiah pulled Isaye close, cradling her head against his chest as she wept.

Cobiah looked down at Macha. "What did you see?"

The asura was covered in ash and soot, her once-bright braids a mélange of grays. "I was on the *Pride*. A messenger from the city stopped by—I didn't get a good look at him, just some human dressed in normal clothes—and said he had a package for you. I told him to leave it, and he wouldn't. After he left, I followed him here."

"I'm glad you did." Cobiah gently squeezed Macha's shoulder, trying to ignore the way his hand shook. "You saved our lives." Macha's face reddened, and she nodded mutely.

Yet again, Cobiah thought, smiling down at the asura, *a little angel saved my life. Biviane, Macha . . . Isaye. I'm fortunate to have them in my life.*

The fire was out aboard the *Nomad,* and the ship's crew moved across her deck numbly, assessing the damage. "It's going to take weeks to repair," Isaye said, shaking her head. "Hundreds of gold."

"I'll help pay for it. It's my fault that this happened aboard your ship. They were targeting me, not you.

You're still a captain, and the *Nomad* will sail again."
Cobiah struggled to focus his emotions. Anger, pain, frustration, and shock fought for his attention, but right now, Isaye needed him to be stoic. He managed a reassuring smile for her sake.

"Who did this?" Isaye met his eyes frankly. "Was it Yomm?"

"Possibly. Or Grimjaw. Both of them have good reason to be angry at me."

"So does Nodobe. I could probably think of two or three others who've sworn vengeance against you over the years," Macha chimed in helpfully. Cobiah made a face. "What?" she chided. "C'mon, Coby. There's an old asuran saying: you can judge an inventor's success by his enemy's firepower. Yours happen to be pretty well armed."

Cobiah stayed on topic. "If it was a bomb made of sparks and oil, I'd guess that a charr made it. If it was magic, it'd more likely be of asuran make. Did you get any kind of look inside the package before it blew up, Isaye?"

"Not really. It was shiny, I remember that," she sighed. "I don't think I'm going to be much help."

Macha glared at Isaye. "Shiny? What, did you think it was a Wintersday present?" Isaye bristled, and fearing for his life, Cobiah stepped in.

"I'm going to have a talk with Yomm and Grimjaw. It's likely one of them was behind this." He clenched his fists and grinned. "If they were, they're going to regret their part in it."

"Just barge in and *ask*?" Isaye admonished him. "Do you really think they'll tell you the truth?"

"Why not? I've never been afraid to go straight to the source. I think the word you used was 'incorrigible.'"

Cobiah winked. "Are you coming with me?" Isaye had little choice. With a frown, she turned to follow. Glaring and ducking her head, Macha trotted along behind the pair.

The three walked through the village toward Yomm's general store. Although dawn brightened the horizon, they could see that workers had been inside the store for some time, loading the shelves and readying the day's inventory. Cobiah pounded on the closed door of the shop, his thudding fist shaking it so furiously that it creaked on its hinges. When those inside didn't respond at once, Cobiah banged on it again, yelling, "Yomm!"

A young asura opened the door a sliver, staring at Cobiah with wide eyes. "What do you want?"

"Where's Yomm?" Cobiah pushed the door open, shoving his way past the boy. "Go get him. Tell him Cobiah Marriner's here, and I'm not leaving 'til we have a chat."

Gulping, the nervous youth rushed into the store, weaving through piles of imported cotton, foodstuffs, and trade goods toward a light in an office behind the main counter. Cobiah followed. Other asura scattered before him, stumbling and dropping their wares in surprise as he strode angrily through the store.

Yomm sat in his office behind a wide desk, three pencils tucked behind his ears. On the shelves surrounding him were books, stacks of paperwork, small trinkets and tools, and a pile of rucksacks waiting to be repaired. When the young asura pushed open the door, he scowled and snarled, "Blipp! What is your *hypertrophic malfunction*? I said I didn't want to be disturbed!"

Cobiah didn't wait to be invited. Pushing past the asuran lad, he strode to Yomm's desk and slammed his hands down on the tabletop. "Tell me about the bomb, you sniveling little skritt."

Yomm yelped, aghast. One of the pencils fell from

behind his ear. Macha and Isaye stepped into the doorway behind him, the first scowling fiercely, the second eyeing the asura and his surroundings with a studious gaze. "What do you want?" Yomm protested with a squeak. Regaining his equilibrium, the shopkeep pulled the other pencils from his ears and tossed them down onto the paperwork. He fixed Cobiah with a withering gaze. "I could have you arrested for breaking in here."

"And I could have you hanged for murder." Cobiah's voice was cold. Slowly, as if he were talking to a child, he leaned in and repeated, "Tell . . . me . . . about . . . the bomb."

The asura's ears twitched. He glanced at Cobiah and Isaye, and lastly, he scowled at Macha. Turning to his young apprentice, the shopkeep snarled, "Blipp, go adjust the golem pattern so they'll stack ale kegs. We have a norn freighter coming in this afternoon. I want those kegs marked up by fifty percent and placed prominently in the front of the store." Eager to leave the room, the youth rushed to obey, not daring to look back.

Yomm reclined smoothly in his chair. Picking up one of the pencils, he spun it through his fingers with nervous energy, much like a drummer boy on festival day. "I don't know anything about a bomb, Marriner. You've gone completely off the deep end. Are you planning to blame me for some imagined perfidy simply because you disagree with my appointment to the council? Shame on you."

Cobiah reached out and grabbed the asura by his ears, lifting Yomm bodily from his seat. Yomm squawked, reaching up to grab Cobiah's wrists. He hung there, kicking and squirming, his feet flailing above the ground. "I'm telling you—I don't know anything about a bomb!" Yomm shrieked.

"You're lying." Cobiah bounced the asura up and down. "Talk, you mangy, gold mongering—"

"Static sucker!" Macha encouraged. "Shake him again, Cobiah!"

"Cobiah." Isaye laid her hand on his arm. "Take a look at this." She spun Yomm's logbook around on the desk, running her finger down the entries. "Every captain in town owes him something. Grimjaw's not the only one. Nodobe and Hedda . . . even Moran."

Macha stood on her tiptoes and studied the numbers. "Maybe everyone who voted yes on the council owed Yomm."

"Well, that would explain part of it. But if they paid him with their votes, where'd he get the retainer money?" Isaye mused. "And why set the bomb?"

Yomm kicked free of Cobiah's hands. He landed on the floor with a heavy "oof" and scrambled to his feet. "I don't make bombs! If you're referring to the fire down on the docks last night, I had nothing to do with it. I was here all evening."

"You could have sent the messenger. That doesn't prove anything." Macha poked him, and Yomm squawked.

"I didn't send any messages, you nitwit. You and your captain both have heads made of oak!" Seizing an opportunity, the shopkeep kicked her viciously in the shin. Macha yelped and grabbed her leg. While she was hopping about and cursing, Yomm rounded on Cobiah. "I don't know anything about bombs, or explosions, or murder. I spent my youth in a *respectable* laboratory, building packing golems like the ones I use to stock my store. I've never built an incendiary device in my life."

"Look at this." Isaye was still reading the ledger. "Grimjaw's last shipment was a load of construction materials to a charr outpost. Charr use explosives to plant deep poles for building foundations. He could have kept some of those to make the bomb."

"Aha! Aha! See?" Yomm rubbed his aching ears. "You're barking up the wrong tree, bookah. I don't care about your politics, but when you march in here accusing me of attempted murder, you've gone too far." He smoothed his ears back, wincing. "I'm calling the city guard!"

Cobiah narrowed his eyes, ready to pick another fight, but Macha stepped between them. "Come on, Yomm. They've just been in an explosion. Isaye's ship took a pounding, and somebody tried to murder Cobiah. Give them a break." She took another step toward the older asura, helping him straighten his clothes. "We're all friends here, right?"

"Friends? Are you delirious? I should . . . What's that you're doing, woman? Is that some kind of . . . what is that?" While Yomm was talking, Macha had reached for the wand at her belt and murmured a few words of magic. Before he could blink, she passed her palm in front of Yomm's eyes. Her hand moved away, his eyes unfocused, and the shopkeep began to wobble on his feet. "Oh . . . oh. Oh!" he said, staring blithely at the empty space between them. A slow, droopy grin plastered itself on Yomm's features and his voice took on a woozy tone. "Councilor Flax! Why, yes, I *would* like an award . . . and here I didn't think you'd noticed. How wonderful . . . It comes with a research grant, you say? Marvelous . . . just . . . uumph . . ." Yomm's eyelids drooped. He muttered something indistinct, and his body sagged toward the floor.

Catching him, Macha called, "Help me get this idiot back into his chair." Coby lifted the small asura and placed him in the seat behind the desk. Before he was even completely situated, Yomm was snoring. Macha thumped his head with her finger for good measure. The tap put Yomm off balance, and he slumped face-first onto the top of his desk. "He's completely down for the count, but it'll only last a few hours. Sadly, he'll probably be up and around for the council vote at noon." Macha went over to the weathered rucksacks in the corner of the room, where Yomm kept his storage goods. Noting a sailor's name stitched to one shoulder strap, Macha swept up a heavy bag and looked at the letters appraisingly. "Henst," she read. "Heh heh heh." She lifted Yomm's head and shoved the heavy bag like a pillow between the asura's face and the desk. Patting the sleeping asura's cheek, she smirked. "Boy, I really hope Yomm drools."

"Good work, Macha." Cobiah crossed his arms grimly. "Darn. I was really hoping it was him."

"Me too," Isaye sighed. "Cobiah, I think we're working against the clock. Whoever did this had to have worked fast, or the attack wouldn't have been so sloppy. It would be far easier to spend a few days looking for the opportunity to get a bomb hidden in the berth of your ship than it was to track you down on the spur of the moment and hope for the best. They could even have planted charges on your keel and set it off after you took the *Pride* out of harbor. You'd be lost at sea. Nobody would have found out about the bomb."

"Maybe they weren't willing to wait that long," Macha muttered as she draped a lace doily over Yomm's head. "Could have been years."

Cobiah shot the asura a stern look and then turned back to Isaye. "You're right. There are easier ways to kill one person if that's your target. It's messy and designed to work even if you can't get close. They could have hired a mercenary to attack me at night on the streets."

"True." Isaye added, "Or sneak aboard your ship and set a fire by hand. A bomb does seem like a pretty obvious way to go about things." Isaye's brows furrowed in thought.

"What does that mean?" Macha asked.

Isaye wrinkled her nose thoughtfully. "It doesn't add up."

Bombs were hard to make and harder to design effectively. It had to be a makeshift plan, based on something scavenged and used as an attack rather than planning out a better strategy, which meant that Isaye was right: the attacker had been in a rush. Cobiah frowned. Yomm had good reason to want Cobiah dead, but he didn't have the materials or the skill to put this plan together so quickly. Moreover, now that he was on the council, it didn't seem like he'd be in a very big rush. He'd gotten what he wanted: a voice. Yomm could afford to take weeks to slowly get control over trade.

Cobiah looked at the ledger, once more noting Grimjaw's recent cargo. It had to be more than a coincidence. He set the book back on Yomm's desk. "We need to have a chat with a certain ill-tempered charr."

"So." Macha trotted behind him as Cobiah left the office. "Tell me we're not going to use the same tactic with Grimjaw. You don't grab a *charr* by the ears. We'll just talk to him, right?" When Cobiah didn't answer, Macha asked more stridently, "You've got a plan, right?

". . . Cobiah?"

21

Now the darkness comes, and the stars above
Circle 'round like sharks at sea, O
Instead of fighting for our lives
We should be sitting at our ease
But I chose the strife of a sailor's life
And the ocean, she chose me, O.
　　　　　—"Weather the Storm"

The *Brutality* was moored at the southernmost dock, sitting low in her berth like a shark prowling still waters. Her shape, long and lean, reminded Cobiah of the *Havoc*, but no engine chugged in this brig's lower decks. She had two masts standing fore and aft rather than parallel, and her sails were square-rigged in the way of charr military vessels. Her hull was painted a dark charcoal gray, like raw primer left to dry. Xeres Grimjaw and his warband bragged that it made her harder to see against the ocean. Sykox claimed it was a tribute to their legion: Ash.

The ship had two decks, with a thick hull designed to ram; she could take plenty of damage and still remain afloat, but that didn't leave the *Brutality* with much space to carry freight. As with most charr vessels, it was lightly crewed, and only two warbands—the Grim warband, and another called the Zeal warband—kept her running on long journeys up and down the coast. Those two warbands comprised fifteen sailors between them, plus three more that Sykox and Fassur snidely referred to as "honorless gladium" because they didn't have a warband. Cobiah understood what that meant. Most humans didn't.

The charr were also in the habit of maintaining a guard on their wharf. Day and night, at least two armed soldiers stood watch at the beach end of the pier. The *Brutality* had few visitors; charr ships were relatively rare, as the great cats weren't a particularly seagoing people, and other races didn't tend to make social calls on Grim-jaw's men. Cobiah stood in an alley across from the dock, rubbing his hand against his cheek as he contemplated the *Brutality*.

"What are you thinking?" Isaye whispered, pressing back against the wall.

Macha interrupted, "Tell me it's not the ear thing. Even if you could lift a charr, Coby, you just don't have hands enough for all four of their ears. Please tell me—" Cobiah clapped a hand over the excited asura's mouth before her chattering could attract attention. The sun was up over Lion's Arch, and the streets were filling with people going about their morning chores. Shops were opening, fishermen were gathering their nets and head-ing out on the tide, and the charr were changing guard on their pier.

"Hush," Cobiah hissed. Sullenly, Macha nodded, and he let her go.

"Force won't work. We have to use guile," said Isaye.

"Macha, can you make us look like charr?"

The asura nodded, braids bouncing. "Sure, but it lasts

only about five minutes. We wouldn't even make it to the end of the dock."

Cobiah cursed and struggled to think of another way.

"I've got an idea," said Isaye. "Give me a few minutes and then head for the ship. You'll know when to move." She smiled, glancing down the street with sudden enthusiasm.

"What are you going to do?" Macha snorted. "Sex it up to distract them?"

Isaye glared at the little mesmer. "By the Six Gods! These are charr, not wharf rats. Get your mind out of the gutter." She poked her head around the corner and took another look at the dock. "I'm going to give them the one thing no charr can resist. When that happens, you get in the water, slip up the anchor chain, and see if you can find anything that tells us whether Grimjaw made that bomb. I'll meet you at the Captain's Council later.

"And, by the way," Isaye added, "I'd recommend you cover your faces in case you find yourself creeping into their sleeping area."

"So they won't recognize us?" Cobiah asked.

"No." Isaye winked, slipping around the corner. "So you don't get knocked unconscious by the smell." She blended into the crowd easily, striding toward the wharf. As she approached the wharf, she singled out in the crowd someone along the way, raising her hand to catch the man's attention.

"What's she doing?"

Macha tugged on his sleeve. "No time. Whatever that crazy Isaye is doing, it won't distract the charr for very long, so we'd better be in the water before she gets rolling." The two edged through the crowd to the harbor. The *Brutality* was on a shared wharf, and three potbellied asuran schooners were also docked down its length.

Macha waved to one, passing the time as if nothing of importance was happening, while Cobiah kept a watchful eye on the *Brutality*'s guards.

Contemplating what Isaye could be doing, Cobiah leaned over the railing of the pier. He looked at the ocean churning far below, frothing in shades of white and gray against a cold, sandy beach. The wood of the railing was hard and cool, thick enough to walk on . . .

Did you really see a mermaid, Cobiah? A really-real one?

"Cobiah? Are you all right?" Several moments had passed while he stood in fugue. Macha waited at his elbow, her black eyes wide with concern. "It's time to go. Isaye and Henst are making a distraction—"

"Henst?" Cobiah shook himself and raised his head.

The two charr at the end of the wharf were slouching, weary from a long night's watch. Their hands rested on the hilts of their weapons and their conversation was kept low. Cobiah could see Isaye and Henst sauntering past the pier, talking a little too loudly. Although he couldn't catch the words, Cobiah could hear their tone— snarky, taunting, and cruel. "By Balthazar," Cobiah said, faltering. "She's *provoking* them!"

"Using Henst as bait? Oh, that's genius. Imagine if old Grist was here to see this! He'd have joined in faster than you can say 'legerdemain.'" Macha eyed the fight with pure joy. "Isaye's right, though: if there's one thing those charr can't resist, it's battle. Better still if it's an opportunity to get their claws on ol' Mr. 'I'm the prince of Ascalon'!" Macha jumped up, grabbing the rail and pulling herself up to stand on it. "Shrewd. I would never have guessed that human woman had the brains to come up with a plan like that—it's positively asuran. Who knew? Let me get up here, and I can get a better look—"

Instinctively, Cobiah grabbed Macha around the waist

and swung her down. His reaction was swift and violent. "What the blue blazes are you doing? That's dangerous! You could slip!"

"Cogswallop!" Macha yelped, shoving him away. "Coby! Ow, that hurt! What's your malfunction? I was just trying to see what they're doing!" Wincing, she grabbed her side where Cobiah's arm had slung her.

"You can see just fine from down here." Now that the adrenaline rush was passing, Cobiah felt vaguely sick to his stomach. Images passed before his eyes—a tiny black shoe with a rusty silver buckle beneath an old green blanket. A crowd of faces on the beach. His mother's curses . . . Cobiah stifled the thoughts, trying to calm down. Macha stared at him furiously. Awkwardly, he added, "I'm sorry if I hurt you. I was just trying to keep you safe."

The asura's demeanor softened. "I'm fine." Macha might have added something else, but she never had the chance. A roar on the charr dock grabbed their attention. As they watched, Henst slammed the butt of a boat hook into a charr's belly. The second one charged the black-haired human, but Isaye hefted a huge coil of heavy rope at him. The wrist-thick strands of the coil, bundled together, slammed into the back of the second charr's knees. He buckled, toppling forward with a yelp of pain. Whatever Isaye and Henst had said to the charr, it had apparently worked. They were certainly distracted.

"Now, Coby," Macha insisted. "We have to go now!" She grabbed the rungs of a ladder that led down to the beach, but Cobiah stopped her.

"There's still a guard. Look there, on the ship." He pointed, and they could see a gruff-looking charr standing on the deck of the *Brutality*, watching the fight on the dock—but not moving. "I need you to cover me with an illusion, so he doesn't see me swimming out to the ship."

"But, Coby, I was going to go with you—"

"No time. You can't cast that spell and swim, can you?" When Macha shook her head despondently, Cobiah grabbed the ladder. "I need you here. Cast your spell and then keep an eye out. After I'm on board, head for the drunk tank. Isaye and Henst are going to need you to bail them out of jail." He shot her a smile.

Jumping onto the dock ladder, Cobiah climbed down, speeding along its length with the nimbleness of a moss spider. He pushed off the end of the ladder into the ocean, where the water was crisp and frigid, filled with the deep chill of the past night. He gasped as he sank into it. "Melandru's waggling arse, that's cold!"

"Shhh! Swim quietly!" On the dock above, Macha began casting. Cobiah looked down and saw his hands, his arms, his entire body turning the same color as the sea. He paused to give Macha a thumbs-up, then realized she probably couldn't see it.

As Cobiah swam toward the ship, he could hear Isaye and Henst brawling with the two charr at the end of the dock. A crowd had gathered around them, taunting them and cheering on the fight. Henst had broken his boat hook in half and was pummeling one of the charr with a stick in each hand, while Isaye clapped the second guard over the head with the lid of a trash bin. Her opponent fell to the ground in a stupor, while his companion— momentarily escaping from Henst—tackled Isaye and bore her to the ground. Nobody was paying any attention to the docks or the *Brutality*.

Cobiah wrapped his arms around the anchor chain and pulled himself up out of the water. "By Grenth." He hung there, shivering. "I think it's colder *outside* the water." Looping his arm through each chain link in turn, Cobiah pulled himself up toward the *Brutality*.

By the time he reached the ship's hull, his clothing had begun to dry, and the coloring that made him near invisible was fading. The fight on the docks had started to peter out as well. He could hear the Lionguard breaking things up on the pier, and the charr replacements for wharf guard duty were taking their places. Isaye, Henst, and the two night guards were clapped in handcuffs and dragged off to the town jail. Macha stood on the dock, watching him with dismay. Unable to soothe her worries, Cobiah pulled himself through a nearby porthole, rolling forward in an effort to be silent as he landed inside. She'd just have to trust that he'd be safe.

The darkness of the *Brutality's* cargo hold seemed impenetrable after the bright light of morning. Cobiah tried to see, but the room was little more than a dark blur after the brilliance of the morning sun. Sparkles of dust danced through the porthole window, glittering on the puddles of water around his feet. Kneeling behind a crate, he took a moment to let his eyes adjust, trying to pick out the details of the various boxes and kegs stacked within the *Brutality's* hold.

As Cobiah's eyes finally adjusted to the gloom, he could see that many of the crates in the hold were marked with warnings—"no fire," "no impact," "be careful around heat," and so forth. Near the stairs to the upper deck stood a workbench covered with tools. Cobiah edged his way toward it, glancing up at the sealed hatch in the ceiling, above the narrow staircase. Once there, Cobiah ran his hands over the implements curiously.

Cobiah studied the tools, trying to find something incriminating among the screwdrivers, pliers, clamps, and . . . other . . . things. Some of the devices looked like those he'd seen in Sykox's toolbox, while others were completely foreign. He picked up one of the rods and twisted the handle, watching the tip rotate with a metallic buzzing sound. "Ooooh. Interesting."

The hatch above creaked open with a sudden slam, and heavy boot steps pounded on the stairs into the hold. Thinking quickly, Cobiah ducked beneath the workbench. Realizing he was still holding the strange tool, he shoved it into his pocket with a silently mouthed curse. The sunlight had half blinded him when he first came into the hold. Maybe he'd get lucky and the charr would be similarly impaired. Or just not notice it was missing.

Voices bellowed from above as two charr made their way down into the hold. "A fight? By the lost Claw of the Khan-Ur. Can't I trust those Zeal warband morons with the simplest tasks?" The voice belonged to Grimjaw, and he was complaining broadly as he stormed down the stairs. His first mate, a burly charr with a spiked orange mane, carried a lantern as he followed Grimjaw into the hold. "Every single time I ask them to take duty, they end up in a brawl."

"What did you expect?" The first mate shrugged. "They're Blood Legion. You knew that when you signed them aboard."

"Yeah, I knew it. But I figured they'd at least need to take breaths between fights. This has been a nonstop problem, Krokar. They're a complete waste of good munitions. We should have hired crew from our own legion, Ash." Grimjaw walked among the crates in the hold, but the first mate paused at the bottom of the stairs. "Then we'd be on task for silent sailing."

"Couldn't find 'em," Krokar said. "Blood was all the fort had to offer." He watched as Grimjaw moved through the crates, opening one after the other. "What'd ya need down here, Legionnaire?"

"First plan didn't work." Grimjaw scowled, pushing

crates around. "Well, the bomb we sent to the *Nomad* worked fine, but that skritt-sucking courier screwed it all up. Now we've got a new plan, and that means we need another bomb." He stuck his muzzle inside one of the boxes, sniffing its contents to detect what was inside. "Blew up a whole damn ship and still missed the target. We're in for it if we don't come up with something else—and quick. The meeting's this afternoon, and if that vote goes the wrong way, we could lose everything."

"Look, we did everything the boss wanted. What more can he ask?" Krokar complained.

"He asked us to do it *right,* and we chumped it, Krokar. This guy may not be a tribune or even a charr, but he's dead-on dangerous. We screw this up again, and he just might toss a torch into our hold himself."

The first mate groused, "C'mon, Grimjaw. This is ridiculous. Why can't we just *seize* the ships we want? If we commandeer them, we don't have to work with this human at all."

"Commandeer them with what crew? We had a hard enough time finding troops to sail the *Brutality.* We're only eighteen charr, and we're promised six more ships. You think three charr can crew a clipper? A galleon? How about the *Pride*—do you think three lone charr can sail *that* ship? That engine's the key to my promotion to the rank of tribune, and I'll do whatever I have to do to get it."

"Shut up and bite your tongue 'til this thing's over. We've got to have his help if we're going to attack Orr, tub face. Use your brain," Grimjaw groused, ripping another crate open to poke at the contents.

Cobiah stiffened. His hand clenched the table leg as he willed himself to stay silent. He didn't think he could take the two charr in a fight, but he was still willing to try.

They wanted to steal his ship? What was this "plan," and who were they working with?

"Aha. This'll do the trick." Grimjaw held up another bomb, this one made of gunpowder rods that the charr used for deep mining. The captain rolled a length of fuse around his wrist and tucked the explosive into his vest.

"What're we going to do with that?" Krokar tilted his head as Grimjaw stomped back through the hold.

An evil grin curled the charr captain's muzzle. Grimjaw clapped his first mate on the shoulder as he headed back to the stairs. "We're improvising, Krokar," he said, gloating. "The first bomb failed. But I'm going to go one better. I'm going to set *this* one where it can do us even more good."

"Where's that?" Krokar asked.

"Inside the Captain's Council. When all the captains are dead, he'll be able to take over the city. Then we'll get our ships. Good, huh?"

"Kill the other captains?" A slow dawn of comprehension rose over Krokar's dull features. "Hey, that's good! Then you'll be in control of the council!"

"Right you are. We'll make him king of Lion's Arch, I'll get the ships and crew we need to attack Orr, and I'll have the *Pride*." The snaggletoothed charr laughed, low and dangerous.

The first mate chuckled with him. "Then we attack Orr."

"Then we attack Orr, right. Trust me, the boss's going to love this plan." Grimjaw's boots shook the boards of the staircase as he marched toward the *Brutality*'s upper deck. "Come on. We've got to get to the pavilion and set this bomb before the others arrive."

Krokar followed, and the two charr slammed the hatch behind them, locking it from the far side. Cobiah wriggled out from under the workbench. "Those murderous sea sharks!" he seethed. "I've got to get back to the docks and . . ." As he made his way toward the porthole, the depth of the problem unfolded in his mind.

Once Grimjaw knew the jig was up, he'd stop talking. The charr had powerful friends, and whoever was behind this plan was willing to go to great lengths to make sure it worked. If he didn't handle this just right, he'd lose his only lead toward finding the real traitor. Cobiah slowed, bowing his head in frustration. As much as he wanted to rush after Grimjaw and attack, that wouldn't solve the problem.

Cobiah squared his shoulders and looked out the porthole, watching as the far dock cast its morning shadow over the turquoise waves. *King of Lion's Arch.* Cobiah pondered the words. Whom had Grimjaw meant? Nodobe, probably, but it could have been anyone. By the Mists, it might not even be a captain. Grimjaw's "boss" could be anyone with a vested interest in the council's vote. Cobiah's mind filled with scenarios, but with little time and few avenues of information, he kept coming back to the same thought.

I have to let Grimjaw set the bomb. Cobiah pondered. *He's not going to blow himself up. When Grimjaw finds an excuse to leave the council meeting, I'll see who goes with him. That's how I'll be able to tell whom he's working with.* Cobiah gripped one of the crates angrily, closing his eyes at the thought.

They'll be leaving the rest of us to die.

I t was nearly noon by the time Cobiah escaped the *Brutality*'s hold. He was forced to wait until harbor traffic slowed before he could slip back down the anchor chain into the sea. Wet and angry, he swam to shore a few piers down from the charr dock. There, Cobiah pulled off his boots with a grimace. He dumped two long streams of water onto the sand. There was no time to change his clothes or shower. The captains' meeting would begin in less than an hour, and he had to get there quickly. Cobiah shook the sand from his clothing as best he could and headed into the city streets.

Lion's Arch was filled with hustle and bustle: merchants selling their wares and eager crewmen on leave spending time in the city. Cobiah would usually have enjoyed a stroll through the alleys, but today he had no time for pleasantries or idle curiosity. He made his way toward the pavilion on the cliff with hurried steps.

Near the center of the city, he detoured to pass the primary Lionguard outpost, where Captain Duserm's militia was releasing two battered charr into the street. "You're lucky!" Duserm scolded them. "Next time I catch you fighting on the docks, I won't let you out of the drunk tank for three days!" He chuckled at their discontent, his portly belly bouncing over a tightly cinched belt. Noting Cobiah, the captain stiffened and managed a halfhearted salute. "Captain M-M-Marriner," he stammered, "what brings you down here?"

"Captain Isaye," Cobiah answered. "Is she in there?"

"No, sir." Duserm gave him a lopsided grin. "Got bailed out a half hour ago by your asuran pilot, both the captain and her mate. They headed that way." He gestured vaguely toward the pavilion.

"Right." Ignoring the man's attempts to make polite conversation, Cobiah renewed his haste toward the council building. He could hear Duserm's voice fading behind him; he was muttering something about the discourtesy of those in charge.

Cobiah took the steps to the pavilion three at a time, bustling up toward the high cliff. He could see some of the captains already gathered at the front door of the building. A voice caught his attention, and he paused to look along the building's side.

Henst stood there, bristling, hands on his weapons. In front of him stood Macha, a sword belt wrapped over her shoulder, the cutlass poking out like Bronn Svaard's ever-present greatsword. "How dare you try to blackmail me!" Henst snarled. "You conniving little runt!"

"I got you out of that mess."

"You got me into it!"

"What the hell are you doing, Henst?" Cobiah strode up to them angrily. "Leave her alone."

"Marriner." Eyes flashing, Henst rounded on Cobiah. "Don't tell me what to do."

Impulsively, Macha seized Henst's distraction to stomp on his foot with all her might, causing the dark-haired warrior to let out a screech of surprise and pain. "Show some gratitude, you fish-livered blackguard, or next time"—she shoved him backward—"I'll leave you in prison where you belong!" Henst hopped up and down, looking for a moment as if he might draw his swords, but Cobiah stepped close to meet the Ascalonian's eyes.

"Do we need to have this little lesson again, Henst?" Cobiah's voice was calm, but his eyes were fierce. "Leave my crew alone."

"You heard him," Macha added smugly from behind Cobiah's legs.

Visibly losing his eagerness for the fight, Henst gathered himself and stepped back. His black eyes were heated and his face red from anger, but he managed to speak in an even tone. "Fine," he said tensely. "But I don't owe you anything, Macha. If I have to pay, then so will you." He shot a nasty glance at the asura.

Cobiah glowered. "That's *enough*, Henst."

Henst turned on his heel and limped toward the pavilion, trying to salvage his pride. Cobiah mused smugly, pleased at his rival's discomfort. Few things put him in a better mood than taking the wind out of the Ascalonian's sails. "What was that all about?"

Macha smiled sweetly, hugging Cobiah's legs. "I told him that he had to pay me back the money for his bail. He didn't agree." She stuck out her tongue at the man's back as he retreated. "Oh, and I brought your sword." Macha slipped the belt over her shoulder and held out the weapon in its scabbard. "I thought you might need it, given how today's going."

Cobiah laughed out loud. "Thanks, Macha." Before she could dart away into the building, Cobiah reined her in by the braids. "Hang on. I need to tell you what I found on Grimjaw's ship." She paused and looked up at him inquisitively, and Cobiah pitched his voice low. "We were right. Grimjaw made that bomb. And it's not the only one. He had another, and he's hidden it somewhere in the Captain's Council."

Macha's eyes flew wide open. "Inside the building?"

"Yeah." Cobiah nodded, buckling the sword belt around his waist. "It's all right, though. I have a plan. Grimjaw's not going to set off the bomb while he's inside the building. All we have to do is wait until he tries to leave and then see who he takes with him. That's how we'll know who he's working with." Macha started to protest, but Cobiah cut her off. "Yes, I know it's dangerous. But it's our only hope to find out who's really behind this."

"Cobiah, this isn't someone you can bluff or a ship you can outmaneuver. This is a *bomb*. What if Grimjaw set it wrong? What if the real villain isn't even in there and sets it off before Grimjaw's ready?" Macha grabbed Cobiah's sleeve. "This is a crazy plan, Cobiah. We should tell the others what's going on and get out of here. Why are we risking our lives?"

"If we do that, we've foiled one plan, but we haven't caught the culprit. They'll try again, and next time they'll catch us by surprise."

"Is this city really that important?" she pleaded. "Enough to get killed over? Look, we could just sail away and let this all sort itself out. The *Pride*—"

Cobiah put his hand on Macha's shoulder. "Macha, you're a good friend, and you've been with me through some very difficult times. I don't know if I ever really told you how much you mean to me. I've been busy lately, and it's taken me away from you and the others. I'm sorry. Maybe that makes me a bad friend. If it does, I hope you forgive me."

Macha placed her hand over his. "You've never been anything but good to me, Cobiah. I'd do anything for you. I'd die for you. Like Verahd did for Isaye. You're my captain."

"Then you understand how important this is. Lion's Arch is the first city that's really been a home to all the people of Tyria, no matter what race they are, or where they come from. It's known real freedom." He slid his hand away and headed up the stairs. "That's worth fighting for."

As Cobiah walked toward the building, Macha looked up at the sky, pursing her lips, and then down at the cobblestones that ran through the city streets. Then she followed him, dragging her feet reluctantly up the stairs toward the pavilion.

Hedda and Moran were already seated at the table, arguing over some point of seafaring lore. Grimjaw was sitting near the others, his long claws tapping the table in a slow, calculated rhythm. Isaye was there, too, sitting beside Nodobe, their seconds chatting pleasantly behind them.

Isaye appeared no worse for wear from her fight on the docks or her time in detention. She'd apparently been able to arrange a change of clothing, and she had placed a small bandage over her eye where a blow had split the skin. Nodobe took her arm as they laughed over some story, his broad smile shockingly white against ebony skin. The familiarity rankled, but Cobiah was so glad to see her alive and well that the feeling washed away like water over a drake's back. She noticed Cobiah at the door and gave him a joyful smile.

As soon as Cobiah entered the council room, the asuran captain, Tarb, strode toward him, muttering in a dark tone. "Marriner, I want to talk to you," Tarb said. "Right here and right now."

Cobiah slowed. "What's the problem, Tarb?" he said

cautiously, struggling to appear interested while keeping an eye on the five at the table.

"Why aren't you willing to compromise on the Claw Island thing? It's been years since they started building on the island, and it could be years more before they're done. What I'm calling for will help the city *now*. A bank. More shops. Are you deliberately stifling the city's growth?" Tarb puffed up like a little rooster. Behind him walked his second, Gamina, carrying a tablet on which she was taking notes.

Cobiah tried to follow the asura's argument, but his mind was on other things. "Can we talk about this during the meeting?"

"I want an answer *now*. An honest answer, not one prettified for politics." Tarb shoved his finger up toward Cobiah's face. "Are you getting a cut from the contractors? A promise of military authority to back you on the council? What is it?"

"What?" Cobiah's attention snapped fully to the asura. "No. Nothing like that. I just want the city to be safe."

Tarb fixed him with a steely gaze. "Whatever you say, Marriner," the warrior grumbled. "But I know payoff when I smell it. I just want you to know: I'm *watching* you." Tarb pointed at his eyes, then at Cobiah, and then stalked off toward the table, unslinging the war hammer from his back with a resounding *whump!* Gamina paused, looked up at Cobiah awkwardly, then shrugged and followed her captain to his seat.

One by one, the seats at the table were filling. Cobiah deliberately took the chair across from Grimjaw, meeting the charr's eyes without shrinking. Grimjaw grinned, showing all of his snaggled, uneven teeth. It turned Cobiah's stomach to smile pleasantly back, but he managed. Yomm was last to arrive, shuffling along in a heavy new robe ornamented with anchors, gold braid, and shiny buttons shaped like lions' heads. He waved his arms as he walked, deliberately showing off the ornate trim on the sleeves.

Macha rolled her eyes. "I was hoping he'd sleep through the meeting," she muttered, a little too loud. Yomm shot her a nasty look.

"Are we all here, then?" Nodobe made a show of counting chairs. "Eight. Good. Then let us all sit and discuss the future of our city."

Cobiah tensed, watching Grimjaw out of the corner of his eye. The charr shifted in his seat but showed no sign of leaving. She looked at Cobiah questioningly, and he gave her a smile. There was no opportunity to tell Isaye what he'd found aboard the *Brutality*, and even if he could, it would only worry her as it had Macha.

"This council was called to vote on the future of the city's monetary concerns." Nodobe reclined comfortably in his chair, looking for all the world as if he were addressing a room filled with his personal followers. Yesterday, it had rankled Cobiah to see Nodobe act like he was in charge. Today, Cobiah had far too much on his mind to try to compete. Nodobe continued. "Thanks to Yomm—excuse me, *Captain* Yomm—the city's treasury currently has enough gold to address some significant issues."

"Like finishing the fortress," Hedda chimed in.

Tarb said, "Or building a bank! By my golematronic grandmother, can we talk about that? I'm tired of keeping my money in my ship's hold. I'm a sailor, not a banker."

Laughing softly, Nodobe held up his palms. "We could do any of these things, assuredly. But we cannot do them all. The question before the council is, which should we choose?"

"Should we vote first?" Cobiah said quickly. "It seemed we were tangled in argument yesterday. I'm curious to see where the council stands this morning. If we have a tangible majority, then it will save us time spent flapping our jaws."

"An excellent point, Captain Marriner," Nodobe agreed. "Shall we vote on the primary allocation, then?"

"All those in favor of spending the majority of the money on our city's defense—more guns on the northern cliff, finishing the fortress on Claw Island, and increasing the city guard—raise your hand." Cobiah lifted his as he spoke, holding his palm above his shoulder.

Moran's hand shot up. "I've seen what those undead freighters can do. I don't want to take any chances." Hedda raised hers more slowly.

After a moment, Nodobe said, "Three. Very well, all those in favor of using the revenue on necessary internal upgrades: a bank, better roads into Kryta and through the Shiverpeaks, more buildings to house shops and trade." He lifted his hand, looking around the table expectantly.

Tarb was the first to join him, which was no surprise at all. Yomm's hand waved pointedly in the air as the shop-keep puffed up in smug contentment. Grimjaw made a show of pretending to consider both sides, rubbing his whiskers and flapping all four ears. At last the charr captain lifted his hand in affirmation, claws glinting in the sunshine that streamed down through the high windows.

"Isaye?" Tarb asked. "Your vote?"

"What does it matter?" Grimjaw jeered. "Four to three in favor."

She exchanged a glance with her second, and Henst put his hand on her arm reassuringly. "I think Lion's Arch needs upgrades in multiple areas if the city is going to thrive. I don't see why we can't split the money between the two."

"An abstention is still four to three." Grimjaw lowered his hands to the table, claws sinking into the thick wood. "We win."

"One moment, one moment, let's hear her out. If Isaye casts her vote in agreement with us," Moran argued, "we'd be tied at four to four until someone changes sides."

"That could take weeks!" Tarb groaned. "I have a vessel to run. Shipping deadlines to make. If I'm stuck here until Wintersday, how'm I going to pay my crew?"

The charr rumbled angrily and turned toward Isaye. "Look, Isaye, I know we've had our differences, but as you're the one that started the fight that landed my crewmen in the clink this morning, I figure you owe me some consideration." Grimjaw forcibly relaxed his fists and placed his pawlike hands on the table. "I want a word with you about your concerns, to see if you and I can come to a compromise. Then we'll have another vote. This time, no abstentions."

Nodobe tapped his fingers together. "Fine. We'll recess for five minutes. But let me tell you this, Grimjaw." Nodobe leaned toward the snaggletoothed charr and put ice in his voice. "If you bully her . . . if I hear one *whiff* of trouble . . ." The Elonian narrowed his eyes. "I'll see you in chains, pulling at my ship's oars. Understood?"

Visibly disturbed at the thought, Grimjaw nodded brusquely. He rose from the table and gestured to Isaye to follow him toward the front of the pavilion.

"There he goes," Macha hissed. "It's *Isaye*! We have to follow her."

Cobiah's breath caught in his throat. "What? It can't be Isaye. She wouldn't blow up her own ship—especially not while she was on it. She wouldn't leave me here to die."

"Maybe you care a lot more for her than she does for you, Cobiah," Macha said bitterly. "She's Krytan, remember? She works for Baede. I bet *he's* behind this. C'mon, we have to follow them."

He'll be king of Lion's Arch. Cobiah considered the thought fleetingly and then shook his head. "Isaye loves me. That was *her* ship. Verahd was her friend, and that bomb killed him. It doesn't make sense; there's no possible way it's Isaye. Grimjaw's going to come back into the room and then leave again with the real traitor. If we go after him now, we're giving ourselves away. I trust Isaye, Macha. We just have to be patient." Refusing to consider the alternative, Cobiah crossed his arms and settled into his chair. Around them, the other captains had broken into small talk and pleasantries, discussing the weather and their next trade runs.

Macha tugged harder at his sleeve. "Maybe I'm wrong, but can we take the chance? Get up, Coby. We can't stay here. *Please,* Cobiah!" A bead of perspiration ran down the asura's forehead, trickling across her temple and vanishing into her braids. Cobiah'd never seen her so jittery. Something was definitely wrong.

"Calm down, Macha," he said, taken aback.

"No, really, trust me—get up, we have to go. To follow them, I mean."

He twisted in his chair, staring at Macha in confusion. Why was she so insistent? Unless . . .

She wasn't just worried; she was panicking. A similar image leapt into Cobiah's mind: Macha, racing down the dock just before the bomb exploded, the same frightened look on her face. She said she'd merely followed the messenger, but when Macha was running up the *Nomad's* gangplank, she was yelling a warning.

"Macha." He gripped her arm. "How did you know about the bomb?"

"There's no time to argue, Cobiah. They're getting away. We have to go after Grimjaw . . ." Her voice trailed off urgently.

"The package on the *Nomad*. How did you know it was dangerous?" Instead of answering, Macha stammered, and Cobiah tightened his grip on her arm. "It was just an ordinary brown-paper package, Macha. It could have been anything. It didn't look like a bomb. Why were you in such a panic if you *didn't know what it was?*"

"Cobiah, you're wasting time." She trembled. By now, everyone at the table was staring at them. Macha yelped as Cobiah's hand clenched her wrist. "Isaye could be in danger—"

"*You* were Grimjaw's courier. You snuck onto Isaye's ship and placed the bomb in front of her cabin. You must have seen my coat on the pylon as you were leaving. That's when you realized I was aboard. That's when you started yelling for me to get off the ship."

"Cobiah, I'd never do anything to hurt you." Macha twisted in his grasp. The others couldn't hear the whispered words, but they could see that Cobiah's face was flushed with rage.

"Not me, maybe. But Isaye?" Cobiah's mind was racing. He jerked the asura closer, growling in rage. "By Dwayna, now I understand! Without Isaye, I don't have any reason to stay in Lion's Arch. In fact, I'd *want* to leave. Isn't that what I told you the morning before the bomb was set?" He shook the asura roughly. "Are you behind all this, Macha?"

"No!" Macha protested. "But I know who is. And yes, I helped him. But that's why we were arguing; I changed my mind. I was going to tell you the truth. You have to believe me, I didn't know there was a bomb here! He was willing to kill me, too." Tears ran down the asura's cheeks, falling on her robin's-egg-blue robe. "Please, Coby, you have to understand. I wanted to get out of this stinking city. I just wanted our life back—sailing on the *Pride* with all of our friends. Like it was before Isaye."

"Who sent the bomb, Macha?"

With tears still running down her cheeks, Macha pointed across the room. "*He* did." Cobiah turned to follow her accusatory finger and saw Isaye and Grimjaw, headed out the front doors of the pavilion, their seconds at their sides. Isaye. Grimjaw. Grimjaw's second, Krokar, and Isaye's second, Henst. And just like that, everything fell into place.

My grandfather was a member of the Asculonian nobility.

Mr. "I'm the prince of Ascalon."

He'll be king of Lion's Arch.

Cobiah hurled himself up out of the chair, still gripping the asura's wrist. "Isaye!" he shouted. The small group paused at the doorway. "Henst sent the bomb. He was trying to kill you and inherit your seat on the Captain's Council. If you let him leave the room, we're all going to die." Everyone in the room froze in surprise, and Hedda let out a little gasp. Isaye stared at Cobiah in utter disbelief.

Nodobe was the first to speak. The dark-skinned captain said slowly, "That's a serious accusation, Captain Mariner. Do you have any evidence?"

"Yeah. Looks like I do," Cobiah said, pulling Macha forward. He rounded on the asura. "This is your one chance, Macha. Explain, or I swear, I'll sit down, Grimjaw will blow that bomb, and we'll all become fizzy-widgets in the Eternal Alchemical . . . thingy."

"The Eternal Alchemy," Macha breathed, dabbing at her tears. "Oh, Coby. You *were* listening."

"Spill, Macha!"

Macha jumped nervously. "It was his idea!" she said,

pointing at Henst. "He made a deal with the king of Kryta. If Henst could take over Lion's Arch, King Baede would recognize his authority as a fellow royal and lend him troops and ships to secure the city and drive out all nonhumans. Lion's Arch would become a 'new home for displaced Ascalonians,' and Henst would be their king."

Cobiah prodded her again. "Now the part about Isaye, and the bomb on the *Nomad*."

The asura's shoulders slumped, and her voice fell. "Henst told Grimjaw to make the bomb that was supposed to take out Isaye. My job was to put the bomb on the ship, because I could get there without anyone seeing me." To the asura's credit, she looked as chagrined as she did bitter. "Originally, Henst was going to buy a ship and get his own seat on the council, but one vote wouldn't have been enough. He needed more. So we came up with a plan.

"Henst gave his money to Yomm to buy a seat instead, and then he planned to kill Isaye. Henst was her first mate; he'd inherit her seat on the council. With Isaye dead, I could convince Cobiah to leave the city. Henst, Grimjaw, and Yomm could all vote against spending more money on the city's defenses, and once Lion's Arch was unprotected, King Baede's troops would sweep in and declare Henst king of the city . . ."

"What was Grimjaw getting? How did Henst convince him to help?" Cobiah pressed her ruthlessly.

"Henst made Grimjaw a deal. Once Henst took over the city, he'd use Baede's backing to give Grimjaw ships, and Grimjaw would convince the nonhumans leaving Lion's Arch to crew them. He'd get what he wanted— an armada to go attack Orr. I'm betting neither Henst nor Baede would give a flap at that point if those ships were successful, so long as they left Lion's Arch." Macha's ears wiggled despondently. "Henst also promised to give

Grimjaw the *Pride*." She shook her head. "Stupid charr believed him."

"This is all ridiculous!" Grimjaw bellowed from the other side of the room. "The asura's lying. Not a word of it is true. If Macha put a bomb on the *Nomad* and she wants to admit it, then that's her concern. I had nothing to do with any of it, and neither did Henst." For his part, Henst stood silently by Isaye's side, looking like a thunderous storm cloud. He kept his hands on his sword hilts, and his eyes glittered with anger.

"Henst wasn't going to give you the *Pride* anyway, you drooling git. He was going to give it to King Baede." Macha snorted derisively.

"The *Pride* was mine! He promised!" Grimjaw said, his temper flaring. "You take that back!"

In the echo of his words, Cobiah felt rather than heard every person in the room turn to stare at the charr. "And there, ladies and gentlemen," Macha said, gesturing with a flourish, "I give you the ancient asuran legal tradition of Testimony by Idiot."

"You can't prove anything," Henst snarled. "You have no evidence."

"Where were you when the bomb was placed on the *Nomad*?" Cobiah said accusatorily. "You were off-ship, weren't you? Because you knew the ship would be attacked."

"Most of the crew was off-ship. We were on shore leave," Henst retorted.

"True. But I'll bet 'most of the crew' didn't take their rucksack ashore that night. Unlike you, they were planning on coming back to the ship. But you knew the *Nomad* would be on fire, didn't you, Henst? So you took all your important possessions off the ship and stored them somewhere safe." Cobiah's eyebrows knitted together with anger. "Unluckily for you, I saw your bag at Yomm's shop, though I didn't connect the two at the time.

"Nodobe, Tarb—Henst stays here." Cobiah directed them. "Moran, go to Yomm's and search that rucksack. If Macha's story is true, we'll find proof there. Letters, I'd imagine, signed by King Baede."

In an instant, Henst drew his swords. "You are too clever by far, Cobiah Marriner." Grimjaw's weapons followed in the blink of an eye, a dagger in one hand and a pistol in the other. Isaye stood trapped by a field of weapons, her jaw tensed and her face pale. "Not a move, Captain Isaye. I wouldn't want to spill blood on the council floor." Henst spoke quietly, raising one of his swords to Isaye's throat as his eyes flicked to Cobiah and the others. "We're going to back out of the room, and you're going to let us—or I'm afraid she dies."

"If you leave, Grimjaw sets off the bomb, and we all die anyway. That is, if I'm understanding all this madness." Old Captain Moran pushed his chair away from the table, rolling to his feet with the sway of a practiced sailor. He drew his mace and tamped the heavy spiked ball rhythmically into his hand. "The hell if I'll just sit on my thumb and go quietly."

"Nobody's going anywhere," Cobiah growled, his cutlass already in his hand.

Nodobe rose as well, and Hedda and Tarb, the first cracking her knuckles and the second reaching for the hilt of his heavy war hammer. With a smile of grudging admiration, Nodobe said, "For once I am forced to agree with my associate Captain Marriner."

Henst snarled, "Then it would appear we're at an impasse."

"Not on my account." Before Henst could react, Isaye thrust her elbow into his rib cage and grabbed for the sword in his left hand. Henst staggered, relinquishing the weapon, but when he snapped back, he was twice as angry. He shoved Isaye, knocking her newly seized sword aside, and cracked his fist viciously against her jaw.

Grimjaw and Krokar paused, exchanged a swift look, and ran.

"Get them!" Hedda yelled, lunging over the captains' table. "Don't let the charr escape!" Several of the others raced forward, joining in the fight.

Cobiah spun Macha around and shoved her toward Moran. "Osh!" he yelled to his old friend. "Tie her up— we'll deal with her after this is handled."

Moran quickly stripped a long sash from his waist. Ignoring the asura's protests, he bodily lifted Macha and placed her in a chair, twining the sash through the heavy wooden arms and around her wrists. With a seaman's quick knots, he secured the rope, locking her inside the chair. "What if the bomb goes off?" Macha wailed.

"Then we're all done for," he retorted gruffly. "So you better stop complaining and start praying." With that, he turned his back on her and stormed across the room toward the fight.

"Asura don't pray!" Macha screamed after him, jolting about in her chair. The old gray captain ignored her and kept walking. "Let me go! You hear me? Moran? Moran, don't walk away from me! There's a bomb, didn't you hear? Let . . . me . . . go!"

23

The brawl in the pavilion quickly spiraled out of control. At Grimjaw's shout, his warband from the *Brutality* poured in the front door, weapons at the ready. Tarb, Hedda, and Moran charged the warband and blocked Grimjaw's path out the door, preventing his escape. Isaye and Henst faced one another in battle, their swords flashing back and forth as each tried to find a hole in the other's guard. Nodobe stayed well back near the table, reaching for the dagger in his belt. He chanted grim words of magic, and a sickly light began to coalesce around his fingers. Still, the captains were outclassed— even with their seconds, they were fighting against ten battle-hardened charr.

Yomm huddled under the edge of the captains' table, pulling his glittering golden robe close about him. "I thought you said you could fight!" Cobiah mocked him, charging toward the battle.

"I *can* fight!" the shopkeep whimpered. "But it's madness out there!"

Krokar, Grimjaw's second, bore down on old Captain Moran with a vicious-looking hooked knife. Moran blocked the blow, cracking his forearm against the charr's wrist midthrust. The captain was not all he had been in his youth, and the blow did not make the charr drop the knife. Instead, it slashed through Moran's guard, sinking deeply into the old man's shoulder. With a yelp of pain, Moran pulled out the knife and then resheathed it in Krokar's chest.

To the side, Captain Hedda took on three charr at once. She'd picked up a heavy oak bench, her arms rippling with massive strength beneath the softness of her chubby body. When all three charged her, Hedda set her feet and held the bench crosswise in front of her chest, setting her entire weight against it. Even with all three charr pushing as hard as they could, the buxom norn woman walked forward step by step, shoving them back with each stride. When she reached the edge of the pavilion, Hedda gave a roar and slammed the bench back even farther, pinning all three squirming soldiers against the wall.

Nodobe's hex left his hand in a blaze of sickening greenish light as he finished the spell. It swirled through the air, leaving a trail of smoky ash in its wake, and then cascaded toward the captain of the charr. When it reached them, it exploded into a buzzing mass of insects, biting and digging into Grimjaw's skin and expanding to encompass those nearby. Immediately, all three charr started howling in pain, scratching at their skin. They scratched so hard that their claws tore away hunks of fur. "Necromancy?" one of the charr roared toward Nodobe. "You disreputable human *scum!*"

Fighting the urge to continue tearing at his itching skin, Grimjaw raised his pistol and fired toward Nodobe, but the shot went wild. The ball of iron careened toward Tarb and caught the asura warrior in the ribs. Tarb gasped but didn't falter, swinging his war hammer like a striking hawk. The heavy iron of the weapon's head cracked solidly into Grimjaw's knees. The charr howled in pain, staggering, but fired the pistol again. The second shot hit Tarb's forearm, and within moments, the asura's sleeve was covered in blood.

Cobiah slashed at Grimjaw's pistol, trying to cut off the arm that held it. Grimjaw blocked the strike using the dagger in his other hand, then raised the same fist to punch Cobiah in the jaw. Spinning, he kicked Tarb in the belly with the same motion. The charr's boot struck the asura's hip and knocked Tarb sprawling. The asura climbed back to his feet slowly, never losing his grip on the war hammer. While he was recovering his balance, Cobiah stepped in to deflect Grimjaw's next blow. Cobiah bullied the charr backward, away from Tarb, keeping Grimjaw's weapons engaged and his line of fire to the asura blocked.

Nearer to the door, Isaye and Henst continued their combat. Isaye's leg was bleeding from one of Henst's attacks, pale skin and a red wound showing through a long cut in her breeches. Henst taunted her with each exchange of blows, drawing Isaye ever closer to the pavilion door. Cobiah understood why. With the bomb still somewhere inside the building, Henst was trying to escape so that he could set it off himself, leaving the rest to die. Although she was good with a sword, Isaye was not a match for Henst. She was surviving on sheer anger and dexterity, but eventually her luck would run out, and Henst's skill would determine the victor.

Cobiah pushed away his instinct to leap to her defense and tried to focus on Grimjaw. He ducked as the charr ferociously lashed out with his dagger, trying to force Cobiah away. Tarb, still behind Cobiah, swung over Cobiah's back and slammed his war hammer into Grimjaw's elbow. While the charr captain was shouting and flapping his arm in distress, Cobiah seized his chance. He grabbed the charr's massive horn and wrenched Grimjaw's head to the side. When Grimjaw stumbled, Cobiah kneed him in the stomach, but the charr's return punch knocked away Cobiah's sword. The weapon clattered to the ground at their feet, but Cobiah couldn't afford to let go of Grimjaw's horn, not with a pistol still waving in his enemy's hand. Rather than pick up the sword, risking a gunshot wound, Cobiah bent over and grabbed one of Grimjaw's four ears in his mouth. He bit down viciously.

Grimjaw howled in pain. "Marriner!" he shrieked. "You don't fight fair!"

"I fight like a charr!" Cobiah retorted through clamped teeth.

While the charr's attention was diverted, Tarb swung his war hammer behind his body. He twisted forward and swung the hammer in an underhand arc, first down and then up—straight between the charr captain's legs. Grimjaw's shriek transformed into a guttural, choking sound. His pistol fell from numb fingers, and his legs clamped together. He fell to his knees, and Cobiah scooped up his fallen sword and cracked Grimjaw across the back of the neck with the hilt. With a whimper, Grimjaw crumpled to the ground.

"The concept of 'fair' relies on an inaccurate understanding of physics," Tarb sniffed. "And I fight like an asura, thank you very much."

"Marriner!" The voice was shaky, but it was clearly Moran. Cobiah spun and saw two of Grimjaw's warband facing the old captain. Moran had raised a guardian shield of blue magic, but the energy was flickering and fading as the charr pounded on it with their weapons. Losing its cohesion, Moran's shield finally crumpled and dissolved.

"No!" Cobiah screamed, starting toward them, but he was too far away. One of the charr thrust his sword through the last shreds of Osh Moran's magic, spearing the gray-haired captain with the full length of his blade. The other slashed at Moran, intending to cut off the human's head before help could arrive—but before the blow could land, Tarb's assistant, Gamina, chucked a flowerpot from the far side of the room. Her aim was true, and her arm was good. The pot caught that charr dead in the muzzle, knocking him unconscious to the ground. Gamina lifted another pot to her shoulder, a solemn, grim look on her face, and Tarb shot her an approving smile.

Just then Cobiah reached them. He leapt onto the still-standing charr, enraged and slashing wildly with his cutlass. The soldier fell back from Cobiah's onslaught, surprised by the attack. Cobiah knocked him back farther and swept his cutlass twice, ending the charr's life in a quick instant.

Dropping his sword to the ground, Cobiah knelt next to the old captain. "Moran . . ." Cobiah's voice broke with sorrow. It was too late to help him. The old captain's eyes were already fixed in death.

Swords rang as they clashed together, Isaye still pressing Henst to his utmost. Her first mate was falling back now, struggling to keep up with her last wild blows, and Isaye knew her time was running out. She used every dirty trick in the book to gain an advantage. First she toppled a chair, kicking it at him; then she spun low and slashed at his ankles, forcing Henst to defy gravity if he wanted to keep his feet attached to his legs. For his part, the black-haired man fought determinedly, refusing to admit defeat even when Isaye's sword cut a deep gash across his chest and arm.

Isaye tried for another, hoping to spear him with her sword. Henst dodged to the side, spinning out of the way of her blade, and caught her shoulder with his hand. He jerked her off balance, his weapon hurtling through the air to cut her open in a single slash. Isaye saw the danger and pulled her weapon down to block it, ending up inches from Henst with the two swords crossed between their bodies. They paused there, steel on steel, locked in a battle of will and strength.

With a shout of anger, Isaye drove the heel of her foot into Henst's instep and shoved with all her might. It may have been that he was growing weary or that Macha's similar move in the alley outside the pavilion had already injured that particular foot, but Henst staggered, suddenly overbalanced. His arms pinned by the weapons, Henst toppled, his sword slipping away from Isaye's. With a sickening crunch, he landed amid the broken chairs and pottery, scrambling to find his footing in the mess. Isaye raised the sword in her hands, ready to finish Henst while he was off balance, but her surety flickered, and her blade wavered in the air above his chest. He was her first mate, after all.

Nodobe, on the other hand, was in no way conflicted. Chanting, the Elonian captain extended his hand, and a sickly green miasma rose from his fingers like steam on a summer day. The smoke whispered from Nodobe's fingers and clung to Henst's fallen form, slipping around the Ascalonian's arms and legs, creeping into his nose, ears, and mouth as he screamed. Henst thrashed as the spell lifted him from the stone floor of the pavilion, and gurgled as his throat closed. Isaye stepped back and lowered her sword, horrified, as Henst's skin paled and his flesh rotted from the inside out. Retching and clawing at the air, Henst writhed back and forth, trying to rid himself of the awful sickness, but his body only grew more withered and more desiccated with each passing second.

Moments later, the corpse fell to the ground. It was shriveled and dried to the core.

Revolted, Cobiah turned away. As the others lowered their weapons and accepted the surrender of the rest of Grimjaw's warband, he walked back to the table and placed his hand on the arched back of Macha's chair. She sat with her head bowed, staring down at her bound hands. "I'm sorry it came to this, Macha. I'll do everything I can to make sure you have a fair trial. No one is going to forget that you helped us today."

Quietly, the asura whispered, "I'm sorry, too, Cobiah. I just wanted you, and the *Pride*, and all the wonderful adventures we used to have. Every day, this damn city eats more and more of your soul. I can't be like that, Cobiah. I need to go on wandering. Inventing. Solving problems. All I do is sit around on an empty ship and think about how things should have been. I can't do that anymore. Not even for you."

"You've always been welcome by my side, Macha. You could have come into the city and helped . . ." Cobiah suddenly noticed that the asura was sitting completely still. Her lips weren't even moving. "Macha?" He reached out to touch her. As his fingers passed through the asura's shoulder, the entire illusion gave way in a delicate wash of smoke and twilight, revealing beneath it only Moran's sash tangled on the seat of the chair. "Macha!"

Her voice murmured sadly into his ear, "Good-bye, Cobiah. I'll see you soon."

The lie was a cutting reminder of a day on the docks when he'd made his sister the same promise. Cobiah bowed his head and he unashamedly let tears roll down his cheeks. "Good-bye, my friend."

In the quiet aftermath of the fighting, Yomm's voice rang out from a hidden cubby at the back of the room. "Hey, everybody!" he yelled. "Guess what? I found the bomb!"

"From the sacred text of Lyssa, goddess of love: *The road may be long, but you can walk it together. | There may be storms, but you can shelter one another. | The cold may come in winter, but you can be each other's warmth. | Each companion to the other: two souls, united. | May no weapon sever the bond that holds your hands together, | And may no word sever the love that keeps your hearts as one.*"

The priest tied a red wedding cord around the couple's wrists and made the sign of the goddess over their joined hands. "I now pronounce you, Cobiah and Isaye, married in the eyes of the Six Gods and within the laws of Lion's Arch. Congratulations."

Isaye pulled Cobiah's face down to hers, pressing a gentle kiss to his lips. "Hello, husband," she murmured. The crisp morning wind ruffled the long sheath of her white dress. Her dark hair, long and unbound, rippled like a banner, and summer flowers had been braided into a thin circlet atop her head.

"Hello, wife," he said in turn, his heart light with pride. Standing tall in one of the new captain's uniforms designed for Lion's Arch, Cobiah beamed down at her with joy.

A great cheer went up from the crowd gathered on the docks. Guns were fired into the air, both pistols and a few of the carronades from ships in the harbor, echoing like celebratory thunder across the sparkling waters of the bay. Sailors waved their hats and citizens waved flags in bright shades of blue and gold.

Waving to salute the crowd, Cobiah continued to hold Isaye's hand as he addressed them. "The city of Lion's Arch stands as a monument to the resiliency of the people of Tyria—no matter what race and no matter what their background. Although the city was destroyed, it has been rebuilt. Where lives were lost, new families will be raised, and new futures will be found.

"On behalf of myself and my wife, Isaye, I want to thank all of you for being part of our joyous day." Cobiah smiled. "It was in the spirit of cooperation that Lion's Arch was founded. Our hope was to create a safe haven for all races, but we must also ensure that the city is prosperous. I am proud to announce that we will be breaking ground on a new project: a bank to help our citizens raise money, store valuable items, and further our city's future." The crowd applauded warmly. Cobiah could see Yomm beaming from the porch of his shop.

After the speeches were over, Cobiah made his way through the crowd, shaking hand after hand. Isaye stayed behind to help with the great feast that had been planned in the city plaza. It seemed as though everyone in the city wanted to give him their best wishes, stopping him every few feet to pat him on the back or invite him to stop by their shops, eager to gain his attention. Word of the fight at the pavilion had also spread over the last few weeks, and the story had grown larger with each retelling. He'd saved the city from a takeover. He'd defended the captains against an assassin sent by King Baede. He'd stood up to an angel of Balthazar, come to force the city to return to Kryta. On the day of his wedding, especially, everyone wanted to shake his hand.

It didn't matter if Cobiah had wanted this future. He was the master of this ship, and he couldn't leave Lion's Arch midsail. He'd become indelibly linked to the city's spirit of freedom and hope for independence. A symbol of its future. Some of the citizens had even begun calling him "Commodore." He was flattered by their trust, and he planned to live up to it. He'd moved all of his belongings from the ship into the house he was building for himself and Isaye. It was a tall manor built from the hull of a ship, with sails in the Lion's Arch style and a wide view of the inner harbor. They could raise a family there. The thought made Cobiah smile, but it faded when he reached one of the gangplanks on the dock.

The ship moored there was the *Pride*, and she was readying to sail without him. Cobiah cupped his hands around his mouth and called out, "Ahoy, the ship! Permission to come aboard?"

Aysom leaned over the rail and waved enthusiastically. "Permission granted, Commodore! Come aboard; Cap'n Fassur's been waiting for you."

"When do you set out?"

"Soon," Fassur answered, shifting uncomfortably. "The tugs are already here to take us into the harbor. We sail on the next tide."

"You'll do well. You're ready for command, Fassur. You have been for years. I'm just glad you didn't have to kill me to take my place. There are some charr traditions I'm not eager to take part in."

Fassur chuckled but quickly sobered. "It'll be tough without our little mesmer. I still can't believe . . . I mean . . . I knew Macha was unhappy, but I never would have guessed . . ." Awkwardly, the charr shook himself as if to dismiss a bad feeling.

"She made her choice. We can't focus on it. We just have to move on." Cobiah reached out and clapped the big charr's shoulder, changing the subject. "Take care of my ship, Legionnaire. Take care of my crew. I expect them all to return in one piece, with profit enough to share."

Fassur laughed. "You'll get a share, Commodore. I promise you that. I may be the *Pride*'s commander, but you'll always be master of her heart." He seized Cobiah's wrist in a fierce clasp, his claws wrapping gently around Cobiah's forearm. "Steel won't yield, my friend."

"Steel won't yield," Cobiah repeated, giving Fassur the traditional handclasp of the Iron Legion. "I'll see you when you return." With a sigh, Cobiah stepped away. He walked down the gangplank, calling a fond farewell to the sailors aboard the clipper, and leaned on the dock railing as the *Pride* lowered her sails to half-mast and cast away her lines. Slowly, gracefully, the clipper slid into the harbor, a blue-and-gold flag with the new symbol of Lion's Arch fluttering above the crow's nest on her highest mast.

"She's always been a handsome ship." A burly, rust-colored charr leaned next to him on the dock's crossbar, his leopard spots dark against the unruly softness of his fur. "Scarred up here and there, but like any charr woman, that just makes her prettier. Too bad her captain's so ill tempered."

Cobiah started in surprise. "Sykox! You didn't go with the others?"

"Bah." The engineer shrugged humbly. "Fassur's got a good crew, both human and charr. I even think he talked Grimm Svaard into going with them. The ship's engine is running so well, an Iron Legion apprentice with two wrenches and a hammer could manage it, and anyway, I'm needed here. They're building a bank, you know," he said conspiratorially. "I bet it's going to have a *vault*. With turny-cogs and leveraged suspension, weight-balanced for a door as heavy as three dolyaks, and probably even some sort of mechanical locking device." He smiled dreamily. "Somebody is going to have to build that beast of a thing. Can't trust just anyone to do it."

"That's true." Grateful, Cobiah ruffled the charr's orange mane.

"Anyway, you're still the *Pride*'s representative on the Captain's Council, so you're going to need a second."

"I thought you hated council meetings."

"Yeah, I used to. But I heard they've gotten more interesting lately. They have brunches *and* combat." Sykox winked.

Cobiah couldn't help laughing out loud. "Thank you."

The afternoon sun was bright, and the smell of the sea tingled in Cobiah's nose. He could feel the spray in the air, invigorating and fresh. Cobiah took a deep breath and felt the tension in his body drain away. Back on the beach, peals of laughter caught Cobiah's attention. Isaye was taking a moment away from her work with the feast. She had her white bridal gown pulled up around her knees, and she was chasing waves back and forth with some of the town's children. She noticed Cobiah staring from the pier and stopped to wave at him with a wide, delighted smile. It was a beautiful image, and Cobiah waved back.

The charr rumbled with contentment. "Tyria's begun a new era, Coby, and I'd wager it'll be a good one. Lion's Arch needs a firm hand on her rudder, but she'll come through like a galleon with the wind at her back. You'll see."

"Do you really think so?" Together, they watched as city tugs towed the *Pride* out past the island in the bay. Her sails unfurled to catch the wind, and Cobiah could hear the faint chug-chug-chugging of her valiant engine, making a wake behind her through the waves.

"I do." Sykox nodded. "I really do."

ACT FOUR

1256 AE

(AFTER THE EXODUS OF THE GODS)

The wind, it howled, and the thunder boomed
Thought the storm might just prevail, O
But we shouldered on 'til the break of day
And we tamed that fearsome gale
Held to courage and to honor
And we lived to tell the tale, O.
—"Weather the Storm"

24

Agale swept over Sorrow's Bay and into Sanctum
Harbor. It whistled through the arches of the
Gangplank Bridge—a wide stone structure that
crossed the narrow strait between the city's outer and
inner harbors—and darted toward the Postern Ward
like a child playing hide-and-seek. It smelled of heavy
rains and sodden canvas as well as the salt of the open
sea. Somewhere offshore, there were storms, but the
sky above the bustling streets of Lion's Arch was free of
clouds.

Twenty years had made quite a difference to the growing city. The docks around Gate Hub Plaza were filled
with ships, and the Trader's Forum bustled with shop-
keeps, mercenaries seeking work, and traders bringing
their wares from Kryta, the Shiverpeaks, and even as far
away as the Black Citadel of the charr. Within the last few
years, the asura had finally resolved their embargo on
the city and built magical gates to link Lion's Arch to the
other major cities of the continent. With the gates, the
city had truly begun to flourish.

As the trade poured in, so did the gold. Lion's Arch
had swelled to four times her original girth and pop-
ulation but kept her own sense of style. The old ships

converted into wharf buildings were iconic to the city, and had more than doubled in number, housing trade stores, shops, warehouses, and businesses within their still-watertight bellies. Tall white lighthouses looked over the cliffsides where the harbor blended into Sorrow's Bay. Beyond that, at the edge of the ocean, the Claw Island fortress stood ringed in sunset's golden light.

With nearly every race in Tyria contributing to the city's structure, Lion's Arch cut a distinctive silhouette against the sky. Among the ship-buildings stood thatched human houses, rigid-looking charr metalworks, and asuran laboratories shining with magical power, all surrounded by the lush tropical forests of the Tarnished Coast. Norn tents dotted the landscape on the shore, and guards dressed in Lionguard tabards patrolled the thoroughfares for miles around, keeping travel safe. They'd even begun to build a series of "havens," or traveler's waypoints, along the country roads.

The Captain's Council had become a hub of activity centered around the prominent ship-building where they now met. The council had outgrown its small pavilion, and as its numbers increased, so had the city's laws—and its need for guidance. Cobiah walked down the great hall of the building, smiling and tipping his tri-cornered hat to the citizenry. "Good day, madam," he said to one. Another he greeted by name, remembering the man's employment and the recent issue he'd brought forward. One and all, the citizens puffed up as he shook their hands, proud to be remembered by such an important figure.

"Commodore Marriner?" A youth of perhaps fourteen pushed his way through the crowd. The boy had sandy-brown hair and wore the hallmark of a city messenger, a blue sash emblazoned with the city sigil: a lion's head in a compass wheel, over a scimitar and an anchor crossed together. "Commander Sykox is looking for you, sir. The scout ship *Gabrian's Comet* has returned. The commander said you'd want to know right away." The boy saluted stiffly, his eyes shining with the significance of his duty.

"I do indeed," answered Cobiah. He took off his hat and ran a handkerchief over his forehead, wiping away a trace of sweat that lingered from the hall's stagnant air. He stood straight and tall, arching his back to stretch stiff muscles, and pushed a lock of still-thick gray hair out of his sharp blue eyes. Although wrinkles distinguished his features, Cobiah was still handsome. He smiled down at the eager lad. "Is Sykox at the quarter house?"

"No, sir. He's waiting on the Gangplank Bridge. Said you might want to get the measure of the tide while you were down there."

Cobiah chuckled. "Measure of the tide, hmm? Thank you, Benedict. On your way." As the boy scampered off, Cobiah put his hat back on and turned southward toward the massive stone bridge. He clasped his hands behind his back and walked with a rolling step, considering the implications of Sykox's message. Ships docked and sailed based on the turn of the tides, but as a man who spent his time captaining keels of trade moved by sails of paperwork, the tides were rarely Cobiah's concern.

Still, when Sykox talked about tides, it usually meant he needed to talk to Cobiah about something serious. Something he'd prefer to discuss at a more private location than the council chambers. The Gangplank Bridge was very near the manor house Cobiah had built on the northern edge of the inner harbor. It was quiet, used mostly during business hours, and empty most of the twilight and night. It was a meeting place they frequently used, and Cobiah enjoyed the walk there.

Cobiah made his way through the city as the evening cooled around him, looking about with a casual air. He paused to nod to Yomm, seated in a rocking chair on the porch of his shop. This time of day, most shops were closing, and everyone was going home for dinner. Sailors were taking their leave at inns and pubs across the city. He climbed the steep slope from the Grand Piazza toward the Gangplank Bridge, gazing up at three towering arches as he passed through them. Each of the arches was ornamented in blue and gold, with massive sea horses curling to either side. They'd been completed only a few seasons ago as monuments to the city's twentieth year.

The bridge was wide enough for large carts, with thick wooden flooring decorated with swirls of blue and high poles along either side from which brilliant blue flags waved. The wind here was fresh and chilled by the ocean, and the view was magnificent. Off the left side of the bridge was the inner harbor of the city: Deverol Island and the Eastern and Postern Wards. To his right, Cobiah looked out across Sanctum Harbor, toward the lighthouse known as Lion's Gate. That view included one of his favorite parts of the city: a tall marker stone placed on the beach just past the docks. It had been carved in the shape of a lighthouse, and on the northwest side, the pillar had been inscribed with Osh Moran's name in shining gold. In the years to follow, more names had been added to the column, commemorating the brave men and women who had given their lives for Lion's Arch.

A familiar, rust-colored form limped heavily along the length of the Gangplank Bridge. Trotting toward it, Cobiah grinned when he saw his best friend but slowed when the smile was not returned. "What's wrong?"

Cobiah put his hand on the engineer's shoulder, grasping Sykox's wrist with the other hand in the manner of the charr legions. "Is your leg bothering you?"

"No, no. Leg's fine. Hardly notice it at all these days." Sykox huffed, shaking his foot obstinately. It'd been injured years ago during one of the Dead Ship attacks, but Sykox refused to acknowledge that the stiffness slowed him down. The burly charr had lost none of his impressive weight—though it had reshuffled itself from his arms and chest to his belly. His fur, too, was now a comfortable blend of rust and steel, the gray swirling in among the brightness like smoke in a forest fire. "*Gabrian's Comet* made harbor today, that's what's bothering me," he said. "Cobiah . . . trouble's coming."

"Dead Ships? We've handled those before. Nine assaults on our city's harbor, and all nine rebuffed by our defenses. Don't worry, Sykox, we'll manage." The charr lowered his head, and Cobiah stared at his friend quizzically. "What is it, fuzz ball? Something worse?"

The old charr nodded. "The *Comet* was carrying a dispatch from Kryta." Rather than soften the blow, Sykox spoke plainly. "King Baede is dead."

Cobiah leaned against one of the bridge poles, folding his arms in contemplation. Baede, King of Kryta, once the king of Lion's Arch . . . before the Orrian wave destroyed the city. The aged dignitary was renowned throughout the continent. Cobiah'd even dealt with him once or twice, though only through intermediaries and ambassadors. There was a tense peace between Kryta and Lion's Arch, broken on occasion by skirmishes or trade embargos, but generally respected. "We knew that was going to happen eventually. Baede'd been sick for years. Hell, the ministry's been ruling things while he degraded. Still . . . this could change the tenor of our treaty negotiations. He had four kids—who'd the old man of the mountain name as heir to the throne?"

Sykox's lip curled in disgust. "That's the problem. He named Edair."

Cobiah choked, the breath spilling out of him in surprise. After a few moments of raucous coughing, he spluttered, "Three fine sons and daughters to choose from, and Baede chooses *Edair*? That . . . that . . ." Words failed him.

"Young, spoiled, pompous *fool*." Sykox filled in where Cobiah couldn't find words. "Yeah. Edair's barely better than a mercenary. The Black Citadel was forging a peace with Ebonhawke until Edair was assigned the captaincy there. Now the southern fields run with blood—both charr and human—just so a human boy can play with real soldiers instead of wooden ones." The engineer's disdain was palpable. "I suppose those 'victories on the field of battle' earned his father's approval . . . or made Baede believe that Edair would be able to defend Kryta. None of the others ever joined the service as far as I know."

"They're scholars. The oldest boy's an elementalist . . . What's the princess? The girl with the really curly hair?"

Sykox concentrated. "Emilane. She's a ranger. Trained by the Tyrian Explorer's Society. Spends most of her time in the northern forests, I think."

"Oh, yeah, now I remember her. She's the one with the big hound."

"Right, right." Sykox chuckled. "Gigantic dog. Really massive. Still, she'd have made a fine heir to the Krytan throne."

Cobiah shook his head ruefully. "Baede was so ill at the end, he probably wasn't even reading the reports from the front. It's likely that all his advisers told him was that Edair was winning glorious victories in Ebonhawke. They probably didn't mention the cost in lives."

Sykox nodded. "Well, now Edair's planning to rule Kryta. News is that he's looking to increase the kingdom's holdings even before he's formally crowned. He's made no real headway in Ascalon, though. The charr are simply too much for his soldiers there." The engineer smiled proudly. "They're mostly Iron Legion, you know. Ascalon's ruled by our imperator, Singe Seigemourn. Heh heh heh. Forgive me while I indulge in a little bit of personal pride."

Rolling his eyes, Cobiah continued. "So the boy king will look to Lion's Arch, hoping to prove his worth by seizing a jewel for his shiny new crown."

"He'll have to justify an attack to his asuran and norn allies. He'll say that Lion's Arch was once part of Kryta. If he wins, the norn will respect that argument—and the asura won't care either way, as long as the trade routes stay open." As he talked, Sykox idly scratched his name into the wood with one sharp claw.

Cobiah swore out loud. "Balthazar's balls! We haven't come this far—worked this hard—for Kryta to swoop in and claim everything we've built." He looked out over the water, watching as the horizon shifted through sunset tones. "Where were the Krytan galleons when the Dead Ships came? Where were the Seraph when we needed soldiers to defend our docks? When the snows locked the mountain passes and grain rotted in our warehouses because we didn't have the manpower to shovel the roads? Kryta abandoned Lion's Arch after the flood, and we learned to survive and prosper without them." He clenched his hand on the stone. "How do we convince this boy king to stay out of our waters?"

"Prince Edair is a warmonger, Coby," the engineer

sighed. "He's angry. Maybe he was born angry; maybe something happened to him when he was young. I've seen his type. If he'd been born charr, he'd have been taught how to control that anger. How to use it on the field and how to leave it there. The tribunes would have sent him to the front lines, where he'd have either learned to control his anger or been killed by the enemy."

"Maybe that's what Baede was doing when he sent Edair to Ebonhawke," Cobiah said.

"No. Your folk didn't put Edair on the front lines; they let him stand in the back and order other soldiers to die. That didn't temper his anger. It just made him disregard the cost." The gruff charr ran a hand through his mane, ruffling the silvery fur sprinkled among the rust. "A man like that will go to war, and he'll stay at war, and he won't turn back until his people's blood pools around his knees." Sykox shook his head, his mane rippling as his long ram-like horns caught the air.

"That's profound, old friend." Cobiah eyed him with respect. "Did you replace the worn-out cogs in your brain while I wasn't looking?"

"I'm not kidding, Cobiah. Once Edair gets started, he won't stop for anything. He won't care that we worked hard for this city, and he won't care that people are dying on both sides. He won't stop until he's either captured Lion's Arch or burned it to the ground."

Cobiah drew in a long breath of cool air. He struggled to imagine his city as it would be if it were ruled by Kryta under King Edair. All the charr would be imprisoned or displaced, the norn paid half as much for their work, the asura gates used to ship supplies and troops for the war against Ascalon. The human citizens of Lion's Arch would be drafted to serve in the border forts in the western badlands. Krytan flags on every mast, and Edair—that hotheaded nincompoop—preening on a throne in the center of it all. "I am *not* okay with our projected course, Sykox. We have to shift the rudder."

"Wait 'til you hear the next bit." Sykox leaned his head against the bridge pole and looked up at the newly emerging stars. "The *Comet* reported seeing a Krytan ship sailing for our port, flying the flag of the king's emissary."

"Oh, by Dwayna's pointy golden hat—"

"It's the *Nomad II.*"

Cobiah's complaint froze in his throat. He stared down at Sykox, wide-eyed, a chill running through his veins. "The *Nomad?*"

"She'll be in the docks by morning." Cautiously, the charr asked, "Think you'll be up to greeting the ship? It's been years since . . ." His voice trailed away awkwardly.

"Since Isaye left?" With a snort, Cobiah finished the sentence. "You can say the words, Sykox; it's not a secret. Hell, everyone in the city knows. She all but fired her cannons at me on the way out."

"Well, yeah, but I'd hoped . . . you know, she might have mellowed." Cobiah glared at him. Sykox cocked his head and snorted. "Guess not. Damn. That woman holds a grudge like a norn." He cleared his throat uncomfortably. "Though you did call her a 'mutinous, grog-snarfing murellow' during a full meeting of the Captain's Council."

"I was angry."

"I think the words 'dump you in a bucket of honey and roll you in moa feathers' may have been uttered. And then you threw a paperweight at her." Sykox twiddled his clawed thumbs.

Cobiah closed his eyes and sighed deeply. "I was an

idiot, wasn't I?" Opening his eyes, he turned away from Sanctum Harbor and headed back toward the city. "Look, it was years ago. We had a fight. She got mad, she left, and it's done."

"Yeah, and now she's coming back, thus leading to my question." Sykox followed him down the slope toward the massive archways. "Are you going to talk to her, Coby?"

Sighing, Cobiah avoided the question. "Maybe I'll send Nodobe."

"That old snake? Are you mad!" Sykox bellowed a laugh. "You want him negotiating with Prince Edair's emissary? He's more likely to slaughter them all and question their corpses." The charr waved his hands about mockingly. "That's no way to go about diplomacy!"

"He's not that bad."

"You've got to take this situation seriously, Coby. Isaye's been working for King Baede, carrying his messages and shipping his most precious cargo. He trusted her enough to invite her to his court on multiple occasions." Ignoring Cobiah's scowl, the charr rumbled hopefully, "She might be able to help us handle Edair."

"Just because Baede liked her doesn't mean she can stop Edair."

"Stop him? No," the charr agreed, "but Isaye may know the prince well enough to arrange a fair deal. Can it hurt?" He rubbed his muzzle with the back of one hand and then said hesitantly, "I guess we could turn her away and send our own emissary to Divinity's Reach."

"We do that, and he'll use the insult as reason to turn more people against Lion's Arch," Cobiah grumbled.

"Right. Now, do you hate that plan more or less than talking to Isaye?" Sykox held his hands out like scales, pretending to weigh each side of the decision. "Eh? Eh?" Cobiah shot the charr an evil glance, and Sykox ducked mockingly. "Don't punch the messenger, mouse. I'm just trying to figure our chances."

Stomping down the bridge's stairs and onto the cobblestones of the city street, Cobiah muttered, "They're low, fuzz ball.

"Very, *very* low."

The *Nomad II* rested in her lines at the Lion's Arch pier, sails half-furled and the Krytan flag waving proudly from her highest mast. The Captain's Council had placed a guard on the dock, supposedly to make sure the Krytans didn't enter the city and cause trouble—but Cobiah knew the guard was more to protect the *Nomad II's* crew than to keep the city safe. The news that Prince Edair was gathering a navy in Port Noble had spread, and Lion's Arch was buzzing like a hornet's nest.

It had taken them two days to decide where to meet, but Cobiah stuck to his guns and insisted that the Krytans come to the main pavilion rather than having the meeting aboard their ship. Isaye'd replied—through messengers—with a caveat: she'd come ashore and speak with the commodore only in the company of two other captains, Nodobe and Hedda, rather than at a full gathering of the council. Remembering the paperweight incident, Cobiah had given in to her demand.

The pavilion where the captains met was larger now, old wooden pillars and thatched roof replaced by smooth plaster walls within the graceful framework of a ship of the line. With a regal view from the top of a high incline, the council windows looked out over the busy harbor.

The building's balcony on the other side provided a view of the city's trade area.

Cobiah stood on the balcony, watching as a tight-knit group approached through the broad city streets. They paused in the plaza, where the tall statue of a lion leapt over a fountain shaped like the Tyrian coast. Cobiah leaned over the railing, watching as they drew closer. The Lionguard escorted a small group of sailors from the *Nomad II* to the pavilion, ignoring or shouting down the detractors who lined the city streets. Cobiah spied Isaye at the center of the group. She wore the pale coat of the Krytan navy, with a wide baldric of green across her chest and a broad-brimmed hat atop her smooth mahogany hair. Her baldric was light on trinkets, holding only two, an indication that she was newly appointed to her position in the navy.

Despite the twisted emotions running through his veins, Cobiah couldn't help staring. She was still beautiful. Though her dark ponytail was streaked with gray and her face was creased with a gentle serenity, Isaye's green-gold eyes still struck the core of Cobiah's heart. What had happened on that day? When he'd found her in an inn room with another man . . .

Cobiah knew several of the sailors walking with her, but it was Isaye's new first mate who drew his attention. He raised an eyebrow. The Krytan man was tall and strong, broad of shoulder with caramel-colored eyes and a light mustache. His hair was curly, a dark brown shot through with sun-bronzed red. He had a rifle strapped across his back, and at his side he wore a macelike scepter made of iron and brass. He, too, wore the Krytan uniform—but his baldric had far more small medals and trinkets than Isaye's. The man might not have outranked her, but he'd clearly been in the military far longer, and far more notably, than she.

"Who's that?" he asked Sykox.

"First mate . . . huh. His name's . . . eh . . ." The charr grunted, looking at the crew manifest they'd been given for the meeting. "Tenzin Moran?"

Turning to look at him, Cobiah blurted, *"Moran?"*

"Hey, yeah, I've heard of him! That's ol' Osh's son. He's, what, fifteen or so years younger than you?" The engineer chuckled to himself. "Old Osh used to brag that his kid back home was some kinda Krytan hero, a real gold star with lots of medals for valor and bravery. Earned them for fighting centaurs in the Shiverpeaks. Osh used to say he was one of their best sharpshooters. Now I guess he's in the Krytan marines."

"Marines? Feh. Those aren't real sailors."

"Best watch it. Marines are mean. They'll wait 'til us 'sailors' take them to shore, and then they'll turn around and eat our faces off." The charr winked.

Pausing to think for a moment, Cobiah asked hopefully, "Did Tenzin ever fight in Ascalon? Does he have any problem with charr?"

"No." Sykox shook his head. "Not that Moran ever mentioned."

"Damn," Cobiah muttered. He glanced back down at the small group now climbing the steps toward the pavilion. "I guess I'll have to find some other reason to hate him." Downstairs, the wide oak doors swung open to allow the clustered knot of Krytan sailors entrance. The Lionguard held the citizens back until the doors could be closed again, but through the gateway Cobiah could hear the loud jeers and angry yells of the crowd. Cobiah walked down the stairs, grateful—as he rarely was—that Nodobe was nearby. The Elonian captain nodded in friendly greeting as Cobiah reached the bottom.

"I'm certain this will be a pleasant meeting," the necromancer said with a grin, rubbing his cheek.

"About as much fun as trying to put a collar on a skritt." Cobiah straightened his coat and tried to look assured.

Isaye and her entourage walked to the center of the room, pausing there as Cobiah and the others crossed to greet them. Cobiah's hands clenched in his coat pockets, and suddenly he wished he hadn't worn his hat.

"Isaye. My dear friend, you grace us with your presence." Nodobe's words were as smooth and pleasant as silk in a breeze. He reached to take her hand and wrap it about his arm. "It has been too long."

Isaye smiled and greeted the dark-skinned captain in return, but Cobiah didn't hear a single word of it. With that one smile, she'd transported him back to the day she'd left—her hair flying in the wind, tears reddening her hazel eyes, anger curling her rich, full lips. Whatever pleasantries she gave Nodobe, they were lost in the memory of words from over seven years ago.

"Why, Isaye? How can I ever trust you?"

"How could you even question?"

"Hedda." Isaye moved on and took the plump norn's strangely delicate hand. "You look wonderful. I think you've lost weight!"

Hedda laughed. "Lost it? By the Spirits of the Wild, woman, have you gone blind? If you have, you're missing out on a feast for the eyes—tell me, who is this handsome cabin boy you've got beside you?"

With a twinkle in her eye, Isaye answered, "Captain Hedda, may I present First Mate Tenzin Moran."

"Well, well, you're a Moran to boot." Hedda looked the young man up and down rapaciously. "If you were a bit taller, you might give my husband, Bronn, a challenge for my interest!" Everyone laughed, and the Krytan's decorated baldric glittered as Tenzin swept her a bow. As they did, Isaye's eyes met his, and Cobiah's heart froze into ice.

They hadn't faded a single shade, the rich hazel of moss-covered trees staring back at him with controlled interest. "Cobiah." Isaye nodded briefly, and he returned the gesture. His throat was too dry to say anything.

"Come, my dear." Nodobe patted Isaye's hand that rested on his arm, drawing her close. "Let us go upstairs. I would be remiss if I did not try to woo you back to us with our city's beauty." He tugged at her gently, and Isaye followed. "We can talk on the building's high deck, where the wind will sweep away the day's heat."

The two, and Hedda, made for the stairs. Sykox was standing there, twisting his new hat in his hands until it looked like a shapeless mass of blue felt. Cobiah saw Isaye greet the charr with a gentle hug, the spotted engineer's sharp claws hovering lightly over her slender back. Wishing more than anything that he were a charr, Cobiah sighed.

"Commodore Marriner," a gentle voice said at his side. Cobiah glanced to see Tenzin at his elbow. "A pleasure to make your acquaintance, sir. My father spoke highly of you and of your city. I'm glad to have the opportunity to see Lion's Arch for myself."

"You're welcome here, Tenzin." Cobiah nodded more sharply than he'd intended. "Your father was a good man and a stalwart friend."

"He said the same of you, sir." Without intention, the young man's charm soothed Cobiah's temper.

"Did he? Well, perhaps your captain gave you a different impression."

"No, sir." Before Cobiah could smile at that, Tenzin

continued blithely on. "She never speaks of you at all."

Grumpy again, Cobiah gestured toward the stairs, and the two men headed toward the top level of the building. The high deck was above the balcony, and the view was one of the finest in Lion's Arch. A full turn showed the city to fine advantage, from the teal-blue water up to the greenery of thick jungle on the hills. Isaye, however, wasn't interested in any of it. "I'll cut directly to the issue," she said, sitting down on one of the wicker chairs about a small table. A servant brought out a plate of tropical fruit and several tall glasses of punch. Cobiah was grateful to smell rum in his; the waiters of the council building knew him well. "The Krytan navy is assembling to the west. Prince Edair is planning to sortie into Lion's Arch if the city doesn't sign over its authority to Kryta. He's sent me to offer terms." Isaye took a sip of her drink, letting them consider her words. One mark in her favor: she didn't look any happier about delivering the terms than the others did in hearing them. "All human captains of the council will be paid ten thousand gold coins for their labors in rebuilding the king's land. They are offered lordships and titles if they swear fealty to Kryta. If they do not swear an oath to Prince Edair, they must quit Lion's Arch immediately, never to return."

Cobiah wasn't the only one gritting his teeth. Even the courteous Nodobe soured, his brows knitting over shining black eyes. Hedda was first to speak, rumbling, "And those of us who are not of human stock?"

Isaye closed her eyes and said, "You are ordered by Prince Edair to leave the city without argument, quitting claim to any land, title, or authority in the city."

"By Wolf's bloody muzzle!" Hedda exploded, banging her drink on the table. "I won't go. I have three young sons—born and raised here! This is our home. I'll see your prince hanged before I give up even a stone of our house's foundation."

Nodobe was quick to calm her down, reaching to touch the norn woman's arm soothingly. "Hedda, be at peace. No one's going to let them drive us out of Lion's Arch without a fight." He looked at Isaye, pursing his lips so tightly they appeared bloodless. "Isaye, sweet lady. Prince Edair must know that his demands are unreasonable. You know as well as I that he has no intention of letting us surrender in peace, even if we are willing to give up the city."

Isaye looked down, swishing her drink uncomfortably. "His Highness would protest that his demands are entirely reasonable, given that the land has always been Krytan. He says you're 'squatting' upon it without leave." A murmur of disbelief rippled through the assembled captains, and Hedda had to choke back another exclamation. Isaye continued as if saying something she'd been made to rehearse. "It's his very public opinion that the Captain's Council should be paying *him* for the years you've been living in Kryta without paying taxes."

Hedda banged her empty glass on the table, making the servants scatter.

"Please, hear us out." Tenzin raised a hand to quiet the angry norn. "I can assure you that if we agreed with him, we wouldn't be this explicit with you. We aren't here to extract your surrender, nor do we expect you to bow down and kiss Prince Edair's feet. Isaye and I . . ." He glanced at her, but the dark-haired captain kept her eyes lowered. Tenzin hesitated and then went on. "Please believe us, but as much as we can be, the *Nomad* is on your side."

Feeling stifled for too long, Hedda burst out, "What in the blood-soaked Mists are we supposed to do? Fight a naval battle against Kryta?"

"That would be a battle they'd lose." Nodobe glowered darkly. "Lion's Arch has the strongest navy in Tyria. We've fought Dead Ships and won. He can't honestly believe—"

"Prince Edair has no plans to fight at sea." Deprecatingly, Isaye crossed her arms over her chest, and the little medals on her baldric jingled. "The Krytan navy isn't going to fight yours in some kind of grand and glorious battle. Edair's going to blockade the harbor, driving off all trade, and soon enough, Lion's Arch will starve. That's when he'll send in the Seraph."

Cobiah felt as though he'd been punched in the stomach. "The Seraph? They'd bring the whole damn Krytan army? Lion's Arch is a naval power. We've never had to raise more than a city guard. They won't have to wait for us to starve; they'll overpower us in a month when the majority of their troops arrive." Tugging off his hat, he tossed it on the table. "Damn it, damn it, damn it. What can we do?"

"Ask for reinforcements from the charr High Legions?" Sykox asked helpfully.

"And once the charr are done rebuffing Edair and turning our city into a war zone, the plethora of warriors in our streets will seize Lion's Arch in the name of your imperator instead." Nodobe shook his head gravely, slumping more deeply into his wicker chair. "No."

Silence fell as they struggled to find other ideas. The wind swept over them, tugging at coats and rippling fur with chilly, salt-touched fingers. Cobiah struggled to keep his tongue. Isaye was right. Edair's plan would work. If the Krytan prince managed to blockade the harbor and the roads, there'd be no supplies. It would be only a matter of weeks before the city had to give in.

Long moments later, Isaye concluded, "There's one more possible option. The city could surrender to Kryta through us. Tenzin and I have the prince's ear. We could make a bargain to allow time for nonhumans to leave the city, maybe even keep their wares or get some kind of recompense, even if it has to come from the Lion's Arch treasury. It's possible that—"

"No!" The shout ripped from Cobiah's throat before he knew it. Everyone at the table turned to stare at him, and Cobiah felt his face growing red. Nevertheless, he glared at Isaye. Through gritted teeth, he said, "We're not giving up on this city. We fight for the things we love. We don't sell them out, we don't betray them, and we don't run away from them."

Isaye flinched, her face paling. "Betray them?" Her eyebrows raised meaningfully, eyes flashing.

"Unfair." Tenzin came to her defense, rising sternly from the table. "Your personal issues aren't welcome at this table, Commodore Marriner."

"And you're not welcome in this city. Get out." Cobiah's tone was final, but Isaye was already yelling.

"Cobiah, for once in your life, think about someone other than yourself!" She rose from her chair to engage with him. "Prince Edair isn't kidding around. He's willing to order thousands of his soldiers to die meaninglessly. Can you say the same? Think of the innocents who live here. Do you really want to drag them through a useless, one-sided war?"

"We can't just give in!" he roared in return, rising as well. Pounding one fist on the table so hard the fruit jumped in its bowl, Cobiah bellowed, "This is our city. We founded it. We built it. Maybe you don't understand what loyalty means, Isaye, but by the Six Gods, *I do!*" The two glared at one another, and Isaye's hand fell instinctively to the pistol at her belt—only to find her wrist gently caught in Sykox's paw.

"Ease down, pretty lady," the charr engineer murmured softly. "Everybody here's on the same side." She glared at him but nodded and slowly pulled her hand away.

Biting off his words sharply, Cobiah repeated himself: "Get out of my city."

"And I believe that signals the end of today's negotiations," Nodobe murmured regretfully, rising from the table with a graceful motion. "Captain Isaye, please allow me to escort you to the Lionguard, who will ensure your safe return to the *Nomad.*" His dark eyes were unusually kind as he offered her a hand. Isaye shot a final look of reproof toward Cobiah but said nothing and took Nodobe's arm rather than continue the argument. Tenzin managed a stiff but polite bow, thanking the council for its hospitality without meeting Cobiah's eyes. When he was finished, Nodobe ushered the two Krytans to the stairwell and below.

Once they had left the deck, Cobiah slumped in his chair. Hedda stood up, walked over to him, and punched him in the shoulder. "That's for being rude," she growled. Cobiah winced, but he couldn't blame her. "By Raven's wing, this is convoluted," the norn woman muttered, pacing back and forth. "If we stay here, we risk being slaughtered by the human king. If we go, we leave behind everything we've fought and struggled for, all the wealth and security we forged." Her blue eyes were wide with anger and disbelief. "How can he make me choose between my children and my city?"

"Nobody's choosing. Nobody's leaving." Cobiah struggled to believe the words even as he said them. "We've driven off nine fleets of Orrian ships—"

"But never an army! And never in a land-based attack!" Hedda exploded. "Even if we arm every man, woman, and child in the city, we don't have half as many soldiers as the Seraph."

Sykox stepped in quickly, laying his hand on Hedda's shoulder with a gentle restraint. "It's all right, Hedda. We'll call a meeting of the full council. Those who wish to leave the city can do so by the asura gate."

"No." Cobiah felt his stomach churn. "That'll be the first thing they manage. Dark tides! If Isaye came here by ship, that means it's probably already done."

"What?" The others turned to stare at him.

"Lion's Arch was built on gold stolen from the Arcane Council of Rata Sum when they built a gate in King Baede's city Divinity's Reach. The asuran colleges have always held a grudge against Lion's Arch for that. If Edair's seriously planning to attack us, he's already negotiated with the asuran council."

"They'll shut off the gates." Sykox's eyes widened. "We'll be stranded."

"Hedda, send young Benedict to the asura gate platform. Tell him to check with Gatekeeper Yokk and Apprentice Roinna and see if the gates still work." A deep anger plagued him. It felt as if the sand of security was being washed out from between his fingers. Frustrated, he said, "Heck, check and see if the two of them are still in the city. I bet they're not." Hedda nodded, and the gesture made her heavy braids thump against her wide shoulders. She spun and strode toward the stairwell, her massive bulk making the deck shudder with each heavy step, hands unconsciously balled into fists.

"Devious wretch, that Edair," Sykox snarled. "He's been planning this for a long time, hasn't he? He was just waiting for ol' Baede to die to kick it all off. Stupid human." He looked up quickly, adding, "No offense intended, of course."

Cobiah pulled off his hat and tossed it disdainfully on the table. He ran his hands through his hair, mussing it up with frustration. "None taken. I don't want to be related to the man, either, even if just by the mutual ancestors of our race." He sighed, struggling with the idea of a Krytan armada poised at the edge of their harbor. "From what Isaye says, Edair's so eager that he's willing to put off his own coronation just to hurry the seizure of Lion's Arch. I'm surprised he didn't lurch through the asura gate screaming, 'Hello, city! I'm your new king!'"

Once more, Nodobe climbed the stairwell to the deck, this time with a weary step. "I instructed two of our port guards to escort the *Nomad* on the next tide," he said. He gave Cobiah a slow smile and sat down in one of the wicker chairs. Taking up a piece of fruit, Nodobe pressed his fingers into it, allowing the juice to run over his fingertips as he picked away the peel. "Also, there was a scout downstairs from the lighthouse at Lion's Gate. He's already noted sails on the horizon. It appears that Prince Edair's armada is assembling. Apparently, he wasn't willing to wait and see if Isaye's mission would prove fruitful." Nodobe's usually broad smile was wan. "It seems we're already trapped."

"It'll be a fight, then." Cobiah crossed his arms grimly. "But that's all right. So long as Lion's Arch has a fleet, we have a chance."

26

People were shouting, soldiers bellowed commands, and the bells at the docks were ringing and clattering in cacophonous noise. Cobiah's eyes flew open. He was in the large, half-empty bed at his manor house, and darkness still surrounded him. The night was still late, then. Not yet morning. For a moment, Cobiah's mind was still tangled in a dream: he was on the *Indomitable*, surrounded by the still-moving corpses of drowned friends. In a panic, he rolled over and reached to grasp the sword that lay on the ground tangled in his pants belt, but his hand fell instead upon a limp rag doll. Polla. She'd been tucked beneath his pillow, but apparently, he'd tossed and turned so much that he'd knocked her onto the floor. In a moment of curious pause, Cobiah lifted it, tucking the faded yellow curls behind her shoulders.

Then the world shifted into focus around him.

The city's alarm bells were ringing, and a heavy smell of smoke filled the air. Quickly, Cobiah set the doll down and snatched up his coat and sword. He rolled out of bed and landed with his feet in his boots. The shouts were coming from the docks, and by the sound of it, trouble was already so far along that half the city was running about in the night. Cobiah rushed to the balcony door, throwing open the curtains and stepping out onto the half-circle veranda that looked out over the inner harbor and the Gangplank Bridge. Black smoke hung thickly in the air, covering everything with a layer of fog. Lionguard—both in and out of armor—raced through the streets, carrying buckets of water. Cobiah lifted his head and followed them with his eyes as they headed west, toward . . .

The docks were on fire.

Massive flames leapt from ship to ship at Macha's Landing, encompassing the levees all the way down to White Crane Terrace. Across the bay, the city's main portage area was flaring up in brilliant shades of orange and red. A sudden explosion rocked the Gangplank Bridge as a charr frigate on the docks went up like a firecracker, armaments exploding with a blinding flash of white light. Sailors scurried like ants, desperate to stop the flames before they could spread farther, but more than three-fourths of the ships at dock were already suffering damage from the blaze. Without thinking, Cobiah leapt over the balcony rail, climbed down the tiered roof, and dropped to the street below.

"Commodore!" The shout came from a slender figure in the Grand Piazza. Through the haze, Cobiah recognized Benedict, the messenger lad. He was carrying an armload of empty buckets back along the fire-brigade line.

"What's happened?" Cobiah grabbed half of the youth's load and ran with him toward the water, where other citizens were filling them with sea and sand to douse oily areas of the blaze.

"Gamina said it was Krytans. She was on watch at the docks and saw four men dressed in black setting fire to fuses. They hurled the bombs into the portholes of our munitions ships—the ones we were readying for an attack on the blockade. I heard her yelling right before they exploded." Benedict dropped the buckets on the sandbar and tried to wipe smoke from his eyes. "She called the Lionguard, but the men ran across the Gangplank, and we lost sight of them."

The *Nomad II* had sailed back out into the Sea of Sorrows four days ago, and Prince Edair's ships had blocked all passage into or out of the city's harbor. Clearly, the impatient prince wasn't going to just sit by and wait while the city readied a defense. "Did Gamina see their faces?"

"Yeah." Benedict brightened. "She said she saw them real well by the light of the first fires. She went across the Gangplank to the portage, in case they had a rowboat there."

"Clever girl. She'll need our help. Come with me; we'll go see if we can lend her a hand."

"Aye, aye, sir." Benedict saluted.

Yomm stood on the long slope that led up to the Gangplank, standing in the shelter of one of the massive seahorse arches. The asura rocked back and forth on his feet, rubbing his ears in distress as he stared down at the fire. "Oh, Cobiah. What are we going to do?" he whimpered.

"We'll keep fighting," Cobiah said.

"I wrote to Rata Sum. I wrote the Arcane Council. I wrote every genius-level asura I knew, even the bad ones. Surely *someone* will help us." Covered in soot, his ornate robes blackened by smoke and wet with seawater, Yomm looked like a drenched cat. "There's got to be a way." Over the years, Yomm had become an excellent quartermaster for the city. When he'd been told that the harbor was going to be blockaded, the shopkeep-captain immediately created a detailed system for organizing what food was left in Lion's Arch, apportioning it, and ensuring it would last as long as possible. Cobiah paused to pat Yomm gently on the shoulder, wondering how asuran parents consoled their children. Probably by giving them crystal wands and mechanical widgets to chew on. "There, there, Yomm," Cobiah said awkwardly. "It'll be all right."

"Will it?"

"Can you fix the gate? Turn it back on?" Cobiah sat up hopefully.

"No. I graduated from the College of Statics," Yomm said, pressing a three-fingered hand to either side of his forehead. "If the gate had, say, fallen over, I could get it back up, build a house around it, and shore up the architectural supports so that even an ettin couldn't knock it over again! But I can't fix the etheric ambulation. You need a graduate of Dynamics, and Captain Tarb's half-senile. If you let him fix it, it'll start teleporting people's parts to random locations! Imagine it! Your head's in the citadel, your feet are in Rata Sum, and your butt's all the way up north among the glaciers! Nobody wants that."

Cobiah stared at him, alternating between bemused and annoyed. "Go back to your shop, Yomm, and take inventory. We've lost everything stored on the docks, and that means we'll have to start rationing."

Yomm clambered to his feet, still muttering. "Fine, I can do that." The asura grumbled and turned, slogging down the slope toward his shop in the Trader's Forum. "'Fix it, Yomm, fix it.' Hmph. What does he think I am?"

Benedict grinned. Cobiah rolled his eyes and hurried across the wide wooden bridge.

On the far side of the bridge was a massive plaza, larger than the main trade terraces in the city square. It was far less ornamented as well, covered with scuff marks where the Lionguard prepared for duty. Racks of weapons stood beneath shady awnings topped with gold flags, their edges blunted for use in training exercises. Cobiah was passing the archery range when Gamina stepped out of the shadows, her snub nose and impish smile far more suited to meadows than murder.

"Benedict said you were tracking the saboteurs?" Cobiah asked, trying not to look too surprised by her sudden appearance. He was good at stealth—or had been in his youth. She was better.

"Keep your voice down, Commodore," she warned him. "I doubt they've gone far."

When Captain Tarb had retired, the pixielike blonde had left the old asura's service and joined the Lionguard. Bronn, now the captain of the guard, praised her to the skies. He even kept trying to give her command of one of the major traveler's Havens, but Gamina always refused. She rarely accepted honors and often chose to work in the background.

Cobiah had discovered the reason she preferred a low profile when Gamina approached him with an offer from the Order of Whispers, a legendary underground agency of spies, infiltrators, and scouts. If he gave her access to the Captain's Council—not to vote, just to watch and stay informed—she and her fellows would keep him apprised of activity happening in the underbelly of the city. He'd agreed. Since then, Gamina had proven to be even more valuable, rooting out thieves, smuggling rings, and other dangers in the newly established city. Without the order's aid, Lion's Arch might have fallen to any number of petty tyrants willing to trade the city's future for their own gain.

"They headed out toward the tugboat dock," she said

quietly, pointing with the blade of her dagger. "I haven't seen a boat leave. Unless they swam, they'll be down there."

"You can't swim out that far. They're still here, probably waiting until the area's clear before they try to make for the ships offshore." He glanced at Benedict. "Can you wield a sword, Ben?"

"Yes, sir." Benedict grinned. Cobiah gestured to the training weapons, and Benedict picked one up and strapped it to his waist. "Might not be very sharp, sir, but it'll do."

Gamina murmured, "That charr ship dropped a bellyful of oil when she went up in flames. It's spread across the harbor, and most of it's alight. The Krytans can't row out right now, or they'll be seen; the city's bombard guns would make short work of them." She gestured lightly toward the gun emplacements on the cliffs. "Keep to the shadows and stay quiet." Cobiah and Benedict followed her into the shadows of the tugboat docks as Gamina continued. "The order got word that the Krytans might try something like this, but we had no timetable. We thought Prince Edair would wait at least a week before he tried to torch the docks." She glanced back at Cobiah. "You must have really gotten on his bad side."

He scowled and didn't answer.

They moved from building to building, peering through windows and checking doors for any sign of forced entry. Gamina's slippered feet passed silently over the cobblestones, leaving Cobiah and Benedict to scurry behind like hounds in the wake of an alley cat. Once again, Cobiah blessed his childhood on the streets; if he hadn't learned thiefcraft, it would have been incredibly difficult to keep up. "It's not surprising that Edair's overreacting," Gamina murmured. "Even his father was afraid of you. Didn't you wonder why Baede never tried to take Lion's Arch?"

"I assumed he didn't care for the climate," Cobiah joked.

"No dice." She chuckled. "He didn't have the guts to take on the finest navy in the world—or their commander." Gamina glanced back at him. "Taking this city by force requires an attacker to be ruthless. You'd have to destroy the navy and slaughter the populace before they'd kneel to a ruler who's not born and bred in the waves."

"Which ruins the point of taking the city in the first place," Benedict surmised. "Isn't that right?"

Gamina nodded. "Baede respected that and tried to deal with you, hoping Lion's Arch would return to Kryta in time. Edair doesn't care. He's not that patient. Remember that, Cobiah, and remember that pride is Edair's weakness."

"Remember?" Cobiah peered out past the edge of one of the buildings on the wharf, ensuring that the way ahead was clear. "Gamina, I'm not exactly planning to have tea with the pox-faced prince of Kryta."

"You might not be planning it, but I can assure you, *he* is." Suddenly Gamina dropped to a crouch and scooted behind a pile of cargo. "Look—over there." She pointed toward the other side of the wharf. Cobiah and Benedict scrambled to either side of her and peered down through cracks between the cargo crates for several minutes, looking quizzical. Growing impatient, Gamina pushed Cobiah forward, indicating the slope that led beneath the pier. "You go that way and get their attention. I'll come up behind them."

Moving silently, she glided around the far corner of the cargo pile and vanished into the night. Cobiah and

Benedict shared a glance. "Uh . . . do you see a . . . 'them'?" Cobiah asked. Benedict shrugged and shook his head. Cobiah sighed. "Me neither."

Awkwardly, Benedict drew the longsword he had gathered from the training ground, holding the weapon as if it were a club. Cobiah frowned in concern, but there was very little he could do about it. Hopefully, Benedict was better in action than he looked standing still. Cobiah drew his cutlass and gestured for the youth to follow him down the slope. "You can't use a sword at all, can you?" Cobiah asked. Benedict shook his head sheepishly, and Cobiah sighed. "All right. Stay close."

As they approached, Cobiah slowly began to make out four men beneath the pier, all huddled around a rowboat hidden beneath the shadow of the farthest dock. They'd been talking in low tones, voices barely audible over the hush and swell of the ocean waves, but Cobiah saw one of them gesture quickly, pulling his fist close to his face in warning. The others instantly fell silent.

In the light of the oil fires scattered over the water of the harbor, Cobiah saw that two of the men were holding daggers. A third pulled a thick-handled mallet from his belt. Looking inquisitively at the fourth, he tapped the heavy work hammer in his hand the way a tree cutter might swing his axe. The fourth moved around the rowboat, peering in Cobiah's direction. Cobiah reached back and gripped Benedict's hand, making sure the boy wasn't moving. Both groups stood in silence for a moment, and then the fourth bandit scowled. He'd seen them.

Raising his voice in the tongue of magic, the fourth bandit pulled a strange-looking dagger from his belt. The blade was twisted like an animal's horn, and the hilt was embellished with blue stone. The man cast a quick spell, and a clawlike burst of fire shot forward from his weapon. The talons raked Cobiah's flesh, searing his skin—and more important, showing exactly where he was standing.

"Get them!" the saboteur elementalist demanded. "Don't let them flee."

"Flee?" Cobiah said, challenging them. "Hadn't even crossed my mind." He charged directly into the group, hoping to scatter them. One on one, Benedict might have a better chance against the Krytans . . . and it would give Gamina an opportunity to do whatever she was planning. The elementalist skittered aside, and the two dagger-wielding thieves darted in opposite directions, planning to flank Cobiah and Benedict. The scruffy-looking man with the mallet blocked Cobiah's cutlass with the hilt of his weapon, a surprised "oomph" of effort escaping him. Cobiah smiled as his sharpened cutlass bit deep into the wood. Surprised at his opponent's skill, the ruffian scowled.

The warrior spun the hammer, and where Cobiah's blade was stuck in the wood, the metal of the cutlass shrieked, bent, and then shattered. "The old geezer's all yours, boys." The scruffy thief said mockingly, "A little bit of a breather, and he might have another solid hit left for you."

The two dagger-wielding thugs approached Cobiah, one to either side. Benedict pressed forward, his back against Cobiah's back, and Cobiah could feel the youth shaking. As is, they were no match for these saboteurs. "Give me your sword!" Cobiah ordered, reaching back to take it from his young friend. Benedict paused only a second before obeying.

"But, sir, what am I supposed to fight with?"

"Give me a minute. I'll get you a dagger." Cobiah shrugged off his coat and began to twirl it in one hand, slapping the ground in circles as he warded off the attacker on his left side. Before the two saboteurs could formulate another plan, Cobiah swung his sword viciously at one of the dagger men. The thug ducked, lunging in beneath the reach of Cobiah's weapon. The dagger cut through the fabric of Cobiah's coat with a vicious swipe, but the old captain was too quick for the steel to touch his flesh. He tugged the coat aside, nearly pulling the dagger out of his opponent's hand, and swung again. This time, he felt his sword scrape against the man's leg. A good blow but hardly crippling.

The bandit elementalist changed his footing and chanted another spell. This time, heaviness pressed in the air around Cobiah, weighing on his shoulders with a damp, cold pressure. Recognizing the spell from his time with Verahd long ago, Cobiah reached back and thrust Benedict aside, jumping forward himself as a spike of ice coalesced above them both. It drove into the ground where the two men had been standing, showering the area around them in chunks of frozen snow.

Using the distraction as an opportunity to attack, one of the other brigands thrust in with his dagger, but this time, Cobiah swirled his coat around it, fouling the blade. Letting the coat fall over the dagger, Cobiah grabbed his assailant's wrist through the fabric. He jerked forward and drove his other fist—still wrapped around the hilt of his borrowed sword—into the man's face. Cobiah struck once, twice, then a third time, following up with a knee into the thug's extended arm. There was a sharp crack, and the man fell with a howl, clutching a broken wrist. Cobiah scooped up the assailant's dagger and tossed it to Benedict. "Better?"

The youth smiled. "Yes, sir! Thank you, sir." He gripped the lighter weapon more assuredly than he had the sword. Clearly, the messenger's childhood had not been so different from Cobiah's own.

Near the rowboat, the brigand with the mallet had been planning an attack of his own. He swung the hammer over his head to gain speed, and as his companion fell, the scruffy-looking warrior slammed it down. The earth and sand beneath the pier rumbled from the mighty force of the blow. An explosion of earth and rocks burst up in all directions, showering Cobiah and the rest with blinding sand.

Emboldened by the dagger and farther from the epicenter of the explosion, Benedict yelled a reedy battle cry and dove past Cobiah. Ignoring the others, he drove his shoulder into the belly of the caster. The man had nearly finished another spell, the tide nearby swirling upward into a geyser—but Benedict's tackle knocked them both backward over the rowboat. The geyser popped like a bubble, drenching the rowboat, combatants and all, in salt water as Benedict and the caster fell into the rising tide. Benedict managed to stab the other man, scoring a solid hit to his shoulder with the knife; the blade snagged and tore out of Benedict's hand as the bandit screamed. The dagger fell into the tide as Benedict grappled with his enemy, rolling and kicking in the water beneath the pier.

First an earthquake, then a downpour. Scratching at his eyes, Cobiah stumbled as he tried to regain his balance on the still-shifting sand. He could hear the other bandit cursing a few feet away. Reaching out for the dark form at the edge of his vision, Cobiah managed to grab the other man's head, tangling his fingers into the thug's hair. The man struck out with his knife. A white-hot flame ignited in a line along Cobiah's rib cage. He ignored the pain long enough to jerk the thug's head forward, cracking a fist into the man's nose. The thug yelped, his body going suddenly limp, and fell forward into the sand.

Benedict twisted in the sand, fighting hand-to-hand with the bandit spellcaster. Thinking quickly, Benedict kicked the other man's dagger free, leaving both to fight purely with their hands. The elementalist quickly pulled out an off-hand focus as he clutched Benedict's arms, his fingers sinking deep into the youth's flesh. Benedict countered with knee-kicks to the body, and the two rolled in the shallow water. The elementalist shouted another spell. With a flash of light, his hands burst into flames. The spell was weaker than if he'd been using his dagger, and splashing water absorbed the worst of it. Benedict's flesh seared, blisters rising on his biceps where the elementalist squeezed.

Aware that Benedict was in trouble, Cobiah pushed himself away from the two whimpering, injured bandits fallen in the sand at his feet. Intending to throw himself forward to join the fight, Cobiah raised his sword and lunged forward—but where he expected to fly to the boy's aid, his body suddenly refused to obey. A second wave of force from the scruffy-looking bandit's hammer knocked him back again, and Cobiah found himself stumbling, pushed aside as easily as a wave knocks away a bit of foam. He could hear his own opponent laughing, feet crunching in wet sand as the Krytan strode closer.

The man with the hammer was a problem. Worse, his blow had shaken Cobiah's body, exacerbating the dagger wound. Cobiah put a hand to his side and drew it away covered in blood. It burned from immersion in salt water and gritty sand, and Cobiah's breath came in short gasps. He was bleeding heavily, and being soaked in water only made the situation worse. Cobiah forced himself to stand.

Benedict was screaming, the elementalist's fire flickering with ghostly flame up and down the youth's arms. "I'm coming," Cobiah managed to say—but he wasn't entirely sure that was true.

"I didn't recognize you at first, you know," the scruffy bandit taunted. "I wouldn't have expected to meet the famous Commodore Marriner under a rough-side pier." The man spun his heavy wooden mallet in his hands, giving Cobiah a snaggletoothed grin. "You're nothing like the king's advisers described. They told us to be careful about you. Said that if the master of the city got involved, we'd be done for." His laugh of disdain echoed with Benedict's cries for help. "But here you are. Nothing more than a weak old man stumbling in the tide. Your 'legend' is nothing but a waste of breath." The man with the hammer paused and eyed Cobiah up and down, taking in the bloodstained shirt, his faltering steps, and the sword hanging heavily in the commodore's hand. "Prince Edair paid us a chest of gold to turn that fleet to ash. I bet he'll give us ten times more if we bring back your head, Commodore." The warrior hefted his weapon again, the heavy mallet moving ponderously in his burly grip.

Cobiah tried to raise his sword for another attack, but it was as if iron bands circled his chest, squeezing all the breath out of him. Where was Gamina? He glanced about but saw nothing in the shadows, nothing in the movement of the waves beyond the pier. As the bandit strode closer, Cobiah's thoughts flitted to Isaye. Macha. His mother, who should have loved him—but treated him like trash. Once more, he'd trusted someone—and they'd repaid him with treachery.

Urgency spurred Cobiah forward. He had to get to Benedict before the saboteur elementalist burned the youth to death. Desperate, Cobiah chopped at the mallet-wielding brigand. The wound made his sword arm as slow as winter molasses, and the bandit dodged easily. Cobiah tried again, but the Krytan batted his weapon aside like a feather. "Just die, Commodore," the man said, grinning. "You're no hero. You're no great leader. You're *nothing.*"

The words were like a slap in the face. *Nothing,* he could hear his mother say, over and over again. *You're worth nothing.* Rage swelled in Cobiah's heart. His vision blurred, turning red, and he ignored the pain to swing his sword with a far younger man's anger. Taken by surprise, the brigand stumbled backward, his hand loosening on the heavy mallet. Cobiah's second swing knocked it free, and the mallet tumbled to the ground. "Out of my way!" Cobiah roared. His heart was pounding. Blood flowed between the fingers of the hand pressed to his rib cage. Clenching his other hand around the hilt of the sword, Cobiah shoved past the scruffy-looking bandit and ran toward Benedict.

Raising his sword, Cobiah stabbed down at the elementalist and felt his weapon strike flesh. As the brigand screamed, Benedict raised his feet and kicked the other man in the chest, pushing him farther onto the weapon until, at last, the fire died, and the man's body went limp. Cobiah sagged, forced to let go of his sword as Benedict rolled out from under the dead man. "Are you all right?" Cobiah managed to ask. Benedict nodded gratefully, shoving the body off him and into the ocean waves.

"Commodore!" Benedict scrambled in the waves for his lost dagger. The seared flesh of his arms was blistered and raw, but he raised a hand to point over Cobiah's shoulder. Wide-eyed, he yelled, "Watch out!"

Cobiah looked, knowing what he'd see. He'd been forced to leave the last bandit behind in order to get to

Benedict before the messenger was burned to death. It'd been a conscious choice, and he was prepared for the consequences. Behind him, the brigand with the mallet swung his weapon in a wide swath. Cobiah heard the whisper and crackle of magical force around the weapon's head. He had only time enough to spin around, placing himself between the injured Benedict and the brigand's strike as the massive bludgeon swept forward.

But the hammer never landed.

Behind the brigand, Gamina's blades flashed like lightning strikes. First one and then the other plunged deep into the thug's back. The bandit warrior staggered, hammer tilting forward and falling out of his hands as he collapsed to his knees. Gamina twisted her blades and jerked them out with a disdainful snarl. He fell lifeless to the ground.

"Sorry I'm late." Gamina smiled into Cobiah's slack-jawed stare. "There were two more up on the dock, and they slowed me down."

"No problem. Looks like . . . you were . . . just in time," Cobiah managed to say. Waves rolled up around his boots, splashing gently against the silver buckles and dark soles. Something struck him, some memory he couldn't quite place. Cobiah's knees gave out, and he fell, sitting in the tide. He felt Benedict's hand on his shoulder, saw the worried look on Gamina's features, but before Cobiah could ask what troubled them, everything went dark.

27

"**Y**ou've got to stop acting like this, Cobiah. Gallivanting about after saboteurs half your age, risking your life in scraps with bandits out at the dock. You're not as young as you used to be."

Cobiah grimaced. "A charr's scolding me about being too eager to rush into combat. What's the world coming to? Look, it's been three weeks since that fight. I'm fine."

Sykox grumped, folding his arms over the lighthouse rail and enjoying the warmth of the afternoon sun. "You know I appreciate a good fight as much as anyone, but you've always been the one who leapt before you looked. In the Iron Legion, we don't leap until we've built three sets of siege engines and a tank to go in ahead of us. If Isaye were here, you know she'd say—"

"Yeah, well, Isaye's not here." Cobiah shot him a dirty look. "So can we stop bringing her up already?" Below them, the streets of the city were splayed out like a thick rug, with citizens traveling here and there, huddled in their cloaks as though afraid that simply being in the open would put them in danger. Although Edair's ships were still far from the city docks, the Krytan prince's bullying presence could be felt throughout Lion's Arch.

Sykox sighed. "A pity, that. She's the only one who can

talk sense into you when you get like this." Understand-ingly, the charr changed the subject. "So, what's Edair up to now?"

The old friends stood on the balcony of the tall light-house at Lion's Gate, looking out over the bay and into the Sea of Sorrows. From here, they could see the Kry-tan fleet surrounding the mouth of the harbor, gold-and-green flags waving atop both high-masted ships of the line and swift scout vessels. All of the ships bristled with armaments. Cannons glistened on the decks and through portholes in rows of ten, twenty, and even thirty, metal gleaming amid the oak hulls of massive ships.

Cobiah raised his sextant again, peering through the scope toward Prince Edair's massive armada. "Not much. They ran off two trade vessels early this morning that were trying to sneak through the barricade. Since then, it's been quiet." Two ships in particular drew Cobiah's eye. One was the sleek *Nomad II*. The other, sailing beside her, was the burliest galleon in the group—probably the largest ship in the world and easily the fattest and slow-est glutton of a boat Cobiah'd ever seen. He could read her name in gold letters on the ship's stern: *Balthazar's Trident.* From the crown that ornamented her prow and the long pennants of green silk flowing from all three of her masts, Cobiah guessed the chubby warthog bore a member of the royal family of Kryta.

Edair.

"The ships won't take action until he's ready. Edair's not the kind to let someone else claim his glory." Cobiah snapped the sextant back into his hand, closing the deli-cate instrument before pushing it into his pocket. The activity stretched the skin across his ribs, and he flinched instinctively. The wound on his side had been slow to heal, leaving a long mark across his ribs where the brigand's knife had sliced him open. He still bandaged the area, applying a healer's salve to numb the ongoing pain. Sykox was right: when he'd been a young man, such things barely slowed Cobiah down. Lately, things were different. It felt like everything in the world had sped up—while he was standing still.

The blockade had been in place nearly a month, and the city was suffering. Krytan Seraph gathered on the roads to the north, threatening land routes; though they'd been unable to fully block the roads as yet, incoming trade had stagnated. Warehouses along the docks tightened their guard in fear of rioting over food supplies. The Lionguard were working long shifts, going house to house where necessary to keep the peace. The fire had destroyed more than 80 percent of the ships at harbor that night, along with all of their wares and stores.

The fire had also cut off the city's hope for a rebuttal against the blockade. The ships that survived were a motley assortment of frigates and carracks—none outfitted for war. If the Krytans hadn't torched the docks, Lion's Arch might have been able to punch through the blockade. Now there was little hope of defeating the Krytan armada, and the citizens of Lion's Arch were rapidly losing morale.

With little choice and plenty of reason to fear, every wagon and cart in the city had been commandeered. They'd loaded each wagon with women and children, and then, under a flag of truce, the caravan was sent along the northern road toward the Shiverpeaks. With luck, they'd reach the mountain passes before the first icy rains of the season made the road too treacherous to travel. The Seraph agreed to give them an escort. If they made it that far, the caravan could reach the norn waycamp known as Hoelbrak before winter. From there, the refugees could travel via active asura gate to Divinity's Reach, the Black Citadel, or Rata Sum—anywhere safer than here.

Cobiah looked out at the sea again, the bright light of the setting sun glinting like a river of silver. Without the sextant's clear view, the armada gathered on the horizon looked like ravens clustered on a tree branch, waiting for the city to die so they could pick its bones clean.

"C'mon, Sykox. Let's take the lay of the land." The old charr nodded, matching his stiff, slightly limping stride to the commodore's. Down below the lighthouse, they entered the city streets. While the city had yet to be physically harmed by the Krytan blockade—other than the docks at the landing, of course—it had clearly wounded its spirit. Desperation hung like a gray shroud over Lion's Arch.

Forsaking his typical cheery greetings, Cobiah nodded briefly to those he passed as his mind spun through every possibility. Could they bribe the Krytan captains? Pay Prince Edair a high price to keep the land? Would he even consider ransoming Lion's Arch's freedom like that, or was he dedicated to the idea of ruling the city? Nodobe had already given good reason not to request the intervention of one of the charr legions, but what about the norn? Were there enough mercenaries in Hoelbrak to take on the Seraph?

Every option seemed worse than the last.

"A word, Commodore." Sidubo Nodobe's smooth voice was impossible to mistake.

Sighing, Cobiah slowed his pace. He muttered an old saying: "Think too hard on Grenth, and he'll come riding on your coattails."

"What's that?" The Elonian fell into step with them, his forehead creasing with confusion. Cobiah waved the comment away, and Nodobe went on. "I hate to interrupt your concentration, but I have bad news."

"Worse than the harbor fire?"

Nodobe paused to consider, and Cobiah immediately regretted the question. "Perhaps not that bad," Nodobe said at last. "But not particularly auspicious."

Cobiah pinched the bridge of his nose. "What is it?"

"Yomm's missing."

"Missing?" Sykox tilted his head and snorted disdainfully. "Hiding, more likely."

"Possible, but I don't think so. One of the merchants in the plaza saw light on the asura gate platform, just before dawn. It was active this morning." Nodobe lifted his hands in an elegant gesture. "We've checked. It's not working now. Whatever—or whoever—turned it on managed to turn it off again before the Lionguard reached the platform."

Cobiah blew out a long breath of air. "That weasely little traitor. I guess he did find a way to resurrect the . . . discombobulated . . . fidgit-casters. Or whatever the hell was keeping those things closed." Shaking his head, Cobiah met Nodobe's eyes grimly. "Check his shop. There's a chance he's hiding under his desk, but it's likely we won't see him again unless the city's recovered. At the least, you can take a tally of whatever stores he's got left at the mercantile."

"Aye, aye, Commodore." Nodobe gave him a dignified bow and strode off toward the plaza.

Sykox grumbled, "This just keeps getting worse. If we don't catch a break soon, we're sunk." Cobiah didn't respond. There was no need to restate the obvious, and the charr's tail was already thrashing like an angry serpent.

The two continued their trek through the city, from the empty shopping areas, past the blackened dock, toward the fort on the far side of the gangplank. There, several young men and women of the city were training ferociously with weapons. Although they'd likely be little match for the Seraph (if it came to that), it gave them something constructive to do, and Cobiah approved of their initiative. He could make out Captain Hedda and her husband, Bronn, in the middle of the pack, schooling four eager young sailors with training swords.

Too young, he thought as he watched them, far too young to be at war. Although he'd been the same age when he boarded the *Indomitable,* surely he'd never been so fresh-faced and naïve. "Commodore!" One of the boys waved toward him. Long brown hair, an eager smile, and loping, slightly bowed legs. Cobiah couldn't make him out. Surely it wasn't . . .

"Sethus?"

"Who, sir?" the young man asked cheerily as he trotted out of the glare. "It's me, sir. Benedict. Remember?" The young man smiled and reached to shake his hand.

"Benedict." Relief washed over Cobiah. Sethus had died more than thirty years ago. How could he have made such a ridiculous mistake? "What are you doing out here?" he asked.

"After our little adventure, sir, I figured it was time for me to learn how to use a sword." Benedict reddened, rubbing his forehead with a nervous hand. "If I'd been trained—if I'd known how to fight, sir, that fight might have gone better. I could have protected you."

Benedict? Protected him? Cobiah chuckled and patted the youth on his shoulder. "You did fine, young man." Still, although the words hadn't been meant badly, they stung a bit: another reminder of Cobiah's age. "Are you healing up all right?"

"Completely, sir. Just a few scars to help me remember

the tale." Benedict showed Cobiah his upper biceps, where a few thin white trails marked the otherwise tan and muscular arms. He'd healed rapidly, another perk of being young. That was a blessing, Cobiah thought, considering that the outcome of their fight against the saboteurs could have been far worse.

"He's doing very well." Bronn followed the youth, carrying his massive greatsword in one hand. The norn didn't appear to have aged a day since Cobiah had first met him aboard the *Salma's Grace*, though now he and Hedda had children of their own. Three sons: Geir, Tryggvi, and Kaive, all of whom were among the pack of young people learning weapons on the field—but who clearly had the advantage, even against charr and humans their own age. Bronn saw Cobiah's gaze and said proudly, "Warbands fight as a team, so charr learn group tactics from a young age. Humans prefer to negotiate, so they instinctively concentrate on defense. Norn are taught from birth to be heroes." Bronn smiled through his lush beard. "So we fight as heroes!" He laughed with good-natured pride, rich and hearty. It had been a while since Cobiah had heard the sound, and he smiled in gratitude.

Cobiah tousled Benedict's hair. "You're a brave lad. Get back to your training. Apparently, you're representing our entire race out there." He winked at Bronn. "Pay attention to Hedda's lessons. She's a hell of a fighter, and you'd do well to remember what she teaches you."

"Yes, Commodore. I will." Grinning, Benedict hurried back into formation, practicing his slashes and thrusts as Hedda called out each move.

"He's none the worse for wear." Bronn chuckled, shoving Cobiah with his shoulder. The norn's blue eyes lost their twinkle as he asked more quietly, "Can you say the same, old friend?"

Before Cobiah could answer the question, he noticed two burly charr marching across the Gangplank Bridge toward the training plaza. Sykox, whose eyes were keener, recognized them first, and all four ears pricked forward in glee. "Fassur! Aysom!" With a wave, the engineer bounded forward to clasp their wrists in greeting. "You old blackguards. How did you get here? The *Pride* was at sea!"

Bronn greeted his old companions with a bellow of goodwill, thumping their backs even as Cobiah gave them a somewhat more restrained greeting. Though the cunning old charr's fur had gone from black to darkly tarnished silver with age, Captain Fassur's grin was just as sharp as ever. Sykox and Aysom burst into challenging, friendly roars, each determined to outdo the other in the ferocity of his greeting. At last, Fassur raised a hand to ask his friends for silence. "I bet you're wondering how we managed to sneak the *Pride* through the blockade." Fassur snickered and brushed his claws through the fur on one arm, so pleased with himself that he might as well have been about to spit up a canary.

"Indeed! How in the realms of torment and travail did you do that?" Cobiah brought his attention back to the topic of their feat. Aysom cracked his knuckles as he answered the question, his face studiously bland. "A good pilot gave us some tricks to slip through against the tide. It was touch and go 'cause we didn't want the Krytans to hear our engine, but we managed to push through while they were eating dinner. I guess they thought it'd be impossible for a boat to enter the harbor when the tide was flowing out." He shook his golden mane, his unusually deep voice resonating with maturity and respect.

"It *is* impossible,"—Cobiah slapped his leg in amusement—"For everyone but the *Pride*! Well done on sneaking past. Engine or no engine, if the Krytans'd seen you—or if you'd hit the shale or high ruins below the waterline—you'd be driftwood by now. And you did it in the dark to boot? Your new pilot must know these waters darn well. Or be darn lucky." Cobiah ran his fingers through his hair, shrugging it back as he admired the sheer difficulty of such a task. "Is he charr or human? No matter. Whoever he is, I owe him a bottle of Black Citadel whiskey. Bring him 'round my manor, and I'll—"

"It's not like that, Cobiah." Fassur gave a sober toss of his iron-tipped horns. He measured the commodore cautiously, and then, as if he'd come to some silent resolution, he added, "It was Isaye. Isaye gave us the information we needed to come through." Beside him, the younger Aysom stiffened, looking much like he was tensing for an inevitable if undesirable fight.

Cobiah's blood went cold. Sykox was the one who spoke first. "Did she come with you? Is she—"

"No." Fassur shrugged, his eyes shifting right to left. "She contacted us out at sea, beyond the barricade. She knew our old hiding places, guessed where we'd be holed up, and came to talk to us. Without her, we'd still be out there. She told us when the Krytan patrols were moving, where the tides were turning, where to avoid the hidden reefs."

"And you trusted her?" Cobiah retorted.

"Coby." Bronn admonished him in a booming tone. "Such rudeness is beneath you. Let them tell Isaye's tale and judge her actions by them alone." His beard wagged with disapproval as he thumped Cobiah's shoulder again, this time hard enough to leave a bruise. "My dainty love, Hedda, told me of your discourtesy to the lady Isaye when the *Nomad* visited our city. There's an old norn saying: 'A cleaved head no longer plots.'" Bronn paused meaningfully. The others stared at him in confusion. Tilting his head, the norn blinked and rethought his words. "Nope, no, wait, it's the other one, sorry." He cleared his throat, trying again. "'Be not the first to speak angry words, or you shall be the first to feast on them.'" Bronn nodded, conviction returning along with his volume. "That's the one.

"Now let us hear what the charr have to say."

Fassur's smile was all teeth and no amusement. "She asked us to bring you a message, Coby," he said with a touch of his old savoir faire.

"A message?" the commodore grumbled. "Keep it. I don't care to hear what she has to say."

Sykox smacked the back of Cobiah's head, sending his ponytail flapping about his shoulders. "Ow!" Cobiah swatted back, but Sykox growled warningly.

"Will you cut that out, Coby? The woman's not one of your infernal gods. She's your *wife*—"

"Ex-wife."

"*Wife*," Sykox said firmly, correcting him. "The priests never separated you, and from what I hear, you humans do whatever your priests say, so get over it. I don't care if she's your wife, your ex-wife, or your goldfish; if Isaye's risking herself to help Lion's Arch, then you'll damn well hear what the woman has to say." He rubbed at his cheeks, his jowls and muzzle distending in a sad clown face. "I don't care what caused the fight. Just fix the problem!"

Chastised, Cobiah said, "I wish it were that easy." Seagulls circled overhead, their shrill cries echoing. Young voices called out in mock battle cries, and Hedda's low alto broke in here and there as she corrected a grip or straightened a footing. The sun was overly warm for the afternoon, blazing down on Cobiah's head with an uncomfortable heat. Sighing, Cobiah gave in. "Go ahead, Fassur. I'm listening."

Fassur's stare was strangely piercing, his tawny yellow eyes both judging and consoling in the same moment as only a cat can manage. He shifted on his padded feet, sinking his claws into the earth between the cobblestones. "Isaye wants to meet with you, Cobiah. She said that she has political blackmail on Prince Edair, and she's willing to hand it over."

"Did she say what it was?" Interested despite himself, Cobiah tried to keep an open mind. "Or how it could help us? Or why me?"

"No." Fassur lowered his head. He picked at one paw with the claws of the other, choosing his words carefully. "I haven't always gotten along with Isaye, Cobiah. You know that. Titan's blood, I'm the one who got you drunk as a skale when she left." A sharp grin. "But she was willing to risk a lot to get the *Pride* to harbor, and she managed it despite our personal history. I believe she's sailing true." When Cobiah remained silent, Fassur carried on. "The route she gave us is clear both ways. If we go out while the tide's coming in, after dark, the Krytans will have their backs to us. More than that. Isaye told us where the patrols will be tonight so we can make it by without alerting them."

Cobiah took a moment to consider. He struggled to trust Isaye, but every time she did something positive, he saw again the image of finding her that day. She'd been meeting with a Krytan agent at one of the havens north of the city—carrying a copy of Cobiah's notes from the council meeting the night before . . . He squeezed his eyes shut against the bright sun, willing the image to fade into spots and flashes. "Is that all?"

"She said that she needed your help, Coby," Fassur added offhandedly, shoulders rippling in a shrug. "I said I'd tell you." Cobiah tried not to show how the words infected him, charged his spirit with a sudden desire to rush to her aid. No matter how they fought, Isaye always had that effect on him. The charr's yellow eyes crept up from where he'd been staring at the stones on the ground, this time judging Cobiah's reaction. *Damn it, Fassur. You know me too well.*

Feeling equal parts amused and manipulated, Cobiah looked around at the others. Bronn jabbed the commodore in the ribs and nodded encouragement. Aysom gave Cobiah a bobbing, reassuring smile, his long horns tilting back and forth. Sykox's ears flicked back and then forward again as his tail kept up a steady rhythm of annoyance. *Thump-thump-thump. Thump-thump-thump. Thump-thump—*

"Fine!" Cobiah threw up his hands. "I'll meet with her. But not on the *Pride*. The *Nomad's* in the blockade with the others, and even Edair's not dumb enough to miss my ship when he sees it. We'll have to use an unknown ship. Then they might think we're Krytan . . . *if* we're lucky."

"I can help with the 'luck' part." Fassur grinned. "I still have that old Krytan flag in the hold, from the time we took the *Salma's Grace*. Remember? Ol' Moran let me take it as a trophy. If we fly that on our mast and they don't see which side of the blockade we came from to start, we should be able to get close enough to signal the *Nomad*."

"Just might work." Cobiah felt his confidence building. "We'd just need a ship."

Sykox brightened. "Use the scout ship, the *Gabrian's Comet*. She's small, low to the water, and her captain's a friend of mine. I bet I can talk him into loaning her to you for the night."

"Now we're getting somewhere." Cobiah grinned, feeling the tension leave his body for the first time in weeks. Finally, a plan! They were *doing* something. Something insane, but something proactive, and that made up for three weeks of pent-up frustration. "Sykox, commandeer the *Comet* and crew her with the absolute minimum needed to keep her moving. I'll need you to find five sailors. I won't risk any more lives than that on this wild goose chase."

"Four. I'm your first mate," Fassur growled. "No argument, Coby. My mind's made up. I'm the one who trusted Isaye and brought you the message. If it turns out she was using me . . ." Fassur's claws snapped in, then out again. "I'll be the one who carves repayment out of her hide."

"Danger, adventure, possible betrayal—by the mighty claw of Bear! I'll not leave you on such an adventure, Coby," Bronn preened. He leaned close and said sotto voce, "Besides, the wife'll have me teaching swordplay all day and all night if I stay here. Spirits of the Wild, protect me from the jaws of yapping pups!"

Aysom nodded. "I'm coming, too."

"Have fun." Suddenly, all eyes turned to Sykox. The orange-furred charr crossed his arms over his spotted chest and lashed his tail belligerently. "What? I'm sure as the Mists not going with you! All this yammering's reminded me that I have some very important work to finish at the docks."

"Work?" Cobiah exclaimed. "What in the Six Gods do you have to work on? The piers are burned! The ships are gone! It's like a Grenth-blasted graveyard down there."

Sykox sniffed. "You say 'graveyard,' I say 'opportunity.' Lion's Arch still has plenty of men and women ready to crew an armada." The charr smiled, and his long white fangs gleamed in the sunlight. "I just need to find them something to sail."

28

The *Gabrian's Comet* was a small schooner, less than two hundred feet long and dwarfed by pinnaces such as the *Pride* and big clippers such as the *Nomad II*. Although she typically carried a crew of around twenty, tonight she had only five sailors working amid her rigging. One of them was a human. Two were charr: Fassur and Aysom. The other two were norn. When Bronn's brother, Grymm, heard about their plan, he promptly stormed into the Crow's Nest Tavern and challenged his brother to a fight to decide which one of them would go. After they spent two hours arguing, breaking chairs over one another, and wheedling the barmaids for more alcohol, Cobiah gave in and brought both. It was far easier than paying their bar tab.

Sanctum Harbor rippled with a wayward southern wind that bled cold from the Shiverpeaks. They kept the sails closed as they pushed off from the pier, letting the last of the outgoing tide draw them from shore. Only when they were completely surrounded by the waters of the harbor and the tide began to turn inward did they unfurl the sails: dark canvas, stained black with oil from a midnight yew. Harder to see against the night sky.

The wind sang in the taut rigging, swelling the

canvases that swayed against the two small masts. It had
been years since Cobiah'd been at sea, and the salt spray
and rolling bow of the deck invigorated him despite
the circumstances. He stood in the aft of the ship, looking back at the lights of the harbor, searching for the
spires of the little chapel on Deverol Island. They'd
built it only a few years ago, and Cobiah'd feared the
other residents of the city might not take kindly to
Krytan religion in their midst. To his surprise, the nonhumans had been supportive. Several of the city's norn
helped carve the great oak beams of the ceiling, and
an asuran inventor had engineered self-illuminating
stained-glass windows just so the little shrine would be
hospitable at night. Fixing his eyes on it, Cobiah murmured a prayer to each of the six gods of his people,
wishing for the best. Grenth, god of death. Balthazar,
god of war. Lyssa, goddess of beauty. Kormir, goddess
of truth. Melandru, goddess of the earth. And on the
highest point, Dwayna the Merciful, sweet and gentle
comforter of the soul.

He could still hear the priest's voice, trying to console
him. *"Pray to her, young man. She will bring you peace."*

Without meaning to, his mind leapt back to the day
he'd first left Lion's Arch, remembering how the white
sails carrying him out of the city had looked like an
angel's wings. It seemed right that he'd tied Biviane's doll
to his belt today, as he'd done in the past when he cap-
tained the *Pride*. Cobiah smiled and brushed his fingers
over Polla's faded yarn hair. All the time that had passed,
from then to now. All the years. All the adventures.

So much had changed.

"We'll be at the edge of the blockade in fifteen minutes, sir, if the wind holds. Even if it doesn't, the norn are
moving those oars like mad things. The steerage's made

for six men to a side, and we've got Bronn and Grymm. I think those two have a bet going as to who can pull harder." Fassur yawned and stretched his arms up over his head with a whining, grunty noise. He tugged on each wrist, loosening the muscles, and then shook himself all over like a dog rising from a nap. "After that, we're oars-only for another ten or so, and that should get us to the eastern pyramid marker. Isaye said she'd sail there for three nights, waiting to see if we showed. There'll be a red lantern hung on her bow so we can tell the *Nomad* from the others." The pyramid marker was a set of stones piled high in the ocean, the top of the stack jutting out well above the highest tide. It marked the edge of safe sailing. If a ship sailed any farther toward the eastern coast of the bay, it risked tearing the bottom of its hull against unpredictable ruins, coral, shale, and other dangers beneath the waves.

Although the prince's ships might notice the *Nomad II* sailing close to that edge, they wouldn't think much of it. Isaye was one of the best pilots in Tyria, and she knew Sanctum Harbor like no other. The other Krytan captains might even assume she'd been told to watch for ships moving in the currents along the dangerous edge. The *Gabrian's Comet* was small enough that it could hide on the *Nomad II*'s port side, keeping the clipper's bulk between the *Gabrian's Comet* and the rest of the ships in the blockade; she'd be hard to spot under casual inspection from afar. The ruse wouldn't have to last long. Cobiah didn't plan to stay.

The tide moved beneath them precisely as Isaye's rough-sketched map indicated. Every piece of wreckage beneath them had been drawn out, with careful timing marked in seconds to indicate when they should turn their rudder. Each time Fassur gestured to him, Aysom pulled on the rudder, shifting the boat's elegant glide through the calm waters of the bay. Although the currents in Sanctum Harbor were a morass of unpredictable fluctuation, Isaye's map always seemed to predict where the draw would be. Cobiah busied himself by adjusting the sails, and when Fassur called for them to ease, he climbed the mast to the low yardarm and rolled her rigging down. He secured the dark canvas with sailor's knots, trying to ignore the stiffness that plagued joints once fluent with such labor.

"Stay silent, everyone," Cobiah murmured to the crew. "The water carries echoes. We don't want the Krytans to hear us coming."

Slowly, her oars piercing the water like sharp-edged knives, the *Gabrian's Comet* slipped to the edge of the blockade. Lanterns glittered in the distance, tied to the gunwales of clippers and larger galleons. Now and again, Cobiah could hear a watchman call the time or make out fragments of conversation from sailors on the Krytan ships. Most of the armada was stationary, and the patrols moved as Isaye had indicated. Buoys were fanned out between them, with ropes and nets splayed from one to another, designed to foul the keel and tangle in the rudder of any ship that tried to punch its way through the blockade. The *Gabrian's Comet* avoided them all—thanks to Isaye's carefully drawn map.

"She's precise," Fassur rumbled, his voice so soft that Cobiah, standing next to him, had trouble hearing it.

Cobiah couldn't help giving in to a little bitterness. "You think that's something?" he whispered coolly. "You should have seen how methodical she was about copying my notes. The Krytans must have been very impressed." Despite himself, Cobiah felt the tension in his shoulders ease. Whatever crazy plan Isaye was going to propose, thus far her information had been reliable. That eased his mind—a bit. Now he could turn his worry toward wondering exactly what she'd felt was so important in the first place.

Nodding in agreement, Fassur folded the paper and tucked it into his belt pouch. Squinting, he lifted a hand and pointed across the sea with one long claw. "There. Red lantern."

Slowly, carefully, the schooner pulled up alongside the *Nomad II*. The waves knocked the *Gabrian's Comet* against the much larger ship, tossing it back and forth in a softly bumping rhythm. Cobiah had deliberately kept his craft dark, and the *Nomad II* dimmed her lanterns along the port side, ensuring that the *Gabrian's Comet* would be further hidden from view of the Krytan ships floating some distance away on her other side. Cobiah tightened his sword belt nervously, watching a sailor on the *Nomad II* throw a long rope toward them. Aysom caught it, wrapping the end around one of the cleats near the edge of their deck. Once they were tied off, the larger ship slid a board down to them: a makeshift gangplank so they could come aboard.

Fassur took Cobiah's wrist in a gesture of brotherhood. "Take Bronn and Grymm with you. Be careful. Aysom and I will keep our weapons out and the *Comet* ready to push off. The minute you're done, don't waste any time with kissy-poo or lovey-dovey stuff. We need to be back through that blockade and into the city's harbor well before dawn."

"'Lovey-dovey'?" Cobiah stared at his old friend skeptically. "Fassur, women really are a foreign species to you. You realize Isaye's more likely to kill me than kiss me, right?"

"Speak for yourself," the charr grunted. "I married

that Blood Legion minx, if you remember. I know fore-play when I see it."

"Don't worry." Cobiah had to stifle his laugh. "This won't take long." He gestured to the brothers and headed up the slippery gangplank.

Assembled on the deck were four human sailors wearing linen shirts and breeches, a kerchief in green and gold tied about one man's neck. As the three visitors made it up the plank and onto the *Nomad II*, the sailors on the deck kept their hands near their cutlasses, taking no chances. "The cap'n's stateroom is this way." One of them crooked his arm for them to follow and walked toward the oak doors on the quarterdeck at the rear of the ship.

Although most ships kept hands active, even at night, the clipper's deck felt all but abandoned. No one was straightening the ropes on the capstan, nor washing the boards, nor standing guard at the bow or the gunnery. The silence unnerved Cobiah, and their footsteps across the broad ship's promenade felt overloud and strange. Bronn frowned as well, exchanging a glance with his brother, and the two closed ranks to stay with Cobiah and the sailors of the *Nomad II*. Bronn subtly loosed his greatsword in its back sheath. Grymm cracked his knuckles, exchanging pleasant smiles with the Krytan sailor walking beside him. Just before the sailors opened the doors to the captain's cabin, Cobiah realized something else: none of the men escorting them across the ship had tattoos—not an anchor, or a mermaid, or a pair of crossed swords between the lot of them. They walked stiff legged rather than rolling with the motion of the waves against the ship, and all four fell into the same rhythm, arms swinging in time, footsteps thumping regularly on the deck boards.

These were *not* sailors.

Cobiah paled. Before he could speak, the large doors on the quarterdeck swung open from the other side. Beyond them, he could see the *Nomad II*'s stateroom. The area was more than a cabin, built to serve as a meeting-room for the officers while the ship was at sea. The area within was lit by hanging lanterns bolted to the beams of the ceiling, their tinted panes casting colored light across the well-scrubbed floors and shining brass ornaments.

Yet there was no central table for meetings or meals, no sign of a captain's desk or personal effects other than a few wall hangings that Cobiah recognized as Isaye's. The furniture had been removed completely save for a tall, ornamented mahogany chair with opulently covered pillows that rested in the center of the chamber. Even though they had never met before, Cobiah instantly recognized the man seated there.

Prince Edair.

He was young, only a few years past twenty, with a deeply privileged smile and an athlete's graceful form. Soft hands gripped the hilt of a bejeweled sword clipped to his gleaming patent-leather belt. The man's skin was olive toned, his hair the rich auburn common to Krytan nobility. Handsome, but the way he lolled on the chair spoke of conceited superiority in every self-satisfied posture. From his shining black boots to his immaculate green-and-gold uniform, the man appeared every inch a Krytan soldier—but not a speck of the clothing looked worn or broken in. Edair straightened his sleeves, keeping his eyes gleefully fixed on Cobiah and the others in the doorway.

Isaye and Tenzin Moran stood to either side of the throne, her hazel eyes unreadable and his gun holster empty. Marines wearing the uniform of the Seraph lined both walls of the chamber, weapons already in their hands. The escorts drew their swords and fenced their three captives in the doorway. Hatches on the deck behind them sprang open with a clatter, and Cobiah could hear thumping, pounding footsteps barging up from the hold.

"Can't go backward," Cobiah conceded. "Might as well charge."

In a flash, he drew his sword. He heard the ringing sound of Bronn's two-hander coming free of its scabbard as Grymm bellowed a challenge. "Villains!" the younger twin shouted, his voice carrying like a foghorn. "Fight us one on one, if you dare!" He swatted away a sword pointed in his face and charged into the line of guardsmen to their right, plowing one Seraph with a haymaker as he drove his knee into a second soldier's gut. It didn't take Grymm long to turn that side of the room into a six-on-one brawl.

Bronn turned to the left, swinging his greatsword in broad strokes over his head to drive their opponents backward. Cobiah took advantage of their escorts' surprise to punch one in the jaw with his cutlass hilt. Before the other Krytans could react, Cobiah grabbed one by the shoulder and hurled him into the third, knocking both of them to the floor.

With the norn twins handling the company of marines, no one stood between Cobiah and the Krytan prince. "I might not make it out of this room," Cobiah said threateningly, storming toward Edair, "but you sure as hell won't."

"Cobiah, please!" Isaye begged, stepping in front of the throne. "I can't let you hurt him." The gesture was baffling, and Cobiah froze midstride, struck by the tears in her eyes and the desperate tone in her voice.

"Damn it, Isaye!" Cobiah grabbed her shoulder roughly, pushing her aside. "This is no time for national loyalty!

The man's trying to kill me. He's trying to destroy our city."

"I know," she whispered, tears running down her cheeks.

That wasn't the response he'd expected. He thought she'd fight him or argue—call him names or defend the Krytan prince's actions. Instead, Isaye stood mutely in his path, willing to take any abuse he'd offer. It wasn't like her at all.

His hand softened on her shoulder, cupping it gently instead of gripping with force. "Isaye . . ." Cobiah wavered, taking in her distress. "What has he done to you?"

Just then Krytan soldiers rushed into the room, flooding past Cobiah and hurtling protectively into position around the prince. One of them knocked Isaye aside, leveling his blade at Cobiah's heart. The blow was so violent that she tumbled to the ground, striking her head against the floor of the cabin. Isaye fell limp, dark hair tumbling across her shoulders to cover her face.

More troops pushed through the doorway, overwhelming the twins with sheer numbers. Three guardsmen forced Bronn's sword out of his hands, backing him against a wall with the barrel of a pistol shoved under the norn's bearded jaw. Grymm struggled to cross the room to reach him, dragging two men on each of his legs and another hanging behind him from his broad shoulders. He swung wildly, trying to knock his captors off him, but more and more piled on. A few moments later, there were so many sailors on the norn that Cobiah couldn't see him anymore—and then the entire pile collapsed to the deck, kicking and wriggling in defiance.

"Your Highness!" a guard reported from the *Nomad II's* deck. "The schooner's cast off. They're getting away!"

"Burn it to the waterline. Use the flaming oil," the

prince said lazily, barely bothering to raise his voice. "Do I have to tell you people *everything*?"

Other soldiers relayed the command, and soon Cobiah heard the twangs of shortbow fire and thuds of oil packets fired from handheld slings. The Krytans stripped Cobiah's weapon from his hand. Keeping their swords pointed at his chest and throat, they forced him against the wall beside Bronn. Cobiah didn't take his eyes off Isaye. Tenzin pushed his way through the soldiers to kneel at her side. The young marine pressed a torn piece of cloth to a wound on Isaye's head, where blood was beginning to mat the silken strands. "Did you have to hurt her?" he said to the soldier sharply.

The man stiffened. "Just following orders, sir."

Even at a distance, Cobiah could hear Isaye mutter something smarmy as her eyes fluttered open. Despite the bleak circumstances, her voice was full of life and fire—and Cobiah eased back against the wall with a sigh of relief.

"Slap the traitors in irons, including the *Nomad*'s officers." Prince Edair gave a lackadaisical wave of his hand. "Take them aboard the *Balthazar's Trident*. We'll handle the interrogations there."

29

The *Balthazar's Trident* was a heavy, broad hulk of a ship, wallowing in the ocean like a pig in mud. She was the very picture of great wealth, with gleaming brass railings, lily-white sails, and carved ornamentation on every door, hatch, and railing. The ship's name was plated in gold, blazoned in two-foot high lettering beneath the balcony of her stern galley. The figurehead on her prow was of the human god of war after whom the ship was named. Twice as large as any other figurehead in the fleet, the statue portrayed him from the waist up as if in battle, raising a brass trident challengingly toward the sky. The ship had four great masts, so large that the trees themselves must have been over a hundred years old, positioned in a straight line from fore to rear along her deck and rigged with a thick span of interconnecting lines that made up her superstructure. A massive golden crown had been embroidered on her forward jib sail, and a series of fifty-foot-long gold-and-green pennants spun from the high points of her mastheads. She even dwarfed the *Indomitable*.

The Krytan soldiers loaded Cobiah and the others into a rowboat the size of a fishing vessel and sailed them from the *Nomad II* under heavy guard. They pulled up against the galleon's starboard wale under the watchful eye of more than twenty riflemen with guns pointed and ready to fire. Instead of a gangplank or a rope ladder, the *Balthazar's Trident* had two elementalists dressed in gold and green standing at an opening in the gunwale railing. One of them raised his voice as the rowboat took hold of tossed lines from the *Balthazar's Trident*, chanting a spell upon a box of slat boards. The wind wrapped itself around each plank, rolling them out of the box to balance solidly upon the air. One by one, they moved past each other over the side of the ship, creating the firm shape of a curling staircase.

Prince Edair, seemingly unimpressed, bounded up it eagerly, calling greetings to his men aboard the ship. "Today," he proclaimed, puffing up as all eyes turned toward him, "is a day that will go down in history! Today, Kryta brings to justice the thieves who have defied her. With the blessings of our patron, Balthazar, we have captured the leader of these traitorous pirates. Behold, Cobiah Marriner!" Prince Edair balanced on the edge of the ship's dock, pointing down at the rowboat while those around him cheered loudly, taunting Cobiah and waving their hats in the air. "Next," Edair said, raising his voice as the ribaldry faded, "we shall make right the indignity done to our fair nation.

"Today, Cobiah Marriner! Tomorrow, Lion's Arch!"

Whatever the prince's other failings may be, Cobiah griped silently, *the boy's father clearly taught him how to galvanize his followers.*

The sailors on the massive galleon repeated the chant, firing their guns in the air and whooping in celebration. Edair grasped the railing and leaned over the side of the ship. "Take the traitors to the royal stateroom." His antic-ipatory grin turned Cobiah's stomach. "Tell Mercer to ready his bag of tricks. We need more information about the city defenses before we give orders to attack."

"I'll handle the transfer, Your Highness." A woman in red, her body molded by a formfitting, coat-like leather bodice over a tight pair of pants, moved through the crowd to the prince's side. The scarf tied about her waist swayed as she gave a bow, brilliant blue eyes peering out beneath a curl of shoulder-length scarlet hair. One paler lock flashed at her brow, glinting like the brightly colored warning of a poisonous fish. "All will be as you command." The prince smiled and nodded, and the two exchanged quiet words that Cobiah could not overhear.

"Snow Leopard, clever and wise spirit, shield my eyes," Bronn said. He sat in the rowboat beside Cobiah, staring up at the woman in frank appreciation. "Kill me if you must, boys, but don't leave me alone with a seductress like that! Hedda'd never let me out of her sight again."

The woman inclined her head once more, and the prince smiled. Prince Edair turned away and strode among his swaggering crew, delighting in their admiration, as the red-garbed woman gave a signal to the soldiers on the rowboat. Obeying with alacrity, the Krytans grabbed all five prisoners—Cobiah, Isaye, Tenzin, and the two norn—and began to force them up the magical stairway onto the galleon.

While the Krytans were figuring out the various difficulties of getting recalcitrant norn up a tightly wound spiral, Cobiah took stock of his surroundings. The *Balthazar's Trident* was the largest ship he'd ever set foot on by far. She was heavily crewed and carried nearly as many combat-trained marines as she did crew. He saw at least two elementalists, though he suspected there were more aboard, and several of those following Edair across the deck wore armor much like Osh Moran had once worn:

magic-wielding guardians, Cobiah suspected, as his old friend had been.

Cobiah could figure out everyone aboard except the woman giving them orders. At first glance, she looked like a plaything, someone the prince might have brought along for personal entertainment during the long nights of the blockade. Listening to her iron-in-satin voice, watching the way the marines leapt to follow her orders without question, Cobiah knew that this woman was no one's toy. An adviser, perhaps? A cousin of the royal line? She seemed distinctly out of place, yet the prince had all but deferred to her suggestions. Cobiah stared at her, trying to reach a conclusion as to her purpose and abilities.

A sharp elbow thumped into Cobiah's rib cage, forcing the breath from his body in a pained exhalation and drawing his attention sharply away from the woman in red. When he looked, Isaye was glaring at him. "If you have to hit me . . . hit the other . . . side," Cobiah wheezed, his still-healing dagger wound throbbing with new pain. He'd been lucky not to tear it open again during the battle on the *Nomad II*. Then again, he hadn't made it close enough to Edair to start a fight.

Isaye grabbed his shirt in her manacled hands, surreptitiously pulling it up and noting the bandages underneath. "You're *wounded*?" Isaye blinked, shocked. "What on Melandru's green earth were you doing out here if you're hurt? Are you insane? You might have ripped it open again. An enemy could find out and use it against you. The wound could have gone septic—"

"My wife needed me." Cobiah met her gaze evenly. "How could I not come?"

Unspoken implications hung in the silence between them. Breath catching in her throat, Isaye regarded him more gently. "Scamp." Nevertheless, a smile teased the corners of her lips, and she looked away before it caught hold.

Once all five prisoners were on the deck of the galleon, the soldiers herded them through a double-doored hatch in the deck and down a short flight of stairs toward one of the lower holds. Judging by the size of the *Balthazar's Trident*, there were at least three levels within the ship's body. At least one of them, Cobiah guessed, was solely for housing all the marines. At the end of a long wooden hallway stood a door guarded by two soldiers who were not wearing the standard gold-and-green uniform. Instead, their clothing was simple, a matching dark blue and silver, uniform in coloration but diverse in fabric and pattern. Their dress looked more functional than showy; tied tight with laces, the fabric was kept close to their bodies so it would not hamper movement, and both men carried swords with well-worn hilts. Guards, then, not footmen.

Cobiah hadn't heard the woman in red walking behind them, and he jumped when her voice seemed to appear as if out of thin air. "His Highness will be interrogating the prisoners in the stateroom." She stepped through the group of captives confidently, completely unconcerned that anyone might make an attempt to do her harm. The two guardsmen, one pale and one dark, stood straighter as she approached. Unlike the Seraph, they seemed perfectly comfortable with her presence, watching the woman in red with the ease of long familiarity. Still, she was clearly in charge.

To the pale-haired guard: "Kaj, go to the prince's quarters. He'll undoubtedly ask to see his prize, and I want you there for protection." To the dark-haired one: "Glenn, see that the brig is prepared for five and be sure there's food and water available. Regardless of their current situation, these people are our guests."

"Yes, ma'am." The door wardens snapped to attention, eyes bright with respect.

"Keep your eyes open. The Shining Blade will be expected to help me ensure good behavior while our new friends are aboard." There was a subtle implication in her words, and both guards seemed to relax in their stances. The woman flicked her eyes over the prisoners, not caring if they overheard. "I will be protecting the prince personally."

"Yes, Exemplar." The two young men gave her courteous salutes and quickly began their tasks.

The Shining Blade? Cobiah struggled to identify the reference. At last, he remembered something Isaye had mentioned years ago: the Shining Blade were an elite branch of the military in Kryta. It was said they were complete fanatics, willing and even eager to die at the king's command. If so, and if she was one of them, why was this woman treating the prince's captives so well?

The broad door opened, and the woman in red stepped into the room without another word. The marines shoved the prisoners after, not caring if they stumbled or fell flat as they entered a large audience hall. The stateroom within was enormous, easily the largest hall Cobiah had ever seen within a ship. Wide, red-carpeted stairs flowed down from the main doorway to a ballroom floor, and to either side of the entryway, a shelflike balcony wrapped around the body of the room. The ceiling had been painted to look like a night sky, with glittering, enchanted stars illuminating the upper area, while lanterns hung in tidy rows along the edge of the balcony to bring a warm glow to the lower part of the room. Marveling at the opulence, Cobiah picked his way down the stairs in the wake of the woman in red, trying not to scuff the magnificent Elonian rug. The wall opposite the staircase held six large stained-glass windows, each patterned after one of the human gods, the whole looking down over a stagelike dais. On that dais stood a massive golden throne.

He was so overwhelmed by his surroundings that it took Cobiah a moment to realize there were people in the room. Indeed, there were at least fifty, all dressed in exquisite and expensive clothing, hair done in elaborate braids and decorative twists, their faces painted with the hauteur of nobility. Cobiah's eyes widened as he realized he must have been walking through the crème de la crème of Divinity's Reach. Although a few of them wore weapons, most were decorative, bejeweled—and had probably never been drawn. The music of stringed instruments faded and died to a hushed silence, broken only by soft, titillated whispers through the crowd.

Each step felt like it took an hour. The crowd parted, their eyes raking over him, hiding murmurs and smothering laughter behind their hands. Cobiah felt his face grow warm with humiliation; here he was in ripped breeches and an untucked linen shirt, bearing the obvious stains of sail and brawl, walking among people whose silken skirts and golden coronets were worth as much as his entire manor. An old anger pricked within his chest. He passed a table laden with punch and fluffy pastries, his stomach rebelling at the oversweet smell. These privileged idiots were dancing and feasting, playing politics while Lion's Arch starved.

A herald at the front of the room sounded his trumpet, and the nobles quickly turned toward the dais, sinking into curtsies and bows. As Cobiah watched, Prince Edair, newly changed from his soldierly uniform into clothing more suited for a royal ball, strode into the room across the dais followed by three more blue-garbed Shining Blade. The crowd burst into polite applause at the sight of their prince, loudly admiring the pattern on the sleeves of his golden doublet, the deep color of a purple shirt made of rare Canthan silk, or the immaculate shine of his high black boots. Apparently, extravagance was in. Personally, Cobiah thought Edair looked like a dancing peony.

Turning away from the stage, Cobiah used the time to count his opponents. Two Shining Blade at the door. Three more onstage. Perhaps twenty Seraph marines standing guard around the room and, of course, the woman in red. Grymm noticed him glancing around and gave the commodore a tense smile. Isaye caught him as well, but her reaction was less approving. She kicked his ankle surreptitiously, saying, "They *will* kill us."

Edair took the time to pause and speak with a few of his supporters at the edge of the stage. He smiled and shook hands, exchanging pleasantries with the nobility while the prisoners waited in a clump at the center of the room.

"What is Edair *doing*?" Tenzin stared at the prince in frank disapproval.

"Making an ass of himself, it seems," Bronn grunted disparagingly. "Is that man seriously wearing *silk* to a *war*?" The norn spat on the floor derisively, causing nearby courtiers to shrink away and stare in disgust.

Cobiah shook his head. "No. He's humiliating us. Deliberately. Letting the nobles stare their fill at his 'prisoners of war' . . . all the better to inflate his pride."

After a few more minutes, Edair made a great show of draping himself onto the throne. "Bring the traitors closer. If they tell me all I want to know, I may choose to be merciful," he said in a tone that was anything but. The Seraph escort dragged the prisoners to the front of the room, lining them up in a row before the dais. The exemplar climbed the dais, her red leather coat brushing the edge of the stairs, but paused before she reached the throne. She took up a position there, her eyes resting thoughtfully on Cobiah. Aware that he was the focus of her steady contemplation, Cobiah felt his neck heat and his cheeks color, and he turned away. He was too old to fall for such an obvious ruse.

"Very well, then." Edair straightened the five-pointed crown on his head and fixed a stern glare at the captives. "You will tell me the best methods of attacking Lion's Arch from land and sea. Where the defenses are positioned and a summary of their capacities." Glancing at the woman in red, he finished graciously, "I will use the information to seize the city with as few casualties as possible. Your people will be spared and even allowed to leave. But they cannot remain in Lion's Arch unless they submit to Krytan rule." A smattering of polite applause rippled through the assembled crowd.

Before any of the others could answer, Isaye stepped forward to address the prince. "Prince Edair," she began. "I served your father loyally for nearly eight years. He trusted me. Until a few days ago, you trusted me as well. I ask you to trust me now." She stood, tall and proud, her dark hair tumbling down her back and the sober look of conscience weighing on her features. Although still in irons, Isaye had the bearing of a noble, her shoulders back, her chin held high as she looked Prince Edair in the eye. "I was there when your father forbade you to attack Lion's Arch. I was the one who convinced him that attacking the city would not be worth the losses Kryta would take. Moreover, I helped your father understand the duty this city performs, for Kryta and for Tyria itself.

"These people are Kryta's allies. They hold back the risen undead of Orr, and we should be *supporting* that effort, not removing their ability to defend us." Isaye's hazel eyes flashed. "I ask you to stop this. Now. Make a treaty that recognizes Lion's Arch's independence and make peace with her citizens. It's the only way Tyria will survive the coming storms."

Edair sat forward in his throne, thrusting his finger toward Isaye. "You're defending them? After they burned your ship. Threw you out! By Balthazar's fire, you cling to your loyalty like a child hiding under a cloak, thinking blindness will keep you safe." The audience had fallen completely silent, watching the exchange breathlessly. This was exactly the kind of theater Edair wanted. "I don't care what information you gave my father over the years. He was a fool to listen to you. Kryta should have attacked Lion's Arch years ago." Isaye's cheeks flushed red, and Edair tapped his fingers rhythmically on the arm of his golden throne.

"Lion's Arch is a *Krytan* city. For too long we have swallowed their fables about 'the dangers of Orr.' They tell tales of this mythical undead force so that we will be too afraid to attack the pirates and smugglers who stole Krytan land!" Leaning back easily, Edair let his gaze play over the room, taking in the opulent wall hangings and the golden decorations. He smiled to a group of maidens on the upper balconies and then returned his stare to Isaye. "I've heard men say that charr are twelve feet high with star beams shooting from their eyes. They can jump so far they might as well be flying, and when they hold their breath, they're practically invisible. They have fur of iron and claws of fire, and they can't be harmed by human blades." The prince shook his head disdainfully. "I've fought in Ascalon. I know the difference between legends and truths. Charr are made of flesh and blood. They're nothing more than animals, barely capable of walking on two legs.

"These pirates tell us stories of an undefeatable Orr. They say it's a living dragon-island, that hundreds of thousands of undead roam there, unkillable, with magic so powerful we can't begin to understand it. And we're supposed to be *grateful* to Lion's Arch for the 'protection' they provide." He smirked. "I'll tell you what else I know. Orrian zombies wash up on the beaches in Kryta, too, and just like the charr . . ." The prince of Kryta took a deep breath and intoned harshly, "They can be destroyed."

Edair rose, holding his hands up in reassurance. "Don't listen to the lies told by these pirates. Orr isn't a cursed kingdom; it's nothing more than a waterlogged, desolate lump of stone. Yes, there is some magic within its shores, but it is old, withered, and impotent, or why else was it lost for so long? The kingdom of Orr was destroyed hundreds of years ago, cast to the bottom of the ocean, and it's no more dangerous now than it has ever been.

"They say we should be grateful to Lion's Arch. For what? Fighting off zombies? Sinking a few rotting ships? These traitors preen about insignificant victories won against feeble opponents. For that, we should give these brigands Krytan land and say thank you? I say no!" Several members of the audience raised their voices in agreement, and a wave of applause rippled through the nobility. Edair shook his fist and accepted their laudations with a calculating smile. The Seraph guards pushed Isaye back into line, warning her to keep silent unless spoken to again.

Cobiah clenched his teeth, his hands twisting against

the iron manacles that held him bound. He was on the wrong side of this situation, unable to fight while every instinct urged him to attack. It was galling to stand silently while someone tore down his accomplishments, threatened his friends, and called him a liar. Yet Cobiah reined in his temper. Twice, Isaye had asked him not to attack the prince. He didn't know her reasons, didn't entirely trust them given their past, but something in the way she'd asked still gave him pause. There was more to this than he knew.

The exemplar swayed across the dais to the prince's side, placing her hand on his arm. "Your Demetran crystal-wine is here, Your Highness." She gestured to one of the Shining Blade, and the man approached, holding out a goblet etched with the sigil of the royal family.

Blinking away his spontaneous ferocity, Prince Edair lowered himself once more onto the golden throne. He took the glass from the silver tray and balanced it in his hand, smelling the fresh bouquet of the wine. "Ah, yes. Thank you, Livia."

Livia.

That name was familiar. He'd heard rumors—everyone had. Livia was the self-appointed protector of the ruler of Kryta, and if whispers were true, she'd been so for *generations*. Some tales said she'd sold her soul to become an immortal lich. Others claimed that Livia sacrificed prisoners in the dungeons of Divinity's Reach and used their blood to give herself eternal youth and beauty. He'd heard a hundred legends, usually during the autumn festival when children were trying to scare one another with spooky tales. Still, all the stories agreed on one thing: Livia was *powerful*. Cobiah felt a chill run through his body as the woman glanced toward him again, her smoky eyes obscured by the curtain of her white-streaked hair. Maybe she was the reason Isaye was so frightened.

"Commodore Marriner." Edair singled him out. He paused to swirl his expensive wine while the Seraph pushed Cobiah forward. A shadow darkened the prince's face as he considered his next words. "Once the majority of the Seraph, my army, is gathered to the north of Lion's Arch, we will march on your city, and we will be victorious. If that happens, I assure you, Commodore . . ." Edair examined him as though he were an acquisition he was deciding whether to buy. "There will be a great deal of bloodshed.

"Although I would enjoy the excitement of honorable battle, I realize we would be marching seasoned military troops against civilian militia. Exemplar Livia has convinced me," he said, setting the goblet down, "that we should first seek other ways of resolving this conflict. I've gone to great lengths to get you here in the hopes that you can help me avoid such an outcome. I had my *loyal* friend Isaye watched by spies. I intercepted her messages. I gave her good reason to think I had an assassin in your city, and to save your life, she did exactly as I'd hoped. She brought you here." Edair laughed lightly. "Really, Cobiah. You should be flattered at the amount of trouble it's taken to make you a guest aboard my magnificent galleon."

"You should have saved the trouble and stuffed this galleon up your—" Grymm didn't get any further. One of the marines rammed the butt of a spear into the norn's belly, doubling him over and knocking the wind out of his words. The Seraph struck him across the back, forcing him to his knees, and shoved the point of the spear against his chest. Blood trickled down from a wound where the spear cut into the norn's flesh. Bronn growled and tried to step toward his brother, but in a flash the guards had their swords at his throat. Around the ballroom, Seraph and the Shining Blade stood at the ready, weapons out and magic coalescing as elementalists concentrated their will in preparation for battle.

"Enough!" Edair snarled. His face had reddened, and he clenched his fists so tightly the knuckles turned white on the arms of his throne. Clearly, the prince was used to getting his way. "This is not a discussion. *This is a royal command.*

"Either you tell the Lionguard to stand down and disarm the city defenses, or I will show you why you should fear the Krytan throne, Marriner." He rose slowly and took a step forward, using the height of the dais to tower over Cobiah and his friends. Edair's body was as tense as a bowstring, his voice brittle with the fraying of his temper. "I assure you, I am not bluffing."

"You can do what you want, Edair; the answer is still no." Cobiah's heart pounded, all fear replaced by the certainty of impending death. "I wish I could. I wish you understood what you were doing, and by Dwayna's white wings, I'd like to find a way to keep my people from harm. But I'd rather have you kill them quickly by the sword than take the city and underestimate the Dead Ships. If that's the choice, then I believe every living being in Lion's Arch would wish for the death you'll give them over the blasphemous unlife they'll receive at Orrian hands."

"You filthy, dishonorable blackguard!" At last, the prince's control broke, and Edair raised his voice in a ferocious shout, like a child being denied a toy. "You *will* do what I tell you! If you don't, your friends will suffer my wrath one by one."

Bronn growled, low in his throat. Stiff and unyielding

despite the weapons arrayed against him, the bearded norn declared, "My brother and I would gladly die rather than submit to a coward such as you."

Edair reddened further. "I'll kill her!" He pointed at Isaye. "And him!" His finger moved on to Tenzin. Seeing that Cobiah wouldn't budge, Edair lowered his hand and paced across the stage. Livia tried to catch his attention with a subtle gesture, but Edair strode past her without even acknowledging the exemplar. "You're so self-sacrificing. So very stalwart. I'm offering you a chance to save the lives of innocents—women and children—but you'd rather have a knife through your heart. Fine. Let's see how much solace that is when the repercussions are staring you in the face."

Spinning away, the prince made a sharp gesture. "Get the boy."

The guardsman snapped a salute, hurrying across the dais to the door through which the prince had entered the room. A terrible light flashed in Edair's eyes. Livia approached him, murmuring softly, but the prince dismissed her words with a quick chop of his hand through the air. Cobiah frowned. What cruelty was this? Thinking that perhaps Isaye knew more than she'd had time to reveal, Cobiah turned to whisper to her—but the words froze in his throat as he took in the pale, horrified look on Isaye's face.

The door opened, and the pale-haired Shining Blade guardsman from before entered the stateroom, leading a small child by the hand. The child was young, a boy not more than three years old, with a mop of dark hair and bright blue eyes. Burbling happily to himself, he kept one hand in his mouth, the other wrapped around the Shining Blade's fingers, toddling along despite his drooping eyes and sleepy smile.

"Commodore Marriner," the prince said, his voice holding a note of cold-blooded pride, "may I present the *Trident*'s newest visitor? He arrived just two days ago." Edair settled back into his throne, keeping his eyes on the prisoners standing before his dais.

There was no chance for Cobiah to respond. Fighting to be free of her restraints, Isaye shoved her way toward the dais despite the Seraph, not caring if their swords dug bloody gouges into her skin. "Dane!" she called out, stretching her manacled arms toward the boy.

At the sight of her, the child brightened. "Mama!" He pulled the hand out of his mouth and waved at her eagerly. Spotting Tenzin, the boy tried to pull away from the Shining Blade and run toward them both, but the guard prevented him from escaping by sweeping the child gently up onto his hip. Tears leapt to Isaye's eyes.

So this was what she'd been protecting.

Cobiah's chest tightened. He couldn't breathe, his heart pounding so hard that he could hear the blood thumping in his ears. It seemed as if the world around him had stopped turning, shrinking down to one small, dark-haired boy. He whispered a prayer to Dwayna and the Six Gods, begging for their forgiveness as he took in the meaning of the scene before him. Isaye's son. Isaye had a son. His wife . . . had a child by another man.

All of the warmth that had been regrowing toward Isaye suddenly withered inside Cobiah's heart. Justifications leapt into his mind. She'd been gone for years. He'd even called her his ex-wife. She deserved to be happy. But the one thing that kept returning and returning to his thoughts was the image of Isaye, meeting alone in an inn room with a Krytan agent, carrying copies of Cobiah's council notes. How long had she been meeting with him in secret? Cobiah didn't even know who the man was;

he'd barely gotten a glimpse before the agent leapt out the window and escaped.

What if they had been meeting for more personal reasons?

Edair stared down at them as he spoke, lingering over the words with obvious relish. "I sent for him several days ago, Isaye. My spies had been watching you for some time to see if you were loyal, and you'd proven yourself to my satisfaction. As a reward and an apology for my lack of trust, I planned to surprise you with my thoughtfulness. Imagine my chagrin when my spies brought me concrete proof that you'd betrayed me and allowed a ship through the blockade with a message for Lion's Arch.

"*Steadfast* Isaye. *Loyal* Isaye. Always playing the part of the devoted Krytan. You fooled my father, and you nearly fooled me." Scorn dripped from every word. "How easily you were discovered."

"Don't you *dare* hurt him!" Isaye bristled. She pushed forward. The Seraph's weapons drove into her skin, forcing her to step back again. As blood stained her linen shirt, Tenzin's hands flexed, reaching automatically for a weapon that was no longer at his side. Behind her, Cobiah's face darkened, making the connection. Tenzin was younger than Isaye, yes . . . but he was old enough.

"Be still, both of you." Bronn clenched his hands around the iron chain of his manacles. "Your actions bring even more danger to the child."

"Listen to your gargantuan friend, Isaye," Edair said quietly. "None of us want to endanger the boy. Isn't that right, Commodore?"

All around them, the nobles of Divinity's Reach stood in rapt attention, captivated and perhaps fearful of the scene playing out before them. Women pressed their hands to silk bodices, and men questioned the king with their eyes, afraid to say anything that might draw the prince's attention. The *Balthazar's Trident* rocked gently in the water, lanterns swaying from the balcony, casting mercurial shadows from wall to wall. Cobiah set his mouth in a grim line, understanding the threat implicit in the prince's words.

"This doesn't have to end in bloodshed, Cobiah. Not here and not in Lion's Arch." The prince smiled victoriously. "I give you my word of honor. Not a hair on the child's head will be harmed . . . so long as you cooperate." Resting easily on the throne, Edair straightened the sleeves of his golden doublet in smug satisfaction. "You'll tell me about those defenses, you'll order the Lionguard to stand down, and furthermore, you'll sign a formal treaty acknowledging Krytan rulership of Lion's Arch.

"I'll give you a little time to reconsider your answer, Cobiah." Edair's smile broadened. "Take them to the brig."

30

The prince snapped his fingers, and the Seraph around the room stiffened to attention. "Give the prisoners water and allow them eight hours' rest. If they haven't come to their senses at the end of that time . . ." He eyed the group thoughtfully. "I'll be forced to do something rash." Isaye let out a soft moan. Bronn and Grymm bristled, but the Seraph guard jabbed them warningly, and the norn held in their retorts. For his part, Cobiah met the prince's eyes with a steady, hateful gaze.

"As you wish, Your Highness," Livia said, stepping in quickly. "Allow us to be your hand." She nodded to the Shining Blade holding Dane, and the man nodded at her unspoken command. Without a word, he turned and carried the boy away. Isaye made a soft sound and stepped after them, but Tenzin caught her arm and pulled her back.

"They won't hurt him," Tenzin told her quietly. "Don't give them a reason to hurt you."

Cobiah wished he'd been the one to say it. Gritting his teeth, he watched as the guard in blue carried the little boy away. Livia strode down the stairs toward the gathered prisoners. "I'll escort them personally. You are relieved." Four more Shining Blade, one of them the dark-haired guard who had been stationed at the door when they arrived, surrounded the group of prisoners. The Seraph marines stepped back, but not without a few more taunting pokes at their hostages. Livia gestured, and her agents led the captives from the stateroom.

The brig of the *Balthazar's Trident* was on her lowest deck, beneath the cold waterline. They were pushed into small chambers with the curve of the ship's hull on one side and iron bars on the other. Cobiah could tell at a glance that the hull here was reinforced lest any prisoners take out their rage on the boards, trying to sink the ship or drown themselves in the attempt. There were no cots or furniture in any of the cells, only a small tin chamber pot with a lid. A faint dusting of straw covered the floor, musty with dampness. The Shining Blade locked each of the five prisoners into a separate cage, removing the manacles from Isaye, Cobiah, and Tenzin. They left the chains on the norn. Livia simply stood in the hold outside the brig cells and watched as they were shoved inside and the doors locked behind them.

After the other Shining Blade left the hold, Livia paused as though she might say something. With a shrug and a sigh, she appeared to decide against it. Her heels made a distinctive clicking sound as she headed up the long rise of stairs. The door to the hold slammed shut behind her.

Tenzin sighed, leaning back in his cell. "We have to escape."

"Escape?" Grymm rumbled. His voice was gruffer than his garrulous brother's, lower and rusty sounding, as if he did not choose to talk often. "Strange words, coming from you, Krytan. Isaye is implicated in treason. Myself, my brother, and the commodore are prisoners of the state. But you . . . I can't figure out why you're here. To spy on us, perhaps?"

Tenzin shot the norn a nasty look, rubbing his wrists where the manacles had chafed the skin raw. "I'm loyal to Kryta, yes. But not to Edair. Truth be told, I was hoping Princess Emilane would be Baede's heir. When he chose Edair . . ." Tenzin shook his head. "My father was right. Power makes you crazy."

"That still doesn't explain why you're here," Grymm said, pressing him.

The Krytan lowered his head. "I asked for the post of first mate aboard the *Nomad* when I heard Edair was planning to blockade Lion's Arch." Tenzin shoved a lock of brown hair away from his eyes. "While I respect Captain Isaye greatly, my father was my hero. He died to protect the city of Lion's Arch. I won't let his sacrifice be in vain."

Cobiah tried to tame his jealousy, focus his mind on the problem, but his thoughts kept leaping to dark places. Great respect for Captain Isaye? Cobiah had seen the warmth in Tenzin's eyes. That didn't come from sheer respect. Neither did a three-year-old child.

"So what do we do now?" Bronn asked, shaking the chain links of his manacles to see if he could find a weak spot. "Break out of the brig? Sneak into the prince's quarters and fight him one-on-one? Capture that red-wrapped enchantress and demand an exchange of hostages? Swim to Lion's Arch and warn the defense?" Cobiah noted that none of the norn's options included "surrender and sign the treaty." Bronn wasn't even considering it. Why, then, was he?

Isaye slid heavily to a seat on the floor of her cell. "They have my son."

The pain in her voice shot through Cobiah's heart.

Despite himself, he said, "There's got to be a way to get the child out of here."

"He'll be more heavily guarded than the prince—and unlike Edair, the guards around the boy have no reason to care if *he* survives. They'll kill him the moment we enter the room." Grymm scowled. "Point us toward the princeling, Cobiah, and I'll gladly join you. But I don't want a child's blood on my hands."

"You're right. I'll think of something else," Cobiah said dryly, sinking down onto the floor. The cell smelled like moldy straw and old bacon, somehow both familiar and disconcerting all at once.

Hours passed in relative silence. Through high portholes, Cobiah watched night turn into morning, dawning gray and dim with no hint of sun. Cobiah could hear the ocean lapping against the side of the boat, but he had nothing to mark the passage of time except the heavy snores of his companions.

Finally, a key clicked in the hatch to the deck above. The door opened, and there was movement on the stairs. It had certainly not been eight full hours—less than four, by his reasoning. This wasn't the prince summoning them, unless Edair had grown impatient. Food, perhaps? Cobiah listened to the movement on the stairs as it approached, and his brow furrowed. The *click-clack* of heels upon the stairwell told him exactly who it was.

"Come to taunt us?" Cobiah asked as the woman in red entered the main room of the brig. "Where's the fun in that, Livia?"

"Taunt you?" The exemplar carried no lantern, nor a torch. Instead, her delicate features were lit by the pale light of a necromancer's ghost candle, the magical light illuminating the appeal of her curves. "How you misjudge me, Commodore." She reached up to close the hatch above her with one hand. The magical light hovered at her side, neither changing nor wavering as she walked slowly in front of their cells.

"What are you here for, then? I seriously doubt you're here to help us." Cobiah glared, trying not to be impressed by the woman's beauty—or her obvious skill with magic.

She tossed her head, and the stripe of pale hair flowed against her high cheekbone like silk over porcelain. "In fact"—Livia's dark lips curved into a smile—"I am."

Isaye was already on her feet, her hands clenched into fists. "If you want to help us, give me my son and let us go."

Livia's eyes were shadowed. "No, my dear Isaye. There's nothing I can do about your son. Prince Edair's orders are very clear, and the boy is under heavy guard."

"Then you can't help us." Isaye turned away bitterly.

"You don't agree with what's going on," Cobiah guessed. He stood and walked to face Livia through the iron bars of his cell. "If you did, you wouldn't be here." Cobiah pressed his luck, relying on instinct to gauge the woman's reaction. "You're older than the prince. You were alive when the sea swallowed Lion's Arch. Hell, you might have even been in the city at the time, in the king's palace. You were probably with him when King Baede and the others were whisked away while the city was destroyed around you. You know what I know . . . you know how dangerous Orr really is.

"I . . ." She paused, sizing him up.

"Don't play games with me. You're not the kind who sits in pretty throne rooms and tells yourself the world turns on your whim. You've been alive for a very long time, haven't you? I'd be willing to bet you saw Port Stalwart destroyed; or other agents of the Shining Blade did, and they reported to you. You've seen the monsters that sail those Dead Ships. That's why you're here."

Livia nodded. A faint smile touched her elegant lips. "You're quite right, Commodore. I do know Orr better than most. Some years ago, I came into possession of an artifact of great power, a remnant of that lost civilization. A scepter. I've spent many years studying it. Yes, I know what Orrian magic could do when Orr was alive." The smile faded, and Livia's stance took on a greater posture of authority. "I can guess what it is like now that they are undead . . . and under the command of an Elder Dragon."

"So what the hell are we supposed to do?" Cobiah wrapped his hands around the bars and leaned toward her. "Give him control of Lion's Arch? That would be akin to handing the entire nation of Kryta to the undead. Possibly all of Tyria!" His voice shook with intensity. "You've got to convince Edair that he's wrong."

"I have attempted to discuss these matters with my prince, but Edair is not a practitioner of the magical arts. He is a warrior. Furthermore, he is very young and utterly convinced of his superiority based on the success of his conflicts with the charr." Livia shrugged, the movement rippling appealingly across her sleek form. "If I cannot convince Edair of the truth, then I must protect him from his errors."

"That's why she's here," Tenzin surmised quickly. "The Shining Blade's oath is to the throne . . . but it's very specific. Her oath is to ensure that the royal line continues to rule. I've heard rumors that the Shining Blade doesn't care who sits on the throne, so long as it is a descendant of Salma the Good. They ensure that Kryta and the line of Salma continue. Shining Blade can't let Kryta fall to Orr . . . but they can support an alternate heir to the throne." Tenzin looked back and forth from Cobiah to the figure in red.

"Essentially correct, Colonel Moran." Livia nodded courteously, as if they were in a formal courtroom and not standing in a ship's brig. "I take my oath very seriously, and I am loyal to Prince Edair . . . but my primary loyalty is to Kryta and the Salmaic dynasty. Prince Edair is the inheritor of the throne, and I support him as such. However, I will not allow his pride to doom the country. But . . . he is only the heir, and a prince. Thus, he does not yet have the authority to countermand orders given to me by a king."

"You still have orders from King Baede." Isaye grasped her meaning first. She looked up, a faint hope lighting in her eyes.

"Correct. Edair rushed to take Lion's Arch immediately upon his father's death. It is his plan to be coronated in Lion's Arch. That is where all the kings and queens of Kryta have been elevated, since the days of Queen Salma the Good. He doesn't plan to be the first to change that tradition."

"He's a prideful snot, isn't he?" Grymm rumbled under his breath.

"What were King Baede's orders?" Cobiah asked.

Livia paused before she answered. Her eyes flicked to Isaye, then back to Cobiah. "Some years ago, King Baede began plans of his own to invade your city, Commodore Marriner. It was his intent to recapture Lion's Arch. However, his mind was changed when Lady Isaye sent him notes . . . documentation . . . proof that your forces were uniquely capable of defending this port against the Dead Ships. King Baede had more than enough militia to invade and seize your city. Because of the information Isaye provided, he abandoned those plans."

Cobiah's mind raced. "That was why you were meeting with the Krytans?" he asked Isaye, numbly aware that she wouldn't meet his eyes.

She nodded, a small, sorrowing movement. "I discovered Baede's plans. I couldn't let him invade Lion's Arch, but I also didn't want to tell the council. Either way, I would have started a war. Taking Baede your notes was the only way to make sure he understood the threat Orr represented. The number of vessels they'd destroyed; the great lengths we were going to, ensuring that our city had a chance against those Dead Ships. I had to prove to him that Lion's Arch—as it was, with the united forces of all races of Tyria—was vital to keeping Kryta safe. Baede would never have been able to arrange charr engineering to enhance the fort at Claw Island or convince the asuran colleges to enchant ships against Orrian fire.

"After he read your journals, King Baede agreed with me." Isaye kept her eyes low, twisting her fingers back and forth in her lap. "He told his army to stand down and leave Lion's Arch alone."

"Well . . . damn," Cobiah said ruefully. It didn't answer all of his questions, but the explanation put an entirely different spin on Isaye's activity—and the man she'd been meeting in the inn room that day. The thought of all the lost years, the distance between them . . . "Why didn't you tell me?" he asked more softly, forgetting for a moment that there were other people in the room.

"You were right." She shrugged. "I was betraying Lion's Arch. I turned your notes over to Kryta, and Baede might have used that information to attack the city. I had to take that risk." Isaye looked up, temper sparking in her eyes again. "Anyway, I wasn't exactly eager to explain myself to someone who called me a grog-snarfing murellow." Cobiah heard Bronn snicker from the floor of his cell, the sound quickly cut off by Grymm's elbow through the bars into his brother's ribs.

With an impatient tap of her heel against the wooden floor, Livia broke in. "I hope I'm not interrupting this touching scene, but there's still the matter of your release to consider." All eyes turned toward the exemplar again. Livia crossed the hold and reached to take a key ring from its hook on the wall, sliding her fingers lightly against the cold iron in contemplation.

Suddenly, a bell began to ring out on the upper decks, its strident clatter echoing even this deep into the hold. The *Balthazar's Trident* began to shift, and Cobiah could hear the crew rushing to unfurl the sails and man the rudder, shouting as heavy boots thumped on the boards over their heads. "What's going on?" Cobiah gripped the bars of his cell more tightly. The norn, quick to respond to the sounds of battle, rose to their feet with grim frowns.

"It's begun." Livia spoke more quickly now. She looked up toward the sound of storming boots. "One hour ago, our spotter on the crow's nest noted a fleet of red-masted ships approaching from the south."

"Dwayna's mercy," Cobiah breathed, listening to the shouts and thuds above. "The Orrians are taking advantage of the blockade. The Dead Ships are coming." The others fell into silence as the chill of Cobiah's words struck them all.

Grimly, Livia stalked toward the iron bars, the keys in her hand jingling softly. "King Baede's orders were that Lion's Arch must be kept sacrosanct so that the combined might of all the races can gather under one flag to fight against Tyria's greatest enemy: Orr." As she unlocked each cell, she continued. "Edair does not have the knowledge to fight them off, Commodore. You do.

"Go to the *Nomad* and lead our defense. You must find

some way to fight them off, or Lion's Arch—and Kryta—will fall to the forces of Orr."

"I'm not leaving without my son!" Isaye pushed past Livia as soon as her cell door was open. The exemplar grabbed her arm, jerking the dark-haired woman back with an iron grip.

"Yes, you are." The exemplar's tone brooked no argument. Seeing the fire in Isaye's eyes, Livia continued more gently. "The *Trident* will be the most protected vessel in our armada. Prince Edair is no hero. He will not be at the forefront of the battle."

"He's a coward, you mean," Isaye snapped.

Livia narrowed her eyes, choosing to ignore the insult. "Your son will be fine. If the city falls, he will return to Divinity's Reach with us, and I will personally ensure his safety. But if you are ever to see him again, we must trust one another." Livia let go of Isaye's arm with a narrow smile. "Are we agreed?"

Isaye bit her lip and managed a nod of agreement.

Livia's strange, pale eyes scanned Cobiah and the rest. "Kryta has a fleet, but no commanders with knowledge of how to defeat this threat. You are a commander with no fleet at your disposal." Despite the bells clanging and the shouts and curses of the *Balthazar's Trident*'s crew, the exemplar of the Shining Blade maintained her calculating composure. "You must do what you do best, Commodore. Bridge the divide."

It was a bitter pill to swallow, but Cobiah nodded. "I don't see that we have much of a choice."

Livia looked over her shoulder at him, the stripe in her scarlet hair falling around her face. "Precisely so, Commodore." The exemplar turned on her high heel and strode toward the stairway. "Make your way toward the lifeboats. The *Nomad* is not far. You'll have to avoid the Seraph, but if you can make it to the lifeboat, you should be able to reach your ship. We'll speak again once the Orrian fleet has been defeated. Otherwise"—Livia crossed the room and ascended the stairs, heading for the upper decks—"I suppose I'll see you in the Mists."

31

The small group made their way through the ship, ducking from room to room, hiding behind swaying hammocks and piles of cargo. It was fairly easy to avoid the Seraph, who were all rushing to the gun ports and the upper decks to defend the ship. The noble passengers fled through hallways, some screaming, others trying to take command of the situation—mostly by ordering everyone else around. Cobiah ignored them.

Tenzin reverted to his military training, bluffing the few soldiers who crossed their path. The *Balthazar's Trident* was as fat on the inside as she'd seemed from without, with layers of labyrinthine passages that led to opulent chambers, private dining areas, and at last, a balcony. Bronn looked up, pointing at a lifeboat that hung some distance above them. "If we could cut that down, we'd have our way back to the *Nomad*." The norn's words met silence. "No?"

The others weren't listening. They were looking out across the ocean, where the armada of Orr was under full sail. Though still some distance away, Cobiah could tell it was a massive fleet—larger than he'd ever seen arrayed against Lion's Arch in the past. The Orrian ships had blackened hulls dripping with broken coral and clinging barnacles, the wood broken and rotting where the sea had taken her due. Some rose from the waves even as he watched, black sails unfurling with the wind as they broke the plane of seawater. At their fore sailed three mighty ships. Two were xebecs, ships of ancient Orr, with scarlet silk hung in long triangles and lateen sails upon their tilted masts. These were far larger than the clipper, the *Harbinger*, that Cobiah had seen in the Fire Island straits so long ago. These two were warships, warded with magic so foul that Cobiah could see the buzz of lightning and the rise of viscous steam wafting from their hulls.

The third vessel, the one leading them all, was the *Indomitable*.

At Cobiah's side, Tenzin murmured, "My father told me of the day he fought the Orrians at your side, when the *Pride* captured the *Salma's Grace*—and then turned to fight the true enemy. He described it to me in great detail. Even though he'd fought waves of their ships defending Lion's Arch, he told me that the first time you see them—the first time you realize that 'Dead Ship' is more than a fanciful name—you're never the same." The Krytan had gone pale, his eyes wide and staring at the dark vision on the horizon.

"Don't worry." Cobiah gulped, trying to calm himself even as his knuckles turned white on the balcony rail. "You never get used to it." The two men shared a terse smile.

Creatures with wings of sea-foam and spittle glided above them, distant voices singing maddened, ancient songs. The stink of fetid flesh rolled in on the wind, striking Cobiah's nostrils with a fearful stench.

In the distance, a swell of magic rolled up like a tide before the two Orrian galleys. Even from here, Cobiah could see dead men in articulated armor swarming their decks. Sixty cannons glowed like demonic eyes, thirty to a side, rolling out thunder and balled lightning from the snarling mouths of their guns. "What are those?" Tenzin pointed, squinting to see them more clearly through the cannon smoke.

"They're Orrian vessels called xebecs. Like our ships of the line, but instead of cannons, they rely heavily on ancient magic. I've fought one before, about half the size of one of those."

"And you defeated it?" the Krytan asked hopefully.

"I defeated *one*. Half as big," Cobiah repeated. "And it nearly took us without a scratch on its hull." He shook his head wearily, watching the massive red-sailed ships cresting the waves amid the Orrian armada. "I can't imagine defeating two of them that size. Their enchanted guns alone . . ."

As if speaking of them had triggered the weapons, one of the xebecs fired a broadside at a nearby Krytan brigantine. Green lightning flickered and danced over the water, floating neither high nor low, but rushing forward in a straight line. Like relentless motes of pollen, they raced toward their target, exploding huge sections of its wooden hull from upper deck down to the waterline. From the crackling explosions, great arcs and tentacles of lightning burst outward to cascade over the deck of the ship. Cobiah could see figures leap from the deck of the xebec to the brigantine, dark shadows launching themselves onto screaming Krytan sailors. Weapons swung and pistols cracked as howls erupted from the combat. Cobiah could imagine what was happening to those sailors. Flesh melting from electric assaults, souls shriveling. Just like the sailors aboard his ship. Like Tosh, and Vost, and Sethus . . .

Isaye grabbed Cobiah's arm and twisted him to face

her. "I know what you're thinking. You think it every time the *Indomitable* is part of an attack. Don't look, Cobiah. Those things aren't your friends."

He stared at her, trying to pull his thoughts away, but all he could see was death. A death he'd escaped, a fate that had taken his friends and turned them into monsters. "They were," he whispered.

"You aren't responsible for their deaths, Cobiah," Isaye said, her hands bracing his shoulders. "Don't think about the dead. Concentrate on the living. We need you."

"I won't give up if you don't." He blurted the words without thinking, and his face reddened with the admission. "I—"

"Deal," she said immediately, and smiled.

Despite everything, so did he.

"Heeee-*yaaaaah!*" Bronn and Grymm had climbed up onto the rails of the balcony, untying the boat above from its moorings. As the little boat fell, they pushed it out, away from the *Balthazar's Trident*, fighting with gravity and balance to make sure it didn't crash against the balcony, get stuck on a porthole, or crack its keel falling into the water. Unfortunately, in the tumult, Bronn slipped off the balcony, arms spinning over the railing. He tumbled, howling all the way down into the waves.

When he came up again, the mustached norn threw his hand over the rowboat's side and waved. The norn's smile faded as he cast a look back at the two doomed ships. "The *Nomad*'s waiting. Come, let us away!"

The small craft made good time, plowing through rising waves in the gray of a cloud-covered morning. When they reached the *Nomad II*, Isaye's crew was rushing about in a furor, loading the cannons and readying her wide sails.

Her bosun stood at the gunwale, a thin, reedy woman whom Isaye greeted as Rahli. She had neither Verahd's creepy style nor Henst's burly sense of threat but carried herself with the chilly, straightforward efficiency of a schoolmarm.

"Captain!" Rahli grasped Isaye's hand and helped her up onto the deck. "We received a message from the Shining Blade to expect you. I've never known them to lie, but I have to say, I didn't believe it until I saw the rowboat approaching." Bronn boosted Cobiah up, helping him scramble aboard the *Nomad II*. Tenzin followed, and after him, the two norn climbed up as easily as if they were scaling cliffs in the Shiverpeak Mountains. "Even so, Prince Edair left several of his guard aboard the ship to 'watch' us. We 'watched' them to unconsciousness with belaying pins and detained them in the hold. I hope that's acceptable."

"I'd have thrown them over the side, armor and all," Isaye growled. She paused to sigh and rubbed her eyes with a shaking hand. "No, I wouldn't have. But I'd have wanted to. That's fine, Rahli. Be sure our sailors are armed, ready the sails, and await my command."

Rahli hurried off to carry out her orders. Isaye turned to Cobiah as a sailor brought him a sword. "What do we do?"

The Krytan fleet had engaged the Orrian armada but fought in scattered clumps. Here and there, a captain had enough hold over his crew to keep them fighting, but other ships broke the line, fleeing, the rotted ships of Orr at their heels.

"Sail straight for the Orrian line." Cobiah drew the sword. "We've got to get their attention."

"Who?" Isaye's eyebrows shot up. "The Krytans or the Orrians?"

"Both. We need the Orrians to concentrate their fire

on the *Nomad*, and we need the Krytans to see that we can withstand it. If the Krytans get their courage back and start to follow our tactic of assault, we can still turn the tide."

"What's our tactic?" Tenzin had grabbed a long-barreled rifle, packing it with gunpowder and shot as he listened to Cobiah's plan.

"Draw their attention and pull them into the city's harbor."

"Toward Lion's Arch?" Grymm looked concerned.

"Toward Claw Island," Cobiah clarified. "Toward the guns and the fortifications of the city. Even if the Krytans can't fight worth a damn, the fort can still hold its own."

Isaye considered. "There are only two flaws in this plan. One, the city guns weren't built to hold off a fleet by themselves. They can't load fast enough, and if the Dead Ships storm the city, they'll get within firing range and be able to blow out the cliffs. That'll be the end of the gunnery emplacements.

"Two." Isaye pointed out at the two massive, red-sailed Orrian xebec. "The *Nomad* has no elementalists. Those ships wield immense magics. If they catch us, we'll have no defense at all."

Cobiah could see only one path through. "The *Nomad* has to close and fight at close range with the *Indomitable*," he replied. "Her guns are larger, but she doesn't have the support of Orrian enchantments. If we're brushing her hull, the xebecs won't be able to use their magic against us without damaging their flagship."

"Just like baiting a snow cat." Grymm smiled broadly, cracking his knuckles as the *Nomad II* turned in her traces and spread her sails against the wind. "Once you're up against its belly, you can gut it without fear of the claws."

Bronn frowned. "If we have to stay that close, how will we get them to follow us to the city's fortifications?"

"The hooks!" Isaye snapped her fingers. "On one of our last runs, we towed a stranded asuran paddle ship. We ran lines to it: ropes, tied off with iron grappling hooks stuck through into their hull. Tenzin." She spun to him, her hair swinging, gray and mahogany, against her muscled back. "If we set those grapnels in the harpoon guns, can you hit the *Indomitable*'s low rigging with them? Tangle them around the masts or sink the hooks into their hatches?"

"I can use a harpoon just fine. It's not so different from a rifle, once you have the weight and heft of it. I once used one to bull's-eye a bosun's pin from three ship-lengths away. Won fifty gold." Tenzin tossed back his hair cockily and set the rifle on his shoulder. "I'll have to set position somewhere high, maybe up on the yardarm. Keep the hook-loaded guns coming, and I'll see that the grappling irons are placed solidly."

"With the lines in place, we can tow the *Indomitable*." Isaye turned back to Cobiah, her gold-green eyes alight. "We'll never leave her side . . . and we'll draw her straight into the city's guns. When we're close to Claw Island, we cut the lines, the *Nomad* pulls away into the harbor, and the fortress can open fire."

"Won't the undead sailors cut the lines?" Tenzin asked. "It's what I'd do."

Cobiah shook his head, considering Isaye's idea. "They're bloodthirsty. They *want* us close. One thing I've learned fighting Dead Ships for so many years is that most Orrians don't do a lot of long-term thinking. If they see a target, they attack, and they don't think about much else."

Tenzin looked skeptical. "But what about leverage? Our ship's smaller. All we'll do is pull ourselves closer to the *Indomitable*."

"It won't matter who's towing who so long as we can keep both boats within the current. The *Nomad*'s weight will pull them with us toward the island," Isaye replied.

"There's another problem," Cobiah said. "We need to keep the undead aboard that flagship from slaughtering us all while the *Nomad* gives her a tow."

"Leave that to my brother and me." Grymm folded his arms, the muscles standing out as if they were carved from granite. While the others were talking, Bronn had demanded the sailors bring another massive sword from the *Nomad II*'s armory to replace the one the Seraph had stripped from him. He slid one hand up the glistening blade, testing the sharpness of the steel.

Cobiah turned to the norn. "You think you can keep the undead from swarming our deck?"

"Just tell the sailors to hold their own, Commodore." Grymm Svaard smiled, tugging on his braided beard.

His brother's teeth flashed beneath a thick mustache. "We'll do the rest."

As the sun began to break through the gray fog of morning, Sorrow's Bay was a tossing expanse of whitecapped waves, racing from the distant shore toward the depths of the sea. The tide was outbound, carrying with it traces of driftwood and washes of lingering foam. The chop of the sea was extreme, curdled by a thrashing wind and the wakes of multiple ships tacking left and right either to engage or to escape.

The *Nomad II* valiantly split the waves as she sailed toward her opponent. Her sails were fully extended, shifted against the wind to set her forward at full speed. All around her, white puffs of smoke rose from Krytan ships, their cannonballs hurtling toward the enemy. Orrian ships returned fire, but instead of leaden balls, they fired skulls set alight by dark magic. Isaye gave orders to the sailors working the rudder, but the captain's eyes continually followed the *Balthazar's Trident* within the Krytan armada, though the galleon was still far behind the line of fire.

Ships were taking damage on all sides. Although the Krytans were excellent hand to hand, the Orrian ships weren't closing. Only a few of the human ships had fighting aboard their decks, and those were the ones being swarmed by the undead crawling up their hulls from beneath the dark waves. Off the port bow, a Krytan frigate was shoved forward on the waves, masts collapsing, sails set alight by wicked purplish fire. She careened slowly into an Orrian clipper, smashing her prow into the rotted ship's side. The fire quickly spread from the frigate's masts onto the Orrian ship. Clearly, the Dead Ships were not immune to their own flame.

Isaye was giving orders to adjust the ship's rigging, shift the rudder, and watch for undead rising from below. Her sailors leapt to the task, their faces white but their hands steady on the till. "Watch to starboard. There's a shadow beneath the waves!"

"Acknowledged, Cap'n!" Bosun Rahli yelled, calling to the ship's sailors. They rushed to the side of the ship and met the assault with flashing swords.

The things that crawled and slithered onto the *Nomad II*'s deck weren't human. It wasn't clear from their forms whether they had ever been human. Tentacles swayed from sockets, and reverse-jointed knees bent as their huge, hooked claws sank into the ship's pine hull. One of the monstrosities had the rotting head of a shark, while another was made of seaweed-bound bone and sharp shards of coral.

Grymm strode into the beasts, gripping the shark-headed one by its wretched arm and driving his fist into the monster's nose. His brother was close behind him, greatsword slashing out in a wide arc. It caught one of the tentacles as it passed by, severing the festering limb. Sliced away, the tentacle twisted and snarled on the oak boards of the ship's deck.

Gunfire rang out from the yardarm, and the creature of bone and coral jerked and spun from a blow to the shoulder. A second shot cracked almost immediately thereafter, and fragments of skull exploded from the monster's head. It howled in rage, but Bronn's sword caught it, lifting it as the blade cut through and tossing both halves of the horror back into the sea.

"There she is." Isaye pointed just ahead of the *Nomad II*'s bow. "The *Indomitable*."

The mighty ship of the line crested the waves before them. Her hull had blackened over the years, rot spreading in dark patches on the ruined wood. Fleshy mold clung to the keel and hull boards, and long threads of kelp fluttered like banners from the horizontal spars of her three masts. Her black sails shivered in the wind, pulling the galleon forward with the might of a foul-smelling gale. Rotted sailors hung from the *Indomitable*'s rigging, some firing pistols and others addressing the set of her yardarms. They sang, and howled, and cater-wauled, the cries drifting across the rolling waves in an eerie cacophony. At the ship's wallowing prow rode the brass lady, the demon with six arms spread wide in malicious glee, green tarnish blighting her features like a disease.

The dark galleon's guns roared a challenge, blasting through a smaller ship in the Krytan armada as the *Indomitable* rolled toward the *Nomad II*. Her hull struck the side of the schooner with enough force to crack its keel, twisting the boards until the Krytan ship's frame gave way. The brigantine broke apart, scattering boards to the tide and pouring her crew into the grasp of gruesome undead horrors beneath the waves.

They were running perpendicular to the *Indomitable*, and the larger ship was slower than the *Nomad II*. Still, the sea between them was wide and filled with writhing monstrosities. "Can we catch them?" Cobiah shouted to Isaye. She didn't respond, glancing back at him with worry in her hazel eyes as the valiant clipper bore forward into battle.

"May Grenth shatter their bones!" Cobiah cursed, running his hands through his graying hair. "I wish we had the *Pride*'s engines," he said, striding to Isaye's side. "Or even that old clunker we had on the *Havoc*. I wish we had Verahd to give us the gale! We need more *speed*." He glanced to the port side, where one of the Orrian xebecs was disemboweling a Krytan galleon.

"We'll catch them," Isaye said through gritted teeth. "Come on, come on . . ."

"We have to!"

"We *will*." Throwing a glance down at her pilot's compass, Isaye grinned fiercely. "There! We just crossed into the harbor current. Now it's *our* turn."

"Our turn to what?" Cobiah asked, but as he got the words out, he felt the *Nomad II* shudder. The ship began to pick up speed, slowly at first and then faster, her prow rising as it bit deeply into the harbor's waves. "What's happening?"

"We've caught the warm inbound current, the one that heads westward. It'll push against the *Indomitable*, slowing her down. That'll make it damn hard to steer the *Nomad*, but she'll be faster in her passage, that's for certain." Though the increase in speed built slowly, it was notable. Bit by bit, the distance lessened between the two. "Make ready!" Isaye called to the sailors on the deck. The norn had cleared it of creatures, but several men and women aboard the ship were injured. Even Bronn was hurt, twisting a scrap of sail around his arm to bind a long slash. "Tenzin?" Isaye shielded her eyes and looked up.

From the upper yardarm, the dark-haired Krytan waved. The sailors had rigged a bucket of harpoon rifles near him, each loaded with a thick grappling hook and a long reel of hemp line. Grymm and Rahli prepared the sailors: one group under the norn, ready to fight off the undead, and a second mustering at Bosun Rahli's command to heave the lines once hooks pierced the enemy's deck. "Once we get the ropes clamped down," Isaye commanded, "we turn the *Nomad* west, toward Claw Island's fortress. We'll still be in the current, and that should help with our leverage. We need to get the *Indomitable* within range of the island's guns."

"Acknowledged, Cap'n." Rahli relayed the orders to the crew.

Before she'd finished speaking, the *Indomitable* opened fire. The boom of cannons rang in their ears and the smell of scorched gunpowder filled their noses. Shrill whistles accompanied the heft of cannonballs as they hurtled through the air, hurling up white-foamed spray where they struck the water, ripping wide rifts in the *Nomad II*'s sails and landing with shuddering explosions against her hull.

"Return fire!" Isaye shouted, and her crew was quick to obey. The *Nomad II*'s guns were fewer than those of the *Indomitable* but had greater range, and Cobiah saw breaches tear open along the black ship's hull where Isaye's gunners struck their mark.

The wounds to the *Indomitable*'s hull wouldn't slow her, nor would the Dead Ship take on water as the *Nomad II* would. But as they closed on the black-sailed ship of the line, Cobiah found himself counting. They had nineteen seconds until the Dead Ship's cannons could fire again.

The *Nomad* reached her in sixteen.

With a steady heave, the smaller clipper ship pulled alongside her enemy's deck and blasted her first grappling lines through the *Indomitable*'s hull. The proximity prevented either ship's cannons from doing damage;

neither could fire their big guns on such a close target without doing equal damage to their own hull.

Her crew was another matter. Undead sailors swarmed the gunwale, leaping across the gap between the vessels before planking could be laid between them. The rotting, filthy corpses of once-living men had no fear of falling, nor of water, nor of the beasts that lashed about beneath the fetid waves. They wielded rusted swords or swung bare fingers with sharpened bones protruding through the tips of greenish flesh.

Pistols fired aboard the *Nomad II* as the living sailors defended themselves. Bronn followed the first rush of flying lead with a long swipe of steel. His massive great-sword sliced through flesh, bone, and all, chopping through undead as they leapt onto the ship. He managed to skewer one on the tip of his sword, but it did not stop him—after a few more chops, the zombie body fell in pieces from the blade.

Not to be outdone, Grymm plowed into the fray with a yell, sounding for all the world like an avalanche tumbling downhill. He lifted one zombie bodily, snapping it in half with his bare hands. The big bearded norn shoved another of the walking dead from the ship, but its clutching hand gripped his shirtsleeve. Defiant, Grymm placed his hand on the zombie's shoulder and heaved, ripping dead cartilage from shattered bone. He grabbed the dead sailor's arm and began to beat another zombie with it, caving in the rotting sailor's skull.

Cobiah emptied his pistols into the enemy, aiming for eyes and joints. The bullets would do no significant harm against raw flesh, so he had to use them sparingly. Once the guns were empty, Cobiah drew his cutlass from his waist and set his feet firmly.

He could hear Tenzin's harpoon gun above him, its

unmistakable report cracking through the sound of battle. The sharpshooter lay along a high yardarm, reloading and firing the rope-bearing harpoons as quickly as he was able. Already, six ropes stretched from the *Nomad II* to the *Indomitable*, their far ends tangled tightly around the galleon's rigging, sunk into her hull or through the rotting boards of her ribs. Another flew out as Cobiah watched, the sharp hooks of the grapple shredding sail and wrapping tightly around the *Indomitable*'s rear mast.

"Make ready to pull!" Rahli yelled as she cracked another zombie with a belaying pin. "On the captain's command!"

But as she called out the order, a terrible voice cut through the chaos, with power behind it enough to rattle the ship's boards. *"There's only one captain here, mortal woman."* The sound was inhuman, chilling Cobiah's blood to ice. *"I am he."*

On the deck of the *Indomitable*, a horrific figure lowered the flintlock it held in a putrid hand. Its skull was square of jaw, the flesh rotted from it entirely, leaving greenish bone open to the salt of the sea. A once-pale coat, now stained with seeping black blood and festering mold, clung to muscles stretching tautly over jagged bone. Ruffles hung at the nape of the creature's neck and at its wrists, antique lace fluttering in the bitter ocean wind. No more the sheepish schoolboy, Captain Whiting had, with the corruption of Orr, become an abomination.

Cobiah staggered back, his breath torn from his chest. *"Chernock,"* the captain hissed. *"Do your duty."*

A second figure approached the gunwale. This one had skin like taut leather, a dried mummy of flesh stretched over a warped skeletal frame. Her grin was frozen in a rictus and her hands glowed with a sickly magical chill. "Aye, Captain Whiting. It'd be my honor."

Aubrey Chernock still wore her service medals, but now they were sewn to her skin, the Krytan coat lost somewhere to the sea. She hissed and leapt high above the gunwale, arching up like a shot and then down again, claws spread wide with feral glee. Grymm managed to get his fists in the air before she landed, but her claws seared through flesh and bone, ripping the norn's forearms open with the barest touch.

The norn yelled in pain, lashing out with a fist. The strike caught Chernock's jaw, snapping her head to the side with a jarring crack of bone. But instead of falling to the ground, the vicious creature simply paused and cracked its head upright once more, the sinews and broken vertebrae in her neck restoring themselves as wormy ropes of flesh crawled out of her skin and lashed themselves around the wound.

"Grenth's mercy," Isaye choked out, falling back to the ship's wheel.

"The ropes are in place!" Tenzin cried out above them.

Though she was clutching one of the wheel spokes in a white-knuckled hand, Isaye quickly took up the cry. "Haul the lines, men, and draw her close. The current will do the rest!" She grabbed the hoop of the rudder line and wrapped it over the wheel spoke to hold course northward into the Lion's Arch harbor.

Captain Whiting fired his gun, the pistol's report cracking like the snap of a rigging line. The bullet hurtled through the air, leaving a trail of black fumes in its wake as it sped toward Grymm Svaard. "Grymm! No!" Bronn Svaard leapt in front of his brother. The shot struck the swordsman, spinning him in a complete circle, knocking him to his knees.

"Brother!" howled Grymm. He tried to push past the snarling Chernock, but her claws carved deep into his flesh. Pinned by the awful wight, Grymm struggled and fought but could find no way to reach his twin.

"Haul the lines!" Isaye was yelling over the chaos, and her sailors risked and lost their lives to obey. But with every heave on the thick hemp rope, the *Indomitable* and the *Nomad* shifted closer together, drifting along the tide toward the fortress on Claw Island.

Cobiah spun, unloading his pistols at Captain Whiting. Both shots tore into the rotting captain's coat, shattering bone and spewing pus from beneath the putrescent flesh, but the Orrian monstrosity didn't flinch. Instead, it began to laugh, recognizing Cobiah at last.

Captain Whiting extended a filthy, blackened finger toward Cobiah. *"Marriner."* The beast's eyes glowed, greenish pinpricks within the skull's dark, moldy sockets.

"You swore to serve my ship for a full tour, Marriner. Her voyage has not yet ended. You escaped the Indomitable *once, at the mouth of Orr. Again when we seized Port Stalwart.*

"You will not evade commission a third time."

33

The crew pulled with all their might, hauling the ropes so fiercely that their hands left bloodstains on the fibers. The *Indomitable* scraped against the *Nomad II*'s side, her hull leaving stripes of black mold along the *Nomad II*'s weathered boards. Creatures crawled across the deck, rotting hands tearing at any sailors they could find. Red water drenched the deck as blood and salt mixed beneath churning boots.

The *Indomitable*'s canvases hung in ruined tatters from her masts, and the wind swelled only the clipper's sails. The *Nomad II*'s guns continued to tear at the *Indomitable*'s rigging, shredding the rotting fabric from her yard-arms. On the deck, Chernock slashed at Grymm again and again with her taloned claws. The norn was berserk with rage. He punched the wight directly in her face, and bones cracked beneath leathery skin as he forced her to retreat across the deck. She was quick, though, and clever, leaping to attack at any opportunity, her claws slashing open the skin of his arms and raking across the pugilist's chest. Grymm grabbed Chernock by the neck and snapped it roughly, and at last, the wight fell limp. Disgusted, Grymm hurled the creature away and raced toward Bronn.

Chernock landed with a thump on the deck. Within moments, her head twisted back around, the bones in her neck crackling loudly, her flesh reweaving itself as the creature struggled to heal the wounds she had been dealt. She was down—but not yet out.

Across the deck, Grymm fell to his knees, hands reaching to clasp his brother's shoulders. He lifted his brother from the floor, tipping Bronn backward onto his knees. "You'll be fine, old cuss," Grymm said firmly, denying any other possible outcome. Bronn writhed in his arms, dark steam issuing from the gunshot wound in his chest. His mouth fell open, and more smoke wafted from his throat and poured from the norn's nostrils. He made a low, guttural sound deep within his chest.

"Bronn?" Grymm let go, drawing his hands back. His arms were bloody from Chernock's aggressive strikes, and his long beard was matted with salt foam. "Bronn, can you hear me?" His brother's head tipped forward awkwardly, and his eyes closed. Grymm wept openly, cradling his brother's body to his chest. "My brother . . . my brother," he murmured in grief and pain.

But as it had been in the fight with Chernock, death was not the end of Bronn Svaard. His body twitched in his brother's hands, startling Grymm, who stared down at the bearded norn in renewed hope. "Bronn?" he asked softly, touching the side of his brother's face.

The body in Grymm's arms went stiff with a sudden rigor mortis, the limbs twitching and spasming as muscles contracted and released beneath the surface of the norn's skin. Slowly, a hideous smile spread beneath Bronn's mustache, a smile that was not his own. The swordsman's eyes snapped open, a solid, inky black, and his hand lifted to clench tightly around his brother's throat. "Brother!" Grymm choked out, horrified.

The thing that had been Bronn gave a sick-sounding laugh. "No more."

Near the gunwale, Cobiah raised his sword and focused on Captain Whiting, refusing to allow the green pin-pricks of light within the monster's skull to unnerve him. "I *outrank* you, Cap'n," Cobiah snarled. "You can swab your own decks!"

Dawn's rays shone palely from the bone of Whiting's skull and the exposed bone beneath his torn frock coat. "*Bosun Vost,*" the undead captain said with a smile. "*Give him thirty-nine lashes as penance for his insolence.*"

A scuttling creature rose from the masses aboard the *Indomitable.* Its hands, from the wrists down, had been replaced with leathery tentacles, not suckered like an octopus's, but serrated, like the teeth of a shark. His white hair hung in torn lumps from parchment-like skin, and beneath the skin, the muscles that shifted the creature's frame were a moldy shade of bluish-white. "Aye, sir," it rasped in a voice like sandpaper. "I'll teach the boy a les-son, a'right."

"Cobiah!" Isaye screamed from the fore of the ship. Her sword swung free of one of the *Indomitable*'s undead sailors, tearing through its sternum. She placed her foot on the writhing corpse's chest and pushed, heaving the body overboard.

Cobiah struggled to keep down his bile as Vost crawled over the gunwale and onto the *Nomad II*'s deck. "I'm a bit busy, Isaye—" Vost's arms lashed out, the tentacles slash-ing across Cobiah's chest. Although he jumped back, the blow tore open his shirt, and where the undead bosun's tentacles touched his skin, boils rose as if he'd been splashed with acid. It scalded fiercely, burning through his skin with incredible pain. Furthermore, the knife wound on his side had begun to bleed again, spotting the bandages across his rib cage with scarlet. This fight was not going well.

Out on the open sea, the Krytan vessels were falling, one by one, to the Dead Ships. The two scarlet-sailed xebecs led the charge, their magic lashing out against the living fleet. As Cobiah watched, the red sails of one ship shivered and burst into flame, heat waves rippling out toward a Krytan galleon. The Krytan ship caught fire as the surge of heat passed, its hull spontaneously bursting into flame. He could hear the distant shouts of the sailors as they hurried to put out the fire with the pumps before it could spread, and saw them targeted by a hundred arrows launched from the xebec's wide deck. Though the Orrian ships were less advanced than the *Indomitable*, their magic made them even more dangerous.

Bronn Svaard surged to his feet, lifting his brother by the neck. His black eyes blazed in sharp contrast to the deathly pallor of his skin. "Don't worry, Grymm," he snarled. "You'll join me in the service of the dragon, and we will again fight as one. *We will serve Zhaitan forever!*"

In panic and fear, Grymm raised his hands above his shoulders, bringing them down in forceful chops onto his brother's collarbone. Once, twice, three times, he struck to either side of Bronn's neck. On the third blow, the bone cracked, and Bronn's hands loosened around Grymm's throat. With a lurch, Grymm raised his feet to Bronn's chest and kicked, separating the two with a massive shove. Grymm fell to the deck, and Bronn staggered back. Rolling to his side, Grymm roared to his brother. "Bronn! Fight it!"

"No, my brother." Bronn reached for his bloodied sword. Shaking the stain from its blade, he lifted the weapon and strode toward Grymm. "You cannot fight the inevitable. I feel it in my bones—in my blood. Zhaitan's will is my will. His strength is my strength." Bronn's black eyes flashed. "The world will be reborn by the dragon's will. Death is the beginning!"

He swung the greatsword in a mighty arc, and Grymm was forced to roll aside. As the blade completed its forward sweep, Grymm gathered himself, lunging to his feet in the wake of his brother's sword.

"No!" Grymm raged. "You are not my brother!" In fury, Grymm lifted his hands, screaming a prayer to the Spirits of the Wild as tears welled in his eyes. "Bear, give me strength! Snow Leopard, lend me speed! Raven, let my hands be your talons!" As he shouted the words, his flesh began to transform, his body shifting, growing larger. "Ever-running Wolf, I am your son. Let me die if I must, but I cannot abandon my brother to this fate!

"Spirits, be with me!" The last words were an almost inhuman roar. Grymm's body had swelled to nearly twice its original size, standing eight feet high with massive shoulders. Silvery claws erupted from his overlong fingers, and cold starlight shone in his eyes. Part man, part wolf, Grymm raised his muzzle in a woeful howl. Then, with a surge of motion, he charged toward his undead brother once more, pitting claw and savagery against steel.

Two smaller Orrian ships cut across the *Nomad II*'s wake, guns blazing. They were chasing a swift little ketch flying the colors of Port Noble, her crew struggling desperately to keep up their speed. As the ketch tacked back and forth, the Dead Ships tried to follow, but their sails grew tangled in the constant shift of rigging and line. Foundering, they blasted their deck guns in a desperate attempt to slow their opponent, but the ketch spun on a lofty roll of wave and danced back toward them, evading their fire. She took one out with a full broadside of her nine-pound guns, the cannons rocking back on their braces.

Yet for every victory, there were multiple defeats. One of the Dead Ships rammed the hull of a wide-berthed Krytan clipper, throwing lines over her side as the Krytans fired their guns, trying to ward off the Orrians. Chunks of the Dead Ship's wooden frame blew off with each assault, but beneath the hull was a structure of bone and muscle, like a living underbelly that absorbed the shots from the Krytan guns. Although the wood peeled like flesh, the underside remained sturdy—and the brave little clipper could not be rid of her. Strange meaty tentacles, like mobile intestines, lashed up from clefts between the bony ridges and attached themselves to the deck of the clipper. The suckers on the flabby lengths clung to every inch of wood as the tentacles contracted, crushing the ship with hideous strength.

In the harbor, the xebecs were making thin lines toward the *Indomitable*, apparently aware of the flagship's distress. With sails of flame, they cut through the billowing waves, leaving a trail of white foam and black ash behind them. "Cobiah!" Isaye yelled. She pointed with the blade of her cutlass. *"Something's under the water!"*

Past the *Indomitable*, a shadow moved beneath the waves. At first, Cobiah dismissed it, thinking it nothing more than the monstrosities he'd already seen, the kind that clawed their way up the *Nomad II*'s hull or walked on the sandy beaches beneath the white-foamed waves. But this one was different. It wasn't just the sheer size—though large, the mass could have been made up of sunken ships or a crowd of undead moving across the ocean floor. But this one moved in a way that was unlike the others; it was no ship, no swimming human or near-human form. The purplish shadow moved like an eel, undulating and twisting in the current that pulled the *Nomad II* toward the island in the bay. As it rose toward the surface, the long shape took form—flippers, each as large as a small ketch; a tail as flat and massive as the deck of one of the Krytan galleons. The head that broke the waterline was triangular and long, with sleek rivulets of hardened flesh to shunt the water from the creature's black, beady eyes. Its mouth was wide and long like a shark's, and rows of teeth—each the size of a man—slit the water into bloodstained froth. Cobiah stumbled as the ship tilted, water rushing before the monster like innocents before an invading tide. He knew that creature.

It was the Maw.

"Eyes to port! Watch for a ramming blow from beneath us!" Cobiah yelled in warning. The leviathan rose farther, a bellow trumpeting from its rotting jaw. Once its leap lifted most of the monster's body above the water, Cobiah could see it more clearly—and it was not entirely as he remembered. The monster was as dead as the ships of Orr, its black flesh rotted and fouled by disease. Barnacles clung to the creature's fins, and putrid green spittle blew from its thick, fleshy lips. The thrashing tail slashed through the current. Water rushed through holes in the creature's flesh, revealing bones etched with salt pitting and bloodsucking remoras the size of a lifeboat writhing in the behemoth's innards. A long, pale scar in the creature's cheek marked an old wound where a cannonball had once rent a bloody hole in sensitive flesh.

"The rule of the living has ended," Captain Whiting said

mockingly. *"This is the time of the Elder Dragons. Thus begins the time of Zhaitan and of Orr. The day of their ultimate victory is close."*

"Close," Cobiah said through gritted teeth, "but not today." He spun to look toward the city and saw the fort at Claw Island growing nearer and nearer still. Cobiah could see the Lionguard manning its walls, turning their cannons toward the sea battle. The flag of Lion's Arch whipped in the wind above its highest tower, and the sandy beach outside the wall held two trebuchets standing ready with balls of flaming pitch. "We're here," he breathed, a smile spreading across his features. "We made it."

As if in answer, the fortress opened fire.

34

The morning sun played over the high stone walls of the island fortress, illuminating sandstone and granite barricades—and the heavy black iron of cannons on its gunnery emplacements. The boom of the guns rolled like thunder, pounding heavy ammunition in waves, one immediately after the next, onto the Dead Ships of the Orrian armada. The cannons' muzzles glowed like red eyes, and the smell of powder smoke swirled in acrid plumes around the fortification. The foam on Claw Island's sandy beach should have been white, but instead it was stained red with blood spilled from the ships at the mouth of the harbor. The fortification's cannons cracked a sharp, near-constant retort, and the bombard guns on the cliffsides above the city echoed with the fire of continued gunnery, but while they could destroy the Orrian ships, they could do little against the Maw.

Even with the fortress and city gunnery, the Dead Ships still had an advantage. They outnumbered the Krytan vessels by more than three to one, and the magic of the two Orrian xebecs continued to raze smaller ships. They raced here and there amid the battle, unfettered by tide or wind, shattering clippers with rock-hard buffets of air or setting them alight with the inferno of their blazing scarlet sails. They knew better than to come close to Claw Island, and with magic enough to give them motion and direction against the tide, the guns were of little use against the Orrian xebecs.

The *Balthazar's Trident* remained away from the main swell of the battle, using her long-range guns to aid ships that were suffering under the Orrian attack. Cobiah was glad to see Edair was helping, but happier still to see that the ship was safe. For now.

All around the *Nomad II*, the Maw laid claim to anything that floundered or fell behind. The monster rose from the waves and bared huge rows of teeth, snapping a clipper ship in half. The screams of sailors were soon drowned in the gargantuan creature's wake. Chernock began clambering up the mast, her clawed hands sinking into the thick wood. On his high yardarm, Tenzin let go of the harpoon gun and drew a pistol from his belt, trying to get a bead on her, but the clever wight dodged and hid behind flaps of sail. As she climbed, she snapped rigging lines with her claws, causing the canvas to sag and shift and cover her from his keen aim. Tenzin skittered higher and higher, trying to find an opening for the shot, but to no avail.

On the deck, Isaye's crew fought valiantly against the undead from the *Indomitable*, swords flashing and pistols thundering. They were outnumbered, but the narrow deck kept the *Nomad II*'s sailors from being overrun. They clumped together, pressing back-to-back to defend one another against the horrific enemy. Amid the shambling zombies and shuffling undead, the monstrous Vost laid about with whiplike tentacles, drawling blood with each crack and snap. He didn't bother to choose his targets, lashing the living and undead with equal enthusiasm.

Pushing past those in his way, Vost inexorably drew closer and closer to Cobiah.

At last, Cobiah found himself trapped between Vost and a pile of netted cargo secured to the quarterdeck. On the *Indomitable*, Captain Whiting stood with one foot on the gunwale, laughing at the brutal carnage. His eyes lit with green fire as he relished Cobiah's desperate situation. "*Well done, Bosun,*" he oozed. "*Thirty-nine lashes, if you please.*"

Vost struck, tentacles slicing through the air with a hiss that could be heard even over the clanging of swords. Cobiah caught the first strike on his sword, cutting through one of the tentacles with the sharp edge of his blade. He stabbed forward, but the blade of the cutlass turned against Vost's hard carapace. The slicing sword was simply unable to pierce the rocky armor of the undead bosun's barnacle-covered skin. More tentacles flailed out where Vost's arms had once been, wrapping like wet seaweed around Cobiah's weapon. With a sharp tug, Vost jerked the sword out of Cobiah's hand. As it crashed to the deck, Cobiah lunged to trap the blade beneath his foot before the weapon slid overboard in a wash of water.

The undead bosun's second strike cracked over Cobiah's shoulder and across his back, tearing through his coat, his shirt, and his skin. Long red welts of blood sprayed up in its wake. "Cobiah!" Tenzin yelled from above. "Catch!" He tossed his pistol down through the rigging. Desperately praying to Dwayna, Cobiah lunged—and caught the butt of the gun in his outstretched hand.

Unbalanced, Cobiah fell to one knee and jerked the pistol around. He squeezed the trigger, and shots rang out, piercing Vost's rocky skin. The carapace cracked, barnacles fell away where the bullets had entered, and the bosun staggered, bloodshot eyes turning red. He lifted a hand to touch the brackish blood seeping from the wounds and gave a withering smile. "Nice shot, but your bullets are too small to do me significant harm, Coby." Vost chortled, a sticky sort of sound. "Shall we continue with your lashes?" he snarled, and the undead bosun's tentacles whipped out with murderous intent.

Tossing away the empty pistol, Cobiah put out his hand and allowed the tentacles to strike his forearm. Skin flayed beneath his twisted coat sleeve as the tentacles wrapped about his arm. He clenched them in his hand, gritting his teeth, and then pulled with all his might. At the same time, he flipped his sword upward with the toe of his boot, grabbing the handle with his other hand and praying to Grenth that he still had some luck left.

Unprepared, Vost toppled forward—and Cobiah targeted the area of the carapace where the bullets had broken through. The sword point caught in one of the bullet holes, splitting open the hole with an audible crack. Cobiah tugged again, squeezing Vost's tentacles in his free hand and jamming the sword in farther with the other. The barnacle covering around Vost's flesh fractured farther, allowing the sword to slide in even more. Letting go of the tentacles, Cobiah clutched both hands around the sword hilt and shoved it upward, shattering the rough covering and splitting Vost's torso in half.

Vost shuddered and collapsed, the hideous light fading from his eyes. As the monstrosity crumpled to the deck, Cobiah tore the tentacles from his arm. Blood oozed from long cuts where skin hung like scraps of sail. He flexed his hand to see that all the fingers still worked, then twisted a scrap of cloth tightly around the wound and turned back to the fight.

The Dead Ships in the harbor were taking a pounding

from Claw Island's cannons, and one of the mighty xebecs had a sail listing in its traces. But the rest of the Orrian armada still harried the Krytan ships—and three of the black-hulled vessels were drawing close to Prince Edair's flagship. Cobiah saw Isaye's eyes worriedly following the distant motion of the *Balthazar's Trident*, fearing for the waddling ship of the line.

At the center of the *Nomad II*'s main deck, a ferocious battle was raging. Grymm, rising up to slash with steely claws, struggled against his brother's sword. Bronn's laugh was burbling and rank, filled with the cloying sickness of Orr. Where his sword cut, it left a black trail in the air like the bullets of Captain Whiting's pistol. Already, Grymm had a long gash in his side. Bronn had suffered as well; claw marks trailed across his face, there were bites in the meat of both shoulders, and dark blood flowed over the muscles of his chest. The wounds would have killed a mortal man. Against the undead, they did nothing but add to Bronn's horrific appearance.

Bronn slashed at his brother, sword flying through the air viciously. Grymm sidestepped the blow and roared, the anger in his bestial tone shaking the deck. He lunged closer, clasping Bronn's shoulders in his wicked claws. Bronn howled, unable to move his sword, as Grymm's terrible, wolflike head bowed closer.

"I'm sorry, brother. I tried," Grymm whispered.

"I'll slaughter you!" the undead Bronn roared, fighting to draw a dagger from his belt. The blade slid free of its sheath, on a path toward Grymm's heart.

Grymm didn't give him that chance. Savagely twisting his head, he dug long canines into his brother's throat and ripped it through. Bronn choked. His back arched as his muscles continued to try to fight the enemy, forcing the body to struggle even against such a horrible wound.

Then, with a terrible wheezing sound, he fell to the deck, truly dead. The norn in beast form raised its head toward the last stars of morning and let out a sorrowful, heart-breaking howl.

Cobiah had never seen a wolf cry before. He never wanted to see it again.

The cannon barrage from Claw Island continued to batter the Orrian ships, but now several of them had begun to hammer the fortress with broadsides of their own. The island was taking damage, and smoke rose from the fortress where buildings inside had been set alight. The gunnery emplacements were taking a toll on the Dead Ships, but it simply wasn't enough to make a serious dent in the Orrian assault.

The ship taking the most significant damage was the galleon in the lead: the *Indomitable*. She was closest to Claw Island, and despite the *Nomad II*'s cover, the fortress had concentrated two of its cannons solely on the prodigious galleon. Areas of the *Indomitable*'s hull were completely staved in, and the ocean swirled around the bones of her keel and lower decks.

Captain Whiting saw it, too. Instead of ordering more sailors forward, he was focusing on the bilges, struggling to keep his ship above water so they could finish the fight. The *Nomad II*'s lines prevented them from avoiding the island or using the current to get away from the guns, making the *Indomitable* a sitting duck for the fortress's artillery. Unable to flee or fire effectively against Claw Island, the *Indomitable* turned her guns toward the most notable target behind the Krytan line.

The *Balthazar's Trident*.

Cannon fire rang out in furious tandem, white plumes rising from the far side of the *Indomitable*. The *Balthazar's Trident* was too close, harried by three Dead Ships. Cobiah saw them turn and work together, driving her toward this fate without any sign of communication. It was as if the minions of the Orrian dragon thought with one mind, capitalizing on every advantage that occurred along the battlefield. Those three smaller ships would keep the *Balthazar's Trident* from retreating farther into the city's harbor. If the *Indomitable* kept firing, the prince's ship would break apart and sink—or worse, like other injured ships, become chum for the lurking Maw.

Cobiah thought quickly. If he could distract the crew of the *Indomitable*, they might stop firing on the *Balthazar's Trident*. The king's ship could escape the galleon's guns. But how? He frowned, considering his options. There was only one thing that the undead sailors on the *Indomitable* wanted more than the destruction of Krytan ships.

"Me." Cobiah's mind rushed through a thousand options, settling at last on the tactic he'd always preferred—he'd have to attack. Grasping a loose line of rigging in his uninjured hand, Cobiah ran backward to get a head start. He raced forward, hurling himself up and swinging wildly on the line as he had done in his youth. The line stretched, lifted him from the deck, and swung him toward the enemy ship—but as the rope played out to its full reach, Cobiah's strength failed. One arm was not enough to hold him aloft, nor were his muscles as powerful as they had once been. Instead of sailing gracefully to the *Indomitable*'s yardarm, Cobiah found himself tumbling down onto her sticky black deck. He slid, scrambling, and slammed up against her mizzenmast. The sky spun above Cobiah as he struggled to catch his breath. Something tumbled from an inner pocket of his coat. Instinctively, Cobiah grabbed the limp bundle, barely recognizing the little doll. He stared into its lifeless button eyes and tried to understand how she could still be wearing that stitched-on smile. The sails above him flowed in the wind, black and foul, the purity of long-ago days washed away by the horrors of Orr.

The *Indomitable*.

The horrors of his last moments aboard the galleon rushed into Cobiah's mind, blotting out his purpose with cruel memories. This time, there were no charr to save him, no *Havoc* to draw him from the sea. He was alone with the shades of his past.

An all-too-familiar figure loomed over him. Although its pockmarked skin was filthy with mold and the limp ponytail slick with rotting kelp, the narrow brown eyes laughed cruelly down at him. It was Tosh—or what was left of Tosh. "Co . . . bi . . . ah . . ." The broken jaw worked, struggling to get out the word. "Still . . . the pretty little . . . dolly." Tosh's hands closed on Cobiah's shirt, and the reek of his fetid breath filled the air. His fingers clenched the linen clothing with a stronger grip than any living man could possess.

Something primitive snapped within Cobiah's spirit at the sight of his old rival's dead face, and he flailed, punches striking in punctuation with his screams. Other undead sailors clustered tightly around him, their hands grabbing at Cobiah's flesh, jerking him to his feet with avaricious, scrabbling fingers. Shuddering backward against the mast, Cobiah tried to push them away. Another zombie pushed ahead of the rest, a crooked smile rupturing his ruined face.

"Good ol' Coby," Sethus whispered, his voice like the whisper of fog on the sea. Sour, greenish cankers oozed pus across the remnants of his skin. "Why'd you leave me? I thought we were friends." The words struck Cobiah like a physical blow, robbing him of air. He gaped and fell back against the rotted mizzenmast as Sethus murmured darkly, "Together again." Sethus's undead eyes glinted. "*For Zhaitan. Forever.*"

"Take me to the captain," Cobiah said grimly, chills running up his spine. "I'm ready to do my duty." The undead shuffled and smiled, their fetid mouths gaping open in jawless, dripping pleasure. More and more of the undead crew gathered to watch the spectacle as Tosh shoved him forward, heading toward the green-banistered stairwell of the quarterdeck. Taking his time, hoping that more undead would gather—leaving their posts at the cannons to see the captive walk the deck— Cobiah strode solemnly through the clustered, horrific mass of wights. He had to keep their attention, give the undead a reason to focus on him rather than the *Balthazar's Trident*.

Holding fast to his courage, Cobiah glanced up at the ruined sails, and an old, familiar memory returned to him. *Angel's wings. Biviane's wings.* He took a deep breath of air laced with sulfur and rot. *You've always been with me when I needed you most, little sister,* Cobiah thought. *I hope you're watching now.*

Isaye's voice cut through the roar and blast of battle. "Coby!" she screamed from the *Nomad II*'s quarterdeck. He saw her fighting her way across the other ship, heading for the ropes that tied the two gunwales together. Before she could reach them, another shout drew her attention upward.

"Isaye!" Tenzin's voice echoed from the high yardarm of the *Nomad II*. "By Lyssa's veil . . . Isaye, look!"

"I have to help Cobiah!" Isaye screamed, pointing with her sword. Her eyes were wide and her motions frantic with worry.

"The fleet!" Tenzin yelled again, overriding her concern. "Look!"

Beyond the fortress of Claw Island, beneath the wide arch of the Gangplank Bridge, sails were fast approaching. They came in every size, every shape—some were little more than bedsheets sewn hastily together, while others looked like canvas that had been taken half-finished from the weaver. Still, the sails were attached to yardarms, which hung from masts, which were attached to . . .

Ships, at least thirty strong. Ships of all sorts, all sizes, as patchwork and haphazard looking as their sails. Their hulls were brightly painted, colored randomly in blues and oranges, the colors changing down their hulls. They seemed cobbled together, as if someone had collected chunks of ships and nailed them one against the other. Cobiah stared, believing at first that he was hallucinating, but as they approached with guns thundering, the nature of the patchwork vessels became more apparent.

These ships hadn't just been built in Lion's Arch.

They'd been built *from* Lion's Arch.

Every retired boat and schooner, every clipper and galleon that had ever been converted into warehousing or into shops, every building in the city that had a hull and a keel had been pried up, retarred, and sent to sea. Some still had advertisements or names of shops painted on their hulls; others had quickly been refitted with masts of light posts and rudders made of signboard. The ships were ramshackle, afloat with spit and a prayer, but they had one undeniable advantage: they were crewed by the finest sailors in the world.

Despite the wind that was at loggerheads with them and the wild tides that fought any ship sailing Sanctum Harbor, the fleet out of Lion's Arch had sails swelled with power. Magic pushed them, hurtling them forward with the breath of a tempest at their heels. The Lionguard elementalists were strong enough to push more than two dozen ships from a standstill to running speed, keeping a powerful wind blowing at their backs through force of will alone.

As the undead gathered around him, Cobiah's eye fell on the lead ship. She was a brave pinnace, plowing through the waves ahead of the others at a speed none of them could match. Smaller than the galleons, larger than the multicolored clipper ships, the *Pride* was leading the way. Even on the distant *Indomitable*, Cobiah could hear the rumble and pound of a heartbeat in the little ship's hold, the *Pride*'s mighty engine pushing her to the fore. She had her guns rolled out and shining, the crew firing on the Orrians as quickly as they could load the cannons, and standing boldly on her prow, his orange fur rippling in the wind, stood Sykox Steamshroud.

35

A resounding cheer erupted across Sanctum Harbor at the sight of the makeshift fleet. The cheers echoed from the high cliffs of the bay where the Lionguard manned the city's artillery, through the brave fortress that stood against the incoming ships, and all across the scattered Krytan vessels fighting bravely in the harbor. As the morning sun shimmered on cool blue water, the blazing cannons of the patchwork navy rained fire and destruction down on the Dead Ships. Even undead vessels could not withstand such a barrage. Fashioned as they were from broken mortal vessels, the will of Zhaitan shielded them and made them powerful—but this new armada was as large as their own, and the sailors were skilled in exploiting the weaknesses of Dead Ships. Between the firepower of Claw Island and the constant volleys of cannon shot from the patchwork fleet, the undead ships began to break apart and founder. The advantage they'd gained was crumbling, and as the tide swept out from the city, it carried with it the broken pieces of many a black hull.

Aboard the *Nomad II*, the tide of the battle had turned, too. Isaye's crew fought with renewed determination, cutting apart their undead enemies and clearing the deck of the minions of Zhaitan. First among them was Grymm Svaard, still in wolf form, wreaking titanic vengeance on the undead. They fought until the deck was covered in torn, rotting flesh and black blood, hurling their opponents into the sea or tearing them apart.

The Maw, on the other hand, seemed to be delighting in the chaos of battle. It swept through the carnage, eating anything and everything, wherever it found flesh. The jagged teeth of the massive creature crushed hull and keel, shredding sails and dragging sailors to their doom. Nothing was safe from its assault, neither Dead Ship nor living crew. It attacked them all, without concern for the meager weapons leveled by those on the surface. Neither cannon nor land-based bombard seemed to have any ability to cause it harm.

The *Indomitable* had taken heavy damage from the cannons of passing Krytan vessels, and her hull was cracked to the bone. Bits of raw flesh clung to her deck, writhing as fire arched from the cliffs of the city and slammed into her wooden core. Captain Whiting turned his green-flame eyes away from Lion's Arch, cursing in a language that had died long before he was born. *"Continue firing on the large galleon . . . what's this?"* The captain turned to stare at Cobiah. *"What have you brought me, lads?"* The captain's rotten lips burbled in horrible imitation of his living, fleshly quaver.

"It's the deserter, sir." Tosh dragged Cobiah forward.

The captain hissed, stepping to the banister, and all eyes turned to Cobiah. The mighty guns of the *Indomitable* fell silent, and Cobiah felt a massive, weighty presence focus on him, something greater than the ship or the captain; something far away, and impossibly strong. *"The deserter . . ."* Captain Whiting drooled eagerly. *"Come to reclaim your commission, Marriner?"*

"Never," Cobiah said loudly, his answer evoking hisses from the crew.

Captain Whiting's eyes fell on him with pleasure. *"We'll see about that,"* he snarled. His once-soft face had been eaten through by maggots, and his eyes were empty pits lit by flickering green flames. *"Give him what-for, lads, and see if that takes some of the wind out of his sails."*

The zombies obeyed, leaving their posts at the cannons and masts to attack Cobiah with raucous, mindless glee. Cobiah fought back, punching and kicking with all his strength. His right forearm ached and bled where Vost's tentacle lashes had injured him, and the wound in his side spilled a trickle of blood. But despite the pain and the fear, Cobiah kept his gaze on the *Balthazar's Trident*, ensuring that he kept them busy while the king's ship—carrying Isaye's son—sailed toward the slapdash armada of Lion's Arch. At last, she was out of range of the *Indomitable*'s cannons. The distraction had worked, and the *Balthazar's Trident* was safe.

A tremor rocked the *Indomitable*. Her black sails swung limply and then tore free, rippling and whipping into the fierce wind. The bronze figure on the ship's prow began to glow with a sickly green light, her eyes and fingernails blazing with eager malice. The ship trembled once more, then began to sink. *"The ship's taken too much damage. We must return to Orr."* The captain eyed Cobiah scathingly. *"Throw Marriner into the brig. We'll make sure his punishment lasts a very ... long ... time,"* the captain commanded. The undead crew was quick to obey, grasping Cobiah's shoulders and wrists and dragging him bodily forward as seawater began to splash over the sides of the ship. The *Indomitable* began to move—down, into the waves.

"Cobiah!" a voice screamed defiantly from the *Nomad II*. "No! I won't let them take him!"

Isaye. He focused his will on the sound. While the *Balthazar's Trident* had been in danger, he'd been content to take a beating, possibly even die, so that Isaye's son would be safe. But now, with the ship out of combat and the *Indomitable* threatening to submerge, Cobiah's survival instinct surged to the fore. He had to fight, had to find a way to get free of the ship before it dove beneath the waves and returned to Orr. He had to get back to her. Again, he heard Isaye calling frantically, refusing to give up on him. No matter what had passed between them, Sykox had been right. Cobiah still loved her. He always would.

The lines that stretched between the *Nomad II* and her prey, designed to keep the *Indomitable* from separating, now stretched to their limit. The weight of the *Indomitable's* descent pulled at the *Nomad II* with ponderous strength. The smaller clipper, weighed down by the force of the towering ship of the line, began to lurch dangerously to starboard. Bosun Rahli leapt from the quarterdeck, leaving behind three fallen Orrians. Blade ready in her hand, she hacked at one of the thick hemp ropes. "Captain!" she commanded. "We have to cut the stays! The Dead Ship's submerging—she'll drag us to the ocean floor!"

Isaye pulled her blade from a defeated enemy and turned toward the *Indomitable.* Her dark, silver-touched hair blew around her face like a thundercloud threaded with lightning, and her eyes were filled with fear. "Cobiah!"

"We have to free the *Nomad,* or it'll be the death of us all! Captain!" the bosun screamed. "Your orders?"

"Cobiah!"

Cobiah's blue eyes met Isaye's hazel ones, with a hundred dead men in between. There was no time for words, nor could she have heard him over the furor and combat between them. Instead, he nodded to her, absolving her of the decision. Tears streaming from her eyes, fists clenching on the ship's rail, she called to Rahli, "Cut the ropes."

"Aye, Captain!" Rahli did not pause even for a second. "Sever the lines! Free the *Nomad* before we find ourselves in that monster's gullet!" Sailors rushed to obey her orders, but the press of undead kept them from the heavy ropes. Rahli was attacked by two hideous, scrabbling wights even as her blade sank into the hemp, and she was forced to pull her sword from the task to defend her life instead. Back on the *Indomitable*, Captain Whiting laughed. The dragon's will infused the Orrians, coordinating their response—defending the ropes even as the black-hulled galleon pulled them all into the sea. The *Nomad II* was far too rich a prize to abandon.

Nearby, the Maw circled the two ships, its huge mouth snapping up anyone who had the misfortune to fall into the waves. The more their valiant ship listed, the more the living had to fight just to stay aboard—and the more easily the undead, whose clawed feet and bone-spur fingertips bit deeply into the wood, could keep them from severing the lines.

Spying a fallen weapon caught in the *Nomad II*'s cargo nets, Tenzin yelled down to the deck, "Rahli! Throw me that rifle!" Tossing down the harpoon gun, Tenzin caught the long gun when the bosun hurled it into the air. Balanced lengthwise on a yardarm, he drew steady aim on the ropes, planning to shoot them free.

Then Chernock struck.

The wight had been biding her time, moving cautiously among the rigging, all but forgotten in the press of combat. When Tenzin turned his attention to the ropes, she seized her opportunity. Leaping out from behind a spiderweb of ropes and mast, the wight landed on the yardarm, sinking her claws into the Krytan's back with a vindictive glee, her leathery face stretched into the vile semblance of a smile. Tenzin screamed in agony, rifle firing uselessly as she ripped into his flesh like a cat sharpening her claws. Chernock shrieked her bloody victory to the sky, raising one hand to lop away the Krytan's head.

Cobiah saw it all happening from the deck of the *Indomitable*, where the undead dragged him toward the lower hatches beneath their captain's approving gaze. Seizing an opportunity, Cobiah tore a pair of pistols from a zombie's belt, turning them toward the *Nomad II*. He could have used them to end his life before the ship submerged, or to fire on Captain Whiting—but Cobiah never even thought of himself. Instead, he fired across the gap between the two ships, and the bullets ripped through Chernock's body. The impact pushed the wight back, inch by inch, with the pounding force of repetition until at last, she collapsed in final death and fell into the sea. "Now, Tenzin!" Cobiah yelled, desperate to see the *Nomad II* safely away. *"Cut the lines!"*

"Aye, Commodore!" Despite the agony of his wounds, the sharpshooter raised his rifle and fired, reloading with incredible speed to fire again and again. With each shot, a hemp line snapped. It took eight shots, emptying Tenzin's belt pouch of ammunition—but at last, the *Nomad II* pulled free.

The clipper rocked to her port with the sudden release of liberation. Water splashed in thick, blood-touched foam around the *Indomitable*'s gunwale as the sudden sway of the *Nomad II*'s release hurled the Dead Ship to its starboard. Taken by surprise, the undead were toppled left and right—and Cobiah found himself suddenly free.

Leaping up, he thrust an elbow into Tosh's face, cracking the undead sailor's jaw and hurling him aside. Cobiah's foot caught another zombie in the kneecap, and the monster crumpled to the tilting deck, sliding rapidly toward the edge of the ship. With a scream, the sailor tried to grasp the rotten boards, the railing, anything that would keep him from the water, but his clawed hands caught nothing, and he slid into the waiting jaws of the Maw.

Still holding the pistols, Cobiah clocked one of the undead with the hilt of an empty gun. He laid about with abandon, pounding squishy flesh and raw muscle, breaking bones and shattering barnacles that covered rotting, putrid skin. With rugged determination, he fought his way to the railing of the *Indomitable*'s deck and stared across the steadily growing chasm between the two ships. The Maw still thrashed about between them, snapping its teeth in the air where tantalizing shadows fell across the sea. One jump, one massive leap, and so long as he didn't fall, he'd be safe aboard the *Nomad II*. He saw Isaye rush to the railing on the other side, her hands reaching desperately over the gunwale. "Jump, Cobiah," she yelled to him.

Suddenly, pain exploded through Cobiah's body as a knife dragged its way between his ribs. "*Escape? No. You're a deserter, Marriner.*" Captain Whiting twisted the blade savagely before letting go. "*And now you will die.*"

Cobiah turned, grasping the hilt of the dagger. Rage overwhelming the pain, Cobiah pulled it out and reversed the blade, raising it to thrust the edge into Whiting's fleshy throat. The captain's bone fingers clenched around his wrist as the wight struggled to escape the slowly piercing blade. Cobiah grinned wickedly, forcing the dagger to cut through bone and enchantment as the greenish flame in Captain Whiting's eyes quavered in sudden fear. "Deserter? No. The word you want, Captain, is 'mutineer.'" With a fierce twist of the dagger's long blade, Cobiah severed the captain's spine, cutting the monster's head from his rotting body.

As Whiting fell, the *Indomitable* shuddered to its core, and the brass figurehead on the bow let out a long, keening wail as if it, too, felt the blow of the captain's death. The Maw surfaced with a roar of its own, and from every Dead Ship left in the Orrian armada, a cry of unified anguish rose from slavering orifice and torn jowl, as if the dragon itself were screaming.

"Cobiah!" On the *Nomad II*'s deck, Isaye called to him desperately as the gulf between them grew ever wider. He could see that the clipper was dead in the water, one mast collapsed and the other ravaged by grapeshot. Even though the *Nomad II* was free of the *Indomitable*'s pull, Isaye's ship could not give chase, nor even remain alongside the black vessel. Her sailors rushed about, trying to save the *Nomad II* from sinking, but that was the most they could do.

The *Indomitable* was crumbling around him, her black masts cracking from deck to high tip, keel twisting as though the ship was writhing in agony. Cobiah watched the deck boards collapse, creating gaping holes in the upper deck, yawing open to reveal sickly, mold-covered holds below. The smell that rose from within the ship was noxious, like decayed flesh and rancid blood, threatening to choke Cobiah with every breath.

Behind him, another voice whispered, "Coby . . . You were right about Orr. It's so beautiful. The ancient cathedrals, the palace of the gods, the magic . . . Remember how we used to talk about all the riches it contains, all the secrets waiting to be discovered? Come with me, Coby . . . I'll show it to you . . ." Sethus's voice was plaintive, and he extended a rotting, pustule-covered hand. The *Indomitable* was settling into the water, plunging lower with each sweep of the waves. Cobiah remembered the dreams of their youth, the long hours they'd spent talking about just such things. Promising to go there together. "Stay with me . . ."

"Good-bye, Sethus," Cobiah choked out, his wounds aching with a cold more biting than the seawater. He dropped the dagger and clutched Biviane's doll tightly in his one good hand. "Good-bye."

His wounds bleeding, his body wracked with pain, Cobiah looked over the twisted deck railing at Isaye, meeting her eyes across the widening gulf of water between them. Never losing sight of her, he put his foot on the *Indomitable*'s gunwale and leapt into the sea.

The ocean current spun Cobiah around and around, dragging him after the sinking *Indomitable.* He fought against it, but his wounds were grave and his body weary. He could barely even kick his feet through the water, struggling to stay alive despite all the odds. The Maw's tail slid past, but the creature was too eager, the sea too full of lashing bodies and sinking wreckage, and it missed Cobiah by several feet. Just as he was beginning to give up, fearing the light above him was no longer the surface of the waves, Cobiah felt something snag on his body, dragging him out of the sea. It was too hard to be an arm: wooden, tipped with metal. A boat hook, then. One of Isaye's sailors?

But as he broke the surface of the chopping waves, Cobiah realized the *Nomad II* was too far away to be his savior.

"Ready? Heave!" The boat hook dragged Cobiah back against the side of a massive galleon, the wood cracking against his shoulder painfully as he was pulled up her hull toward the topside of the ship. He spat water, kicking off his soaked boots to lighten the load, and clawed his way through the rail onto the deck boards. Once safely there, Cobiah untangled himself from the boat hook and stared up into a white-faced group of Krytan sailors. He was aboard the *Balthazar's Trident*.

"Is he alive?" Prince Edair put his hand on Cobiah's shoulder. "Commodore—are you injured?"

"Yes." Cobiah blinked salt water out of his eyes, shivering from the cold of the sea. "If you're going to make me a prisoner, I'd rather you just kill me now. I'd rather die on deck than drown in the bilge like some kind of . . . of . . . stowaway skritt." His stomach churned with seawater and disappointment.

Edair's brown eyes softened. "I'm not sending you to the brig, Commodore, though I do intend to have strong words with the individuals who took it upon themselves to countermand my orders in that regard." Edair flashed an indignant glance at Livia. "Nevertheless, I watched what you did on that great black galleon—leaping across to face the undead captain one-on-one? I've never seen anything like it." The prince of Kryta grasped Cobiah's hand and pulled him to his feet, supporting Cobiah with his shoulder when the older man's knees failed to gain balance right away. "Your actions saved my ship from destruction. I . . . may have misjudged you."

"'May have'?"

The prince shook his head. "We've no time for argument, Commodore. You're needed." Edair pointed across the ocean, indicating the battle taking place around them. One of the Seraph came forward, and Edair took the man's proffered cloak, placing it on Cobiah's shoulders and wrapping it around his shivering body. "That black-sailed devil of a ship is gone, but my armada's not doing well. We were unprepared for this assault. Though they have fought bravely, you and the *Nomad* have taken on the lion's share of this fight. With the reinforcements from your city—however odd—we may yet have a chance against these Dead Ships.

"But I hold no such hope for victory against *them*." Edair's finger pointed toward the xebecs with scarlet sails. "The *Trident* is uninjured and ready to fight. But I . . ." The prince's voice failed him, and his jaw stiffened with pride. He moved out from under Cobiah's shoulder, allowing the commodore to stand on his own among the Seraph marines. "I saw you command the *Nomad*," Edair added. "I'm asking you to do the same with the *Trident*. Although the fight is going well—"

"It doesn't matter how well it's going. Those Orrians won't leave until you've destroyed them utterly or they've replenished what they've lost and won the day. Every loss for you increases their numbers, don't you understand that?" Cobiah said wryly, pulling the cloak about him. "Macha used to call it a 'zero-sum equation.' There's no such thing as just driving them off. Unless you're winning—you're losing.

"They'll ram your ships, use their cannons, and leave your men to die at sea—and every sailor drowned in the tide, every vessel that sinks in their attack—they'll rise to fight against you." He narrowed his eyes and took a strip of cloth from one of the Shining Blade, wrapping it about his torso to staunch the seeping wounds. His hand had swollen, the flesh torn and ravaged, but everything still worked—for now. Limping to the *Balthazar's Trident*'s railing, Cobiah leaned on the smooth wood and looked out at the firefight on the waves. "You can't fight Orr like you fight charr."

The patchwork ships from Lion's Arch were fighting like nimble piranhas, packing light punches but evading most of the attacks being levied against them. They didn't have much protection, and their hulls, too long out of the water, couldn't absorb a powerful blow. Already several were down, their hulls compromised by a single hit from the cannons on the black-sailed galleons. The Krytan vessels, on the other hand, were ready for a fight, and although they were taking a pounding from the Orrians, most of them managed to remain afloat despite a great deal of abuse. However, they were wasting their blows pounding on the already-ruined hulls of the Dead Ships, a tactic that would work on living ships but did very little to this enemy. "This is what you wanted. Lion's Arch at your fingertips, our fleet at the bottom of the sea. You said the Dead Ships were no danger. You said we were lying." He glanced back over his shoulder with a hostile snort. "You have everything you asked for."

Edair bristled, a satirical reply on his lips. Before he could speak, Livia's hand fell upon the prince's sleeve. He paused and took a long, deep breath, closing his eyes as he regained control of his temper. Cobiah turned and looked out at the waves once more, listening to the pound and flash of cannon fire, the booming of gunnery emplacements on the cliffsides, the high, arching loft of flaming balls of pitch heaved from Claw Island's shore.

"You were right," Edair ground out between clenched teeth.

In a low, angry tone, Cobiah agreed. "Damn straight, I was."

The anger slowly left Edair's eyes, but his shoulders were back, and his stance was still that of a soldier. "Tell me how to save my ships."

"And if I do?"

It took Edair a moment to answer. "I'll leave your city. Take my ships and my army, and renege on the siege." Livia's hand tightened reassuringly on the prince's arm. Lifting his head, Edair said, "We'll . . . negotiate a truce.

Limited autonomy under Krytan rule, with you as the city's governor—"

"Full independence," Cobiah retorted sharply.

"Are you mad?" Edair blurted in shock. Several of the Seraph around them reached for their weapons, anticipating an angry command. The Krytan prince shook free of his exemplar's restraint, stomping closer to Cobiah until their faces were mere inches apart. "Lion's Arch will never survive. The races weren't meant to live together. You'll tear yourself apart!"

"If we do, that's my problem. Not yours." Cobiah met the young prince's fervent gaze with the cold wisdom of years as a ship commander. As shouts and cannon fire echoed off the water and the Maw rose again to swallow one of the smaller pinnaces whole, the two men stood locked in a fierce battle of wills.

As smoke wafted past over the *Balthazar's Trident*'s deck, Edair made his decision. "Fine. I'll recognize the city's sovereignty so long as the Captain's Council remains in charge."

Cobiah put out his uninjured hand. "Done." Unused to such gestures, Edair shook it awkwardly.

Now that they were in agreement, Cobiah turned his mind to the battle. "Your ships need to work with ours. Let our faster vessels lure the Dead Ships to the Krytan line and then use your heavier guns to blow apart their masts, shatter their rudders, and target their guns. Don't waste ammunition on their hulls." Pulling the warm cloak more firmly about his shivering body, Cobiah warned him, "It takes a hell of a lot more damage than your ships can do in a few passes to get through the layers of bone and gristle hidden beneath their rotting hulls." The prince blanched at Cobiah's description but nodded. "If the Orrians can't chase you and they can't shoot at you, then you'll have plenty of time to break them apart."

Edair summoned one of the sailors forward. "Have our mesmer pass those commands to the other ships. Send the same message to the *Pride* and tell them the orders come from Commodore Marriner." The crewman saluted briefly and raced to do the prince's bidding.

"That's a start. But we've got another problem. Those red-sailed ships. The xebecs, the ones with the fire shields and magical artillery." Cobiah frowned. "They're more self-willed than the others. I don't know—maybe they're smarter, or maybe they're better able to interpret the dragon's commands. Those ships won't fall for our tactics, and cannons alone won't take them out. The only way to destroy them is with magic."

Edair understood at once. "We'll have to take the *Trident* in."

37

No, you don't know a storm 'til you ride the wind
Beneath cold and blackened skies, O
'Til you're sailing through a thunderhead
With the lightning in your eyes
Death, he laughs in the sails and the jags
And the bloody sun won't rise, O.
                    —"Weather the Storm"

As Cobiah's battle plan spread among the two fleets, the Krytans and the patchwork armada began to work together. Although neither had the ability to defeat a Dead Ship alone, working as one, they began to turn their advantage into victory. Sykox and Fassur led the charge aboard the *Pride*, plowing courageously into their enemy as though wholly unafraid. Their bravery was contagious; where the Krytans had been flagging, they picked up the fight once more, inspired by the *Pride* and her cobbled-together city-fleet. Acting as one, they drove the Orrian vessels back toward the south. Only the two xebecs held their ground, sweeping the sea with fire and lightning, using their powerful magic to eradicate any living ships that happened to cross their path.

What would Isaye say? Cobiah looked out across the sea at the *Nomad II*, still foundered near a set of moss-covered rocks that jutted up from beneath the sea. He could make out sailors moving on her deck, trying to fix the yardarms of the one remaining mast, firing volleys at Dead Ships that came too close in their pursuit of more active Krytan vessels. He couldn't find the dark-haired captain amid the others, but he knew she was there. What would she say if she knew he was taking the prince's ship—and her son—into battle? The *Balthazar's Trident* could be destroyed if they were outmatched by the ships of Orr. Young Dane could die.

"He's dead if I don't."

"What's that, Commodore?" Livia's voice was smooth and emotionless. Although the words were a question, there was no hint of curiosity in her voice, and Cobiah wondered if she was already aware of his thoughts before he spoke them.

He raised his head to look at her. "I need you to issue a command to the Seraph. Get the nobles and other civilians to the center of the ship where they'll be most protected from shrapnel and other damage to her hull. Keep those people together. If the ship starts to sink, get them to the lifeboats and get them out of here. I don't like going to battle with them on board, but I can't afford the time to get them off—and they wouldn't last long in rowboats. Not with the Maw chewing up everything that fits in its mouth."

Livia nodded. "Of course."

Quick to defend her more fragile companions, the *Pride* engaged one of the ships with scarlet sails. The spellcasters of Lion's Arch were less powerful, their magic less facile, but they'd fought such ships before, and their vessel was the faster. Bit by bit, the *Pride* led their opponent away from the main battle, leaving the body of the armada to dismantle the rest of the Dead Ships without interference from the devastating Orrian spells.

The *Balthazar's Trident* closed on the second, with Cobiah yelling encouragement and tactics to the three young elementalists aboard. Four guardians, like Osh Moran, stood on the *Balthazar's Trident*'s bow, firing orb after orb of energy at the two xebecs. A single mesmer, the *Balthazar's Trident*'s messenger and one of the Shining Blade, used his illusions to hide their true position, causing the xebec to waste attacks against empty sea. Still, the red-sailed xebec was smaller than the prince's galleon and far faster in the water, using widespread area-effect spells to catch the *Balthazar's Trident* and deal damage to her hull and masts. Sickly fireballs exploded from the xebec's cannons, setting the Krytan galleon's canvas alight, and one of the Krytan elementalists was forced to turn her attention from the battle to use water spells to put out the blaze. The impact had another cost as well: the young mesmer used to coordinate among the Krytan ships had been knocked overboard, swallowed up by the Maw.

Suddenly, an explosion rocked the rear of the Krytan galleon. Amid the shouting and furious activity, one of the Seraph marines yelled a report to the commanders. "They're using a wind spell to block our cannons! It's surrounded the lower decks of the ship. If we continue firing, we'll only be damaging ourselves."

"Order the cannons to hold their fire!" Edair called back to them commandingly. "Continue using the deck guns. Load the carronades with grapeshot and fire at their sails." He glanced at Cobiah, and the commodore nodded approvingly. Edair pointed at one of the elementalists. "Doralyn, get below and see if you can counter that wind spell—or divert it to our sails. See if we can use their magic for our benefit." The woman nodded and raced for a nearby hatch to the decks below.

Clever. Cobiah chuckled to himself. *The boy might just make a good commander someday.*

Seeing that the *Balthazar's Trident* was in danger, the *Pride* cut short her attack on one opponent, turning her cannons toward the xebec attacking the prince's ship. So long as the xebec was fighting the *Pride*, she couldn't also assault the *Balthazar's Trident*. But that made two Orrian ships against one small pinnace, and the *Pride* wouldn't be able to hold them off for long. Meanwhile, the Maw zigzagged between the ships, churning the waves and snapping its massive teeth with a sound like clanging iron. The *Pride's* guns harried the xebec, and the *Balthazar's Trident* followed suit as best it could, but the Orrian elementalists continued to hold their ground against both sets of opponents.

"Sykox!" Cobiah yelled at the top of his lungs as the pinnace pulled closer. "Like with the *Salma's Grace*!" He pointed at the closest xebec and grinned.

On the other ship, the rust-furred engineer's four ears stretched forward, trying to catch Cobiah's words. Comprehension dawned on Sykox's face, and he lifted one hand in agreement, turning to yell something to the crew, his words too muffled for Cobiah to make out. Slowly but unrelentingly, the *Pride* pulled alongside one of the xebecs. With the *Balthazar's Trident* on one side and the *Pride* on her other, the xebec was caught in a simultaneous volley of cannon fire—and the xebec's magic allowed her to defend against only one. Hull collapsing, her magic overwhelmed by the spells of the Krytan elementalists, the Orrian ship foundered and broke apart.

Cobiah began to warn Livia: "They'll come at us under the water—"

"No. They won't." The ancient necromancer raised her hands, her fingers arched like claws and her eyes turning black from edge to edge. The language she spoke echoed with murder, and withering green smoke hissed from her palms and her eyes. As the Orrian zombies and wights touched the *Balthazar's Trident*, Livia's magic took hold of them, shredding their putrid flesh into a thick, reddish goo. Cobiah stared at the necromancer in awe and horror, and took a quiet step away.

The second xebec came around, shooting bolts of magical fire at the *Balthazar's Trident*. One caught her side, setting the hull alight and causing the crew to respond with an immediate brigade of buckets and water spells. Before the scarlet-sailed vessel could fire again, the *Pride* dodged between them, firing a broadside to get the xebec's attention away from the slower, wallowing galleon.

Just then, there was a crashing thump, and the *Balthazar's Trident* bucked in the water. Cobiah grasped the gunwale and looked over the side of the ship. The water below them was whitecapped and churning, but through the waves, he caught a glimpse of the Maw rising beneath them. There was a second jolt, and the ship's keel creaked dangerously. "It's trying to break the ship apart!" he yelled to Edair.

Amid the shouts and panic of their crew, Cobiah noted a third ship approaching. For a moment he thought it was one of the Lion's Arch fleet, but something about the vessel bothered him. Taking a second look, he realized the ship was Yomm's, the brigantine the merchant had purchased to qualify for a spot on the Captain's Council. "I can't believe it!" Cobiah exclaimed. "That cowardly old coot used the asura gates to get to his ship in Rata Sum—and then sailed all the way back alone? Has he gone completely mad?"

The asuran brig was no war vessel. Cobiah doubted she had enough guns to spearfish along the coast. Despite her blue-glowing, enchanted masts and her alchemically reinforced hull, the sturdy little caravel was a cargo ship, with an expanded hold and a study hall. "Yomm could have at least brought a few more ships. Or a bunch of asuran elementalists," groused the commodore, trying to catch a glimpse of the asura on the *Nadir Shill*'s deck. "I can't imagine what a little dinghy like that is going to do against Dead Ships—or the Maw." He saw only one robed figure on the deck; the rest were obviously frightened sailors, scurrying about the ship as they prepared to enter the battle zone.

"My lord prince." One of the sailors approached them. "Bad news. The explosion below reached our ammunition stores. Elementalist Doralyn was forced to flood the area with water spells to be sure it didn't catch fire and destroy the ship. We saved most of the munitions, but Doralyn . . . well, sir, she gave her life for the *Trident*."

"Bad news, indeed." Edair frowned. "And the gunpowder?"

The sailor shook his head. "Not in good order, sir. Between the wind stoppering our cannons, the explosion in our stern, and the flooding of the deck, it's all we can do to load the carronades."

"Damn it." The prince stared sullenly toward the second xebec. "We've got one more of those gods-cursed vessels left, not to mention the monster below. By Balthazar's hounds, what are we going to do?"

Looks like you're in trouble again, bookah. The whisper came out of thin air, nearly making Cobiah jump out of his skin. It was high-pitched, snarky . . . and wholly familiar. *I have no idea how you managed to get along without me.*

C obiah blinked. "Macha?"

Yomm snuck through the asura gate to Rata Sum, the voice said blithely. *You should have seen him begging the Arcane Council for assistance! But his request was rejected. None of the colleges were willing to send help. Who knew they'd be so mad over a little counter-appropriation almost twenty years ago? It's not like they didn't make their money back when they double-charged us to build gates in Lion's Arch.*

"Macha, what are you doing here?"

In the last few years, I've spent a lot of time considering the Eternal Alchemy, and I've come to the conclusion that my formula of diverse interaction was flawed. I redid the calculations and found my initial error.

"What?"

An audible sigh. *I said, I came to make things right.*

The *Nadir Shill* pushed its way past the others, cresting the whitecapped waves. As it cut in front of the *Trident*, Cobiah saw four more phantom ships materialize around it. Scarlet spread through the water, and he smelled the overwhelming reek of blood. Apparently the Maw smelled it, too, because the monster broke off its attack on the *Balthazar's Trident* and gave chase. Macha's illusionary ships began to limp and wobble in the water like injured birds pretending to have broken a wing. The Maw eagerly focused its attention on them, teeth snapping through hulls that didn't exist, tail lashing the water as it was drawn away.

That left the *Pride* and the *Balthazar's Trident* to deal with the second xebec.

"I've got an idea." Cobiah brightened. "Helmsman, sail to the west—back where you picked me up. The *Pride* will follow us." He signaled toward the *Pride*, and Sykox waved back. Cobiah gestured for them to unfurl the sails. "Put ours down, too."

"They're burned," Livia protested smoothly. "They'll do us no good."

"Put them down! All of them! Even the ones that aren't catching wind. We need to block their line of sight."

"We have no guns to the rear," Edair reminded him. "We won't be able to fire at the Orrians when they give chase."

"We won't need our guns. Just unfurl the sails and head west—and keep them on the *Trident*'s stern!"

Together, the *Pride* and the *Balthazar's Trident* sailed side by side, sails wide and grasping at the ocean wind as the Orrian ship followed them. The xebec continued to fire, and the remaining elementalists on the Krytan galleon did everything they could to turn the blasts aside. Twice, Cobiah thought they would be blown apart by the Orrian attacks, only to see one of the four Krytan guardians lunge forward, shielding the rear of the ship with a protective blue hemisphere of magic. When the Orrian spells impacted upon their magical protection, the guardian's enchanted shield crumpled, and the protector fell, their life force expended to prevent the blast from reaching the ship—giving their lives to save their fellows.

Cobiah signaled to Sykox. Using charr hand signals designed to coordinate a silent attack, he initiated a countdown. They were almost there . . . almost . . .

"Now! Hard to port!" Yelling, he followed the command with, "Sykox! Hard to starboard!" The charr aboard the *Pride* were ready, and both crews pulled their rudders hard and twisted their sails to draw them away. The two ships parted like a leaf cut in two by the keen blade of a sword. Their unfurled sails had hidden the sea ahead from their pursuer, keeping the Orrians from recognizing the territory into which they sailed. And as the two ships broke to the sides, they slowed, allowing the Orrian ship to rush between them—and onto a massive, rocky outcropping that jutted up above the waves.

The xebec slammed into the promontory, wood shrieking as moss-covered stone pierced through her fire shield and into the hull itself. The entire ship crashed upward, masts giving way with a terrible cracking sound. They fell forward, snapping the rigging and causing the scarlet sails to founder and unfurl across her deck. The undead crew, caught off guard, flew forward, crashing into her forecastle and tumbling across the ship's deck. And as her spellcasters lost their concentration, the xebec's magical protections failed.

"Fire!" Cobiah pounded his fist on the railing. "Now, now, *now!*"

Cannons fired from both ships, taking advantage of the xebec's crumpling prow and her lack of magical defenses. Free of the winds that had been enchanted to shroud the portholes and lower decks, the *Balthazar's Trident*'s massive cannons could fire at last. By the time the smoke cleared, there was nothing left on the rock except a keel, weathered shards of wood, and a wide scrap of singed red sail.

Edair stood in the center of the deck, commanding the Seraph response to the damage that had been done to his ship. The Krytans obeyed his commands earnestly, doing their best to repair the injuries done to the massive ship's hull and sails. "Commodore," the prince called to him. "Looks like the *Nomad*'s full foundered. We should sail by and offer aid while we can—that asuran friend seems to have lost the beast. It could resurface anywhere."

Fully aware that the Maw was still out there, Cobiah nodded. The monstrous creature would see a still ship as a target, and it would take little effort for it to destroy a craft that couldn't move. Across the rippling plain of the bay, Cobiah could see limping Krytan vessels taking aboard rafts of sailors from crushed ships of Lion's Arch and a flurry of small ships taking on a black-sailed clipper that was trying to take advantage of a Krytan ship on fire. The *Pride* was headed to meet with the *Nadir Shill*, pulling alongside the asuran craft to exchange greetings.

Cobiah's breath came in short gasps, his lungs laboring. The damage he'd taken aboard the *Indomitable* was significant, but he ignored it. The leviathan was still out there, and at any moment, it could strike. He scanned the sea, trying to catch a glimpse of the creature's fin or wake, but the waves were so choppy, the number of wrecked and ruined ships so great, that Cobiah could not find any sign of the massive beast.

Battered and weary, the *Balthazar's Trident* pulled alongside the *Nomad II*, its massive bulk making the clipper's small body look like a delicate koi resting against the bulk of a fat sunfish. "Isaye!" Cobiah called to her.

"Cobiah! Thank the goddess Lyssa, you're safe. We thought you'd gone down with the *Indomitable*!" she shouted back from the *Nomad II*. "Is it over? Is Dane . . . ?"

"Your son's fine. The Maw—it's still out there. We need

to get your crew aboard the *Trident*. Without sails to move you, your vessel's a sitting duck." He heard his own voice shaking and struggled to regain his composure. Sailors on the Seraph vessel hurried to extend planks between the ships so the sailors on the *Nomad II* could evacuate. "It's all right. Edair's made a promise; we need to work together. Hurry." He reached to take her hand, helping her across the wooden board.

"And you trust him?" she asked skeptically. Still, she couldn't hide the relief in her eyes as she took his hand. As the rest of the *Nomad II*'s crew came aboard, Isaye made her way across the plank to Cobiah's side.

"No. But when we have a choice"—he pulled her toward him—"I'll let you know."

"What is Sykox doing?" Isaye asked as she stepped across to the *Trident*. Leaning against Cobiah, she raised one hand to shield her eyes and squinted out to sea. "Is that Yomm's ship? Why are the charr going aboard?" Nearby, Rahli helped Tenzin across one of the walkways; he leaned heavily on the bosun. Confused, Cobiah turned to follow Isaye's gaze, spying the *Pride* and the *Nadir Shill* floating side by side. Several of the charr were leaping onto the asuran ship, their weapons at the ready, though there were no undead anywhere that Cobiah could see. Before he could venture an opinion, the *Balthazar's Trident*'s bell began to ring. One of the crew nearby shouted, "I see the beast! To starboard, ahoy!"

Indeed, the Maw was rising once more, tearing one of the patchwork ships of Lion's Arch between its teeth as the monster lifted its massive bulk above the waves. Cobiah heard sailors screaming and wood rending, and saw the vessel's mangled deck shatter in the monster's mouth. The leviathan slammed down into the water, scattering dead bodies and ruined canvas in its wake. Huge waves rolled in all directions from the impact, swelling so high that they knocked the *Nomad II* violently against the *Balthazar's Trident* as if she'd been buffeted by a giant's fist. Cobiah heard boards smash and crack as their hulls crashed against one another.

"Your Highness!" a sailor called out from the far end of the ship. "We're stuck!"

"Stuck?"

"The boards, sir!"

Pulling Isaye away from the edge of the ship, Cobiah looked past the railing. Indeed, jagged boards in the *Nomad II*'s hull had impaled the *Balthazar's Trident*, twisting their boards together where the clipper's broken ones jutted out at an angle from the ship. "Get the boat hooks!" commanded Prince Edair. "Tear them apart. We'll fix the damage after . . ."

Even as he yelled, the Maw rose again, this time on the far side of the *Nomad II*. Its teeth grazed the hull of the clipper, ripping through boards, tearing apart her lifeboats, and catching in her rigging. The blow hadn't been dead-on but rather askew, and the Maw continued on past the two ships, expelling water in a wide arc where it crashed back into the sea.

The galleon and the clipper rolled in the waves, pushed gently by the wind and the tossing of the creature's wake. "We've got to get away from the *Nomad*. We have to keep moving," Cobiah called to the prince. "As long as we're moving, it's harder for the Maw to catch us."

A nearby sailor shook his head. "Those boards are caught together too well for us to lever them apart without proper tools, sir. We're trapped."

"We'll see about that," said Grymm Svaard, grasping a long boat hook in either hand. As he wedged them down between the two vessels, Cobiah heard the sound of small-arms fire. He looked back over his shoulder and saw the faint smoke of pistols rising from the deck of the *Nadir Shill.*

The *Pride* was pulling away from the asuran vessel, her engines chugging full bore. But Cobiah could see charr on the *Nadir Shill*, and he heard Fassur cursing even this far away across the waves. "What's going on?"

"Coby!" Sykox roared from the deck of the *Nadir Shill.* "Coby! That skritt-fink of an asura! She stole our damn ship!"

"Wait– what?" He bolted toward the railing but was forced to stop as the wound in his side flared up agonizingly. "What did you say?" Cobiah yelled back, still holding Isaye close.

"Macha!" The charr pointed desperately after the *Pride.* "She made us think you were aboard the *Shill.* It was one of her crazy, confusing illusions—we came across because you ordered it, but then you vanished. By the time we realized it was a trick, the lines had been cut, and her engine'd already gotten them out of leaping range!" Asuran sailors raced about on the little caravel, terrified by the furious charr warband trapped in their midst. Fassur swatted at one, knocking the little fellow into the ship's hold with a squeak of terror.

"Macha's here?" Isaye's hazel eyes flew wide. "What is she doing?"

Cobiah glowered with barely contained rage. "Apparently, she's stealing the *Pride.*"

39

Grymm Svaard stood with one foot on the deck of the *Balthazar's Trident* and the other foot on the deck of the *Nomad II*, shoving two long boat hooks down between their hulls. Crew from both ships lined the railing, with boat hooks, halberds, and other poles, trying to lever the two ships away from one another. The boards groaned and creaked but held firm, tangled together. The norn's muscles bulged, and he shouted encouragement to the sailors, each hand gripping a boat hook scissored between the hulls. The boards cracked slowly apart under the push of his mighty strength.

"She's taking on water," Edair noted, lending his strength to the task. "The *Nomad's* sinking." The prince labored side by side with his sailors, ignoring the fact that his golden sleeves were torn and his elegant silk shirt was stained with blood and salt water.

"That's the least of our worries," retorted Cobiah. "If the Maw hits, we'll be dead long before she can pull us down." He could see Livia issuing subtle orders to the Shining Blade and noted that they were readying one of the rear lifeboats without commentary. He snorted. If the Maw struck their ship, Edair would likely be spirited away in a wink of Livia's magic—with or without the prince's consent.

But as for the rest of them . . .

"There it is!" A sailor pointed. The Maw broke the surface of the ocean on the far side of the *Nomad II*, its fin splitting the waves in the shadow of the drifting ships. The monster circled, drawing ever closer, and Cobiah could almost sense it deciding how best to attack the enticing morsel drifting in the waves.

The Maw rose before them, its massive teeth pulling apart as its jaws opened, revealing the enormous depth of the leviathan's mouth. Sailors on the *Balthuzar's Trident* screamed in terror as they desperately tried to free the galleon from the *Nomad II*'s sinking grip. "If I can get to the *Nomad*'s cannons, I can try to shoot inside its mouth, maybe hit something vital. I might hurt it enough to make it change its path." Cobiah tried to limp forward, forcing his battered body to carry him onward one last time. But Isaye kept her hands on his shoulders, and the gentle restraint was enough to pull him back.

"It won't make a difference, Coby," Isaye whispered, pressing her face to Cobiah's chest. "Oh, gods. I don't want it to end like this. Dane . . ."

"Shh." Cobiah pressed his hand to her hair, pulling Isaye close and holding her tightly.

"No, I have to tell you." Isaye stepped back, meeting his eyes. "Dane's your son, Cobiah. I was pregnant when I left Lion's Arch. After he was born, I kept him from you because I was angry that you didn't give me a chance to explain. I wanted to say something, but . . ." Tears poured down her cheeks. "I should have. You're his father, Coby . . . and I love you."

Overwhelmed, Cobiah bowed his head and kissed her, tears salting their lips. He stroked Isaye's hair without words. Whatever happened, no matter how short their lives were, he never intended to let her go again.

To the side of the *Balthazar's Trident* came a rumble that swiftly turned into a roar. Cobiah raised his head in confusion, staring as the *Pride* raced past the conjoined ships, so close that the churning of her engine blew up a salt spray that drenched the deck of the tremendous galleon. "Macha's pushed the engine into overdrive," Cobiah said, marveling, recognizing the sound. With her engine booming, the *Pride* bored past, swerving and weaving on a trajectory that would take her directly toward the Maw. "Macha can't crew the ship alone," Cobiah said numbly. "What's she doing? It must be out of control."

"I don't think she plans to go far, Cobiah," Isaye breathed. "Look."

As they watched, the *Pride* slid in front of the *Balthazar's Trident*. Her hardy engine blew sparks in her wake, and her keel lifted up off the water as she crested the bay's rolling waves. The Maw's mouth was splayed open before her, ready to swallow the pinnace whole on its way toward the two foundering vessels.

That leviathan's too big to take down with cannons. Still, I'm a genius first class, and as usual, I've got an idea.

"What? Macha? What are you doing?" Cobiah said aloud, not caring that the sailors on the *Balthazar's Trident* were staring at him in confusion.

I'm sorry, Coby. It wasn't supposed to end this way. I just wanted to balance the etheric transference between our spirits within the Eternal Alchemy. To pay my dues.

"Macha!" he yelled, clutching Isaye close and watching as the *Pride* raced ever faster toward the massive sea monster. A second later, the pinnace plowed directly into the wide-jawed mouth of the Maw. The clipper drove into the back of the leviathan's throat, engine thrumming with immense power. As he watched in horror, something within the *Pride*'s hold caught fire.

Good-bye, Co—

The ship exploded.

Stunned and wounded by the detonation, the Maw could do nothing to save itself. The forefront of the behemoth erupted in the blast, body lashing helplessly as its head and neck were blown apart. Reduced to headless flesh and shattered bone, the monster thrashed in the waves, its death throes churning the sea to red and white foam.

Grief tinged Cobiah's words. "She knew that engine as well as I did. As well as Sykox. It had to be deliberate. She turned the *Pride* into a bomb."

"She killed the Maw," Isaye said wonderingly. "Macha saved us. But why?"

He pulled her closer, wrapping his cloak around them both. "She said she wanted to make things right. And she gave her life to do it." Cobiah watched the vast body of the leviathan sinking into the waves at the mouth of Sanctum Harbor.

"Macha died to defeat the enemies of Lion's Arch." Cobiah looked up at the morning sky, breathing in the scent of the sea and the faint smell of smoke and oil. Remembering what the asura'd said, Cobiah continued, "She paid her dues. Let her be honored as a hero." Isaye nodded in agreement, a sad smile curving her full lips. Although his body ached and his legs felt like collapsing, Isaye was warm within his arms, and the world finally felt at peace.

"Farewell, little angel," Cobiah whispered, though whether he was speaking to Macha or to the spirit of his sister, he wasn't sure. "Thank you for watching over me."

40

The *Balthazar's Trident* dropped anchor in Sanctum Harbor, her sails furled and her long green-and-gold banners waving with wounded dignity from the tops of her tremendous masts. Scarred and burned wood showed how much damage she'd taken, and a narrow hole in her hull just above the waterline marked the spot where she'd been pierced by the *Nomad II*. One of her sails was burned through, and her rear jibs had been broken by the fire cannons of the pursuing xebec. Other ships of the Krytan fleet were even more damaged. Many, both from Kryta and from Lion's Arch, had been lost in the assault.

"That was not my fault!" Yomm shouted from the *Nadir Shill* as she pulled alongside the other two ships. "Macha promised she was going to use her magic to help the city. She said absolutely nothing about stealing a ship or detonating herself in the harbor! It was completely unprofessional of her, and I shall be filing an ex post facto grievance with the Arcane Council of Rata Sum."

"She saved our lives," Cobiah corrected him wryly.

"Yes, well, I shall also be proposing that the Arcane Council award her the Incantrix Luminus, our highest award of honor." The asura captain sniffed disdainfully and crossed his arms. "But that still doesn't absolve her of the indignity."

Isaye and Cobiah helped Sykox across a gangplank that had been placed between the *Nadir Shill* and the *Balthazar's Trident*. Fassur and Aysom followed close behind, keeping their hands on the hilts of their pistols. On the *Balthazar's Trident*, armored Seraph lowered their halberds in readiness, bristling at the charr. The warband snarled, teeth bared, ready for a fight.

"Cut it out, guys," Cobiah managed to say, his breath coming in short gasps. Though he wasn't able to yell, his soft words quelled the charr as if they'd been a tribune's bellow. Cobiah turned to glare at the Seraph, aware that nothing he said could command *them*.

"Stand down, Seraph." As the prince's marines stepped back, confused, Edair shoved his way through the guard. "You heard me," he growled, pushing the blades of their pole-arms to the floor. "These charr and their fleet just saved our lives. They may be our enemies, but you'll treat them with respect, or you'll be swimming home." Properly chagrined, the Seraph relaxed a bit and stepped to the side.

"They aren't." Breathing between taut lips, Cobiah kept his arm around Isaye's shoulders to steady his balance. "Your enemy, that is. These charr are my crew. Citizens of Lion's Arch."

"Whoa, Coby." Sykox stepped closer and gripped him gently. "You're weaving." He frowned, looking his friend over with concern. "You've gone pale, and your eyes aren't focusing. Isaye, help him sit down." Together, they lowered Cobiah to the deck, keeping the bloodied Seraph cloak tucked about him. The charr pulled his hand away from Cobiah's body, staring down at his paw, which was red with more than the rusty color of his fur.

Edair's eyes widened at the sight. He snapped his fingers at the Seraph, auburn hair brushing the tanned skin of his cheekbones. "Bring bandages. We need to tend to his wounds." One of the marines came forward, carrying medical supplies, and began to look at Cobiah's ravaged hand, the bloodied puncture in his back, the wound on his ribs that had again ripped open. The marine's gentle fingers drew a gasp of breath from the commodore, and everything blurred. Cobiah's vision narrowed. "Whoa, there, Cobiah." Edair gripped his shoulder, holding him steady. Cobiah caught sight of a concerned glance between the prince and Isaye, but things had stopped making as much sense as they had before.

"I'm fine." Cobiah tried to push the prince's hand away. "I just need a minute to rest."

"Captain Isaye? I think someone's waiting to see you," Livia said smoothly.

A bright voice keened from across the deck. "Mama!" It was the homesick call of a little boy. Dane beamed as he pulled his hand away from one of the Shining Blade, racing over the boards toward his mother. Isaye opened her arms and wrapped him up tightly, holding the child snugly to her as he laughed. "I saw the prince's crown, and I ate an omnomberry tart, and Livia told me a story about Queen Salma . . ." Dane's voice chattered on eagerly as Isaye kissed his face.

Livia smiled at Isaye. "Your son was very brave."

"He takes after his father," Isaye said, holding the child close. She tousled his mahogany locks and turned toward Cobiah. "Dane, I want you to meet Cobiah." The little boy stared at the commodore and ducked his face into his mother's dark hair, suddenly shy. "Coby . . . this is your son." As he met the child's eyes, which were blue and wide with innocence, Cobiah felt as though he were young again, standing on the docks of old Lion's Arch, teasing a little girl about mermaids and keeping her safe from bad dreams. They had the same pure gaze, the same bashful smile.

Cobiah reached out and put a hand on the boy's shoulder, his heart filled with joy. "He's beautiful, Isaye."

"He's a scamp, that's what he is." Isaye squeezed the boy close. "Just like his father."

With a smile, Cobiah reached into his pocket. "I don't know if it's the kind of thing boys like, but here—I have a present for you." Cobiah drew the rag doll from his inner pocket, pressing it into the child's hands. "Someday, I'll tell you a story about my sister, Biviane. This was her doll. Now it's yours. Keep her close, and she'll keep you safe. Just like she's always done for me." Cobiah folded the boy's hands around the soft rag doll, smiling as the child looked at it with curious eyes.

Although the boy didn't understand the toy's significance, he held the rag doll close, cradling it like a treasured friend. "What's her name?" Dane asked inquisitively.

"Polla," Cobiah replied. Dane ran a gentle hand over her yellow yarn curls and smiled.

Cobiah let out a grunt as fresh bandages were tightened around his waist. His injured hand was wrapped with strips of fabric, blood spotting the white canvas like foam on a still tidal pool. "Your Highness," the medic said quietly. "His wounds are extensive. I've done everything I can to help him, but the commodore's lost a great deal of blood. I don't know if . . ." The Seraph's words trailed off.

"I'll be fine." Cobiah pushed the medic away. "I just need some rest. At home. With my family." Isaye looked at him fondly, and they shared a smile.

"If we still *have* a home," Fassur growled, his voice low and threatening. "The Orrians are gone, but the war's not over. Kryta still holds Lion's Arch hostage."

Edair bristled. Before the prince could speak, Livia's cool voice broke in. "His Royal Highness has come to an accord with Commodore Marriner. I'm certain that no further violence will be necessary."

For a moment, Cobiah thought the pompous Krytan might go back on his word. Edair smoothed the sleeves of his ruined doublet, frowning thoughtfully as he considered the implications of their bargain. At last, the prince nodded somberly. "So I did. Full independence, I believe, was our agreement."

The charr broke into wide smiles and roars of approval, and both the *Nomad II*'s crew and the asura under Yomm's command began to chatter in gleeful satisfaction. Cobiah held up a hand to quiet them. Addressing the prince, he said, "You were looking to make history here in Lion's Arch, Prince Edair. I respectfully suggest that you've done exactly that—though not in the way you were intending." He took a deep breath, feeling the wounds and aches of his body throbbing with the movement. "A conquered people will always resist you, Edair. But allies—allies will fight by your side." Cobiah put a hand on Sykox's mane, ruffling the charr's reddish fur between his fingers. "You'd be surprised what we can achieve together.

"That is the lesson of my city, Prince Edair." Cobiah raised his voice, aware that everyone on deck—charr, human, and asura, Krytan and citizen of Lion's Arch alike—was listening. "Together, Tyria is stronger than it could ever be in parts."

Edair nodded, his features softening. A twinkle of his old impudence sparkled in the prince's eye. "All of you gathered here on this day," he demanded, voice rising to address the gathering. "I call on you to witness my words, as prince of Divinity's Reach and heir to the Krytan throne."

The prince drew his sword and held it sideways, giving his oath on the blade. "On this day, the nation of Kryta hereby recants all authority over the city of Lion's Arch and the lands it claims, so long as it continues to fight against the threat of Orr. With courage, it's earned its freedom—and our friendship." He bent his knee and held the blade out to Cobiah as the others crowded around them on the *Balthazar's Trident*'s deck. "In return, do you, as commodore of this city, pledge your goodwill to Kryta, as her friend in peace and her ally in time of need?"

Cobiah placed his hand on the steel of the prince's sword. "As leader of the council, I, Cobiah Marriner, do so swear."

Livia called out to all those assembled, her dark eyes flashing beneath the silken sway of her scarlet hair. "Let the word travel across Tyria—Lion's Arch shall forever be free."

Cheers erupted from the gathered crew of both ships. The charr roared in approval, and even the Seraph looked relieved and pleased by the accord. Other ships in the harbor, sailing close enough to hear the news passed by eager shouts, took up the cry until the crew of every ship in the harbor were waving their hats and firing their guns in celebration.

"Did you see that crazy asura?" Sykox flopped down on the deck beside Cobiah, his paw resting on the commodore's shoulder, claws gently curved around his old friend's arm. "Tricked us, stole the *Pride*, and then blew up our ship!"

Cobiah nodded. "You should never have taught her how the compression unit worked."

The spotted charr chuckled. "Too true." He shook his head, mane rustling around his brawny shoulders. "That little ear flapper did the right thing in the end. I'd give her the greatest compliment a soldier of the legions can give." Sykox crossed one arm in front of his chest in an Iron Legion salute, looking out toward the area where the Maw had been destroyed. "She died like a charr."

"So she did, my friend. So she did." Cobiah closed his eyes, a wash of exhaustion flooding over him.

It was done. Although there was still much to do to rebuild the city's fleet and restore her trade routes, with this agreement, more and more travelers and merchants would come to Lion's Arch. The city was safe, and there would be peace. As celebrations broke out around them, Cobiah was acutely aware of Isaye's presence at his side, her arms cradling his body and her eyes filled with love. When she spoke, her voice was a soft, welcome whisper in his ear. "Come on, Cobiah.

"Let's go home."

"WEATHER THE STORM"
(A TYRIAN SEA SHANTY)

You don't know a storm 'til you ride the wind
Beneath cold and blackened skies, O
'Til you're sailing through a thunderhead
With the lightning in your eyes
Death, he laughs in the sails and the jags
And the bloody sun won't rise, O.

A sailor's life's filled with toil and strife
The sea's both boon and bane, O
We're Kryta bound on a northern tide
Through the lightning and the rain
We'll sail through all these stormy nights
'Til we're safe at home again, O.

Open sea, and we're homeward bound
Fair or foul the weather, O
The cap'n swears we'll make our port
Though the sun's burned to an ember
If the Dead Ships come and the darkness falls
Then we'll all go down together, O.

She's a restless sloop with a six-armed maid
A-dancing on her prow, O
Her brassy cannons crease the sea
But the weather's chased her down
Her compass spins, and her captain screams
And the crew's all dead and drown'd, O.

The sails are rent, and the engine's blown
The keel is split to stern, O
We lost the rudder to the tide
And the mizzenmast is burning
The rain's like nails, and our harbor's lost
And the compass spins and turns, O.

Now the darkness comes, and the stars above
Circle 'round like sharks at sea, O
Instead of fighting for our lives
We should be sitting at our ease
But I chose the strife of a sailor's life
And the ocean, she chose me, O.

The wind, it howled, and the thunder boomed
Thought the storm might just prevail, O
But we shouldered on 'til the break of day
And we tamed that fearsome gale
Held to courage and to honor
And we lived to tell the tale, O.

No, you don't know a storm 'til you ride the wind
Beneath cold and blackened skies, O
'Til you're sailing through a thunderhead
With the lightning in your eyes
Death, he laughs in the sails and the jags
And the bloody sun won't rise, O.

Acknowledgments

Special thanks to Jeff Grubb, Scott McGough, and David Wilson: three exceptional companions in this journey through the history of Lion's Arch. Your invaluable input, insight, and patience have made Tyria—and this book—come to life.

About the Author

Ree Soesbee is an award-winning writer, game designer, and author of more than sixteen novels in a wide variety of fantastic worlds, including the ever-popular *Dragonlance* saga. She is a member of ASCAP and the Science Fiction & Fantasy Writers of America, and has been nominated for multiple Origins Awards. Ree currently works professionally as a narrative designer for ArenaNet on the internationally acclaimed MMORPG, *Guild Wars 2*.

Her credits include traditional pen-and-paper RPGs such as *Star Trek*, *Deadlands*, *World of Warcraft*, and *7th Sea*. She worked as lead writer for *Legend of the Five Rings* (both CCG and RPG) and was a primary designer for the *Warlord* CCG.

Ree holds a master's degree in Myth and Literature, performed her doctorate studies at UNC–Chapel Hill, and now lives in Seattle, where she spends her time writing, playing RPGs, MMORPGs, and LARPS, and being handmaiden to the Grand Adventuress of Cats.